The Tale of the

Ramajians

Cover design by DARK IMAGINARIUM Art & Design
www.darkimaginarium.com

Printed in the United States of America

ISBN: 978-0-692-25348-9

PROLOGUE

The sun left a brilliant splash of red, pink, and yellow hues as it struck her smooth, golden-brown skin. She reached a lithe arm into a basket full of ripe fruit. The mongpayas were especially delicious this season. She picked one up and raised it to her nose. The sweet aroma of the fruit's flesh, thinly veiled behind its blanket of skin, made her taste buds water.

Velda moved to purchase the magenta-colored fruit when she felt her skin tingle. She grew stiff like a wooden plank and slowly stepped backwards. She moved carefully at first, but threw out all caution and took off with blazing speed, letting everything in her hands fall to the ground in abrupt abandonment. Velda headed for the one place she knew she could find sanctuary – the dark thick of the woods. Her long thick dreadlocks slapped behind her as she ran, faster and faster, until she became a blur to the prying eyes around her.

Armored men gained on her, with the aid of their overheated horses now panting with exhaustion. They were soon pounding at Velda's heels.

"Catch her!" one large guard shouted from the lead, his sword pointed directly at her back. "Be careful, and no marks this time, men. Got it?"

Velda was too valuable to kill, but freedom was no longer hers.

Thankfully, they hadn't found her—yet. She slowed to a tiptoe at a curve in the foliage and hid behind a nearby tree. She held her breath and shut her eyes tight, hoping not to be detected, but it was too late.

"Aha! There you are! Come here you..." The closest guard hopped from his mount, and reached out a thick, muscled arm. He wore the smile of a jackal and prepared to claim his prize when Velda suddenly vanished from sight, disappearing in mid-air. He searched frantically, but she was nowhere to be found. The guard fell to his knees and roared like a beast, pounding his fists into the tightly packed earth like he was denied of a guaranteed kill. They almost had her this time, but like water slipping through a sieve, Velda managed to avoid capture once again.

Secure in the familiar woods near her safe haven, Velda panted. With each breath, her lungs seared as though on fire, but the pain gradually eased. She was finally able to relax, but this was a luxury she could only afford for a few cherished moments.

Once she had finally settled down, Velda spoke out loud, although there was no one around to hear her words. "I swear...I swear on the Soranayum...I will stop you," she whispered with defiance, looking out into the neverending distance.

CHAPTER 1

Athaliah Stevenson sat in the attic of her parents' home, reading through old letters that her father had written to her over the years on her birthday. It was June 30, a little after ten o'clock, and about six months since her nineteenth birthday. Growing up, her father wrote a letter each year to celebrate the occasion. This had been their tradition ever since she could remember. Each letter was sent postdated, so that they would arrive precisely on her birthday or a day before. He always told her that it was a precautionary measure, a "just in case", although he never explained exactly what he meant by that last part. At any rate, Athaliah didn't mind; the message hadn't gone unnoticed. There was never a time when she didn't feel loved.

When Athaliah was twelve years old, her father went missing. It had happened suddenly, and although the investigation had carried on for some time, there had been no breakthroughs or discoveries. There were no leads, no clues, and no answers. When all the trails had grown cold, the investigation was called off, and chalked up as an unsolved mystery. It was as if he had disappeared at the finale of some magician's trick, leaving behind a puff of smoke and a daughter who had suddenly found herself lost in the world.

Frederick Stevenson was gone, and everyone's life had took a turn for the worse because of it. Although Athaliah still had her mother, Janice, the home opened up a large void in the wake of his disappearance.

At the time he went missing, Frederick had been working full-time as a Professor of Archaeology and Engineering at the University of Maryland, College Park. In his spare time, he also enjoyed working part time at an antique store, although that seemed to be more of a hobby than for serious financial gain. He had an avid interest in history and archaeological artifacts, which was the only explanation as to why an esteemed college professor would have been drawn to working at such an unusual place.

In one of his more obscure adventures down a rabbit hole of research, Frederick stumbled upon tales of a woman named Athaliah, whose story enthralled him. Little was known about her compared to other ancient figures, but it was believed that she may have been the subject of a mythological culture. He was so fascinated with her story, he decided to name his daughter after her. Frederick dedicated much of his free time in his later years to learning more about Athaliah, her culture, and the tales of her life.

Around the time Frederick disappeared, he had actually been in the middle of a particularly passionate research bender centered on her long-forgotten civilization.

Yet, however sentimental the origins of her name may have been, Athaliah did not like it. She loathed it so fiercely that in her younger years, she refused to be called by her given name. Instead, she preferred to be called "Jane." This was a simple name, if not plain. But plain was good. It was nearly impossible to butcher and there were never questions surrounding the strangeness or the origin. It was a widely accepted and common name, which was exactly what she wanted early on in grade school—to blend in.

Her father had already established a reputation for being a bit of a community outcast, especially when he began working closely with the eccentric owner of the antique store, Mr. Miller, who had been mocked by her classmates to no end. Jokes about her father soon followed when some of the kids noticed that the crazy old kook in the antique store had found himself a sidekick. Whenever she heard a joke brewing, Athaliah wanted to curl up and die. After all, she already felt like an expatriate for other reasons.

Athaliah was an African-American who lived in a predominantly Caucasian area. Not many other children understood her features, particularly her darker skin, larger lips, flatter nose, and especially her wild, curly hair that refused to be tamed, no matter how important the occasion. She may have been the first African-American that many of her schoolmates had ever met in person. By the time she made it to the end of middle school, Athaliah finally decided to be called by the nickname her parents had used for her as a child - *Alaya*. She had come to love this name over the years, and found it to be quite beautiful, but not only because it distanced her a bit from the mockery. Rather, people seemed to find it exotic, and Alaya agreed. It was exotic *enough*, yet still acceptable. Perhaps most importantly, it was easy to pronounce.

In the attic, Alaya was caught up in the thick mist of nostalgia, but a call from her mother downstairs shook her from her reverie. Alaya moved quickly and shuffled the papers into a loose pile, leaving them in the open box before racing down to see what her mother needed.

Janice Stevenson was a thirty-nine-year-old African-American woman with rich, raven black hair and a smile that could split a storm cloud. Although her appearance was impeccable, her once smooth, youthful skin was beginning look a bit more worn. For the last seven years, she had been plagued with worry and languished over her lost husband, unable to ever fully accept that he was gone. Janice had once been vibrant and full of joy, but she was now consumed by heartache, and often turned to alcohol to dull her senses.

Frederick's disappearance had also taken a financial toll on the family. After Alaya's birth, Janice had originally planned to be a stay-at-home mom. Boredom, however, soon brought her back to the working world as a part-time nurse. However, once Frederick went missing, the weeks stretched into months, and Janice had no choice but to resume working full-time to put food on the table and keep a roof over their heads.

Luckily, Janice's salary as a registered nurse was fairly decent, but with college on the horizon for Alaya, it had become clear that something would have to change.

"Alaya! Come take a look at this!" her mom shouted. Raised voices that echoed through their oddly empty house had been their accepted mode of communication for several years. It was especially useful when Alaya was upstairs, but not particularly appropriate when she was standing right beside her mother.

"Mom, I'm right behind you!" Alaya said, covering her ears with her palms.

"Oh, okay. Sorry honey, I didn't hear you come down. Anyway, look at this." Before Alaya had a chance to sit down, Janice handed her a folded newspaper like it was a college diploma. When Alaya unraveled it, she saw the front page of the classified ads. Several offerings were circled in red ink.

"Just look at you. My little girl is all grown up! Pretty soon, your hair will be gray and there will be grandchildren sitting on your lap." She smiled. Alaya could smell the vodka on her breath, but she ignored it.

"Is that the order of things these days? Thanks, Mom...Besides, what better way to embrace adulthood than by looking for terrible jobs in the classified section?" Alaya's sarcasm wasn't exactly hard to detect. While she knew it was time to start contributing to the household, Alaya wasn't too thrilled about joining the working world. College hadn't appealed to her in the slightest, either. She wished she could have had more time to think about her future path. After all, why rush these things? There was plenty of time to forge a life-long career she'd spend in misery and regret. Just by observation, Alaya learned that much from school.

Janice was steadfast. "My little comedian's always got something to joke about. Anyways, Alaya, I'm worried about you. I know that the years since your father disappeared have been difficult; we've both had to bear that weight."

She held her daughter's hand. "But we've got to move on, in spite of it. He wouldn't have wanted to see you throw away your potential, just because he isn't around to push you along. You sit around the house every day, wandering from couch to couch, but you've barely done anything since you graduated. At the top of your class, no less." The look in her eyes was serious, almost pleading.

This was not like the normal conversations that developed when the topic of Alaya's employment status was brought up. Alaya couldn't tell if that was a good thing or not; deep chats between mother and daughter had never been their forte.

"Alaya, I won't be around forever. I want...no, I *need* to know that you'll be okay if God decides that it's time for me to move on from here. You know what I'm saying, right?" Her mother's brow furrowed in worry, a common expression on both their faces.

Alaya rolled her eyes; she hated it when her mother became so melodramatic. Janice had no idea how much Alaya had thought about losing her; especially since Frederick disappeared.

"Mom, of course I understand. It's in my head almost every day, but I don't want to worry about losing you too. I just can't. I know that's a reality I'll face someday, but why worry for now? You look fine to me." She gave her mom a quick peck on the cheek and thanked her for breakfast.

Alaya sat at the table and began devouring her meal: scrambled eggs with turkey bacon and toast. She was a simple soul, and looked forward to the small pleasures in life. It wasn't that Alaya had no goals; she simply didn't want to pursue them if it meant that she would eventually grow to be miserable.

Ever since she was a little girl, Alaya had wanted to be a nurse just like her mom. She would often play with her dolls and patch them up when they were scuffed or dropped down the stairs. Her mother even joined in when she was younger, but Alaya was no longer sure that nursing was the best option for her future. She couldn't stand to see people suffering in pain, so leaping into a career that involved a lot of that didn't seem like the wisest choice. And Alaya swore on her life that she would never turn to alcohol for comfort, not even once. Seeing her mother passed out on the couch after particularly brutal nights had taken a toll on their relationship. The ups and downs of the emotional tide in their home often made Alaya feel seasick.

It wasn't until she was halfway through chomping on her last bit of toast that Alaya noticed her mother frowning across the table.

"What is it?"

"You didn't even look at the newspaper." Janice said, and slid the folded paper across the table until it was under the front rim of Alaya's plate. "Go on, take a look."

Realizing that this was a battle she would clearly not win, Alaya glanced down and read while she ate. The advertisement encircled with several red lines stated in bold, block letters that an antique store was hiring.

"Oh, come on, Mom. You can't be serious. Mr. Miller's Antiques? That old man is probably two days away from a padded cell." Alaya continued eating. "Everyone knows it – even you."

"Listen, Alaya. I know there are plenty of rumors about Mr. Miller, but he's a good man. And besides, there's nothing wrong with being a little eccentric..."

"A *little*? Mom, listen to yourself. Really? If he was just a *little* eccentric, then why have my friends said that they've seen him talking into a shoe? He was talking like there was someone on the other end. Who knows, maybe he's James Bond in real life." She retorted.

"Stop it, Alaya. You've been nineteen for six months now. You're not starting college anytime soon, unless you've enrolled without telling me, which I doubt. I thought you wanted to pursue nursing; it's what you've always said. You graduated tenth in your class without even trying, but that was a year ago. You have all this talent and you're just carelessly throwing it away like it means nothing. How do you think your father would feel if he could see you like this?" Her mother asked, her eyes gleaming with the painful statement.

Alaya looked at her mother; the words stung like prickly thorns.

"I know you might not like it, but you have to hear it. You've been like this ever since he left; there's just a general...apathy about you. At some point, you're gonna have to get up and start living like an adult." Janice continued, unapologetic and blunt. Her expression turned to stone.

Alaya turned away and stood up to leave the table. She couldn't stand when her mother tried to lay guilt trips on her, but bringing her father into things was too much to bear.

"Look, all I'm saying is that it's time to do something with your life. You have no clear direction right now, and I don't know how else to motivate you. Some days, talking to you is like talking to a rock. All you do is watch television or fiddle with your phone. I assume you're still talking to old friends, but you never seem to go out anywhere and have fun with them anymore. That's no way to live. One day, you're going to look up and wonder what happened. Then you'll realize that these are years you will never get back. Precious years lost, where you could have really made something memorable and started your own life outside of these walls," Janice finished, a motherly tone creeping back into her voice.

Alaya listened with her back still turned to her mother, frozen in her flight to the staircase back up to the attic. She didn't know how to feel; her face was blank while her mind wrestled with Janice's words. Alaya understood the magnitude of her mother's message, but she didn't feel ready to commit to anything. She didn't feel she was ready to make any sudden moves toward a professional career. Perhaps she wanted to hold onto the time when she felt happiest — her early childhood.

In addition to that, Alaya was disgusted by the idea of living a life where she was forced to work a nine-to-five job, just to pay bills that would simply reappear the following month. It seemed pointless. She wanted a different kind of life, something off that well-worn path of the masses. Alaya sometimes wished she lived in the 1960's; she would like to travel across the country in a van, with nothing but the clothes on her back and nature to sustain her.

The only problem was that her mother was right about one thing. Since her father went missing, Alaya's desire to do anything had basically vanished. She used to dream of becoming a ballerina, although this was quickly lost once she learned more about the rigorous training and painful torment that they put their feet through on a daily basis. Then, she wanted to be an archaeologist, like her father, traveling to new lands to uncover the planet's best-kept secrets. This second dream crumbled when her father disappeared while on a work trip. Since then, she hadn't formed any new interests in a career, although she knew that she liked helping others. In the back of her mind, she knew that she would get a job eventually, so she toyed with the idea of nursing, like her mother. But the honest truth was, a career was simply not something Alaya spent much time thinking about.

Janice must have sensed that her words had finally struck a nerve, and offered a reasonable suggestion.

"You can at least try getting into a community college around here. Just get your general education classes out of the way, and then maybe in a year or two, you'll know enough about a few different fields to pursue something that you enjoy. In the meantime, you're getting off your behind and doing something with yourself every day. I'm not here to pour the tea at your pity party, and I can't afford to give you a handout every time you need to buy something. Just give Mr. Miller a call. He and your father were very close. Who knows? That fact alone might get you hired."

"How close were they?" Alaya did not remember much about her father's relationship with the storeowner, except on those rare occasions when he would bring home items that Alaya had never seen before. They were 'special trinkets for special occasions,' as her father would say. She just remembered the teasing from her classmates about her father working with the strange old man.

"Why don't you ask him? I didn't get too involved since I knew Frederick was always looking for the latest and greatest discoveries, but it wasn't exactly my cup of tea. Wherever you end up working, I know it will do you some good to get out of this slump you've been in. And who knows? Maybe spending time with someone who was close to your father can help you accept the fact that he is probably not coming back. He may not even be alive. I know you don't like to talk about this, but if he was out there somewhere, wouldn't he have come home by now?" Janice said, her voice catching in her throat in a strange mix of anger and pain. Although it hurt to accept his disappearance, she had gradually developed a bitter, cynical outlook on the situation, which caused Alaya to despise her at times. Not to mention the drinking, which grew worse by the day.

"It wasn't easy for me to accept either, but one day, I realized that I had to keep on living," her mother said as she stood up from the table and moved toward Alaya. She turned her gaze away from the staircase, just enough to see the tears forming in her mother's eyes. Janice always became hyperemotional when she drank. "I had to keep on living, because there was still someone in my life who needed me." She looked as though she might become a crying heap any second.

Alaya knew her mother was right. It was time for her to take some pressure off her mother's shoulders and see what else life had to offer besides grief and daytime television.

"Okay, I'll give him a call."

***

After breakfast, Alaya called Mr. Miller on her cell phone and surprisingly, he offered her an interview for ten o'clock the following morning. With nearly perfect timing, Janice sauntered into her room, signaling the thumbs up with approval of her landing the interview.

"I'm proud of you!" She mouthed. As Alaya said goodbye to Mr. Miller, she could practically hear his excitement through the phone as well.

CHAPTER 2

The next morning, Alaya awoke to the sound of her favorite morning talk show on the radio. She reached out a lazy arm and slapped the snooze button, but it was too late. A few seconds later, her mother came bursting into the room.

"Time to rise and shine," Janice practically sang as she faced Alaya's window and flung the curtains wide. She turned the blinds open about halfway, allowing slivers of sunlight to sear across Alaya's face like hot pokers. Although it was early, the sun was bright on this clear morning.

Alaya was glad to see her mother in such a good mood. It had been a long, hard road to reclaim some semblance of happiness after her father disappeared. In the first years after it happened, her mom had fallen into a deep depression, which occasionally set her into sudden bursts of anger. Most of the time, Alaya was the unwitting recipient of her rage.

Once, Alaya overheard a friend suggest therapy, but Janice shunned the idea. Instead, she chose to self-medicate with alcohol. After a few rough starts with Alcoholics Anonymous, it seemed that she was doing better, but of course, setbacks were inevitable. Fortunately, today was a good day, and Alaya welcomed all the good days she could get.

"Come on, Mom! Please, I just need ten more minutes!" Alaya said, pulling the covers over her head. She took after her father in that regard. He had been a night owl, while her mother, on the other hand, had an irritating habit of being bright and chipper before the sun came up, even when she had nowhere to go. The schedule of a nurse was constantly in flux, especially when she was on-call, which was often. One of the nurses in her office recently quit, so while they were training the replacement, Janice was asked to take over the night shift. She had accepted since the pay was almost double. And somehow, Janice managed to live consistently off only five or six hours of sleep.

Alaya could never understand this; she much preferred falling into bed around midnight and sleeping in every morning until at least 9 am, but crawling out of bed after 11 o'clock wasn't unusual either. It didn't help that her bed was so warm and comfy.

"Get up, Alaya! You don't want to be late, girl," Janice said, and tugged the covers off the bed. Alaya sprang up, and reached out for them. The room was surprisingly cold on the early summer morning.

"And look at that hair of yours!" She stroked Alaya's frizzy dark brown hair, failing to smooth it down in spite of each stroke of her hand. The unruly coils simply sprang back up in defiance.

"Alaya, you're not going to go into the interview like that, are you? The wild-eyed, bushy-tailed look may have worked for you in high school, but that's not going to cut it in the professional world. You'd better braid it down or something." Janice admonished.

Alaya sighed as she fell backwards onto the pillow, biting her tongue while choosing her words carefully.

15

"I've told you a thousand times, Mom. I like it this way. If he can't accept that, then this job wouldn't work out for me anyway." She said.

"Please, honey, take this seriously, for me?" Janice pleaded. "I don't know why you always have to turn things into an argument. I know how you feel about your hair, but at least make it look presentable. You know all those business professionals aren't just blowing smoke when they say to dress for success. At least *try* to make it look like you want to be there."

Alaya laughed. "That's the beauty of natural hair, Mom. I do make an effort, and it still looks good...even like this." Alaya got out of bed and modeled in front of the mirror across the room, making faces like she was posing for a photo shoot—pursing her lips together, pulling in her cheeks and flirting coyly with her reflection.

"Alright, alright. We've been down this road before." Janice sighed, and glanced down at her buzzing pager. "Just get ready, please."

Although it was her day off, Janice was still on-call for emergencies, which always seemed to come up when she was off the clock.

"I've got to go, do you want a ride?" She quickly asked.

"I'm fine, Mom. Thanks for the offer, though."

Janice kissed Alaya's forehead and patted down her rebellious hair before disappearing out the door. The fact that she was being called in to work on her day off meant that there was someone facing something much more serious than a job interview. Besides, the hospital was in the opposite direction of the store.

Once in the bathroom, Alaya gripped the edge of the sink and stared hard at her reflection in the mirror. She reached for gels and a brush, wondering what to do to with her mass of hair. After fussing with it for a few minutes, she decided to just slick it into submission with some gel and put it into a ponytail, a universally accepted style. It was never offensively huge and was versatile enough to be dressed down or up, depending on the occasion. She slipped on some nice slacks, a loose-fitting blouse, and some small square vintage earrings that her mother had gotten her as a graduation gift. Alaya was about to head out the door when she remembered one final element of her outfit. Back in her bedroom, she opened the vintage armoire near her bed, pulled open a drawer, and put on her favorite necklace. It was a key charm that her father gave her when she was a child.

When Alaya walked up to the door the door, she saw Mr. Miller through the glass. He was pacing back and forth, while poring over a book. He appeared to be mumbling to himself. Once Alaya pushed open the glass door, a loud clang of bells shattered the silence, signaling her arrival like a call for the cavalry. Mr. Miller nearly dropped his book to the floor. His half-moon glasses slid off the bridge of his nose, straight to the floor. He quickly reached down for his reading glasses, and fumbled with them, struggling to regain his composure. He tried to look calm and collected as Alaya entered the store.

"Good morning, are you Mr. Miller?" She asked as she carefully closed the door behind her.

"Oh yes, that would be me. I'm very glad to see you!" He pressed forward, with an outstretched arm. "Thank you for making it on such short notice." Mr. Miller said with a big smile, clapping his book shut and laying it on the counter next to him. Alaya had a difficult time determining if he was genuinely excited to see her or if he was just grateful that someone had actually showed up.

"No, thank you for offering to meet with me." Alaya said, hoping to sound as though she wanted to be there. She took a look around, and realized that her day of preparation might have better suited Mr. Miller, than herself. She was careful not to step on anything as she walked through the claustrophobically cluttered store. The shop was an absolute mess; it was a wonder that he got any business at all.

Random pieces of tin, scraps, and other antiques were scattered across the floor, on shelves, and even in bookcases. It looked as though Mr. Miller had either zero ability to catalogue his wares, or he had been the victim of a powerful earthquake. Since Alaya would have remembered any seismic activity in recent weeks, she went with the former and assumed Mr. Miller simply lacked organization skills of any kind.

"The sooner the better, I say! You know the saying about the early bird catching its breakfast…or something like that." Mr. Miller said, butchering the euphemism.

Alaya didn't correct him; she could only shake her head and smile. This was the Mr. Miller she knew all right. Some things hadn't changed one bit.

"You're my first interview of the day." He said, and gestured towards the back of the store. "Come, come! Don't mind the mess! Please follow me. My office is right down the hall. We can interview there." Mr. Miller waddled as he walked through the "hall", which was just a narrow space between piles of desks, chairs, dressers, elaborately carved headboards, and dozens of other unidentifiable objects. It appeared that his left leg was slightly shorter than his right. Realizing that it was rude for her to continue staring, Alaya diverted her gaze to the stacks of antiques, piled high and balanced like a varnished house of cards.

"This is all very interesting, Mr. Miller. I can't remember the last time I was here, but there seems to be loads of new things." She made sure to avoid commenting about the current arrangement of his inventory.

Mr. Miller's cheeks flushed red at the comment, either in pleasure at her compliment or embarrassment at the discombobulated state of the shop, which she had been kind enough to not mention — at least, out loud.

"Why thank you, Alaya. Yes, it is all rather fascinating. Every piece has a story. And what you see out there is only the half of it. Ah, here we are." Mr. Miller opened his office door, ushered Alaya in, and instructed her to have a seat. The only available chair was an old, tattered piece with clawed feet, upholstered in sea-green leather. It looked like something that just walked out of a 1970's magazine ad.

Only the half of it? Alaya thought with disbelief as she walked into the cramped office. She sat down on the beat-up chair and took a deep breath, preparing herself for the interview questions she was prepared to answer.

"Why don't you tell me a little about yourself?" Mr. Miller asked, as he trundled his way around the desk to sit in his larger, though equally modest and worn leather chair.

Alaya was expecting this, so she was calm and measured in her response. She told him about her interest in working at his store, particularly in relation to her father and the interest he held in archaeology. She remembered how he often brought home antiques, one of which was the piece of jewelry that she treasured above all others.

"I don't believe in luck, but this has always been a favorite of mine." Alaya said, fingering the chain around her neck.

"Oh? And what is that?" Mr. Miller asked.

Alaya pulled the long silver chain from the inside of her blouse, revealing a key-shaped charm. Small, mother-of-pearl-like jewels were clustered in a circle on the handle.

19

"What do you think?" Alaya asked. She took off the necklace, and dropped it into his hand.

"Ack!" Mr. Miller recoiled in unexpected shock and dropped the necklace on the wooden desk.

"I'm terribly sorry, but I'm a bit of a germaphobe." Mr. Miller apologized. "I'll just set it down, right here, if you don't mind," he continued, flustered and red as a tomato. He gently dropped the chain on the desk between them.

Alaya assumed that he must have had a severe case of mysophobia. One of her teachers, Mrs. Wright, had suffered from the same condition back in grade school. It was always entertaining to watch her endure panic attacks every other day when a student would sneeze or accidentally touch her while she walked past. Accepting seemingly benign gifts such as apples were totally out of the question. Alaya had never understood why Mrs. Wright would want to teach school-age kids, who had to be some of the most filthy, germ-ridden creatures on the planet.

Mr. Miller took a closer look at the necklace, with a magnifying glass he retrieved from his top desk drawer. He was silent as he examined the charm, turning it over with the tip of his letter opener, rather than using his long, surprisingly delicate fingers.

"You shouldn't take that off..." He said in a low voice. Alaya leaned in to hear his words; he was practically whispering.

"Excuse me?"

"I mean...it's lovely," he said. "Those gems, they are truly a rarity and perfectly intact. I forget the name, but I know that they are quite valuable. Must be worth a fortune."

Alaya reached across the desk and picked up the necklace with a bit more care. She had no idea that it held such value.

"Your father was a very talented man, Alaya. Brilliant beyond what even you may have realized. It was a true pleasure to have had the opportunity to work with him."

Mr. Miller spent the remainder of the interview explaining the particulars of the job, and what she could expect if she were to become an employee.

They exchanged a few additional words and small talk pleasantries before he brought the interview to a close and told her that she would hear back from him with a decision very soon.

After making it back home, Alaya decided the interview had gone well. While the shop was certainly strange, Mr. Miller seemed nice enough. She assumed it would take several days before hearing from him, so she changed back into her pajamas, made some popcorn, and plopped onto the couch to watch her favorite television show - Maury Povich. Alaya loved outrageous scandals and "baby mama drama", both of which Maury had in high supply. She was dozing on the couch a few hours later when the phone rang. Shaking the sleep out of her head, she picked up, only to hear Mr. Miller's voice on the other end, informing her that she had gotten the job. She thanked him, and he asked if she had any additional questions, but she drew a blank.

"Great! Why not start tomorrow, at 10 o'clock?"

Alaya was stunned; everything was happening so fast. Perhaps this is how things were with part-time jobs. Or, it was because he just really needed the help that badly.

"Sounds good." Alaya agreed before hanging up the phone and turning back to the white noise of trash television.

CHAPTER 3

Around eight o'clock the next morning, the insistent siren of Alaya's alarm clock startled her awake. She proceeded to declare war against the bothersome machine, and viciously smacked the "snooze" button every ten minutes until she finally admitted defeat at nine. It had been a late night; last night she crawled into bed at two in the morning. Alaya made a mental note to stop torturing herself in the sleep department.

Dragging her feet, Alaya moved almost as slow as growing grass while she got ready for work. Each task of her morning routine with done with such deliberate slowness that a sleepwalking octogenarian would have looked spry and even youthful in comparison.

Alaya walked past her mother's room and peered in. Her mother was fast asleep, although Alaya hadn't heard her return from work. Alaya glimpsed at her mother's clock — it read half-past nine. She hadn't scheduled any time for a proper breakfast, so she quickly went into the kitchen and grabbed a pen and a piece of paper.

Quickly, Alaya scribbled a note:

Mom,

I got the job. Mr. Miller wants me to start today. I love you.

Alaya reached into the snacks cabinet to grab a protein bar, and headed out the door.

***

By the time she arrived at Mr. Miller's Antiques, Alaya had woken up a bit and was ready to face her first day. The walk wasn't too bad, maybe fifteen minutes. She opened the door and the bells on the handle once again clanged and chimed long after she had made her way inside. Every bit of the store remained just as it was yesterday. She could only imagine what Mr. Miller would have her working on first, but organization was never her strong suit. Alaya didn't think it was possible so early on, but she was beginning to feel overwhelmed.

Mr. Miller presented himself a moment later, appearing from around a chaotic corner of nearly-toppling gadgets with an outstretched hand.

"Hello, my dear, come, come!" He motioned his hand forward when he saw the apprehensive look on her face. "Don't look so nervous; you already got the job, right? It's okay to look around. Let me give you the full tour."

Mr. Miller proceeded to show her around the store, and explained the hours of operation. Although each wall and corner was packed with antiques like cooking materials, books, furniture, and other knick-knacks, the high ceiling made it feel slightly less intimidating.

"The store is open Monday-Saturday, from ten in the morning to seven in the evening, but this is only for the summer. In the fall, I will only be open until six. I would like you to work most days during the week and every Saturday." He said, while still showing her around.

Alaya was shocked by the small mountains of antiques, which somehow looked even larger than they had the day before. As they passed the door to his office, Alaya saw it was slightly ajar. She quickly glanced inside, and saw there was another door just beyond it. *Had that been there before?*

Mr. Miller pointed to the attic, explaining that some of his unprocessed inventory was stored there. The attic would also need to be catalogued into the inventory once the main room was completed. This was just too much, and Alaya began to have second thoughts. She wasn't sure if she could be a personal maid. The ad specifically asked for an assistant, to help with purchases, and recommendations to customers. Alaya began to make conversation, hoping this would cause Mr. Miller to reconsider her job duties.

"How long have you owned this store, Mr. Miller?"

"Almost eighteen years now. It's been a long time, and I'm honestly surprised that I'm still in business, especially with the place looking like this! You've been very kind, but I know what you must be thinking. This place is a sty—I know." He stepped into his office, grabbed something, and handed a small pile of forms to Alaya. He casually walked over to the far corner of his office, and shut the door.

"This closet door, always popping open." He smiled. "Now, if you wouldn't mind, I just need you to fill these out. They're just formalities for taxes and such. When you're finished, we can get started!"

Alaya sat in the sea-foam green chair and filled out the forms, adding her emergency contacts and other basic employment processing paperwork. Mr. Miller tried to look busy at his desk, but it was clear that he was only waiting for her to finish.

"So, Alaya, tell me more about that necklace of yours. How did your father come to own it?" Mr. Miller asked.

"I think he said he picked it up here at the store." Alaya said. She removed it from her blouse, but kept it around her neck.

"He gave it to me a long time ago. I may have been only five or six years old, but he didn't allow me to start wearing it until I was eleven. Since then, it's been my good luck charm. Whenever I wear it, I feel like I can accomplish whatever I want and things seem to go my way. At least, until..." Alaya trailed off, trying to ward off the particularly painful memory of the time when the necklace failed to work in her favor. She returned to completing her paperwork in silence. After a moment, she said in a soft voice, "I guess it doesn't always work."

"I see." Mr. Miller replied, seemingly unsure of what to say next. "I don't remember having this particular piece for sale, but, as you can see..." Mr. Miller motioned to the boxes full of unsorted items stuffed into every nook and cranny of the office, "...there is quite a bit that I have to keep track of. I hired you, because I was sure you could appreciate what this store has to offer. Your father was not only a great scholar, but an unrivaled friend."

Alaya appreciated the kind words. Once she was done with her paperwork, Alaya couldn't resist and asked how much competition she had for the job. Mr. Miller looked puzzled by the question.

"Why do you want to know?" he asked cautiously.

"Actually, I'm just curious. You did call me back pretty fast," Alaya answered. She secretly wondered if anyone else was crazy, or desperate, enough to try and work at the store. She obviously kept that second question to herself.

Mr. Miller went on to tell her that she was the only one who had inquired about the position. Once he saw her, he realized that she was Frederick's daughter.

"And if you have anything remotely close to Frederick's work ethic, I know things will work out just fine." He assured her. "So, welcome aboard! Now, let's get started."

Mr. Miller took the rest of the day steering Alaya around the store, helping her get acquainted with some of the merchandise and familiarizing her with the layout. Occasionally, he demonstrated how to assist customers, although there were very few. He ended up letting her go a bit before closing time, since the foot traffic coming into the shop was nonexistent. It was the 4th of July, and the town was electrified in anticipation for what promised to be a dazzling spectacle of fireworks, courtesy of the city of Annapolis.

"See you tomorrow, Alaya. 10 a.m. on the dot!" Mr. Miller flashed a toothy smile just before closing the door behind her, and flipping the sign to "closed." The thick humid air of the summer night blanketed over her skin.

CHAPTER 4

Back at home, Alaya found her mother asleep on the couch. The television was on and the first edition of the evening news was about to begin. It was only six o'clock, but there was an empty bottle toppled over on the floor. It was merlot—her mother's favorite red wine. She reached over Janice as quietly as possible and gently plucked the remote control from underneath her arm, and turned off the television. When the background hum was silenced, Janice bolted awake.

"What! What is it?" she said, looking out of sorts and disoriented.

"Relax, Mom. You fell asleep with the TV on again. I just turned it off...nothing's wrong." Alaya sat down beside her on the couch and began smoothing her mother's disheveled hair.

"Alaya? What time is it?" Janice struggled against her daughter's encircling arm. She was groggy, but eventually managed to sit upright. It was clear that she needed more rest than she had gotten. Her eyes were bloodshot, and there were dark rings hanging low beneath her eyes. Alaya couldn't help but hide a small smirk while watching her mother attempt to rise from the couch. Janice pushed her thin blanket aside and struggled to regain some of her maternal presence and control.

"It's after six now, Mom." Alaya was unable to contain her laughter when she noticed that Janice had also managed to somehow put her shirt on inside out.

"Really! Six? Well, then it's almost time for the fireworks!" Janice said, now standing. She nearly stumbled over the empty glass bottle, sending it spinning across the floor. "Oh, my head." She placed a palm on her forehead, and rested her other hand on her hip.

"Careful, Mom! Don't worry about the fireworks. We really don't have to go. I'm nineteen years old...a bit beyond fireworks in the park. I mean it; we don't have to go out tonight. It looks like you could use some more rest. Do you want me to make you something?" Alaya stood up and continued smoothing down a wild patch of her mother's hair. Although her mother's hair was silky and straight, this patch defiantly stood on top of her head. At least they had that in common.

"Kid or not, Alaya, we still enjoy it every year. Let's go...come on. I'll even buy you some ice cream! Your favorite - Rocky Road."

Alaya couldn't say no to that. Her mother's face beamed with excitement, even though it was clear that she was somewhere between the middle and the end of a mild hangover. Alaya decided that it was best to make an effort at normalcy. "Good" days were fewer and further between than they used to be.

"Alright, Mom. You sold me with the ice cream," Alaya responded, knowing that she shouldn't deprive her mother of the joy she got out of this event every year. Considering how stressed and overworked Janice had been lately, perhaps this was exactly what she needed. Alaya was upset that her mother had been drinking so heavily yet again, but decided now wasn't the time to bring it up.

As they walked through the neighborhood, heading toward Shady Tree Park, Alaya grew quiet as she reflected on her earlier years and Independence Days gone by. She remembered how her father had walked with her through town into the park, often with her perched atop his shoulders. After she grew too big for this, she held both her parents' hands. They would often swing her back and forth, feet never touching the ground. Although each year, this took more and more effort on their part. This old memory brought a smile to her face.

Alaya thought back to her final Independence Day outing with her parents. She was twelve years old, and her father had reached out for her hand, but she refused. Alaya remembered the moment like it was yesterday. She had told him that she was 'too old' for that, and didn't need to hold his hand anymore. Besides, her classmates would tease her if they knew that she was still holding her parents' hands at that age.

But now, seven years later, walking through the streets with just her mother, Alaya would have given anything to be able to hold his hand just once more. She wouldn't be ashamed of it...ashamed of him. She felt the tears begin to form and turned her gaze so her mother wouldn't see. She looked far into the distance at the deep hue of orange that was splayed out like a burst of fire on the horizon. She loved it when the sun hid itself beneath the sky, blending with the rest of the early night sky to create a perfect canvas of rich, vibrant colors. It was almost as though the clouds waited patiently until the sun was gone, so they could then follow with their own encore of spectacular reflections to display a subtler beauty all their own.

Alaya was grateful for the slowly darkening sky.

29

Despite her hangover, Janice noticed something was off. Although, as a mother, it was no surprise she was able to see straight through Alaya.

"Your father would have wanted you to be happy right now, Alaya. There's no point in allowing yourself to get stuck in the past. Your father would have wanted both of us to enjoy ourselves. Just like the song says." Janice grabbed Alaya's hands and began swaying from side to side in a dance that Alaya had no desire to participate in. "Don't worry, be happy, right?" Janice gave her a little bump with her hip and began singing; not one note hitting the right key.

"Please, Mom, please. Anything but that! I'm happy now, see?" Alaya smiled a smile so wide that it was almost ridiculous.

"Okay, I get it. Too old to dance with your mom. But a smile is a nice improvement, even if you have to force it. Smiles beat tears every time. Don't ever forget that." Janice gave Alaya a side hug, and they continued walking toward the park. They were just beyond the historic shops district when they noticed Mr. Miller approaching them from the opposite direction.

"Why hello, Mr. Miller! Fancy seeing you here." Janice said and greeted him with a hug.

"Yes, I was just locking up the store for the evening. Hello, Alaya. Long time, no see!" He tipped the oversized brim of his hat in her direction, nodding.

"Hey, Mr. Miller. Are you coming to see the fireworks too? My mom and I do this every year. It's been a tradition in our family." She said, half hoping that he would choose not to join them. This event was supposed to be for family only, but Alaya knew it would have been rude not to at least extend the offer.

"Well, you should enjoy it then. Quality time spent with family can never be replaced, right?" he said, and a warm smile spread across his face. "I'll see you tomorrow?"

"Of course, bright and early," Alaya replied, now genuinely grinning.

"Wonderful! Janice, it's lovely to see you again." He nodded politely, shook her hand, and then headed off in the opposite direction. Alaya watched as he turned left at the next corner and was gone.

"I wonder how he celebrates holidays?" Janice said.

Alaya wondered the same thing. As far as she knew, he had no family.

CHAPTER 5

The next day at work, Alaya dutifully inspected just about every piece in the store, wondering what stories might be concealed in their past. She held up an old, worn cast-iron skillet, which looked so deeply rusted that she thought she might cut herself if she held it wrong. Alaya had always had a fascination with the antique wares and often wondered who the former owners were. That instinct made her happy, since it was also something that intrigued her father throughout his life.

She picked up an old musical instrument that resembled a small wooden flute. However, it was shorter, and instead of keys it had open holes strategically placed along its length.

"Mr. Miller, where did you get all of this stuff?" She asked, gently placing the flute back on the display case.

Mr. Miller looked over his shoulder and smiled.

"I see you found the Tarka flute! It plays beautifully, or so I've heard." He spread out his arm to encompass the scope of his impressive inventory.

"Everything you see here—these items are from unique places all over the world. Flea markets from other countries, estate sales, and the occasional donation. When my supply runs low, I go out on a field trip.

He nodded towards the Tarka flute. "I came across that gem while I was in Peru. Sometimes, I've just gotten in my car and driven until I felt the urge to stop. Once, I drove all the way to Quebec, which is where I got this."

Mr. Miller pulled something from his pocket that looked like a cross between a toothbrush and a medieval torture device. "Early dental hygiene from 18th century Canadians!" He handed it to Alaya, but she quickly placed both hands up.

"Oh, I don't want to destroy something so old. Shouldn't that be in a museum somewhere?" Alaya was feeling somewhere between intrigue and nausea as she inspected the painful looking instrument. She also questioned the cleanliness of the device.

"So, where's the furthest you've ever traveled?" She asked.

Mr. Miller thought for a long time before answering. "That's actually a very tough question. I can't properly say for sure." He paused, as though he was considering something else, but held back.

"I'll get back to you on that one, I promise." He said, although his smile faded.

"Okay." Alaya said. But this response was not okay; it was strange. Why would anyone need time to think about the furthest place they've traveled? She figured she would revisit this question at a later time.

After confirming that it was okay to do some "housecleaning," Alaya continued sorting through the massive piles to determine what was safe for purchase and what was actually junk—or worse—a safety hazard. Some antiques crumbled through her fingertips the moment she picked them up.

Alaya also helped lower the prices of any duplicate items, such as a pair of musty Russian tapestries. She was actually making good progress for the afternoon, and the clock only read half past one.

While sorting through a particularly dust-filled crate, Alaya accidentally inhaled a bit of it, and began a sneezing frenzy. Once the dust had settled, she saw something moving from the corner of her eye. When she looked down at her right arm, she began to shriek and slapped her arms around like a windmill. In an instant, Mr. Miller ran over to see what all the commotion was about. He quickly navigated through the piles of junk he must have known so well.

"It was just a spider...sorry if I was a little melodramatic. I just *really* hate spiders." Alaya said, fraught with panic as she still smacked at her arm. The silky fibers of the spider web clung to her skin with uncanny determination. She tried not to think about how silly she must have looked. After all, someone her age shouldn't still be reacting with such fear.

After she successfully pulled off the last stubborn bits of cobweb, Alaya turned to Mr. Miller.

"How long has this stuff been sitting here?" She asked. Alaya thought it was a miracle he managed to keep himself in business considering the state of things.

"A few years, perhaps...although, maybe it's been a bit longer than that." He mused with uncertainty. "One never really knows these things for sure, do they?"

Alaya rolled her eyes and turned back to her work. Although, she sped up her pace so she wouldn't have to linger with the pesky spiders and their nests. She feared at any moment, she would certainly feel the rumblings of her stomach as it threatened to violently return her lunch. Alaya had never even enjoyed picking up after herself as a child, but in this endless room of junk, cleaning up after Mr. Miller was almost too much. After all, it wasn't her mess, so why should she have to suffer through it? Cleaning hadn't been mentioned as part of her duties in the job interview. If it had been, she probably wouldn't have accepted, no matter what her mother had to say about it.

CHAPTER 6

After a month's time working at the antique store, and despite her initial concerns, Alaya actually developed a fondness for the dump. Sure it was still messy and disorganized, but they were making vast improvements and she felt a growing sense of pride. As the store progressed, they began to attract a few more customers. She was especially thrilled when she would overhear comments such as "what a quaint little place," and, "it's got a charming sort of character." Mr. Miller also seemed impressed and satisfied with the growing business. Alaya liked to think she had a hand in that.

With August brought the beginning of a new college semester. This part-time job soon became a welcome distraction for Alaya, and delayed her from submitting an admissions package for the nearby community college. She and Mr. Miller had been getting on far better than expected, which surprised even her. So Janice agreed that as long as Alaya was happy, it would be okay to postpone for just one more semester.

As far as Mr. Miller, he was a little eccentric, but otherwise harmless. In fact, she was starting to like the old guy, as well as the bizarre stories behind some of the stranger antiques in the store. He seemed to have taken a shine to her as well. He was patient with her questions about the store's inventory, seemingly taking a delight in her interest. There was some sort of background story for everything, so Alaya only asked about the most unusual items. Otherwise, she never would have made any progress – succinct was not a word she would use to describe her new boss.

At the end of another full day of packing, sorting, and pricing inventory, Alaya was preparing to head out the door when Mr. Miller called her name. She stopped with her handle on the door, and the bells slightly jingled.

"Alaya, there's something I'd like you to read tonight." Mr. Miller said as he walked toward her. He was holding a large envelope and wore a broad smile.

"What's this?" she asked, slipping it into her large purse that hung at her elbow.

"Just a bit of light reading. Let me know what you think about it tomorrow. It should answer a lot of the questions you've been having, and probably a few you haven't thought of yet. Have a good night!"

Mr. Miller walked Alaya to the door and she exited, intrigued by the contents of the envelope. But once the warm summer air embraced her, her mind drifted to on one thing: frozen yogurt at the nearby ice cream parlor. She could already smell the intoxicating aroma of warm, fresh waffle cones being made.

***

Back at home, after enjoying her frozen treat, Alaya found a note from her mother. She was apparently stuck at work and wouldn't be home until ten o'clock at night. Alaya took the opportunity to cook for herself - a small steak with home-made fries, followed by a much larger serving of her favorite Rocky Road ice cream straight out of the carton. The creamy goodness and the tingle of sugar in her blood always had a way of making everything else in her life seem irrelevant. Alaya knew that perhaps one day soon, this would all catch up to her and she'd have to change her eating habits. But thankfully, today was not that day. She had to thank her mother for her fast metabolism. It didn't seem to matter what she ate; for now, her clothes still fit the same.

After tidying up and doing a few chores around the house, Alaya went to her room and flopped onto the bed. Her favorite reality television show was about to start when she saw the crinkled corner of Mr. Miller's envelope poking out from the top of her workbag.

Although the latest episode of "Mall Wars" looked promising, Alaya decided to get the "light reading" out of the way. She hadn't expected homework to be a part of a shop assistant's job description, but she couldn't deny that she was intrigued. Mr. Miller did have plenty of interesting stories. She opened the envelope and slid out the pile of papers inside. She picked up the first sheet sitting on top and had only gotten a few sentences in when she heard her mother come through the front door.

"Alaya! Are you here? Can you please get some food together for me? I'm absolutely exhausted." She heard Janice drop her things unceremoniously on the counter. Moments later, Alaya heard the crunch of the leather sofa as her mother sat down, followed by the dull hum of the television.

"Yeah, Mom...I'm coming." Alaya sighed and put the stack of papers on her nightstand. The last thing she wanted to do was go back into the kitchen. However, there was a limit to her irritation with her mother. After all, Janice had been working noticeably harder since the nurse shortage. Even though Alaya now had a job, at least she never had to work double shifts. She wasn't even sure she could if she tried. Sleep — that sweet escape — was far too important.

Besides, something else had been troubling Alaya. Although her mother had tried to hide it, it was becoming clear that Janice had been drinking more often. Her hangovers had gotten so bad that Alaya couldn't help but notice the empty aspirin bottles piling up in the wastebasket, not to mention the clang of wine bottles in the recycling bin outside that occasionally woke Alaya up at strange hours. That familiar, toxic nectar was the only thing Janice trusted to quell the pain. A head filled with wine helped exorcise the demons that haunted her nightmares after brutal late-night shifts. The traumatic vision of bloody children pulled screaming from car wrecks was the stuff of nightmares that followed Janice into her waking hours. Alcohol would get her to sleep, but Alaya feared the toll it was taking.

Alaya prepared some steamed vegetables and quickly seared a steak in the frying pan. When she brought it in to her mother with a glass of water, she found her fast asleep. Alaya gently placed the plate on a TV tray next to the couch and headed back to her bedroom. Nestled into the warm, fluffy blankets on her bed, Alaya was set for some uninterrupted reading.

The first few sentences were non-descript—a summary of inventory from nearly two decades ago. However, as Alaya delved deeper into the pages, her father's name appeared. Alaya sat upright, her heart racing as she continued to read. After another page or two, she realized that not only had Mr. Miller been a friend of her father, Frederick Stevenson, but her new boss had also enlisted her absent father to collect items from distant lands. Some of the locations were exotic, but unremarkable, like Tunisia, Jamaica, and Peru.

The name of one land in particular continued to appear in the text, a name that Alaya hadn't heard since she was a child. It swept Alaya back to many years ago, when her father told her bedtime stories to get her to fall asleep. The place was called Batunia, and she loved to hear tales of the mysterious land.

As a child, Alaya thought it was a make-believe land, just like any of the other stories her parents read to her just before bedtime. But here it was in black and white, being discussed as a real destination. One that was just as real as Mexico or Nepal. Alaya read through a few more pages and her confusion deepened. According to what she held in her hands, it looked like her father had gone to Batunia nearly a dozen times.

Alaya didn't like feeling foolish, but none of this made any sense. Was there any truth to this? Or was Mr. Miller indeed that out of touch with reality? However, if it was the latter, why would her father work so closely with him for so long?

Alaya began to wonder, *did he hire me because of my father? Or is Mr. Miller just a silly old man pulling a prank on his new employee?* Alaya thought about asking her mom, but then realized it may not have been such a good idea just yet. At any rate, Alaya knew one thing was certain: Mr. Miller appeared to have had a much deeper connection to her father than she had known.

Alaya was also beginning to think that Mr. Miller must've shown her the papers for a reason, although there was something missing—an explanation. Crazy or not, she was going to find out more.

CHAPTER 7

Alaya struggled through the front door, sweating more than she would like. Both hands were clutching overstuffed bags of takeout for her and Mr. Miller. The Chinese restaurant spared no expense when it came to extras. They both had two side orders, hot and sour soup, an egg roll, full entrees, and drinks. This was by far the best lunch special around. As an added bonus, it was only a few minutes' walking distance to the shop, so there was no need to tip for delivery.

Mr. Miller switched the sign on the shop to "will return at noon," and the door clanged shut. They both sat at the small table in his back office to eat. At once, they opened the small white boxes and dug in like ravenous wolves. After several minutes, Alaya knew she needed to break the silence. She had been thinking about what she'd read in the pamphlet all morning, waiting for the right time. *Carpe diem*, she thought.

"Mr. Miller, I had some questions about the papers you gave me yesterday." Alaya said, before scooping a large portion of chicken fried rice into her mouth. She was slightly disappointed; although the soup and egg roll were delicious, the rice smelled a lot better than it tasted.

"You've already read through it? That's great! So, what did you think?" Mr. Miller asked with marked enthusiasm as he delicately pulled the flimsy lid off the container for his soup.

"Well, last night, I tried doing some research online, but I couldn't find anything about one place you mentioned — Batunia. I've also never heard of it in history classes or geography lessons, and I couldn't find it on any maps. Is it called something else by the people who live there? Or is Batunia the name that you and my father gave it? I mean, according to the rest of the world, this place doesn't exist. So how could my father have gone there?"

Alaya was unsure how Mr. Miller would answer, but she didn't care. She had planned to approach this subject a bit slower, but the mystery of the past 12 hours had all spilled out of her like water breaching a dam.

He returned her flood of questions with a coy smile. "Well, in school, did you ever learn about Pompeii? Or the lost city of Atlantis?" Alaya nodded in confirmation.

"But Pompeii was real, and Atlantis isn't." She said.

"Well, as far as we *know*, Atlantis isn't real." Mr. Miller clarified. "Just like those two worlds, Batunia is shrouded in mystery. Your father and I believe it is real; although very few others have agreed with us. My thought is, Batunia was some sort of ancient world, where all documentation was destroyed before the Kingdom's history was recorded." He said matter-of-factly.

"A city forgotten by time." Alaya said. "That's interesting, but if it was lost thousands of years ago, then how was my father able to take trips there? Was he trying to find the supposed site of the city? Where did he actually go?"

Mr. Miller's lips were pressed tightly together as he looked into her eyes, seeming to look through her, measuring something inside. He opened his mouth, but said nothing. She felt like she was getting close, so she pressed him.

"Mr. Miller, besides me, you've only ever worked with my father. That can't be a coincidence." She refused to let him off the hook; it was clear that he wanted to say something.

"You're right. There is no such thing as a coincidence, Alaya." He said. A meaningless non-answer, and then his lips shut again, but she was not going to be put off by riddles or cryptic wisdom.

"So why do you need me? I know you trusted my father, but what does that have to do with me?" Alaya was direct; there was no sense pretending to be otherwise. There had to be a reason why he had given her those papers, knowing she would come back with questions about Batunia and her father.

But still, Mr. Miller remained silent. He seemed to be mulling through his thoughts.

"Were you two working with a museum or his school or something? Trying to find evidence or artifacts that prove this place existed?" She tried to put herself in Mr. Miller's shoes. It had been her father's life-long dream to discover new territories and unearth secrets of long-lost civilizations. At least that was what Janice told Alaya when she was younger. *Pieces of the world's past can help shape our future,* he would often say.

Finally, Mr. Miller answered. "Yes." But he did not elaborate. He had a puzzled, suddenly serious expression, which looked out of place on his usual jovial face. He stood up abruptly.

"Alaya, the time has come. There is something I would like to show you. However, you *must* promise to keep this to yourself," he warned. His voice was cold – a stark contrast to his usual light-hearted nature.

Alaya hesitated, but slowly nodded and promised to protect his secret.

"Alright. Follow me." Mr. Miller turned the sign on the front of the store to "closed," and walked to the back of his office. He stopped in front of a worn china cabinet made of rich, knotted oak, and carefully moved this fragile relic to the side. The exposed area of the wall held a small, narrow wooden door. It was the door that Alaya noticed had been slightly ajar a few weeks prior.

This door looked weathered and gnarled, as though it had been exposed to the elements for decades, rather than tucked behind a china cabinet in a dusty old shop. He grabbed the small brass doorknob and gave it a push forward, revealing a dark, winding staircase that disappeared just beyond the threshold.

"Ladies first?" Mr. Miller offered.

"Uh..." Alaya gave him a bewildered look that said he must be crazy to expect her to go first. She remained firmly planted in her spot, unable to move even if she'd wanted. She felt a slightly cooler rush of air coming from the lower level.

"Of course." Mr. Miller smiled and stepped first through the doorway. He reached up to pull on a string that hung unseen from the ceiling just above him, which helped only slightly; the light was faint and sputtered like an old car engine.

"Down we go. And please, watch your step." He warned.

With a bit of trepidation, Alaya followed as Mr. Miller led the way, winding further down the wooden staircase. She didn't say a word, but her mind was on overdrive; each step feeling like she was voluntarily walking into her own grave. *What am I getting myself into?* She thought.

What lay at the bottom of those steps was an absolute mystery, but all she could do was have faith that Mr. Miller was just a quirky crazy, not "torture-dungeon-beneath-his-shop" crazy. She had seen many horror movies develop entire plotlines around this concept. Of course, none of them were any good. All the same, her insides swirled and her heart hammered in her chest as curiosity slowly won over the voice of reason.

The staircase seemed to go on forever, and what feeble light there was grew dimmer. As they descended further underground, the darkness completely choked out the light from the flickering bulb and the temperature took a distinct drop.

Alaya shivered unconsciously and her once sweaty skin, warm from the late-summer heat, now felt cold and clammy. A strange glow still surviving from above mercifully lit their path, holding out as long as it could until the twists and bends of the staircase snuffed out even the memory of light.

Just when Alaya was certain that she would inevitably run into her guide, Mr. Miller clapped his hands, shattering the silence and stopping her in her tracks.

"Here we are."

CHAPTER 8

laya removed her foot from the last step, and was reassured by the comforting stability of the smooth, solid ground. At last, they had reached the bottom level of...wherever they were. The darkness still engulfed them, and she couldn't even see Mr. Miller, although she could sense his presence directly front of her.

Alaya shivered again; her moist skin was now cold to the touch. She rubbed her arms with her hands, wishing she had worn a full shirt rather than a tank top. The air was thick and stale, making it almost difficult to breathe. There clearly wasn't much ventilation down here, almost like it had been intentionally sealed off.

Mr. Miller's footsteps shuffled across the room, but Alaya couldn't follow the direction of the sound. She heard the click of switches and soon thereafter, bright lights illuminated the room along the length of the ceiling. She covered her eyes while they adjusted from the enveloping darkness to the blinding light.

"Oh! Too much?" Mr. Miller asked as a grin spread wider than his face. He flipped one switch back down, which eliminated half the lights in the spacious room. This left only a few rows of softer, tiny white bulbs that were arranged in a circle in the center of the room. Instead of a bright, sterile hospital, the room now resembled a forbidden, secret hideout.

For a moment, Alaya considered heading back upstairs, the sinister shadows gave her an uneasy feeling. The corners were dark once again, except for the eerie outlines of shelves and bookcases, shrouding their secrets contained within.

"How's that?" Mr. Miller asked. Alaya stepped forward into the center of the room and looked around. From the moment she stepped off the staircase, Alaya knew this was no ordinary basement.

The room was massive, yet splendid in its grandeur. As she took in the full scope of the room, Alaya couldn't believe what Mr. Miller had kept hidden away from his regular customers. Judging from the size of the tiny antique store, no one would have ever believed there was a storage room of this magnitude concealed underneath — herself included.

"Mr. Miller, this basement is incredible!" Alaya exclaimed. It was easily three times the size of the store above. Instead of the close, cramped quarters and corridors of junk, the basement was vast. The soaring, vaulted ceilings also dwarfed everything in sight.

"You probably have lots of questions, Alaya," He said before Alaya could even begin with the questions. "But before you ask...yes, this is all part of my store. In response to your second probable question, no...no one else has seen this. No one except your father, that is."

Alaya was slightly stunned by the news, feeling a wave of emotion, as though she had unearthed a new connection to her father. *Dad...? He's been down here...? Why?* Before she could get any of those questions out, Mr. Miller interrupted the spinning wheels of her mind.

"Let me show you around." He said almost instinctively, as though he knew everything that she wanted to ask.

The large room was almost a perfect reflection of the state of things in the store above. Dozens of trinkets were haphazardly arranged on shelves, and nothing was organized in a way that made sense. Alaya could not imagine anything worse than the expansive scene of disarray that lay before her eyes. With Mr. Miller's methods of storing inventory, Alaya already wondered how he ever kept track of anything. However, with the basement, Mr. Miller seemed to have truly outdone himself. Seemingly valuable possessions were stored right beside unrecognizable clutter.

"Mr. Miller, what do you plan to do with all this…junk?" Alaya said, decidedly not mincing words. She stepped forward, carefully traversing a weakly carved path through the clutter littering the floor. It took great effort to not touch anything in the process.

"I once learned about this condition called hoarding from a show. It talked about how some people have a compulsion to keep things, no matter how useless they are. Judging from this stockpile, you won't need anything else for your inventory for years, maybe even decades. This is just unreal." Alaya said, feeling that similar overwhelmed feeling she had when she first began working for Mr. Miller.

"I mean, I can even help you find some places to donate all of this stuff if you want." She began to rattle of additional benefits, such as the potential tax write-offs for donating to thrift stores or shelters.

Rather than take this criticism personally, Mr. Miller erupted into laughter.

"Oh, my young explorer. That's not why I brought you here. I don't need you to help me de-clutter this collection, although I might need some help rearranging a few things."

He pulled up a chair from a dusty old table on his left. The table was missing one of its legs, but he propped it against the wall, where it stood perfectly still. He motioned for her to also take a seat. Alaya eyed a second filthy, unstable chair with skepticism. An intricate puzzle of cobwebs had formed at the top and strung their way down to the seat. She didn't move an inch.

"Oh! How silly of me. Use this!" Mr. Miller said, and pulled out a yellowed old sheet from a crumbled television stand. He fluffed it out a few times, and a flurry of grime, dust, and other bits of unknown particles exploded into the air. Then he placed it onto the chair. After waving the debris away with one hand and covering her nose with the other, Alaya sat down against her better judgment. Besides, she still had plenty of questions bouncing around her head, and was curious as to why Mr. Miller wanted her to see this area.

He began to speak, slowly at first.

"Alaya, when I opened this store several years ago, I had big ideas. Grand dreams...I had ideas that many believed to be ludicrous. Heck, I've even been called crazy more times than I can remember. Can you believe it?" He asked, and his disposition fell flat for a moment.

"Imagine that," Alaya said blankly, staring down at the floor. She suddenly felt a surge of guilt that she had often used the word "crazy" to describe Mr. Miller in her mind.

"When I first met your father, we decided that we could not only store inventory, but we could...no, we *should* keep things down here for safekeeping." His tone turned serious.

"You mean to say that there are things down here you have no intention of selling? Ever?" Alaya asked, completely perplexed by such an idea. "I can hear the commercials now: 'Come on over to Mr. Miller's Antique Shop...the only store with stockpiles of inventory that will never be sold'." She said mockingly, like a spokesperson in a low-budget advertisement.

"That's not quite right, but something along those lines, yes." Mr. Miller said.

Alaya didn't know how he could operate like this. He seemed almost gleeful at the idea that he might never see the bottom of the floor. She could hardly walk beyond the most prominently carved path, which led from the center of the room to the staircase.

"That's ridiculous, Mr. Miller. Why would there possibly be a need to *keep* any of this?" Alaya stood and spread her arms in both directions, pointing to the dusty mess that surrounded her on every side. "Isn't this why you have the store in the first place? Isn't that why you needed to hire me? To *sell* things?" she asked, attempting to make sense of the anger and confusion she felt toward her employer. She had heard the rumors about how strange he was, but this bordered on insanity.

"You know, Alaya, most of the things in here aren't just worthless trinkets and shiny doo-dads. Some of these items may hold a great deal of sentimental value for you. I wanted you to have the chance to see them with your own eyes." Mr. Miller held out a tiny jade elephant in front of Alaya and let it fall into her outstretched hands.

She inspected the tiny sculpture, wonder spreading across her face. "It's beautiful. But how could this have any sentimental value for me? I've never seen it before." Alaya said, as she ran her fingers over the smooth, shiny object.

"Your father told me that you should have it," Mr. Miller said quietly.

"You've held onto this for seven years. Why are you giving it to me now? Why wouldn't he have just kept it in a safe deposit box, or given it to my mom?" she asked, her gaze still fixed on the brilliantly crafted sculpture.

Mr. Miller's expression fell. "Because Frederick disappeared before he had a chance to show it to you."

That stung Alaya like a hornet. She didn't like talking about her father's sudden disappearance, mainly because she didn't want to accept that he wasn't still alive out there somewhere, still fighting to get back to her and Janice. A few moments of silence fell between them, and the room grew thick with tension.

Alaya was grateful when Mr. Miller finally spoke again. He may have sensed Alaya's swell of painful feelings beginning to emerge, because he didn't press her to speak.

"He found it while he was out traveling on a mission for me."

"A mission for *you*? He was collecting inventory, you mean?" She began looking around the room once again. She quickly reconsidered, thinking that it might not hurt to take a second look at all the 'junk' she had previously offered to help Mr. Miller dispose of. If some of these pieces were there because of her father, then that meant they had passed through his hands; she wanted to see each and every one of them.

"He certainly did." Mr. Miller said, and walked over to a bookcase, picking up items from the nearest shelves.

As her eyes traveled along the shelves surrounding her, Alaya realized that there were many items in the room that she had never seen before, neither in books nor elsewhere. For example, Mr. Miller was standing near a trumpet-like device that sported a huge bell connected to the front end of a basic pellet stove. He was adjusting the bell delicately, perhaps because it looked as though it might fall off at any moment.

"What is that?" Alaya asked curiously as she stepped closer.

"This, my young explorer, is one of the grandfathers of the modern space heater. It was believed that the widened mouth at the base would help concentrate the heat to a specific area of the room, depending on where you positioned it. Ahh, take a look at this!" He said proudly as he stretched his short body to reach a higher shelf. He retrieved a small wooden bowl that had intricate designs wrapped around the exterior. It reminded Alaya of symbols often seen on ancient tribal artifacts.

Mr. Miller held it out, and Alaya accepted it with both hands.

"It was a bowl used to grind corn by the Incas. It is centuries old." He said. "I know, it should probably be in a museum somewhere, but can you blame me for wanting to keep it?"

Alaya smiled, humbled by this experience.

"I know that my dad liked to travel. That's why he became an archaeologist. I wish I could've been there with him—to have seen this in its original home must have been incredible." A distant, sad smile imperceptibly touched her lips. "I guess that's probably why you keep calling me 'young explorer.'"

"Ah, so you've noticed." Mr. Miller chuckled. "It's a fitting nickname. Your father's blood runs through your veins, true enough."

Alaya continued to carefully inspect the bowl, when Mr. Miller made a suggestion.

"Now, would you like to know how your father and I did it? How we were able to find everything that you see down here?" Mr. Miller's arms spread to encompass the sprawling room.

"Of course!" Alaya said. "Those papers didn't go into much detail. I still don't understand why you've collected all this stuff, especially if you don't plan on selling it or donating it to museums. I'm sure you could make a fortune, even if you only sold a fraction of it!" Alaya said, providing sage advice as though she was a professional appraiser of artifacts from ancient empires.

Mr. Miller sighed. With a pensive look on his face, he said, "Alaya, there are some explanations that have been kept from you for far too long, but for good reason." He began pacing the room, and his words unfurled with every step. Mr. Miller began to reveal much more about her father's travels than she had ever known.

"Frederick was something else. He would have gone to the ends of the earth if he had the means and the time. When it came to certain destinations, your mother was fully aware of his trips. Others, however…most, in fact…she had no knowledge of." Mr. Miller said, although he must have known how bad it sounded.

Alaya felt herself becoming hot, which surprised her. She never thought this would happen, but she actually felt some anger towards her father. *What would he possibly have had to hide?* Fortunately, the only man who could answer that question was standing before her. She tried to control the accusatory tone in her voice as she spoke.

"Why didn't he just tell us about it? There should be no reason for keeping secrets like that." Alaya chided, and though she tried to fight it, a flush began to rise in her cheeks.

Mr. Miller's head dipped lower in response to Alaya's tone.

"Your father decided that it would only complicate matters and could have even put the mission in jeopardy if your mother knew that he was traveling to a completely unknown land." Mr. Miller said. He looked back at Alaya, as though seeking forgiveness for her father's transgressions. Fat chance. This sort of revelation didn't simply come to light and be immediately forgotten. She needed more answers.

"Well, what country was it in? At least you could have said, 'we're going to Australia.' Here," Alaya reached over to a faded, pockmarked globe that sat perilously crooked on a wooden stand, "Go on and point it out to me. I'd like to know at least that much. Since all of this is in the past, there shouldn't be any more 'danger to the mission.'" She added, unconsciously tapping her foot in annoyance.

"Alaya..." Mr. Miller gave a heavy sigh. "It's not quite that simple."

"What is that supposed to mean?" Alaya retorted, feeling her heart rate quickening. *You opened the door to this conversation, Mr. Miller; I'm just walking through it.* Alaya was beginning to lose patience. Although her temper had gotten better over the years, when her anger began to rise, Alaya quickly lost the ability to censor her speech. She wanted answers, and if that meant hurting someone's feelings, then so be it.

"Mr. Miller, this is my father we're talking about. I'll ask you again: how complicated can it be? You have to know that much. Hell, can you at least narrow it down to a continent?" She asked.

Mr. Miller did her no favors. "Well, you could say the Middle East, where the ruins of ancient Mesopotamia are found. Or perhaps somewhere in Africa, most likely near Maputo, Mozambique. Yet, it is difficult to say with any certainty."

Wow! Alaya thought. *What is it with this guy? Why is he being so evasive?* He seemed completely unable to give a straight answer. "I honestly don't get it, Mr. Miller." Alaya said, shaking her head and pacing, just as he had been doing moments earlier. It was the only thing she could do to keep her anger from boiling over.

"That's a *huge* disparity. How could my father travel somewhere on your orders, and yet you don't know where he went?" Alaya asked. Growing up, plenty of people said that she had been too nosy for her own good, but it had served her well. Her relentless questioning had backed Mr. Miller, who had fallen noticeably silent, into a corner. Alaya was determined to get to the bottom of this, no matter what.

"Well? I'm looking for answers," she said, sounding more like a prosecutor in a courtroom than a new employee.

"My child, please. There is something…something I have to confess. It was foolish of me to think I could keep it from you any longer." He sat back down, and gestured for Alaya to do the same. "You are quite the curious one, if I may say so…just like your father."

Mr. Miller exhaled deeply before beginning, the type of breathing one might expect after dragging a couch up three flights of stairs.

"This is going to be very difficult to explain, and even more difficult for you to hear, but after all these years, perhaps it will be good to let someone else in. The thing is, your father and I….Well, we made a discovery one day, while we were working together in this very room…" He looked all around him, but his eyes were distant, lost in some faraway memory. Perhaps, he was seeing the room as it had been, not as it now stood.

Alaya followed suit, her eyes scanning the room and falling on a far corner, where a statue of a woman stood. She looked like the armless statues of Greek goddesses that populate museums across the world. She had long, thick tendrils that reminded Alaya of Medusa; except these were flat, rather than spiraling onto itself. The blank, vacant eyes stared back at her and Alaya got a strange feeling of déjà vu.

Alaya suddenly felt a shiver down her spine, losing the staring contest that the frozen woman had been playing for centuries.

"This discovery was something that had never been achieved, as far as we knew." Mr. Miller paused for a moment and clasped his hands together. "It would appear that your father and I discovered the possibility to...well, the possibility of time travel. So...right." He wrung his hands and looked up at Alaya, as though hoping for a positive response, perhaps eliminating the need for him to go into any more detail.

"I'm sorry...time travel? What are you talking about? I'm not a child anymore, Mr. Miller," Alaya said curtly; the hot feeling in her face began to return. "You don't have to make up stupid stories to explain why my father disappeared."

"No! No, of course no—"

"Do you think I'm an idiot? Don't you think my dad might have mentioned that? I might not be up on all of my science facts, but I'm pretty sure that time travel is a big deal." She waved her hand dismissively to the room of artifacts. "And don't try to tell me that these artifacts all came from your "time travel" adventures." As she thought about the story he was feeding her, a frightening thought struck her. *What if Mr. Miller had something to do with her father's disappearance?*

"Mr. Miller...do you know what actually happened to my father? Is that what all this time travel nonsense is about?" Skepticism coupled with thinly veiled fury dripped from her voice like lava. Her questions were valid; the connections made sense. Even Mr. Miller seemed to agree: he was nodding, apparently understanding the source of her doubt and acknowledging her right to be suspicious.

"This all began with Frederick flying to locate unique artifacts all across the world. On one of the excavation trips that your father took to the ruins of an ancient village in Mozambique…he found this." Mr. Miller held up several pieces of paper that were frayed and crumpled around the edges, but were otherwise in decent condition.

"What is that?" She asked.

"Instructions for a project," Mr. Miller began. "Your father found it buried among some rubble. There were hundreds of pieces of parchment, filled with nothing but faded characters written in cuneiform. Your father happened to stumble across one piece in particular, however, which surprised him. It didn't belong; in fact, it was thousands of miles from where it should have been. He took several pictures of it before turning it over to his colleagues. They all decided that it would be best to take it back to their lab to determine what its message may have been, since it was written in the text of an ancient language –Sumerian." He said.

"So what were the instructions for? Did he ever find out?"

"Well, your father brought the pictures back here, and we pieced them together as best we could. He took a great risk in doing so. Several other excavators had taken pictures of artifacts, but they had been legally bound never to leak anything to the press until more research had been done. Your father had the feeling that this was something special, though, so he took the chance. As luck would have it, on another trip your father later took to the Congo, he discovered a rough guide, which allowed us to loosely translate the text. It has been widely debated among scholars around the world how to decipher the code of the Sumerian language. We had basically found the Rosetta Stone of this language. More importantly, your father and I used it to translate the true message of the script." Mr. Miller paused, seemingly hesitant to continue.

"And what was the message?" Alaya did not realize it, but her fingers were clenched around the wooden armrest of the wobbly chair; her knuckles lost all circulation.

"Since you're Frederick's daughter, I'm willing to show you, as a courtesy. However, you must keep this in the strictest of confidence. You are only the third person to have ever seen this. I hope you appreciate the magnitude of that." With that, Mr. Miller slowly waddled his way over to the back of the room to a dark corner where neither of them had yet ventured. It was untouched by the light that crept into the far reaches of the massive space.

Alaya's eyes followed him as he made his way into the shadows. He wheeled out a large colorful mural into the light, dragging it straight across the maze of detritus on the ground.

"Allow me to show you..." He tugged the partition clearly into view. "This is what your father and I were working on...right before he disappeared." Mr. Miller pushed aside the colorful mural, which had been partitioning off a large lumpy object that was shrouded by a black velvet cloth. It was completely covered in dust, which was to be expected given the condition of everything else in the room. Alaya would have never noticed this before, as it was safely concealed by the mural, not to mention being tucked into the shadows in the darkest corner of the basement.

"Now, this may be a bit dusty. It's been years since this has been uncovered." Mr. Miller warned as he pulled the black cloth aside, releasing a shower of dust. Years' worth of chalky, sandy particles were swept into the air, dancing in the light.

Alaya quickly covered her face to shield her from the small storm of dirt. Some bits of debris managed to get into her lungs, and she began to cough profusely. Alaya heard Mr. Miller breathing heavily through sputtering coughs; he must have made the same mistake. She'd felt sprays of dirt fall into her hair and on her clothes, but it didn't matter. Her curiosity was piqued, and she squinted through the dust. It was all she could do to not open her eyes fully.

When the cloud of dust finally settled, Alaya was able to clearly see what lay in front of her.

"What is it?" She asked.

CHAPTER 9

Mr. Miller stood next to an oddly shaped vehicle; his arms extended like a game show host presenting the grand prize. It looked like something torn from the pages of a science fiction magazine. It was large enough to carry just two passengers, although even that would have been a tight squeeze.

Alaya cocked her head and warily stared at the machine. "What is it?" she asked. With all that buildup, Alaya was expecting something else. "That thing looks like a busted up car from a theme park ride. How did you get it down here anyway?"

"Well, not everything is as it seems my young explorer. Please, allow me to explain." He said. "This machine is not what you think it is. Yes, it may resemble something from a child's fantasy, but I can assure you, its true purpose is something altogether different."

Alaya's full attention was brought back into the moment. "Okay, I'll bite. What was it used for then?"

Mr. Miller took another deep sigh. "Your father traveled to different worlds in a machine just like this. It was a bit less flashy, but very similar."

Alaya walked over to the machine, taking in the design of the sleek machine. Upon closer inspection, it was unlike any vehicle that she had ever seen. It had several buttons and gadgets, all of which were completely foreign to her, lined across a smooth steel panel. The only things that even closely resembled a traditional vehicle were the modified gas and brake pedals. When she finally spoke, her voice was noticeably softer. "What exactly am I looking at?"

"To be clearer, Alaya, this *is* the machine that your father traveled in. However, I've made some slight modifications over the years."

"It's been years…what else haven't you told my mother and I?" Alaya asked, and began backing away from him, fearing that he may try to silence her, the same way he may have silenced her father seven years ago. "Mr. Miller, do you know where my father is? Were you behind the whole thing all along?"

Alaya suddenly realized that down here, no one could hear her scream. No one would even know where or how to find her body. She instantly dismissed those thoughts. She was going to get out of this junk-filled dungeon; there was no doubt about that. With Mr. Miller's bad leg, she would at least have a small head start and was grateful for that advantage.

The clock in the corner chimed loudly, which gave Alaya a start. It was now six o'clock — an hour before closing.

There was only one problem; Mr. Miller wasn't done explaining himself. He pleaded with Alaya, who was now carefully backing away toward the staircase.

"Please, you must believe me. If there was anything I could have done to save your father, I would have. He meant a great deal to me too. I can only imagine how angry you must be feeling right now…how angry you must be at *me*."

Alaya remained at the foot of the stairs, unsure of whether to speak, run, or stay and listen. She decided on the latter, confident that she could sprint up those winding stairs if she had to.

"Now, there is something you have to understand. There is no way that I can know for sure, but your father...well, he may be alive and well. Before you run off, just allow me to tell you one more thing. I want to explain what happened the night he disappeared." Mr. Miller suddenly sounded old and wounded.

Trusting the sincerity in his voice, Alaya moved closer to the center of the room. Her mind slipped back into an old memory, perhaps her worst memory, from the night her father was reported missing. It was a cold night and the rain spattered at the window for hours, like a leaky faucet; constant and annoying. He had been expected back from his trip earlier that morning, but he had already missed dinner.

Neither Janice nor Alaya had heard from him in days, but that was normal when he was on one of his expeditions, miles away from a telephone. Alaya wondered where he could have been, if the roads were safe enough to drive on in the storm. The sirens whistling down her street startled her from an unplanned nap, quickly followed by a knock on the door. She looked at the clock and saw that it was the middle of the night; she knew that the swirling red and blue lights outside could only mean one thing.

The police spoke with her mother first. They asked how she was feeling and asked her if she had anyone to stay with, fulfilling the obligatory checklist for grieving families. Once that was finished, they quickly got down to business. They mostly asked questions that could provide leads for their investigation. Once they learned of his part-time job at the antique shop, they asked about his relationship with Mr. Miller, who quickly became the prime suspect in her father's disappearance. Mr. Miller didn't have a crime-laden past, by any means, but Frederick had last been seen with him. Due to a lack of any incriminating evidence, Mr. Miller was not considered as a suspect for long. Since there were no other leads in the case, it quickly fell cold. Alaya feared that the resolution would always come someday, blindsiding her and Janice on some random Tuesday afternoon, but it never came. For months, their lives felt like purgatory, always searching and holding out hope, but never reaching a true, conclusive ending.

The few bits of evidence from her father's case now lay on a forgotten shelf somewhere in a crowded storage warehouse, where they had remained for the last seven years. Another unsolved murder, long forgotten, up on the old shelves where no human dared to tread without a darn good reason. Alaya had been twelve years old, but the experience made her grow up fast.

Reflecting on that night strangely brought her back into the magnitude of the moment and she felt determined to take hold of the situation. She was not leaving the basement until she had gotten the truth out of Mr. Miller—all of it.

She sat back in her chair, crossed her legs, and folded her arms resolutely, like an army general confidently hunkering down before a battle.

"Tell me what happened, Mr. Miller—and don't leave anything out." Her voice almost had a threatening ring to it.

Mr. Miller responded appropriately, sensing how serious his 'young explorer' really was. "Your father was going on a trip for himself. I believe he went to Batunia, a place he had been a number of times before. I had told him that there was no reason to go, that we had all we could gather from there, and that it was time to move on. However, there was something else he had been researching. But to this day, I don't know what he had been keeping from me. Anyway, on his way back, something went terribly wrong – I'm sure of it. This machine returned…but your father did not." He had a grave look, unable to face Alaya.

Mr. Miller was quiet for a minute as he kept his eyes locked on the floor. When he spoke, his voice cracked with pain. "I don't know where he could have gone. I hypothesized that there could have been some sort of in-between world, or perhaps he had remained trapped in Batunia. At any rate, without the machine, your father had no way of getting back home to you and Janice. Please believe me; I've done all that I can to try and figure out what to do. I've considered going back to Batunia alone, but the problem is, if I fail, no one would ever know. I also don't trust anyone else to help me…" Mr. Miller corrected himself, "No, that's not right. I *didn't* trust anyone, until I interviewed you, that is. When I saw your father's eyes looking back at me, and could sense the determination in you, I knew that this might be the only chance. You, Alaya, are the one who must help me. That is…if you think you're up to it."

"What…? Why now? Why me?" A thousand thoughts bounced through Alaya's brain, along with everything that could go wrong. Her vision blurred for a moment; she finally realized that Mr. Miller was telling the unbelievable truth.

"My dear, you were far too young before; you were still in high school. No one else would have had a vested interest in asking the right questions, let alone believe the answers. Your mother had worked hard her whole life, and losing Frederick took a heavy toll…I was afraid that this would have been too much for her. I couldn't imagine her taking care of you, being the sole provider for your whole family, and also go traveling to strange, uncharted lands looking for a man that might not even be there. That was always your father's area of expertise, not hers."

Alaya turned away, knowing that he was right. Hearing all of this should have been some sort of good news and it should have provided her with a sliver of optimism, no matter how small. This revelation meant that her father was not necessarily dead, as the detectives and her mother had eventually come to believe. In spite that "good news", all that Alaya could do was think of the supreme sadness she had felt on the day she realized he might never come back. Also, she was drawn back to what his loss meant — that their family would remain broken and incomplete forever. She couldn't accept this absolution. Not then, and certainly not now.

With the uncertainty of his whereabouts once again brought to the forefront of her mind, Alaya felt the fresh, raw wound being peeled open. Could Mr. Miller be cruel enough to tell her such things if they weren't true? *He can't be doing this just to hurt me, can he?* It was as though he had searched deep into her soul to rub jagged salt into the gaping, deep cuts of her past. She suddenly felt drained and was unsure of how to respond to all she had heard.

"Alaya, you must be feeling many things right now, and I'm truly sorry for dragging all of this pain back into your mind. I had hoped that this might encourage you. Trust me on one thing: this is good news. Maybe we missed something somewhere in our planning. Perhaps we miscalculated Batunia's exact location the last time, or maybe he didn't even go there at all," Mr. Miller said, trying to offer some form of comfort.

Alaya suddenly shot back, "And if so, what does that mean for my father? That he's out there lost somewhere in limbo?" She turned around, so her back faced Mr. Miller. "Besides, what good does that do us now? It's been seven years! We have no way of telling exactly where he could be, so what good will this machine even do? Who knows if it even works! He could have died in a hundred different ways

65

by now, for all we know." She was trying hard to suppress the knot swelling in her throat and fight back the foggy mist forming in her eyes.

"However small a meaning my apology may hold for you, I cannot accept anything less than full responsibility for what happened to Frederick, Alaya. There was no easy way to say any of this; you understand that, surely? What I am asking of you now is to put any harsh feelings toward me aside and help me piece together the clues. There may be a chance that we can find where your father ended up." He walked over to her and placed a hand on her shoulder.

She didn't reject it, but she was decidedly conflicted. *I can't bear to go through all of this again...but what if there really is a chance...?* She sighed, knowing she couldn't turn her back on the chance of seeing her father again.

"What can I do...? I mean, what is it that you want me to do?"

Mr. Miller smiled. "Seven years ago, this machine returned to this room, badly damaged, along with this." Mr. Miller pulled an old faded photograph from his pocket and showed it to Alaya. She stared back at a younger version of her family. She stood happily between both parents, their fingers interlocked above her head, her father's arm wrapped warmly around Janice's shoulders. This was the last picture her family took before his disappearance one year later. Her heart felt like it was being stabbed with tiny daggers.

"That's actually not all that returned...it was the machine, this picture, and...this." Mr. Miller held out a badly worn scroll. "I'm certain something must have happened to him, but I think I speak for us both when I say that we need to know the circumstances surrounding that day. This remains one of the most unfortunate events in my life, and it has plagued me for years. I can't even imagine what it has done to you. For your father's sake, I was hoping that you could continue the work he began. As you can see," Mr. Miller pointed to his left leg, "I'm not exactly in peak physical condition anymore."

"What is that?" Alaya asked, reaching for the scroll. She unrolled it carefully and read through it, but it was a jumbled mess, vague and confusing. Faded scribbles spoke of danger, an impending war of sorts, and something else. It spoke of a strange man from a faraway place, but the bottom of the scroll had been torn off. Whatever this was, Alaya was sure of one thing: it wasn't her father's handwriting, but it was referring to him. *What could have happened to him?* She thought of the possibilities, the chances of additional heartache; doubts began to bloom.

"Mr. Miller, how can I just pick up and leave? What do I tell my mother? *Hey, Mom. I'm gonna take a ride in a possibly functional time machine with my new boss to go find Dad, although we don't know where or when he might be...*Yeah, I doubt that will fly with her."

"Well, then allow me to suggest something else. I believe that we'll find the most success if we frame this as a dual-purpose business trip. Think of it as archaeology, just like the trips your father used to take. Your purpose will be to locate and retrieve anything, or anyone, of value in Batunia. However, this is clearly not something you'll be able to accomplish overnight. If we expect any measure of success, you'll need to spend enough time there to search properly. Your mother won't be happy, but she'll understand your interest in getting closer to your father, perhaps finding some peace by delving into his passion."

The way he stated this plan so plainly gave Alaya the impression that this was something he had been thinking about for a long time. Looking at the state of the room, Alaya figured that it was a good thing that no one had seen the mess that surrounded them in the basement. The antique store was well stocked, and had been for many years. He clearly didn't need her to retrieve anything else of value — the only treasure she was committed to finding was her father.

Mr. Miller offered his assistance in the only way that he could. "I will train you to the best of my abilities. We can begin tomorrow if you'd like, but I can't make any promises. Alaya, you must understand that this is not necessarily a search and rescue party. You may have to go to many different lands, if necessary. I'll support you in any way I can, but this entire endeavor could be extremely dangerous, since I will not physically be there with you. I would ask you to search high and low, but only as far as you are willing."

"Yet, with that being said, I want you to stay under the radar as much as possible. I don't want you taking any chances and jeopardizing your life. Are you sure you're okay with this?" he asked.

Alaya looked up at him with a smirk; she was touched by his parental concern.

Her mind began running through the endless possibilities of everything that had just been explained to her. Mr. Miller presented her with an option for life that she could have never anticipated. It would also be an alternative to simply finding a good college to attend and mindlessly going through the motions of higher education. The thought of enrolling in classes in which she had no interest made her want to run away, as far as possible. *My choice is simple, isn't it?*

"Of course I'm up for this. We're talking about possibly finding my father. And we can get started tomorrow?"

"Absolutely," Mr. Miller said. Just then, the cuckoo clock upstairs began to chime, startling them both. It was now seven o'clock, closing time. "How about Monday morning? I just realized, today's Saturday."

"Alright, first thing Monday, then. I'll be here bright and early!" She was slightly upset to have to wait a day, but soon realized that an extra day to wrap her head around the revelations of the afternoon might be worthwhile.

CHAPTER 10

Sunday was one of the slowest days imaginable. Alaya was convinced that by some unknown trickery, each hour had passed much slower than normal, as if dragged through sand. Now that the idea of time travel had entered her reality, she supposed that anything was possible.

That night, sleep was an intangible respite, taunting Alaya as it danced just out of her reach. She knew why she couldn't rest. The idea of possibly finding her father alive was more than enough to keep her energized throughout the night. She thought of her mother, particularly about how Janice would react if she knew what Mr. Miller had been keeping secret for all these years. She knew that for now, it was probably best to keep this to herself.

Just as her eyelids began to droop, the soft rays of sunlight slipping through her bedroom window gently caressed her face, interrupting her journey to sleep. Alaya knew that she had not gotten much rest; it seemed as though she had been asleep for little more than five minutes. She got up and looked at her reflection in the bedroom mirror. To her disappointment, the red, irritated eyes staring back did her no favors. She looked at the clock, only to grimace when she saw that it was flashing 7:45 a.m. For a moment, she contemplated returning to bed, but knew that would have been an impossible task. The second her head hit the pillow, it would take a far greater effort to wake back up than it would take to drain a pot of coffee and begin the day. After all, she'd been madly anticipating the last 48 hours like it was her first trip to Disneyland.

Saturday night had opened so many doors, ones that Alaya was convinced she had closed and sealed off long ago. She thought that she had accepted the fact that her father was missing and would never return. She accepted that she needed to be strong, both for herself and her mother. Alaya did her best to no longer show pain or grief, which unconsciously had turned to staunch indifference.

But her hard work was crumbling right before her eyes. In came Mr. Miller, with all his new revelations. Her shield had cracked, and she was defenseless once again.

While she began to get ready for work, Alaya had a subtle flashback to the bedtime stories her parents had read to her as a child. There were tales of bravery and heroic deeds achieved by regular people who had been dropped into life-threatening situations, yet they emerged triumphant. Alaya wished for that sort of courage right now.

***

The entrance of the antique store clanged open; Alaya was a full fifteen minutes ahead of schedule. Although the store's front door was unlocked, Mr. Miller was nowhere to be found. She wandered into his office and saw the china cabinet pushed off to the side. Below, she could hear faint noises of shuffling feet.

Carefully, Alaya descended the winding old steps. A few minutes later, she found Mr. Miller scurrying about, seemingly unaware that she had arrived.

"Morning, Mr. Miller." Alaya put her things down on an unsteady table next to the foot of the stairs. It was now covered in a white sheet, for which she was grateful. It shifted slightly under the weight of her bag, but the fourth leg was still missing. Mr. Miller did not immediately acknowledge her presence. He was engrossed in an old, dark green journal. It was worn around the edges, and from her vantage point, Alaya could see what looked like handwritten notes scrawled across the tops of the pages. Several additional books were spread out along a shelf; he seemed to be researching something.

Alaya walked directly in front of Mr. Miller when he finally gave a start.

"Oh, hello there! You almost scared the hair off my head! At least what's left of it," he said, patting his bare, shiny crown. "I wasn't expecting you for at least another twenty minutes."

Alaya couldn't argue, she couldn't bear to wait any longer.

"What are you up to?" she asked, glancing over his shoulder.

"I came in early this morning to take care of a few things before you arrived. Before you leave, we must do everything we can to ensure your safety and wellbeing. I've taken nearly every precaution I can possibly think of and have done my best to integrate the most essential items into this pack for your travels."

He pulled a cloth bag from behind the desk, which had one strap and a zipper. It was rectangular; and may have been half the size of a gym bag.

"Your father and I narrowed down a list of provisions that were best for this type of travel. They won't get you any unwanted attention, but they can be good in a pinch." He began removing contents of the bag and displayed them on the table.

"There's no telling how long you may need to be out on your own. There is some dried food, money, and a few changes of clothing. From what your father has told me, there is something you must know: in Batunia, women do not commonly wear pants. The dresses should keep you sufficiently warm, but if not, a scarf or cloak should be fine. Also, money is referred to as *Ikbars*. The largest denomination is called *Leeras*, but they are only used by the wealthiest in society. Alas, I have none." He said.

But there was something else Mr. Miller wanted to ask; Alaya just couldn't tell what it was. He was silent for at least a couple of minutes, nervously looking around the room, for nothing in particular.

"What is it?" She asked.

"Alaya, have you ever gone out on your own before?"

Alaya pondered the question, and a fresh dose of reality began to stream in, all at once. She had been operating on autopilot since the revelations of Saturday night, but in this moment, the significance of what she was about to do suddenly struck with alarming voltage. *What were they doing?*

There had been only one time Alaya had gone camping when she was young. She was six or seven years old, and while her father found it to be a great adventure, Alaya and her mother were miserable. The lack of standard plumbing was more than Janice could handle, so their weeklong trip was cut short after only three days.

Alaya could not remember much else beyond the hazy memories of winding hiking trails and sleeping under the stars with her parents. On their first night, she learned about the North Star and her favorite constellation, the Big Dipper.

That night, her father told her one important piece of advice: if she was ever lost, the North Star could help her find her way home. He called it 'nature's compass.' But this was going to be different. Now, she would be nowhere near home, and she would be completely alone on this journey. *Besides*, Alaya thought, *would the North Star even help her in Batunia?*

Doubts began to collide in her head like melodies in an orchestra, overpowering everything else.

What am I thinking? Alaya asked herself this question several times over, drawing a blank each time. She took a seat on a nearby dust bucket to calm herself. The bell clanged upstairs—it was the first customer of the day. Mr. Miller quickly ran upstairs, allowing Alaya time to silence her thoughts. But there was no need; she recognized precisely what was happening. She was allowing fear to take hold.

Mr. Miller must have had a sixth sense for her anxiety; when he returned, he pulled up a sheet-covered chair and sat down.

"Alaya, we have no idea what type of peril may await you. For someone as inexperienced as you, I know that this whole thing is quite irresponsible of me. Maybe I was going about this the wrong way. It's been so many years since I went back, but..." Mr. Miller trailed off.

"I'm still going to do this." Alaya said. "I have to."

CHAPTER 11

laya wasn't sure if she was going to convince Mr. Miller that he hadn't in fact made a mistake. But it didn't matter. This wasn't going to change the fact that she was still going to Batunia. She abruptly stood and walked over to the time machine. The unit was cold to the touch, yet inviting.

"How did you and my dad build this thing anyway?" she asked.

"That's a very good question, Alaya. You may not have known this, but while your father was a brilliant archaeologist, he was also quite gifted in physics and engineering. I tinkered myself in the past, so we developed this revolutionary new technology. As you might expect, it's based on principles of mechanics and physics, with a healthy bit of chemistry thrown in as well."

He walked to the bookshelf and returned the books he held in his hand, only to retrieve new ones.

"Is it safe?" Alaya studied physics and chemistry in high school, but she wasn't quite sure how many of those experiments would work outside of a formal lab setting.

"Surprisingly safe, in fact. Although your father did notice slight variations in time, he rarely visited the same place twice so that was never a real concern. Batunia was the only place Frederick ever visited more than once. He claimed to be researching a project, but he didn't say much about it, only that he needed to gather more data. Unfortunately, he never got that chance." He stared off into space, as though reminiscing on an unearthed memory. "Whatever he was doing there, Frederick played it close to the vest."

"So, how does the machine work exactly?" Alaya asked. She leaned over the door panel and examined each of the buttons on the machine's control panel, careful not to touch anything.

"To put it simply, it combines the concept of intense speeds with high amounts of energy to create a hyper-speed type of transportation system," Mr. Miller explained, as though this was as obvious as breathing.

Alaya looked around the room. "And exactly *how* do you manage the 'intense speeds' down here?" she asked. "Unless you're going to tell me that the walls are going to disappear and that all of this is just an illusion."

Mr. Miller began to laugh. "Oh no, I don't mean speed in the way you and I interpret it. There are some things in nature that move very quickly. So quickly, in fact, the naked eye cannot detect, so the object appears immobile. Remember, for example, the single atom. It is in perpetual motion, whether we can observe it or not."

Alaya thought back to physics classes, although it was difficult; she never intended on committing any of that to memory.

"I think it sounds vaguely familiar. But what does that have to do with the machine?" She asked.

He answered quickly, as though he had anticipated these very questions. "Well, think about a glass of water. It contains millions of tiny atoms that are constantly bumping against one another."

Alaya nodded. A few more lectures crept back from the recesses of her memory. "Okay, that makes sense, but I can see the water moving if I shake the glass."

"Of course, but these atoms are moving *so* fast that our eyes can't see them. Take this..." Mr. Miller stood, pointing to his chair. "In this chair, there are atoms moving so fast that we can't see them. However, when you break anything down to its smallest components, the atoms will be bouncing around and against each other. Adding heat only serves to increase the atoms' movement." Mr. Miller began to pace the room as his enthusiasm grew; his penchant for teaching was once again renewed.

"Years ago, maybe ten or so, your father and I discovered the secret behind getting the atoms within the machine to move faster than normal...so fast that it could move into a new world, all without breaking through the walls of this store. I know how that sounds, but don't just take my word for it. Allow me to demonstrate." Mr. Miller walked over to a teacup sitting on a shelf.

"This teacup will show you what I mean." He gingerly placed the ceramic cup in the palm of his hand. "Basically, if I harness the combined energy from a specific physical and chemical reaction, it will enable me to access a subatomic particle, called a neutrino. These are unique in the sense that they lack mass and are incredibly small, even in terms of atomic sizes. Are you following me so far?"

Alaya's attention was locked on; this was one lecture she wouldn't be sleeping through.

"Now, you may not be aware," he continued, "but it is believed by researchers that neutrinos are able to travel faster than the speed of light. If that is the case, then time travel would be theoretically possible. This was a game-changing development for most physicists, since it had long been believed that Einstein had it right about the theory of relativity, which said that nothing could travel faster than the speed of light. The theory of relativity essentially rendered time travel impossible. Fortunately, your father had colleagues and friends at the university who were interested in similar work with these special particles. We all put our heads together and decided that if we could harness the power of a neutrino and infuse it into an object, then in theory, we could give that object the ability accomplish the impossible—time travel."

Mr. Miller placed the cup on the table, and then placed a large, clear box over it. "I know that science isn't your favorite subject, so let me try to make this as clear as I can." He took a step back, while Alaya took a few steps closer.

"First, we found a way to introduce neutrinos into the fundamental molecular structure of an object. When this happens, that object loses its mass—no diets are needed. Eh, diets, get it?" He looked over at Alaya, but the joke was lost on her. She was completely unmoved, so Mr. Miller picked right back up, as though he had never tried the attempt at scientific humor.

"Yes, so as I was saying, the only way for something to travel faster than the speed of light is for it to be weightless. So, now that we've removed its mass, we then apply another force known to affect the movement of atoms - heat. When we add heat, the particles will move even faster, allowing the neutrinos to begin vibrating inside the molecular structure until the entire object finally achieves a speed that is faster than light." Mr. Miller then demonstrated by striking a match and placing it in the box where the cup was held. He left a small opening in the corner to allow oxygen into the box.

Suddenly, the teacup began to emit a slow, pulsating glow. Within moments, the entire cup began to transform into white, blinding rays. The powerful beams reminded Alaya of the circling beacons of lighthouses. She squinted her eyes attempting to block the light, but it vanished almost as soon as it had appeared. Once Alaya's eyes adjusted, she saw the box was completely empty—the teacup was nowhere to be found.

Alaya was astounded. "What happened? Where did it go?"

"Well," Mr. Miller began, lifting the box and running his hand over the smooth surface of the table, as though proof that the cup was not just made to be invisible. "It is hard to say for sure, but chances are good that it traveled to somewhere in the past, or perhaps the future. It's hard to say precisely, since we didn't assign a specific direction or destination for that unit. This box is kind of faulty in that way," he said in a blasé manner, like a time-travel snob who didn't have any patience for directionless journeys into the ether.

"Well, I hope you take better care with me!" Alaya said, wondering if it was wise to leave her life in the hands of a mad scientist.

"When you step into the machine, the atoms in your body work with the neutrinos, creating a small nuclear reaction. Combined with the technology your father helped develop to harness and direct that energy, the entire process is perfectly safe."

Alaya found this information hard to believe, yet somehow, it seemed plausible. After all, it must have worked rather well if her father had been able to travel as widely as he did—before he went missing, of course.

"In other words, you aren't going to randomly send me off and hope for the best, right?" she asked half-joking, half-serious.

"That's a great question, young explorer. I'd like to show you something. Follow me!" He waddled quickly back over to the machine, with Alaya trailing behind. "Like I said, your father helped discover a way to safely infuse the neutrino sub-particles into not only the machine, but also into the person who occupies the machine." He said.

"How could that work for a person though? You just covered it up with a box. Would it be dangerous for a human to be openly exposed to these neutrinos?"

"That's what I initially thought as well, but your father determined that the particles are much too small to have any dangerous effects on a human. You may feel a slight tingling sensation in the beginning, but that quickly subsides. Let me show you." He sounded reassuring, like a paternal figure.

Mr. Miller walked Alaya through all the controls. "You see this button here?" He pointed to a small green button with a circle in the center and a short vertical line cutting through the top half. It was the universal 'power on/off' button.

"When you press it, not only does it begin to diffuse the neutrinos through a self-perpetuating series of reactions, but also simultaneously heats the machine, causing the neutrinos to activate, building in speed until you are able to surpass light speed. To me, however, it will look as though you are not moving at all; you will simply disappear."

Mr. Miller continued. "If you find yourself in a particularly cold environment, these two levers control the temperature." He demonstrated this by dialing a lever marked 'Outside' to the highest temperature, and the lever marked 'Inside' to the highest temperature. "Simple enough to understand, right?"

Alaya had expected something far more intricate, but so far, there was nothing particularly complicated about the process. Yet still, this was a thought that made her feel like she was living a dream, and hadn't awakened yet. *Was this really happening?*

"So far, so good, Mr. Miller."

Next, he pointed out the programming keys.

"Here's a new feature; I have installed a keyboard, eliminating the need to speak your destination. Unless you would prefer to use the microphone here." Mr. Miller pointed to a tiny hole near the temperature controls. It was no bigger than a drop of water and labeled 'mic.'

He pointed to the light gray button at the top right corner of the dashboard control panel. "This is how you retrieve the keyboard," he pressed it, and the keyboard slid out. He pressed it a second time, and it slid back into its compartment, sealed by a sliding panel.

"This is all pretty amazing. It seems like you've thought of everything," Alaya said.

Hours passed in what seemed like minutes as Mr. Miller continued showing her the various intricacies of the machine and its inner workings. Thankfully, Mr. Miller was willing to forgo customers today—he switched the sign back to 'closed' after the first customer arrived in the morning.

In total, the crash course in time travel took a little over seven hours, but once they heard the cuckoo clock chimed six, Mr. Miller sent her home for the evening, with a promise to continue where they left off tomorrow.

CHAPTER 12

The next morning, Alaya sprang from bed ahead of her alarm, and headed for the bathroom to get ready. The cool water of the shower felt good against her warm, sticky skin. She had slept with the bedroom window open the previous night, and the humidity snaked its way across her body, covering her like a blanket.

Alaya quickly showered, but it was a blur. Her mind was preoccupied with nothing but thoughts of her coming voyage. Soon enough, she found herself back in the large, cold basement of the store. She was pleased to find Mr. Miller already puttering about.

"Day two! This is becoming a trend!" Mr. Miller said. "I like it!"

Alaya shrugged. *Don't get used to it,* she wanted to say.

"As promised, your preparations will continue. But there is one thing I've forgotten." He handed her a small tube, which looked like regular breath-spray, but after the events of the past few days, Alaya knew better than to assume normality about anything.

"Are you sure about this?" She asked, as she carefully inspected the travel-sized can of pepper spray. It was concealed in a small leather case.

"Just keep it. I will feel safer." He said.

Alaya tossed the can into her travel bag.

"I can't emphasize this enough, Alaya - you *must* maintain a low profile at all times. You are about to step into a new world. You don't know anyone and you know almost nothing about the landscape, the culture, the people, or the customs. I don't mean to frighten you, but you also don't know who can or cannot be trusted. To be safe, I would suggest trusting no one. Try your best to blend in, make small transactions, and keep your wits about you. And if you inquire about your father, I would suggest you do so discreetly." His tone sounded as though he was warning her about boys before her first school dance.

"I'll be fine, Mr. Miller. Trust me," Alaya replied. "If things go south, I'll bail."

"There's something else, just in case." Mr. Miller walked over to the table where he had been working when Alaya arrived. When he returned, he handed her a smooth, glass orb.

"This is a troudare. There are only two of them made, and I have the other. Think of it as a cell phone, but one that *only* makes calls to me. Use it whenever you feel the need. Needless to say, it is far beyond anything Batunia has in terms of technology. You must ensure that it is kept with you at all times." He cautioned.

"A cell phone crystal that can communicate with people in different times? This is amazing!" Alaya exclaimed. Under normal circumstances, she wouldn't have been so easily impressed, but this was an exception.

"Did you make this yourself?"

Mr. Miller only smiled. "I can't reveal all my secrets in one night, can I?"

"Okay, I get it...So how does this thing work?" Alaya rolled the sphere around in her hand, looking for a touchpad or a speaker.

"It's simple. Just hold it in your palm and speak directly into it. I also have one and will keep it with me at all times. The best part—no electricity needed," he said, patting his pocket proudly. "It runs on solar energy."

Alaya got the impression that he would have loved nothing more than to move into a long-winded explanation of the mechanisms that allowed this sort of communication to be possible, but she wasn't interested.

"I'll take your word for it." Alaya carefully placed the glass sphere into her pack. She wondered whether she would even be gone long enough to use it.

"Well, that should just about do it," Mr. Miller slowly spoke, looking around the room as though considering what he could have missed.

Alaya began gathering her things and headed back upstairs. Once again, the day had flown by and it was almost time to go home.

"Oh, Alaya?" she turned around as her foot hit the bottom step. "Tomorrow seems like as good a day as any to head out, don't you think?" Mr. Miller asked, the familiar smile returning to his face.

Alaya was taken aback, shocked that he thought a couple days of prep was sufficient to send her across time and space. She wondered if this was happening too quickly, but then decided that it didn't matter. She couldn't think about it that way. *If I let fear stop me now, it may never happen.* However, one question remained.

"Can I really just leave my mother so abruptly? I'm sure she's going to have hundreds of questions. What should

I tell her?" Alaya asked the hard questions now, since time was running out and there was no reason to avoid them any longer.

"Leave your mother up to me," Mr. Miller said. "Remember how I said that this will be dual-purpose trip? I'll tell her that I have chosen to sponsor you for an internship, and the confirmation just came through today, since your application had been submitted late. I'll explain that you had shown an interest and an aptitude in archaeology, but didn't think to apply since it was such short notice. I already have the letterhead ready, and standard wording for all types of summer internship programs can be found on the Internet. Janice will be concerned, but she'll buy the story, mainly because she will want to believe it. But remember, Batunia may seem harmless enough, but you will have to keep your eyes and ears open. If anything were to go wrong..." he trailed off, not wanting to put words to his fears.

"I know..." Alaya had another wave of doubt, but she couldn't finish the sentence.

"Leave the home front to me. Besides, time works in funny ways," he assured her.

"What do you mean? What if it my trip takes days, or even weeks?"

"For some reason, once you're in another time, the rate of life here slows down dramatically. It is practically reduced by half. Basically, eight hours in another world will be roughly four hours here." Mr. Miller looked directly into her eyes, as though Alaya just stated that she had no desire to return right away. "Please, don't be careless!" He warned; his voice sounding harsh and accusatory.

"Sorry, Alaya. I just mean that it is foolish to gamble with time. It is delicate, and we are effectively manipulating it for our own purposes. I trust that you will respect that. If something were to go wrong, there's no telling what could happen. I couldn't bear it if I lost you, just as I lost your father. Who knows where you could end up? If there is a limbo of time, as I suspect there is, you could be trapped forever." Mr. Miller walked over to the staircase and stood directly in front of her, and gently placed a hand on her shoulder.

"Alaya, you *must* promise me that you will respect time, and return when we agree. This is a watch configured to work on Batunia's time. It may look like it's working double-time now, but it will run normally once you get there. If things look dangerous, or if you feel threatened, get out of there and return immediately." He looked troubled...maybe even afraid.

Alaya read between the lines. "I promise, Mr. Miller. Don't worry." She was silent for a moment, debating whether or not to ask her final question. She also didn't know whether Mr. Miller would trust her enough to tell the truth.

"Is that how my father went missing? He didn't respect time?"

Mr. Miller gave a heavy sigh. "You're a smart girl. I knew that you would figure things out sooner or later. That is what I suspect must have happened to him. Your father left in this machine without telling me. I don't know why he would have done that, but it must have been some kind of emergency. We had already determined that it was becoming too dangerous. He also left without a specific plan to return. The only note he left indicated that he had a long-term mission planned, which he hoped to complete in approximately a week. Obviously, that didn't happen. At the end of that week, the machine returned, but it was badly damaged." Mr. Miller walked over to one of the old bookshelves, opened a hardcover book in the top left corner, and removed a letter from the center of the pages.

"Your father left this brief note just before he left. He wanted me to tell your mother that he was going on a conference overseas. Some say that he was going to Mozambique, but no one knew where exactly to look. So when you add those two elements, it was a disaster waiting to happen." Mr. Miller's voice cracked and he put his head into his hands, and fell silent.

"I've thought long and hard about whether or not I am doing the right thing in sending you away, Alaya. I will not be able to help you beyond the troudare, and the things in that pack. Please don't make the same mistake as your father. The second you notice danger, return...no matter what the cost. Understand?"

Alaya responded simply, in a low voice, "Yes." She struggled to stave off the knot that had begun to swell in the back of her throat.

Mr. Miller tried to offer some comfort after his words. He must have seen that he'd opened some old wounds. "Your father, he had to have had his reasons. But what they were, no one knows for sure. Perhaps you will be able to find the answers to the questions we've both been asking for so many years."

***

Later that night, Alaya dreamed of her father. He was alone, trapped in a void. It was dark and he was frozen, yet always on the move, floating endlessly through time. Frederick was unable to sleep because he was desperately hunting for a way out. If he shut his eyes, he would surely miss his chance for freedom. He kept repeating two names: Alaya and Janice, as though doing so would bring him closer to salvation. Or perhaps, it was because he only wanted one last chance to say goodbye.

CHAPTER 13

The clock read six a.m. when Alaya turned over in her bed. She had tossed and turned all night, almost on the hour, every hour. Although she set her alarm for eight, no matter how hard she tried, no matter how tightly she shut her eyes, she was not able to sleep. The idea of staying in bed, lying there and attempting to fall back to sleep actually irritated her.

Just as Alaya prepared to leave for the shop, a nagging feeling took hold, anchoring her to the house. Janice, her mother, had been left completely out of the loop. Alaya had not mentioned anything to her about the trip, despite the welling desire to spill every story from the past few days. Although, this was by design. There was still no way to approach the subject, although things would certainly become easier once her "acceptance" letter arrived. But still, Alaya was unsure whether she could handle the onslaught of questions. For now, though, she determined it would probably be best if she simply avoided the subject altogether.

Alaya slowly crept into her mother's room. Goodbyes had always difficult for her, ever since her father's disappearance, but this did not really feel like goodbye. After all, Alaya knew she would return.

As she gazed down at her sleeping mother, so unaware and peaceful, Alaya couldn't fight the small twinge of guilt and sadness now rising in her like a fever. It overwhelmed her, unannounced and without restraint. Alaya felt warm tears begin to tumble and roll down the sides of her cheeks. She let them fall, which was something she would have never let anyone see on a normal day. But this was far from a normal day.

Alaya leaned down over her mother and gently kissed her forehead. Janice briefly shifted, but remained fast asleep, secure in the place where dreams kept her blissfully ignorant of the secrets her daughter had purposely withheld.

Alaya took one last look back at her mother before shutting the door. Under her breath, she whispered, "Love you, mom." With that, she slipped out the front door, ready for her new journey.

***

With nothing but the clothes on her back, Alaya made her way through town to the antique store. It was early August, and the late-summer heat wave was in full swing. The bright sun made an early appearance, bathing the street in orange and pink light.

As Alaya walked, conflicting thoughts wrestled inside her mind. She was battling a powerful blend of excitement, anxiety, and fear. It was anyone's guess what awaited her once she crossed into that other realm. Whatever happened, Alaya hoped she could return safely.

Suddenly, Alaya stopped walking. She had made it to the costume jewelry store, three shops down. She was so caught up in her thoughts that she marched right past Mr. Miller's store. It felt like she had only just stepped out of her house moments ago. Thankfully, habit guided her footsteps on that humid morning.

Mr. Miller seemed eager to get started. He quickly made his way to the front door and swung it wide open like he was airing out the place. His wall clock chimed; it was seven o'clock in the morning. Alaya looked around, up and down the sidewalk. She hadn't seen a single person on the street, nor a car moving in the distant intersections. The rest of the world carried on safe and warm in their beds; oblivious to all that awaited her once she stepped inside. She felt her insides begin to churn.

"Well, don't just stand there...come in, come in!" he said cheerfully as he waved toward the back of the room, inviting her into the store. "An early start may be just what we need to give you slightly more time, if you need it."

Once they reached the basement, Alaya was surprised to find that the machine was already running. She was immediately drawn to the low hum emitting from the vehicle, and dismissed the uneasy feeling in the pit of her stomach. Lights twinkled on the main control panel as she ran her fingers along the smooth, polished edges of the door. He had cleaned up the machine quite a bit since the night before.

This was really happening.

Mr. Miller instructed Alaya to change clothes, so she quickly slipped into his office. She tossed her jeans, t-shirt, and tennis shoes onto his desk, exchanging them for simple, more modest clothing. Her dress fell just below her ankles, and made her feel as though she was going to be ordered to confession at any moment. The dress was a drab, lavender hue, lacking any discernible style other than the cinched waist and ruffled bodice. The look was completed by a pair of black ballet slippers. She was pleased to find that they were comfortable at least. Finding shoes in her size, an unusual 11, was never an easy task. She was taking one last look at herself in the small mirror on Mr. Miller's wall when he called to her through the door.

"All set in there?"

"Just about," Alaya shouted. She gathered up her regular clothes that she had tossed haphazardly onto Mr. Miller's desk, but as she turned to leave, she heard something fall to the floor. Looking down, she saw that it was the green journal Mr. Miller had been studying so intently. She instinctively scooped it up and went out to meet Mr. Miller.

He walked her over to the control center of the machine, rapidly reviewing the meters for energy levels, dials for seat controls, visor and windshield functions, weather-proofing, and once again, he walked her through the heating and cooling functions. There was a small panel where Alaya would enter the details of her destination, including the name, date, and coordinates. Finally, he showed her the new feature on the machine, something of which he was particularly proud.

"Let's say that you want to go somewhere in particular, but you don't know the name. Well, now you can also simply describe your destination using prominent landmarks. The machine compiles your data, analyzes the various possibilities, and then makes suggestions. Then, you can make your choice." He smiled, as though he expected a round of applause and a shower of roses.

"I'm pretty sure that cell phones have apps that can do the same thing." Alaya said, noticeably unimpressed. She immediately realized how rude that must have sounded. None of this could have been easy for Mr. Miller. After all, her father wasn't around to help, and besides that, Alaya certainly hadn't created anything this spectacular. "I'm sorry, Mr. Miller, it really is brilliant."

"No harm done," Mr. Miller said, a smile returning to his face. "My ego is not as fragile as you might think. So, are you ready to go?" he asked, hints of enthusiasm and concern blended in his voice.

"As ready as I'll ever be." Alaya said as she strapped herself in.

"Great. And you do have the watch, correct?"

Alaya held up her arm and slid back the length of her dress sleeve, revealing the small watch delicately ringing her wrist. She had almost forgotten she was wearing the device. She had never had a reason to look further than her cell phone for the time, so this would be good practice.

"Well, I suppose that's it!" Mr. Miller was bouncing on his toes; practically brimming with nervous energy. "Off you go then." He assisted Alaya with getting seated into the machine.

"And don't forget, when in doubt, check the marketplace! That's always a good place to start," Mr. Miller suggested. "I promise. I will be here when you return."

Alaya took a deep breath and carefully placed her right finger over the green "destination" button, unsure of what would happen next. She looked at Mr. Miller, who was waving wildly at her from behind his desk. "Such a goof," she said under her breath as she entered the coordinates and Batunia's name into the control panel.

Suddenly, the air seemed to transform into a hazy gray, and began to thicken around her. A small gust of wind picked up pace until it rushed past her face, overwhelming her. Her vision blurred from the force of air, and she squinted. The machine's low hum was now a grumbling roar, and her seat shook like a bucket in the Niagara Falls. The strong, gusty air tore a vibrating tear from her eye, which seemed to be filled with the light of infinite stars.

A strange tingling sensation suddenly appeared in every of her body. It gave her a rush as it jolted through every limb of her body like cold lightning. Then, she felt a dizzying sense of vertigo, as though she had been spun in circles a dozen times in an instant. Alaya tried to pry her eyes open, but she could no longer see Mr. Miller, or the basement. Only the swirling, gray gusts surrounded her and the machine.

Alaya gripped the sides of the seat so tightly that she felt the circulation cease in her hands and fingers. She never asked Mr. Miller what to expect, so she had no way of knowing if this was how it was supposed to feel when traveling through space and time.

The violent rumbling continued on for at least another minute. Alaya felt as though she might be torn from the machine at any second, tossed errantly somewhere in space. She tugged at her strap with one shaking hand, making sure it was still secure. Her mind reeled back to her father. Was this what he had felt? Had he been struck by the paralyzing fear that he was about be sucked out of reality, forever lost in an endless universe? Or worse yet, that he might be separated from his very existence? She tried to be brave. Those thoughts wouldn't help her now.

***

Nauseating twists and plummeting turns tossed the machine, making Alaya feel like she was being thrown overboard from a ship traversing choppy waters. Although she couldn't be sure, Alaya felt as though she was doing somersaults. It was only made worse by the fact that she couldn't see beyond the gray mass surrounding her. Instinctively, Alaya shut her eyes to fight the feeling of nausea. The madness continued without end, until finally, after what seemed like hours, the machine came to an abrupt stop.

Alaya took a number of panting breaths, with her eyes still shut. She needed a minute for her stomach to settle.

Several times, she wrestled down the urge to be sick, and kept a hand over her mouth just in case.

Finally, she opened her eyes. Bright sunlight nearly blinded her, but through slit eyes, she could see a forest surrounding her. Alaya attempted to stand and caught her balance. The feeling of vertigo lingered for just a moment longer.

Once Alaya emerged from the machine, she held up a hand to shield her eyes from the glaring sun that drowned out the landscape. Her mind swirled wildly as she knelt to steady herself on solid ground. Once she felt that she could stand, she took a single step, fearing that even a small movement would bring up her breakfast. Her eyes had grown accustomed to the bright sunlight and her focus shifted to a quite unexpected sight.

A vast landscape of lush, green trees surrounded her on all sides. As she looked out even further, just beyond the edge of where her eyesight could reach, she could make out patches of barren desert. She wondered how the two could coexist within such close proximity to one another. She looked up and marveled at the soaring trees. They each stood three or four stories high; some stretched even taller. They prevented her from seeing the entirety of the sky, but the blinding sun told her that it was daylight.

The setting was unlike anything she had ever seen before in Maryland. Although, admittedly, Alaya had never traveled far outside the range of her childhood bubble. *Had it worked?* Alaya wondered.

Alaya's ear was tickled by the sounds of a brook mumbling eternally to itself nearby, somewhere to her right. She felt drawn almost unconsciously toward the water. The touch of the soft, damp earth beneath her slippers assured her that this was not a dream. Alaya was truly standing in a verdant forest.

That fact could only mean one thing: the machine had worked. However, therein lay the most important matter to address…the machine. She had to ensure that it remained safely hidden. If it was found, her chances of returning home would disappear as completely as she had disappeared from Mr. Miller's basement.

Taking in her surroundings; Alaya noticed the abundance of dead, fallen leaves, perfect for camouflage in the colorful forest. As she worked, building a mound of dead leaves around the machine, Alaya pondered the seasonal differences. In Maryland, it was still the end of summer, but it was clear from the variety of colors on the trees that Batunia was in the midst of autumn.

Alaya made short work of her task and completely covered the tiny machine in less than ten minutes. It now had the appearance of a slightly oversized pile of fallen leaves. Figuring that she could not do much else in the way of disguises, Alaya turned her attention back to her current situation. First, she had to figure out where she was, and secondly, she had to figure out where she was going. *Some things never change,* she thought, and an amused grin cracked her expression.

CHAPTER 14

laya glanced down at her watch. For a long while, nothing happened, and she worried that it might have broken in transit. When she looked more closely, however, she realized that the larger dial had finally moved. It was about half the speed of a regular clock. *It is working! Just like Mr. Miller said it would.* Alaya felt a surge of gratitude as her thoughts fell to the elderly man awaiting her back in the basement of the old, disorganized antique store. How far away it seemed now.

Before Alaya had time to consider her next move, Mother Nature made the decision for her. The once bright sky was now turning to a hazy overcast. A slow, sporadic rain began to fall, which steadily increased until in a matter of minutes, it had turned into a torrential downpour. She picked up her bag and ran into the thick of the forest, without a particular destination in mind. She had to find shelter. Besides the mammoth tree branches hovering above, there was very little she could do to protect herself from the savage deluge. There was no choice but to keep moving.

As Alaya walked, she noticed that the sky had begun to darken. She looked at her watch. *It can't possibly be evening already, can it?* Her watch read 9:30 a.m. Had this been an error on Mr. Miller's end? Alaya didn't think so; he had been so careful about every detail. She realized that she might simply be in a different time zone. It was, after all, morning when she departed on her journey. Alaya concluded that she would have to adjust the time after all; once she found out what time it actually was. She momentarily lamented the intense jet lag, or perhaps *time* lag, that she would inevitably face when she returned home.

Alaya trekked aimlessly through the thick curtain of rain, but she was just as lost as could be. There were no maps, no tour guides, and no compass. She couldn't even look into the night sky towards the stars, as the gray, cloudy mass above did her no favors.

Soon, Alaya noticed something odd. Small, glowing lights began flashing all around her. They reminded her of fireflies, but these were different. Fireflies normally kept their distance and didn't usually travel in packs, while these dancing beacons almost seemed to be traveling together. *But why were they following her?*

Knowing that she couldn't continue without a clear direction, Alaya stopped to get a look at her new surroundings. Once her feet stopped moving, the firefly-creatures quickly took off in a single direction, like a flock of frightened birds. Her eyes followed the swarm; she was sad to see them go. Their bright, gentle light had been comforting in the cold, dark forest. Once they had disappeared from sight, her eyes readjusted and she was able to make out something in the distance.

Alaya initially thought that she was imagining things, but there was no denying it: off in the distance, she saw the outline of a building. It was a few dozen yards away, buried in the thick shadows of the rain and the woods.

It was ever so faint, but Alaya also spotted a bit of smoke rising through the trees in the northeast. Just then, she realized how cold she had become. Prickly goose bumps flared over her skin, and her thin, drenched dress clung to her body. She needed to find refuge from the storm quickly, or she would soon have bigger problems to worry about.

Alaya quickened her pace and headed directly for the building. She could now see that it was a house, and although it was a ways off, she could almost feel the warmth emanating from the fire that was burning.

As Alaya drew closer, she began to wonder whether the owner would be friendly enough to invite her inside. If they were not, she would thank them, and keep moving. *But what if she couldn't find a place? Why hadn't she brought any weapons?*

That last thought nearly brought a laugh to her lips; it wasn't like Alaya knew how to fight anyhow. In nearly 20 years of life, she had never been in a physical conflict of any kind. The opportunity had frankly never come up. She was an only child and her parents had raised her to take the path of least resistance when it came to classmates.

Alaya approached the front door, and decided that it was best to devise some sort of strategy before knocking. What would she say?

Quaking rumbles of thunder and electrifying cracks of lightning interrupted her thoughts. The thunder sounded strong enough to shatter brick and bone. In quick succession, the lightning and thunder struck a second time. Alaya nearly lost her footing as she cowered and shrieked in fright. The heart of the storm was dangerously close; the blinding flashes seemed to be riding her heels.

Alaya realized that she did not have the luxury to sit and weigh the consequences of knocking on the front door, nor the disposition of the person standing on the other side. Her teeth chattered uncontrollably and she crossed her arms, wishing that she had at least packed a raincoat. There was no use complaining now. Considering the current state of affairs, she was left with very few options.

She paused for a few moments on the front stoop and knocked three times on the knotted, dark wooden door. It was far too cold to turn back now. Perhaps the residents were a feeble, elderly couple who were both too weak to cause her any harm. After knocking a second time, she took a step back, preparing for disappointment. Her foot was also turned on a slight pivot, just in case the residents were less than friendly.

Alaya was prepared to walk away when she heard a voice. It was not what she expected - not even close.

"Who is it?" It seemed that the couple was not so elderly after all. There were two voices. One sounded young and friendly - clearly a child. The other was a female, who sounded a little older, but not by much. Alaya fought within herself, debating what exactly to say. In that moment, she saw a sliver of light appear as the door slowly began to creak open.

"Careful! What if it's one of the King's Riders? Or worse..." a hushed voice whispered.

"Don't worry, Max. Why would either of them come to our home? Besides, they wouldn't knock on our door. They would kick it down," Alaya heard the second voice say. It was a female. "And besides, if it is, it certainly doesn't matter now. They have already heard you with your oversized mouth."

Following this exchange, the front door cracked open a tiny bit more, revealing a face. An exasperated young woman with long bright red hair, fair skin, and gray eyes stared back at Alaya. The woman looked to be about the same age as her.

"Oh! Max, it's okay. Come and see for yourself," she said, peering behind her shoulder.

The timid boy snuck out from behind the young woman's legs. He couldn't have been more than nine or ten years old and had dark brown hair. His face was littered with light freckles and he smiled a nervous grin, revealing several missing teeth.

Max stared at Alaya for a brief moment, and then immediately slipped back behind the woman. Alaya quickly surmised that Max must have been her younger brother; she looked too young to have a son his age.

"Hello. Who are you?" the woman asked. "I've never seen you around here before."

Alaya had to think of something to say, and quick. She was not prepared for a lie, although it should have been part of her planning. She decided to simply tell the truth, or at least as limited a version of it as she could. There was no harm in that.

"My name is Alaya. I was just in the area visiting, but I seem to have gotten lost," she said, holding her arms for warmth as her teeth began to chatter; she hadn't moved in a few minutes and what little warmth she had in her bones was quickly fading. The sudden deluge was not doing her any favors, and it was getting colder by the second.

"Hello, Alaya. My name is Hava. Hava Iskinder." She reached out and gripped both of Alaya's forearms. Alaya didn't question it, realizing that it must have been some sort of traditional greeting.

"It is not safe to wander out in the woods alone at night. Please, Alaya, come inside. You must be terribly cold." Hava opened the door wide enough for Alaya to feel an intoxicating rush of comforting heat welcoming her inside.

Just then, far off in the distance, a faint sound was heard. It was very distant at first, but grew louder with every passing second. Something was approaching - fast. The indiscernible rumble soon transformed into the distinct sound of hooves pounding into moist earth.

"Come in - quickly!" Hava whispered as she ushered Alaya in, and shut the massive door behind them. She then bolted every lock, and closed every window curtain, shutting out the darkness.

Alaya wrung out her soaking wet bag and dress before she stepped inside, but was afraid to track water and mud into this kind stranger's house. It looked like a small house from the outside, yet it was cozy and inviting on the inside. Alaya could feel the warmth wash over her and thaw the chill from her face.

Once safely inside, Hava explained her reason for such caution.

"The King recently began a new curfew. It's even earlier than before, and his guards take it very seriously. They are always looking to capture new servants. You are quite fortunate to have come here. If they found you first, you would have surely been forced to serve in the castle."

Alaya simply nodded, but her teeth began to chatter again as a last chill ran through her body.

"Oh goodness, follow me!" Hava said and directed Alaya over to the fireplace. The heat quickly began to melt Alaya's frozen skin. She did not realize how cold she had become until the room had become silent.

"It's about time those teeth stopped chattering," Hava said. "Let me get you a cover, before you fall ill." She rushed out of sight, leaving Alaya alone.

She took this opportunity to explore her new surroundings, but soon realized Hava and Max were not alone. New voices were coming from the room Hava had disappeared into. When she returned, an older woman and a tall, burly man were with her.

"Here you are," Hava said, and handed Alaya a thick blanket. "Also, I'd like you to meet my parents."

The mother was a tall, slender woman who was probably in her early forties. Her drab blonde hair was pulled back into a sloppy bun and she had a plain look about her. Tiny wisps of hair fell out of place, making her appear somewhat stressed and older than she probably was.

"And Max...well, you met him earlier." Max came out of his hiding place, this time from behind his mother's leg.

Hava's parents glanced at each other. Their eyes were full of questions that no one could hear, but were clearly shared between the pair. Several moments passed, and not a word escaped their lips. Alaya tried to read their faces so she could formulate an appropriate response, but their expressions were impenetrable. The woman looked as though she was struggling hard to remember something. The man on the other hand, was a wall of stone—stoic and unreadable.

"Nice to meet you, Alaya," the older woman smiled as she stepped forward to greet her. She followed the same greeting that Hava had done at the door. Alaya took a mental note of this.

"My name is Willemina Iskinder, and this is my husband, Nikolai." She gave him a cryptic look, which conveyed something that went over Alaya's head.

Nikolai was a tower of a man. His muscular arms nearly ripped through the old flimsy shirt he was wearing, which was accompanied by dirty, shabby pants. He might have been in his late forties, judging by the flecks of gray sprinkled throughout his close-cropped hair. An eye patch hid his left eye, accompanying various long-healed scars and cuts to his face. Alaya wondered how he had lost it, but she dared not ask. It looked as though he wouldn't hesitate to rip a man's beating heart out his chest and feast on it right there without a second thought. She looked instinctively down to the wooden planks on the floor, unable to hold eye contact.

"Alaya," Nikolai said with a booming voice and stepped forward. He did not grab Alaya's forearms, but instead, held out one hand with his palm facing up. It looked as if he was expecting something in return, but she doubted that it was a low five. Alaya knew that Nikolai must have been extending a greeting, but she didn't know precisely how to respond. It was clear that men and women greeted one another differently. She stood there, wondering what to do.

Nikolai looked at her with questioning, suspicious eyes. Hava must have noticed this, because she suddenly spoke.

"Mother, father, Alaya's not from this area. From the look of her clothing, she must have traveled a great distance and become lost in the forest. Is that right, Alaya?" Hava asked, looking for confirmation with hopeful eyes.

One thing became instantly clear to Alaya: she would need to quickly learn Batunia's customs. She felt foolish for not reading through the rest of the guides Mr. Miller had given her.

Alaya smiled and tried her best to seem friendly and harmless, although she felt more awkward than anything. She told them how she lost her way and happened to be in town visiting.

As Hava spoke, Alaya noticed that Nikolai only stood back, listening carefully. He observed for a few more minutes before retreating to the back room. All the while, Max hadn't said a word, but had instead hung near his father. Alaya didn't realize that he was there until her eyes caught sight of the small person staring up at her with big eyes.

Willemina provided an explanation for her son's behavior. "You will have to excuse him. He has recently had a terrible fright. He is still a bit shy around strangers now. However, once he gets to know you, you will almost wish that he had not." She gave a low, barely audible chuckle. Of his two parents, Alaya could see where Max had gotten his bashful nature.

"That's a smart way to go about life," Alaya said, thinking about how foolish and trusting she was to step into a complete stranger's house, as she had just done. Things seemed to be going well, but she needed to keep on guard. Alaya sent a friendly smile in Max's direction. She was much more relaxed now that Nikolai had left the room; his presence was like a physical force amidst his family, but it clearly came from a place of protective love.

With the pleasantries out of the way, it was now time to get down to business. Alaya told them a bit more about herself, and as she talked, Max crept out to join the rest of his family.

"Alaya, I cannot believe that you are traveling alone. If I may ask, how old are you?" Willemina asked.

"I'm nineteen years old. But I can handle myself," Alaya said, trying to sound confident.

"And I am nine years old!" Max suddenly blurted out, beaming with pride. The family froze for a moment, surprised that Max had warmed to anyone so quickly, and soon filled the small room with laughter.

"I guess that he has finally found something to say," Hava said, and began laughing.

CHAPTER 15

As everyone began to become better acquainted, Alaya was careful not to say too much. She remembered what Mr. Miller had told her about the differences in cultures and technology, and how even the slightest conveniences of modern society can become an issue.

Since Alaya didn't have a chance to read through Mr. Miller's notes, she keenly observed the Iskinder family, taking mental notes from their social cues. She learned that there was very little in the way of amenities, judging from what little she had seen of the house. However, there was a basic clock on the wall. There was no television, no phones, cellular or otherwise, and no sign of computers. The house was very simple, filled with modest chairs, tables, and a pile of scattered books neatly stacked onto bookshelves that lined the small room.

Alaya also noticed that Willemina and Nikolai did not use contractions when they spoke. Apparently, this was the sign of someone who was educated. This was now a status symbol, with the "upper-class" consisting of individuals who chose to speak with proper diction. Although Hava had received some formal education, she preferred to speak more like her friends, who had never attended. She thought speaking as her parents, would make her seem pedantic and elitist.

"Hava, please do not tell me your father and I wasted our hard-earned money for nothing. Show our guest that you have had proper training," Willemina urged.

"Mother, please. I told you, no one our age talks that way anymore. I tried it, but everyone looked at me like I was crazy. Quit being so old-fashioned. Besides, everyone knows how poor we are now. We can't even afford to send Max to school," Hava said.

Willemina lashed back. "You watch your tongue young lady!"

"Sorry," she said.

***

The night wore on, and Alaya soon realized that it was getting late. It was very dark outside, but the rain still hadn't let up. With the curfew in place, Alaya knew that she couldn't risk going back outside. She also wanted to check on the machine, but that would have to wait. She needed a place to stay, and the Iskinders seemed kind enough.

Though they were kind, the questions were interminable. Alaya began to shift in her seat, unsure of how to answer them. After all, any response out of the ordinary could put her life in danger. She had to think...there had to be a way out of this.

An idea suddenly struck Alaya: amnesia. That could be the perfect solution. She quickly improvised on this new strategy and told them that she was lost. She confessed that she could not remember the reason for her journey, nor where she was headed. And while she knew she was from a distant land, she could barely recall the name, or how to return.

"While I was walking through the woods, I knew I needed help, but I didn't know where to turn," Alaya then rubbed a random spot on her head, pretending to experience a sharp pain.

"Oh, you poor girl!" Willemina exclaimed. "Shame to me, I have not even offered you something to eat or drink. Are you hungry?" she asked, maternal instincts kicking in.

Alaya shook her head. "I can't—I cannot seem to remember anything beyond what I've told you. I'm sorry."

The truth was, Alaya really just wanted to get to the morning as quickly as possible and begin to find something that might point her toward her father. With the blanket wrapped firmly around her, she stood, pretending to do so with great difficulty, and then sat down gingerly on a nearby chair. She gave a dramatic sigh of defeat, and looked down at the floor in silence.

Alaya could only imagine how pitiful she must have looked, with her still-damp hair, clothes, and squishy shoes.

"I have heard of this before," Willemina said in a kind voice. "You seem to be suffering from some type of a memory affliction. We can help find a remedy, but we will need to get to a marketplace. We shall go first thing in the morning."

"She has no place to stay in the meantime, Mother," Hava added. "What should we do?"

Maybe this will work out after all, Alaya thought.

At once, both Hava and Willemina stopped speaking. Alaya saw that Nikolai had returned to the room, as silently as he had left. It was clear that he was the one who would make the final decision on the matter. Alaya was overflowing with worry, wondering what he would say. *What if he says no? Would I have to go back outside and fight through the storm?* The stony expression on his face did little to indicate his leanings. Perhaps he had overheard the discussion and was unconvinced that she had amnesia?

"What did you say your name was?" he asked, looking at Alaya as though she had robbed him blind.

"Alaya, sir," she said in a timid voice.

Alaya didn't know why she said 'sir.' She had never even said this to people who may have deserved it back home. All she knew was this: the decision of where she'd spend the night rested in this man's hands. On top of that, he also struck a fear in her that made it difficult to breathe, let alone lie. She hoped that was the extent of his questions.

"Interesting," he said, and stared her down. "No one has called me 'sir' in many years. How did you know that I used to work for the Guard? You are either very astute, or you are not who you say you are. Also, I didn't mean your first name; I would like to know your family name. Alaya what?" he asked, still wearing the same flat expression.

Alaya began to shiver again, but not from the cold. He could apparently read right through her.

"Um…Frederickson, sir." Alaya said, with an understated sigh. She was quivering on the inside. Lying had never been her strong suit, but in that moment, she decided to settle with a variation of the truth. Alaya tried to control her breathing; hoping that he wouldn't see how terrified she was.

Nikolai was silent for a moment as he slowly crossed the room, slowing when he was mere inches from her face. He extended his hand once again, as he had when they first met. From the corner of her eye, Alaya saw Hava's face break into a huge smile.

Nikolai reached down and gently grabbed Alaya's arm, taking her by surprise.

"Like this," he said, and placed her hand directly above his. But they did not touch.

"This is how you do it. And please, you do not have to call me 'sir.' That was another life," he said. "I hope your memory returns soon." Nikolai turned to his wife, and nodded once.

"Willemina my dear, if you have room for one more, we can allow Alaya to stay with us for as long as she needs. Hava, please prepare a space for her in your room. I will return soon," Nikolai said and headed out into the cold, rainy night.

"Wonderful!" Hava exclaimed and

"I will go prepare dinner," Willemina said, and took her leave.

"Welcome to our home!" Max said, and ran towards Alaya to grab her by the hand. It was clear he had his own way of greeting strangers. "Let me show you around."

With Max as her guide, Alaya received a tour around the house. There were three bedrooms, all of which were very small, yet there was a certain inviting atmosphere that drew her in. She noticed that the smallest room was not in fact a true "bathroom" and actually lacked a proper toilet with plumbing. However, there were two basins. One was for waste and the larger basin was for washing. Max explained how they heated water on the stove for baths. Alaya stared down at the steel basin, imagining how cold it must feel on the skin first thing in the morning. She hoped to keep her stay as short as possible, but while she was around, she might as well know the ropes.

Soon, a blend of wonderful smells began to circulate through the house. Once she reached the kitchen, Alaya's stomach groaned with hunger pangs loud enough to wake a baby.

"Oh you poor thing! It will be done soon," Willemina said as she stirred the contents of the largest pot.

Alaya immediately felt flushed.

"Sorry! I didn't realize how hungry I must've become," She said.

"Do not worry. One of our neighbors will be joining us tonight," Willemina said, wiping her brow as she swirled around to a large, dark skillet over a heat. "I hope this will be enough food for everyone."

"It will be plenty," Max piped in, attempting to snag the first bite of the freshly fried dough that Willemina scooped from the skillet. Alaya caught a whiff of the bread, and more rumbles sounded off from her belly.

Willemina slapped Max's hand away before he had a chance to take a bite of the aromatic bread. "Mom, please can't I just have some? Besides, Hava doesn't eat much when Whalen visits anyway. Isn't that right, sister?"

Hava had just entered the room and didn't speak, but the scowl across her face spoke volumes.

Alaya didn't pay much attention to the sibling banter. She was too entranced by the pots and the delightful scents emanating from their depths. The air was filled with savory smells and spices. She saw that all of the cookware was nearly filled to the brim with meat, sauces, and vegetables. Dozens of sliced potatoes rolled in a rapid boil inside of the largest metal pot. Alaya was lost in the enthralling aroma, only now realizing that she had not eaten since that morning.

Although the kitchen was small, Alaya made her way past the bickering family members and went to take a seat back in the living room. Removing herself from the temptation seemed like the best idea.

"Do you like it?" Max asked, following closely behind. Before Alaya could get a word out, her stomach growled again, making its empty presence known to the whole room. A moment later, the second echoing groan was loud enough for both Hava and Willemina to hear, and they all erupted into a hearty laugh.

"I guess that answers your question?" Alaya said.

"It's one of the best dishes our mother makes!" Hava said, joining them. "Potatoes and monocrant stew."

"Monocrant?" Alaya had never heard this word before.

"You know them, those big beasts that work in the fields? We get milk from them and they also make delicious meat," Max said.

"Oh, yes, monocrant. I thought you said mono*cat*," Alaya said.

She took in another deep whiff. Something else resonated in the aroma as well. It must've been the fresh bread, but it was certainly fresher than the packaged store bought bread that she was used to eating.

"Mmm that smells so good," Alaya said, nearly drooling all over herself.

"Good. This is the best bread you will ever have, if I may say so," Willemina said with a proud grin, and then began delegating tasks.

"Hava, before dinner, why not take Alaya to freshen up? I am sure that she would like some dry clothes to wear before your father arrives with Whalen. You two look to be about the same size," she said.

"Yes, Mother." Hava suddenly grabbed Alaya by the arm. "Come with me, Alaya!" she said with excitement that Alaya couldn't understand, and urgently whisking her away.

Max interjected, "Hava always gets so excited when Whalen comes over. You will see for yourself, Alaya. It is quite funny."

Hava shot Max a vicious look and her face transformed into the color of a ripe tomato, although she did not verbally respond to Max's taunts.

"Come on, Alaya," she said.

In Hava's room, she motioned for Alaya to take a seat on the bed. Hava went through her wardrobe and pulled out an assortment of outfits as potential options for Alaya. Most of the dresses were dull in color with high collars; without exception, the most apt descriptions for the clothes were plain and simple.

Alaya struggled with the fashion selection for women in Batunia; it seemed as though the look of plain Jane was the only option. Mr. Miller must have been right - only men had the privilege of wearing pants.

While Alaya searched for something mildly stylish to wear, Hava attempted to sort out Alaya's hair, which had been savagely tangled in the storm.

It seemed as though Hava declared war against the knots and kinks, attempting to sift through large sections of hair with great difficulty. Although Alaya did not feel any pain, the vicious tugs weren't a good sign for the state of her hair. The relentless brushing nearly pulled Alaya's eyes up to her hairline. She feared that she might not have any hair left if Hava continued her campaign against her delicate coif.

"Father has had a surplus over the last few days," Hava said as she brushed, seemingly unaware of her own strength being applied to Alaya's head. "He often invites people over for a meal to celebrate. It's usually for the less fortunate, but today, he wanted to do something special. For many moons now, Father has wanted to show his support for the Warrior's Council, and he has finally found a way to do that."

"What's the council?" Alaya asked.

"Basically, it's a group of trained warriors. They are mostly men, but there are some women. Years back, father and a few men left the Royal Guard and decided something had to be done. I just became a member not too long ago. He doesn't want many people knowing who has joined the Council, so he trained me himself. Our mission is to work hard to protect the people who need it most, since our King's attention lies elsewhere," Hava said, although she didn't expand on that last sentence.

Alaya's scalp was screaming for relief; she couldn't take it anymore, no matter how kind the intention of the gesture was on Hava's end. She reached up and grabbed the tool, putting an end to the botched grooming session.

"It's okay, Hava. I've got it. Perhaps you can find something for me to wear?" Alaya suggested, grateful for the exchange of duties.

"I'm sorry, but goodness, Alaya! Your hair is massive! I've seen others with curly hair like yours, and I have to ask, how do you manage to live with it?"

Before Alaya could answer, there was a gentle rapping on the bedroom door, and it slightly opened.

"Hava, they are back! I can hear them coming!" Max blurted out, and then raced back into the living room.

"So…any suggestions?" Alaya asked Hava, who began frantically searching through her wardrobe, knowing that the excitement of the night would soon begin.

Quickly, Alaya tried on one dress after another. Some were stretched beyond their normal limits, while others threatened to burst at the seams. After a few attempts, the truth was obvious to them both; Alaya's body was slightly more robust, so fitting into Hava's more petite clothing wasn't going to work.

"Well, how about this one?" Hava asked, extending her arm with yet another dress. "It is a little old, however, so it has been stretched out quite a bit. Perhaps it is just what we need," Hava said, and handed her a pale, yellow dress made of delicate, aged fabric.

Alaya put the dress on, and it gently hugged her body rather than strapped her down like a straight-jacket.

"This will do just fine," she said.

CHAPTER 16

When Alaya and Hava returned to the living room, Max was chattering excitedly with the new guest. He was tall and lean, about the same height as Nikolai, and wrapped in a gray hooded cloak that looked to be waterproof. The man bent down and playfully ruffled Max's hair.

"Hello, Max. How are you this evening?" He asked.

Nikolai interrupted their brief greeting. "Max, leave him be; at least until he gets settled. Come inside, Whalen."

The tall man stepped further into the main room and removed his coat, his back turned to the kitchen. Alaya lost sight of them both as they took a seat in the living room.

"Mother, this is far too much!" Hava said, balancing two large plates like a circus act. Alaya rushed over to help her lower them onto the dining table, which lay adjacent to the kitchen. She returned to the tiny kitchen and brought the large plate of fresh vegetables to complete the cornucopia already overflowing on the table. Once all of the food had been laid out, Willemina asked everyone to take a seat.

Hava chose the seat closest to Whalen, on his left, while Max sat on his right. Alaya sat on the opposite side of the table, across from Max. She found it amusing how the two of them fawned over their guest like a Thanksgiving turkey.

Alaya decided that an introduction was probably in order.

"Hello. Whalen, is it? I am Alaya." She extended one hand across the table, then quickly remembered the custom and extended one palm facing up. Alaya noticed that the room grew strangely quiet, causing her to wonder if she had done something wrong. Whalen returned the greeting after a moment's hesitation and Alaya quickly dropped her hand.

Finally, Whalen spoke. "It is nice to meet you, Alaya."

He greeted her with a genuine smile, which Alaya could only contribute to her awkwardness. Batunian traditions were still foreign to her. His dark hair was cut very close to his scalp, which reminded Alaya of the buzz cut style she knew back home. His eyes were a deep, dark brown. They seemed honest and kind.

"We are among friends here; some old…and some new," Nikolai began, nodding off in Alaya's direction. "We have been blessed by the Soranayum with a good harvest, and are grateful to be able to share that bounty with our friends. Now, let us eat," he declared.

Without another word of formality, everyone dove into the stew. Sounds of pleasant feasting filled the room; silverware clanging into plates, and scooping out seconds from the serving dishes. Willemina blushed at the showers of compliments she received as they all tore off chunks of bread with their teeth, and spooned mouthfuls of stew into their mouths.

It was all Alaya could do to not plow through bowl after bowl of the stew. It was one of the most delicious homemade meals she'd ever had. The meat was wonderfully tender and the potatoes were cooked to perfection. Exotic spices, to Alaya's palate at least, gave the mixture a sharp, savory flavor. Alaya sunk her teeth into the soft bread that filled her mouth like warm pillows, unconsciously murmuring to herself in delight. She devoured the entire piece and reached to fill up her bowl for a third time.

When her stomach neared capacity, she was forced to slow her pace. It was only then that she finally looked up, and saw all eyes at the table were staring at her, thoroughly amused. Alaya felt her face grow warm and immediately stopped eating. She wondered what cultural faux pas she had managed to commit this time.

"There is no need to stop, Alaya. We have plenty more left," Willemina read her mind and encouraged her to continue. "We are only surprised; it must have been a long time since you have had a meal, or perhaps my stew simply has an ardent admirer." Everyone, including Alaya, began to laugh at this. Both statements were true: she was ravenous and the food was delightful.

"I have to admit, it's been a very long time since I've eaten like this." Alaya thought back to her life at home, particularly about her mother's drinking. Janice barely had enough time to prepare a TV dinner for herself, let alone sit down for a home-cooked family meal with Alaya. Life had been that way for quite some time, and Alaya had nearly lost hope that they would ever find the happiness they had once known.

Once the chewing slowed, the chatter around the table began. They all shared interesting stories of their day, clearly enjoying one another's company. Alaya sat and observed with a purpose; she didn't talk much and only smiled or laughed when it seemed appropriate. She knew very little of Batunia so far and wanted to soak up everything she could.

Based on the small bits of information that Alaya remembered from skimming through the guide, she was able to place some of the pieces into their proper context. Alaya recognized the customs of respecting nature, families' reliance upon farming for their sustenance, and other day-to-day norms. Alaya's hosts tried to include her and occasionally directed a few questions at her, but she blamed the memory illness for her lack of participation, which Whalen found intriguing. Conversation began winding down when Nikolai finally placed his napkin on the table. He had eaten more than everyone else, and seemed satisfied, full, and relaxed.

"I saw them again, Nikolai," Willemina said, which froze the room into deafening silence. "They did not say anything to me, but I do not care to ever see them again if I can help it."

No one spoke a word. Although everyone felt it, they were unwilling to break the tension, until Nikolai cleared his throat. His expression was steel.

"Were you seen?" he asked.

"I do not believe so. But one of them did that disappearing trick before they were able to cause any mischief. I hope that was the end of it, but I really doubt it," Willemina answered.

"Yeah, I saw their dreaded Gramongles flying around earlier in the day too, father," Hava added nervously.

Willemina nodded in agreement. "Those men frighten me, Nikolai. It seems they are growing bolder." She reached out to touch her husband's arm, as though that simple contact could inspire courage in her. Alaya wished she knew what they were talking about.

"I know, Willie," he said with a heavy sigh. "When I was out meeting Whalen, I saw a Gramongle descend on someone. We can only pray for that poor soul it has taken.

However, we must all stay on guard. We know what they are capable of. Remember - they are no longer men, and do not deserve to be treated as such," his voice lowered with that last reminder, falling to an ominous rumble.

"The other day, Alfred told me that they have female members now," he continued, staring blankly at the table before him.

"That's not surprising," Max piped up. "Women are just as dangerous."

"Max!" Hava said. "That is not a kind thing to say. What sort of lady would do such a thing? Who would ever want to be that hideous?"

"He is only speaking the truth, Hava," Whalen said, concurring with the small boy. "The Neya Men are no longer limited to men. Women have joined their ranks. I did not believe it either until I saw them with my own eyes. Do you remember Shahara? She and I have been close since birth. Yet lately, she has become like a stranger to me. I told her we could help with her situation, but I think they have already gotten to her. I wonder what talent they offered?"

Alaya, unsure of this new topic, decided to ask before they moved any further, or before she became completely lost.

"Excuse me, this may be a silly question, but who exactly are the Neya...people?" Alaya wondered how Mr. Miller could have missed something as seemingly important as this. Maybe it was in her packet of information. She made a point to remember to check once she was alone.

"You do not know, Alaya?" Max asked; eager to contribute to the conversation. "They are the scariest people in Batunia, maybe in the whole world. They are even worse than the King's Riders. They do bad things to people whenever they want. No one stops them either - they are too afraid of them."

Nikolai interrupted his overzealous son, wanting the facts to be straight for their guest.

"Allow me to clarify. The Neya Men go back as far as anyone in Batunia can remember. Their exact history is unknown, although it is believed that they are the remnants of a race that possessed certain abilities, which many have began to covet as 'talents.' Most consider those abilities to be linked to dark sorcery. They strived for the powers of the Ramajians, but rather than helping people, they obtained abilities far more dangerous — even deadly.

"For this, they paid a very high price. Unlike the Ramajians, the Neya people are not born with these 'gifts' and do not use them for good. In fact, they seem to use them exclusively for evil. Their primary goal has always been ultimate supremacy, but this always proved difficult with the Ramajians around. The Ramajians were the only ones who could stop them, but the conflict was vicious."

"So there was a war?" Alaya felt brave enough to ask.

"Well not exactly. King Ogapallos I tasked Velda, a powerful Ramajian, to do something about this. She and the other Ramajians did their best to seal away the Neya Men, but there are always dangers associated with that kind of magic. Things did not go as planned, and since the Ramajians could only use their power for good, it was difficult to fight back. Eventually, they did retreat, but no one knew why.

"Some say that the Neya Men retreated into a faraway land. I believe that they have only gone into hiding, rebuilding their strength in some sort of underground cult. I am sure that they will do anything to ensure their survival until the time is right to come back above ground, once and for all. It already seems that their courage is growing."

Willemina had been nodding her head in agreement with everything her husband had said.

"We believe that the Soranayum cursed them," She added. "Some also say that they have lost their souls, causing their humanity to simply rot away. However, one thing we do know is that they have lost their human appearance, which is why they mostly come out only at night. They wear dark, heavy cloaks to blend in with the dark of night, which is why it is uncommon to see travelers after sunset. The problem is the Neya Men have grown recently in numbers; we can feel their evil spreading in the forest. I pray that this may end soon, but I must admit that my faith wavers at times. The King and his Riders do not involve themselves with the Neya Men. We have no one to help us..." Willemina's voice trailed off.

Nikolai interjected. "Do not worry, Willie, or fear them. It only weakens your resolve and gives them your strength. It will take more than a cloak to defeat the Council," Nikolai said, but he turned to Alaya and spoke a word of caution. "But she is right about one thing; they have grown in numbers."

Hava added, "Some of the boldest among them wear armor to conceal their mangled faces, which is why you might see them in the day. They are the fighters, and we can usually handle them. That's what the Council is for."

Willemina also spoke up. "The Warrior's Council may be able to help with the Royal Guard, but the Neya Men are different. Some of them use sorcery, ancient magic that is unlike the Ramajians. Some even say that they eat human flesh! Can you believe such a thing?" The question hung in the air like putrid meat; it was far too disturbing to consider.

Alaya was concerned for Max. He seemed too young, but she remembered that this was not her world. Why try to hide the truth of their reality? The more that Max knew of the dangers in the world, the better he could prepare and be ready to defend himself against them.

"We are not saying this to scare you," Whalen explained, "but know this: If you ever see them, do not hesitate—get away quickly and quietly. When they are around, they do not mean well; for you, me, or anyone."

Max let out a wide, uncontrollable yawn that seemed to have taken him by surprise.

"Time for bed, young man?" Willemina asked.

"No! Not yet. I'm not tired, Mother. I only wanted a bit more air in my body. That's all it was!" Max pleaded.

"Clever boy," Whalen said with a smile. He stood up and stretched his legs. "I should head back as well. It is getting late."

Hava sprang to her feet. "Maybe we can go with you, for safety. Right, Father?"

"That is very kind of you, Hava." Whalen said, causing Hava's cheeks to burst with crimson, "but I think the less of us that are out at night, the better."

"He is right, Hava. We do not want to draw any unnecessary attention to ourselves. It is far too dangerous. Plus, it is already dark. Whalen knows how to travel safely when the curfew is in effect. You, my dear daughter, do not," her father said with an air of finality, settling the matter.

"Don't underestimate me. I learned how to fight, and I can learn this too." Hava said very quietly, so that only Alaya could hear.

Max let out another yawn; this one was too wide to deny it—he was ready to retire for the night.

"Come with me, my little warrior. Time for bed," Willemina coaxed, ushering Max to the back of the house.

Whalen stood. "Thank you everyone, it has been an enjoyable evening." He made his way to the exit with Nikolai leading the way and Hava following closely behind.

"It's customary to see the guests off," she whispered to Alaya, who followed suit.

"Take care," Nikolai cautioned. "A few of us have had the privilege to see your training. Your apprenticeship seems to be going very well. Soon the student will be able to outperform the master."

"If I should only be so lucky," Whalen replied humbly. "I would consider it a gift from the Soranayum to become even half as proficient."

"I must feed the animals, my friend. Have a good night," Nikolai said, and clapped Whalen on the back, then disappeared to the rear of the house.

"Enjoy your evening, ladies," Whalen said, with a slight nod. "It was nice to meet you, Alaya." Whalen caught Hava's eye and held it for a long moment, but said nothing. He turned and disappeared into the darkness.

Hava seemed to melt into the doorway; her eyes were glued to the dwindling shape of his body long after he was out of sight.

"Oh brother," Alaya said, nearly laughing at her love-stricken companion who was now red with fire. Alaya swore she saw the stars in her eyes.

As Alaya lay in bed that night, everything she had heard that night replayed over and over in her head. The curfew, the Neya Men, and the frightening products of her imagination wouldn't give her a moment's rest. She shifted back and forth in the small, cement-like bed, unable to get comfortable.

The sun was nearly up before she managed to capture some sleep. Even her dreams were littered with worry. She kept returning to her decision to take this journey. Coming to Batunia at such a dire point in time might not have been the wisest choice. However, she had to stay resolute—there was no backing out now.

CHAPTER 17

After what felt like mere seconds, Alaya was awakened by a string of loud thumping noises that seemed to shake the entire frame of her small bed. A small sliver of light crept through the window, and as she stood up, her head began pounding so hard it felt like it might split at any moment. She concluded that it could have been due to the lack of a proper pillow, but the limited sleep was more than likely the culprit. She moved toward the bedroom window to investigate the source of the raucous crashes that continued to ring through her skull.

She spotted Nikolai a few yards from the window, wearing the same clothes from the day before. He was hammering away at a piece of wood with a massive axe, while Max dutifully stacked more large pieces near his feet. Willemina and Hava were also outside and appeared to be gathering crops from the garden.

Alaya was quick to scope out a change of clothes. The others must have been awake for quite some time, and were simply too kind to wake her. Apparently, sleeping in was not an indulgence for the average Batunian.

Alaya couldn't quite gauge the time difference, but she estimated that more time had passed than her watch led on. Although it read half past three, her body felt strange; perhaps time travel jetlag was more complicated than the normal variety.

Alaya's thoughts shifted to her mother. She wondered what Janice's first night alone must have been like without her there, knowing that her only child wasn't going to be returning home for an indefinite amount of time. It was almost a given that her mother would be thinking about her father's travels, and his unknown fate.

Unwilling to dwell on something that she couldn't control, Alaya refocused to her current situation.

She looked around. There was a fresh towel, clean clothes, and a washcloth stacked neatly at the foot of her bed. Alaya gathered them up and walked barefoot across the stone cold floor in the washroom. It was a sharp contrast from the wooden floors of the bedrooms and halls, and at this moment, all Alaya wished for was a thick pair of socks.

There was an old hand pump connected to a basin, so she lifted the lever and a small trickle of brownish liquid collected at the bottom. Alaya took a step back, thinking twice about bathing in the questionable water. She immediately thought about her fancy showerhead and invigorating water pressure that she was used to; *I'm certainly not in Kansas anymore...*she thought.

Outside, she heard Max and Hava laughing. It sounded as though they were playing. She returned to the bedroom and looked out the window. Nikolai was tossing leaves at his children, who were both double-teamed against their father. Willemina laughed and cheered her children on.

Alaya looked down, suddenly feeling herself growing heavy with shame. The warmth and love in their family was almost painfully beautiful. Brown water or not, they were genuinely happy.

What am I doing? Alaya thought to herself. The Iskinders had been nothing but kind to her. They dealt with horrors every day of their lives, but never thought twice or complained about it. Alaya realized how lucky she was to have found them, and how differently things very well could have turned out.

Willingly swallowing this dose of humility, she returned to the washroom.

***

Once Alaya was fully dressed, she made her way outside and asked how she could help. But Willemina and Nikolai refused; both said that she didn't need to worry about helping, since she was their guest. Granted, she did not know the first thing about gardening or farming, but she still felt obligated to contribute something to her generous hosts. She insisted on helping in some way and Nikolai eventually gave in, promising to teach her everything she needed to know in due time.

Soon afterward, Hava piped up, remembering Alaya's request from the night before. "Mother, remember Alaya wanted to pick up a few things at the market?"

Willemina steadied herself on a tool that looked very similar to a garden hoe and smiled. She wiped the sweat from her brow with the back of her hand. Her hair, which had been kept neat enough and tucked away the night before, was now disheveled and fell haphazardly from her hair clasp.

"That's a good idea, Hava. I plan to visit the Circle of the Soranayum later to pray, but perhaps you can pick up a few things for me as well. Just...be careful. And remember to return before dark. Not even the lufaiyas can keep you safe once the sun goes down." She said.

Alaya felt slightly guilty for leaving the rest of the Iskinder family to work while she and Hava went shopping, but to be fair, while shopping was nowhere near her specialty, chopping wood couldn't have been more foreign. At the same time, Mr. Miller had sent her to Batunia with a purpose and she intended to accomplish it.

The pair of them set off for the marketplace, taking a winding, pebble-strewn path that wound through the forest, occasionally lit by sunlight that snuck through the canopy of bending trees. In the daylight, Alaya could now see what was hidden by the shroud of night when she first arrived in Batunia.

The trees, while tall, curved upon themselves like large brown pretzels, bending in ways that reminded Alaya of the rollercoasters she loved as a child. Yet, they were seemed sturdy enough, and held leaves and branches without effort.

"Do all trees look like that?" Alaya asked.

"Like what?" Hava asked, with a quizzical look.

"Like that, all curvy and bending," she asked again.

"Sure they do, which tree doesn't? Besides, that's what makes them so fun to climb. Mother thinks they're dangerous, but it seems like a good way to travel if you think about it." Hava said.

"It does seem like it could be fun," Alaya said, debating her next question. *What the heck?* She thought, *I've got amnesia. No question is too strange.*

"One more thing, Hava. What is a lufaiya?"

"That memory of yours, it's worse than I thought." Hava said, and stepped with great care through a small brook in the woods.

"Some believe that lufaiyas are special guardians who were sent by the Soranayum to look after us. Mother believes, and she still goes to the Circle of the Soranayum to pray, but I think she's wasting her time. Father thinks so too, but he doesn't want to upset her, so he goes along with it. I believe the Soranayum have forgotten about us, if they ever existed at all."

Alaya was unsure of how to respond. She had no opinion on the matter, since she didn't know enough about them. Growing up, her parents were never big on religion. Her personal belief system was quite simple - live and let live.

Hava returned to Alaya's previous question. "Mother believes that the lufaiyas are special creatures who seek out those who have become lost, and guide us to safety when we are in trouble."

Alaya thought back to the previous night, when she was wandering through the forest alone. The rain pounded without letup, she was lost, and needed a place to stay. That was the moment—when they suddenly appeared. The glowing insects that reminded her of fireflies had come to her rescue. Alaya realized now that they must have led her to the Iskinder's house.

How brilliant, she thought. Perhaps Willemina was right about more than just the lufaiyas.

Alaya and Hava began running into more villagers the longer they walked. Some nodded to Hava, and a few stopped to introduce themselves to Alaya. While a few looked at her with curiosity, most seemed quite friendly.

It wasn't long before Alaya had another burning question.

"Hava, why is there a curfew in the first place?"

"Many of us ask ourselves that same question. When King Negash took over, he established the curfew because he wanted to stop anyone who might try to overthrow him. Of course we him gone; who wouldn't? But the people have learned their lesson – no one has tried to dethrone him for many years. Even so, he became extremely paranoid. Now he keeps himself busy by capturing innocent people who walk through the forest at night."

"Is he that bored?" Alaya asked.

"The King's Riders, an elite group of the the Royal Guard, are the ones who do it. It is truly a sick sport. What I do not understand is, the King is desperate for complete dominance, yet somehow, he does not realize that he has already achieved it." Hava said plainly.

As they walked down the gravely path, more and more people joined them, presumably also headed for the market. Many of them seemed to know Hava, so Alaya met several new townspeople. As they approached a bend in the path, something pulled Hava's attention away.

"We're almost there, just a bit—" Hava broke off. Alaya could hear cheers in the distance, and a large crowd appeared to be gathering.

Alaya inched her way through the tightly packed crowd, trying to keep her eye on Hava's bright red hair as she snaked ahead up to the front of the audience. Standing to one side of the circle was a man hunched over and swaying from side to side on the balls of his feet, as though he was preparing to fight.

Hava's eyes twinkled, and she let out a heavy sigh. "There he is," she murmured to no one in particular, her eyes fixed on the shirtless warrior.

Alaya took a second look as the man turned around to face the crowd- it was Whalen.

"What is he doing?" Alaya asked, steadily moving closer. It was clear that a match of some sort was about to take place, but she couldn't understand why no one was trying to stop it.

Whalen stretched his arms and rotated his neck from side to side. Hava did not answer Alaya's question; she just continued to look on, almost entranced by the figure standing before her.

Moments later, a second man emerged from the crowd. He was welcomed with cheers and applause. A bell was struck, and the two men moved closer to one another. The inner ring of the crowd closed in, hot with anticipation.

"They are about to begin!" Hava exclaimed, holding her hands to her face.

"But why?" Alaya asked. "Won't they get in trouble?"

"They created a brilliant cover story. This is an exhibition! They have been training for a long time now, but it is all part of a much bigger plan. Was it not obvious last night?"

When Alaya did not show any sign of understanding, Hava explained further.

"The Warrior's Council, remember? We have no one on our side anymore. If a crime is committed, no one comes to our aid. Not the King, and certainly not his Riders. There is no justice system in this kingdom. Batunia needs us." she said, never taking her eyes off the duo. Alaya thought she even saw Hava blow a kiss.

"But you were just saying that King Negash is paranoid and cruel. Wouldn't an organized group of citizen warriors just cause more concern?" Alaya suggested.

"That is the real beauty of it. It is of no concern to him if the villagers are fighting among themselves. What harm does it bring him? He pays no mind unless there is a direct threat to him or his rule."

Whalen had caught their sight, and Hava flashed a toothy smile.

Just then, Hava looked around and lowered her voice.

"Something else, Alaya. The members of the Council would be in grave danger if the King learned the truth." Hava's face had grown serious, as though someone had just threatened to steal the money from her pockets.

"I don't remember the old days very well, but from what I hear, they were dark times. My parents don't talk about those days much, but I know that it has something to do with how my father lost his eye," Hava fell silent as she looked back at the men fighting a few feet in front of her. "I hate war, but I do not want to see anyone else get hurt, either. That's why I wanted to fight too. Everyone should be able to protect the ones they love."

Alaya wondered what sorts of tragedies Hava may have seen, but she didn't ask. She could offer comfort, but she didn't want to expose old wounds that were better left untouched.

She glanced down at her watch. "I would hate to keep your family waiting. We should probably get our shopping done and head back."

Hava noticed the watch on Alaya's wrist.

"That is a lovely bracelet you have - very unique. I've only seen one other like it. It was a long time ago, but that one was not nearly as pretty as yours." She gave a heavy sigh, but smiled. "Now come on, let's get to the marketplace before everything is sold."

CHAPTER 18

The entrance to the marketplace was now within sight, and dozens of people were filing in from all directions like water straining through a funnel. Alaya was reminded of the outdoor swap meets that she and her mother had frequented when she was younger.

"Here we are," Hava said, as they stepped onto the paved road. Large tents were overflowing with goods lined up on shelves, while still more wares were spread out on thin blankets. The plaza was bustling with people, and the tents were lined up row after row on opposite ends of the road, facing each other. Everywhere Alaya looked, were eager merchants ready to compete for business.

The center of the graveled street was wide enough to easily accommodate the hundreds of customers who strolled past each booth, casually browsing the array of goods with excitement and intrigue.

"Unfortunately, there is not much money to be spent, but people like to come here to look around and socialize," Hava explained as she glanced down at a table full of exotic-looking fruits. She picked up a purplish one, sniffed the skin, and returned it.

Alaya could relate to this method of shopping. She thought of the malls back home, where she would often go with friends just to window shop. They would usually try on clothes they knew they could never afford, but it was always nice to pretend to have a bottomless wallet, even if only for a few minutes.

Hava suddenly perked up and grabbed Alaya's arm.

"Alaya! Come take a look at this!"

Hava skipped off with her long red hair undulating behind her. Alaya ran after her, navigating the crowd so as to not run into anyone. For a moment, Hava was lost; until at last, Alaya caught her at the edge of a fancy-looking booth. Once Alaya got closer, she saw why Hava had been drawn to it. The vendor featured row after row of glittery gems and jewelry, all hid behind a thick pane of glass.

"This one is my favorite," Hava said, and pressed her finger against the glass.

"Which one?" Alaya asked. She crouched down and peered into the case, mesmerized by the elaborate pieces glimmering in the sunlight.

"*That* one. See it?" Hava pointed again and Alaya was finally able to see the piece. It was a stunning emerald gem, cut in the shape of a heart and centered on a long, silver chain. "It is beautiful, don't you think? Unfortunately, it is four hundred ikbars. It would take a whole year of earnings to pay for it. I do not think there is anyone in this world that could afford such a beautiful thing, except the king, of course. But someday, I will have it." Hava declared under her breath, as though making a pact with herself.

"May I help you with something, child?" the owner of the booth asked, visibly losing patience. She was an older woman covered from head to toe in dazzling jewels. The air of aristocracy that surrounded her was almost suffocating.

"No, thank you. We're just looking around," Hava answered abruptly.

The older woman cocked an eyebrow and looked Hava up and down as though she carried a contagious disease. The threadbare state of her dress did her no favors. It was clear the owner did not see Hava - only that she lacked the adequate amount of funds for any purchase of her wares.

But the woman said nothing more, and turned her attention back to the crowd, searching for potential customers. Hava lingered, but Alaya grew uncomfortable. They were all but dismissed. When Hava finally pulled away from the booth, Alaya could see thick tears brewing in her eyes. They were a single blink from spilling over.

"What else do you like?" Alaya asked as she put her arm around Hava's shoulders. Alaya hoped that Hava wasn't too upset by the rude merchant.

Hava sniffed, quickly regaining her composure.

"Let me think," Hava said, "Is there anything you were specifically searching for?"

Alaya didn't have time to respond. Their attention was pulled by sudden, loud shouts coming from somewhere nearby. They were accompanied by a loud crack.

Everyone in the marketplace was drawn to the source of the noise. Off in the distance, Alaya caught sight of a dark-haired man who was quickly drawing a flock of other curious morning shoppers.

"Come all and listen! I urge you, brave souls, be you men or women. We have all grown weary of this man, Negash. He is no more than a gutless coward who allows his people to starve while his own belly swells!" The man had wild eyes and spat as he shouted.

Dozens of people scattered in the crowd cheered enthusiastically, and the surrounding mob grew, anxious to hear this bold man add a voice to what they were all thinking. Some on the outskirts looked stricken with terror, and occasionally glanced behind their shoulder, as though their lives were endangered simply by listening. Yet, no one left.

"We *must* take a stand, I tell you! For once and all, we must rise up against this evil! Against corruption! Against our so-called king!" He said with added emphasis on those last words.

Cheers erupted all around Alaya. Even though she knew very little of Batunia and its struggles, she found herself wanting to join in this protest and hear more from the passionate speaker.

"No..." Hava whispered. "This is not the place, Jarax."

Alaya wanted to ask about the angered man, but there was no time. Just then, a scuffle from behind Jarax confirmed Hava's concerns. The man's protests were cut short. Uniformed men, most likely Royal Guards, put an end to the treasonous speech.

A pair of the guards roughly pulled him from his crate and he was dragged out of sight, behind a row of the merchant booths.

A bearded guard turned to the crowd. He was strapped from head to toe in leathered armor, with torture-devices masquerading as weapons hanging from his belt. There was an evil sneer plastered across his face.

"Disband! Or you will face the same fate! You are all well aware of the punishment for treason!" He scanned the crowd with a fierce look. His raging eyes soon fell and stayed upon Alaya. It felt like several minutes of burning rays beaming straight through her skull, although it was probably no more than a few seconds. She couldn't stop herself from looking away.

A man rushed forward through the crowd; a few others followed behind him in support.

"Please, let us take him. Jarax meant no harm."

"I have had quite enough of this, Bartholomew! You and your men can watch him pay for his crime, if you like." The guard roared inches from the man's face. He spat while shouting, before turning back to the crowd.

"Unless you want to stay and receive the same punishment as this fool, we suggest you either continue shopping or go home!"

Alaya felt a strange internal battle of wits. She wanted to know more, yet she was happy to escape from the menacing glare of the guard. She struggled to comprehend what she had just seen.

"Batunia has quite the king, don't you think? Father will not be pleased with this news," Hava said and stalked off.

Alaya struggled to keep up and avoid getting lost within the scattering crowd. From a distance, a bloodcurdling scream rang throughout the marketplace, followed by a stunned silence. Not a word came from the crowd, perhaps in honor of their fallen spokesman.

Although every muscle in Alaya's body twitched from wanting to turn around, she dared not look back. It was best if she could shut out the entire memory of that traumatic event. She caught up with Hava, who stomped back through the long rows of merchants.

"Yes, Alaya, before you ask. This is normal. Even though it's believed that King Ogapallos died years ago in an accident, it sometimes feels like he continues to rule us from the grave." Hava said.

"At the very least, it is clear that Ogapallos had a great deal of influence over King Negash. From what I've been told, ever since his brother fled Batunia, Negash has always taken the wrong advice from the wrong people." She slowed in her pace, and began perusing the last few vendors' stalls once again, as though nothing had happened — it was business as usual.

"He had a brother?" Alaya asked, surprised by this new information. She saw an elderly, silver-haired woman watching her from across the road. She could feel the eyes on her for a good length of time. Alaya tried to ignore the unwanted attention and moved further along the stalls. She began to wonder if something was wrong with her appearance that made her stand out. There were plenty of other dark-skinned women around, so her ethnicity couldn't have been the issue.

"Yes, his brother was named Matthias. He was very wise, so King Ogapallos II made him the head of scientific advancements. He always wanted Batunia to stay ahead of neighboring kingdoms. We're going this way." Hava grabbed Alaya's hand and guided her off the main road, veering off from the masses.

They found a relatively low-traffic area of the market that was filled with day-old meat and produce vendors, which might have been fine on a cold, wintry day. However, the seasons had not yet shifted and it was still warm outside. As they neared, the stench became so atrocious, Alaya began to feel nauseous. But no matter how bad it had become, Alaya did not cover her face; realizing it might be rude.

Hava continued talking as if she didn't even notice the noxious fumes.

"There was always a rivalry between Matthias and Fendrel, typical of most brothers. But they had a terrible quarrel after Matthias' childhood teacher, Velda, was murdered. The rumors say that King Ogapallos' men were behind it, but Fendrel Negash defended his actions. I do not know if the truth of the tragedy was ever discovered. What we do know is that Matthias and his new wife, Belina, disappeared a short time later." Hava stopped to inspect some of the monocrant meat; it was marked down with a deep discount.

Alaya thought for a minute. *Belina, Matthias.* These names sounded so familiar, but why? Alaya couldn't remember where she had heard them before, but she intended to do some digging in Mr. Miller's piles of notes to find out.

CHAPTER 19

It was just after 3 a.m. when Alaya jostled awake. It hadn't been a nightmare; instead, it was a dream of her father. It was so vivid that Alaya believed it was real, even after she awakened. It took a few minutes of sitting before she realized she was disillusioned. In the dream, Alaya was once again a child, curled up in the crook of her father's arm, listening to the fairytales he used to make up just for her. She began to wonder; perhaps it had not been a dream at all, but a memory.

There was something else. Alaya began to feel pieces falling into place, although the entire picture wasn't quite yet ready. She rose from her bed and looked around the room. In the darkness, Hava was sleeping deeper than a bear in hibernation, complete with the impressive snoring. Alaya had a bit of time before the sun rose and she fully intended to take advantage of it.

Quietly, she grabbed her bag and tiptoed into the living room. The entire house was quiet and the rooms were frigid compared to her warm bed, but she didn't care. The floorboards creaked, so she slowed in pace, until she reached the long, thinly cushioned couch.

There was only one thing on Alaya's mind right now: Belina and Matthias.

There wasn't enough light on the couch, so Alaya grabbed an old blanket from a nearby shelf, and sat directly underneath the window to catch the soft light of the full moon. A thin layer of dust crept into her nose, threatening the silence of the house with a sneeze. Alaya quickly covered her face with both hands just in time; a mousey squeak was all that snuck out. Waking the entire Iskinder family right now would not be wise.

Alaya got straight to work and dug into her bag. Her hands first closed around the troudare, which she had no use for just yet. She pulled out page after page of her father's papers and Mr. Miller's notes. Her father had called them 'research papers', but Alaya just assumed that they had all been works of fiction. There were far too many unbelievable details for any of it to be historically factual. As she scanned through the sea of papers, her eyes flitted over a few new familiar words. It was one of her father's research papers, handwritten in ink. She sat back and read through a passage:

> Many people have transformed magic into an evil practice of dark sorcery, but it remains the origin of the oldest form of healing the world has ever known. Naturally, very little is known of magic. No one has taken the time to research it with any thoroughness, so I took on the task myself. It has become my personal crusade. I was beginning to gradually understand the true nature of all human involvement with the supernatural. Voodoo, hoodoo, witch doctors, shamans…they are all taboo in most elements of Western society. But why? What they do not realize is that they all originated in one way or another from a single birthplace: the Ramajians. Over time, the

different variations have taken on their own names and details, most likely due to cultural and ethnic differences. They are our doctors, our natural healers…yes, even our physicians may have a bit of magic left in them. Sadly, the more progress a culture makes, the more reliant they are on technology. Their relationship to magic fades as they rely less and less on their link to the Ramajians.

This process slowly but surely reduces their otherworldly abilities and they become less powerful, until eventually, they are just regular people like everyone else. Ramajians were highly respected in the old days. They were admired, envied, and feared. Many believed them to be gods; some even worshipped them. It is clear that some wanted the power of the Ramajians, no matter the cost, while others wanted nothing to do with them.

One Ramajian was immensely powerful. However, rather than worship her, the kingdom of Batunia feared her. The most powerful of all the Ramajians, from my research, seems to be the one named Velda. I believe she is the link…

Alaya put the pages down. There was that name again…*Velda.* She reached her hand back into her bag and heard something fall to the floor. It was the old, dark green journal from Mr. Miller's store. She had forgotten that she'd taken it with her.

With the blanket wrapped tightly around her, Alaya opened the book. She flipped randomly through the pages and began to read:

I have narrowly escaped the King's Riders today, although I do not know how they saw me. I did my best to disguise myself in the marketplace. Regardless, I was able to enjoy

my day in spite of them. There were perfectly ripe
mongpaya's for sale, and I was about to have one. It has
been too long since I have enjoyed such comforts.
But that was disrupted, and my venture quickly came to
an end when I was spotted. Fear began to swell inside me,
and I wondered if this would be it – my end.
Thankfully, the Soranayum gave wind to my legs and
helped me escape. I ran faster than light, and by their
grace, I was able to lose my would-be captors. Oh, the
Riders – their anger was delicious in defeat. I hope they
take their failure back to Ogapallos. I will never be a
prisoner in his dungeons again. I almost wish that I could
see his face...almost.

Mr. Miller had kept Velda's journal in his store for all
these years. But why? The questions continued to pile up, but
the answers still eluded her. Alaya looked down at her watch
- it was 3:45am. She looked down at the stacks of papers,
overwhelmed by how much information she would have to
pore through. Glancing over to her bag, she saw the clear
troudare, reflecting the shine of the moonlight.

Alaya picked it up, and thought to herself, *why not?*
After all, it would cut down on time reading through the
masses of papers in front of her. Also, the Iskinder family
would begin to waken soon, and explaining what all of these
papers were would be difficult, if not impossible. Suspicion
from her hosts would make her mission far more difficult.

With the cold, glass orb in her hands, Alaya
whispered.

"Mr. Miller? Are you there?" she asked into the blank
glass. Alaya whispered to herself, "Man, I hope this thing
actually works."

Silence was her only response. Alaya tilted the
troudare like a fortuneteller looking through a crystal ball,

but there was no change. Mr. Miller clearly wasn't there, but she was compelled to try a final time.

"Mr. Miller...I need to speak to you!" Alaya said, raising her voice a bit higher. She was beginning to grow desperate to make a connection.

As Alaya began to lower the troudare back into her bag, she thought she heard something through the orb, a faint shuffling noise. A moment late, the cloudy glass began to lighten, lit by some inner glow. The swirling smoke in the crystal obscured her vision, but it soon cleared, leaving Mr. Miller's face staring back at her.

"Alaya, my young explorer! How goes it?" he asked, just as cheerful as she remembered. She never thought she could feel so much comfort from seeing the aging man's face. His eyes were deep-set and weary.

"Thank goodness," Alaya said with a deep sigh. "Things are fine, but I have some questions."

"That was to be expected, I suppose. Anyways, it is mid-afternoon, so there aren't many customers."

Alaya thought to herself, *when are there ever any customers?*

"Great. I just wanted to ask you a few things and then I'll let you go," she said. "What do you remember about Belina and Matthias? Those names have come up a few times and they sound familiar, but I don't know why. Any ideas?"

Mr. Miller took a deep breath before he began.

"Of course, Alaya. I wondered when this might come up. As I told you, I am quite old to be traveling across space and time, but there is another reason that I couldn't come with you to Batunia."

"Which is?" she asked.

"Well, there is a bit more to my situation than I initially revealed. I think it is due time to be completely honest with you..." He paused for a minute, perhaps to gather his thoughts or to figure out how best to express them. She waited for him to begin, giving him the benefit of the doubt before getting frustrated at his secrecy.

"I didn't go with you because...Batunia is my hometown."

"Okay...but why is that a bad thing?" Alaya questioned. "You could have helped my father."

"No, my dear. I don't think you fully understand. My real name is not Jeremiah Miller. My real name is Matthias. To be exact, my full name is Matthias Negash, and my wife was Belina Negash." He fell silent, awaiting her response.

Alaya felt as though she had been physically struck in the stomach. She had to remind herself to breathe.

"So you're related to the King? Then that means...you are from the past?" Alaya couldn't believe the words coming from her mouth.

"That is precisely the point. I don't fully understand either. I thought your father and I had created a time machine, but in truth, I'm not so sure. There is no mention of Batunia anywhere in the history books. I couldn't point out Batunia on a globe because I truly don't know where it is located."

"So what does that mean?" Alaya asked.

"More and more, I am beginning to believe that perhaps Batunia is not from the past at all; perhaps Belina and I traveled to an alternate reality all those years ago. That's why I had your father travel for me. He was a well-known historian and archaeologist, so if anyone could figure this out, it would be him," Mr. Miller explained.

Alaya had to admit, it made perfect sense. But it didn't help soften the blow knowing that her father was sent into an unknown world, completely alone.

"You used my father, and led him into the same mess as I'm in now. He is missing, and probably dead, all because of you!" Alaya's voice began to rise; the quiet of the house wasn't in the front of her mind any longer.

"Now, now, Alaya. It was not like that. This was a mutually beneficial arrangement. Your father was more than eager to do the traveling. He was fascinated by the mystery surrounding Batunia. Over time, he became so engrossed in that world that he wanted to learn more about it. He traveled to Batunia at least once a week. Most of the time, I was aware of his trips. Frederick was very careful...at least in the beginning..." he trailed off, pausing before carrying on

"However, one day, I came into the store and saw that the machine was missing. That was seven years ago." Matthias' face looked apologetic and remorseful through the small glass sphere.

Alaya heard a noise coming from the back of the house and realized that she was no longer the only person awake in the house.

"Thanks, Mr. Miller, I mean...Matthias. I have to go. I'll keep in touch..." Alaya quietly dropped the troudare back into her bag and remained perfectly still.

It was Max. She watched from her place near the window as he padded into the kitchen. *Had he heard?* Alaya couldn't be sure, but her eyes remained fixed on him like a lion following its prey. Even in the dim light, she could see his outline perfectly. He poured himself a glass of water from the pitcher on the counter, spilled a little in his sleepy state, and retreated back to his room.

Alaya let out a small sigh of relief and haphazardly shuffled the papers and journals back into her bag. The sun would be up soon, and she needed sleep.

Once back in bed, Alaya curled up against the warm blankets and like a busted light, she was out.

CHAPTER 20

A few hours later, the sun slanted through the trees bright and early. Alaya helped the Iskinders with morning chores, which was surprisingly difficult. But she didn't complain.

Once they were finished, Max decided he wanted to spend the rest of the day outside playing. He had a small round ball and began to kick it around the enormous yard, while Hava and Alaya sat on a patch of grass and watched. They enjoyed the tickle of the warm sun on their skin, and Alaya couldn't help but notice how peaceful everything was around them. Nothing would have indicated the turmoil that Batunia faced after dark.

Max's ball was the same size and shape as a soccer ball, so taking advantage of her limited sports knowledge, Alaya taught Max and Hava how to play soccer and kickball.

"Did you learn how to play those games in school?" Max asked.

"Yes, when I was about your age, actually." She smiled, and kicked the ball to Hava. She clearly wasn't too thrilled as she struggled to kick it in a straight line back to Max.

"How do you *do* this?" Hava whined as she nearly toppled over from a lack of hand-eye coordination.

146

"Usually, the King's men send their children to school. Father says I cannot go, because it costs 100 ikbars for each half-year, and we do not have that sort of money right now," Max said with sad acceptance. "Hava has gone to school before though. She is very smart!" He looked at his older sister with pride spread openly across his face.

Poor kid, Alaya thought.

"I'm sorry, Max. I had no idea that you didn't know what it was like to go to school. But let me be the first to tell you, it's pretty overrated."

"She's right." Hava said. Max passed the ball and it skated past her legs, but she chose to ignore it.

Max smiled at their attempt to cheer him up. "It is okay. I have learned all kinds of things from my family, and of course, from Whalen and his teacher. Alaya, maybe you can teach me too!"

Just then, a loud noise broke in the distance, capturing their attention. Max turned his head in the direction of the commotion.

"What was that?" Alaya asked.

But no one spoke; perhaps out of fear. The unmistakable sounds of battle cries and the clash of weapons were soon heard ringing just beyond them in the forest.

"We should get back inside," Hava said. "There's no telling what that could be, and I don't want to stick around and find out." She slowly began to back away, looking toward the others to agree with her decision.

"No, Alaya, come along! This way!" Max tugged on her arm. "You can finally meet them! I forgot they would be out today." He continued walking toward the noise, clearly not afraid.

"Are you sure, Max? I don't know if this is such a good idea," Alaya warned him, remembering all too vividly what Nikolai and Willemina had said about the Neya Men.

147

"It will be fine, Alaya," Hava said, suddenly standing up straight and fluffing out her hair.

As they drew closer to the fight, Alaya recognized one of the men as Whalen. He was wearing some light body armor, but his opponent sported full armor and a heavy helmet.

Whalen's back was turned to them, but as Max stomped through a patch of crunchy leaves, he immediately swung around, on full alert. In that brief moment, Whalen lost focus and was hit hard in the midsection, and fell flat on his back. Hava began to dart forward to his aid, but stopped in her tracks when Whalen's opponent spoke.

"You must handle the enemy in front of you before you can face a threat from behind. Never forget that, Whalen. Breaking your focus for even a second may cost you your life."

The man withdrew the sword, which hovered only inches from Whalen's chest, and bent down to help him to his feet.

"Other than that, great job. Let's take a break." He said.

Whalen sprang up with minimal assistance and rushed over to Max, Hava, and Alaya.

"Hello, how are all of you today?" To Alaya's surprise, he reached for her hand and gently kissed it. This was not the usual greeting that she had become accustomed to, but she didn't ask questions.

"Well, this is certainly a reunion!" Whalen's teacher spoke, joining the group. "Hava, it's been a while since your last lesson!"

"Yes, well —" she started.

"Whalen, that looked incredible!" Max said, interrupting his sister. He bowed to the strange man as he began to remove his armor.

"But it was also very dangerous. You should warn him about that when you teach him, Whalen," the man said, as he removed the plates covering his chest, arms, and shins. He had dark, golden-brown skin that rippled with lean muscles.

Not wanting to be rude, Alaya moved to introduce herself. She extended her hands, palms facing up.

"Hello, my name is Alaya. Nice to—" Alaya started, but before she could finish, her tongue froze in place. The man had removed his helmet and dropped it gently in the grass.

Suddenly, all eyes were on Alaya, who had stopped mid-sentence. She felt as though her heart stopped. Now that she had a better look at the man in front of her, it was like the earth had been pulled from beneath her feet.

Against every odd, from the shadows of despair, Alaya somehow found herself staring into the face of a man she had believed to be dead. A man who had been declared missing for more than seven years. It was her father—and he was very much alive.

CHAPTER 21

*C*ould this really be him? Alaya wondered. Or perhaps, were her eyes deceiving her? These questions spun through her mind like a broken record; and the needle threatened to bore straight through her heart. *But...how could it be?*

When she was a child, Alaya often mistook other men for her father, desperately wishing that they would have some semblance of familiarity. Sadly, the story had always ended the same. They would tell her she was mistaken, and turn away with apologetic eyes.

Did he know how broken Alaya had felt the last seven years? How hard it had been for her to accept the harsh, cruel reality that he might never come back, no matter how badly she wished for it to be otherwise?

Still, Alaya began to fear something new, something different. *Perhaps this was just another illusion? A sad result of the overactive imagination of a naive, hopeful little girl.*

The man stepped closer, and to her disbelief, he looked every bit like her father as she had last known him, if only a few more grays sprinkled throughout his jet black hair.

"Well, I'll be damned..." his words tumbled out in muttered pieces. He rubbed his eyes in disbelief. "Am I dreaming...? I have not looked upon your face for seven years, three months, and ten days. But I could never forget that curly head of hair."

The man stepped forward unconsciously, as if pulled toward her by an invisible force.

"Alaya, do you know who I am?" He asked.

No matter how hard she tried, Alaya could not bring her lips to form words. She had been dreaming of this day for many years, but she had never expected reality to reflect those sad fantasies. Now, here he was, standing mere feet from her. All of the things she played over in her head, everything she ever wanted to say, were suddenly lost.

Without further delay, Alaya held out her arms and almost collapsed into her father, but he caught her and held her tight. She didn't say a word. Instead, her tears spoke volumes, flowing unchecked down her cheeks onto his armor.

"Ha-ha! My girl has finally come to me!" Frederick laughed, also misty-eyed, and scooped his daughter up. He swung her in wide, looping circles like she was a child again, young and weightless.

"Are you real?" Alaya finally managed to whisper to her father, still clutching him fiercely, taking in his familiar scent that still clung to his body. To think, a person could smell the same after all those years. She lost track of time. But Alaya wasn't ready to let go. In fact, she wasn't sure if she would ever be ready.

"You better believe it. I'm as real as a man can get," he answered in a blubbering cross between laughing and weeping.

The others looked on, still completely confused as to what was happening.

Max frowned, feeling left out of some grand secret. "Miss Alaya, what is going on? How do you know Mr. Stevenson?"

"Yes, please tell us. Has your memory illness been resolved?" Hava asked.

Frederick spoke on her behalf. "Why don't we go speak to your parents? There is a great deal to explain," he said, and took Alaya by the hand, leading her out of the forest.

As they walked back to the Iskinder's home, Alaya felt an overwhelming sense of grateful for Mr. Miller, for insisting that she return to Batunia. If she had not done so, none of this would be happening and she would have never found her father. She would have to find some way to repay him for this incredible gift.

***

Willemina and Nikolai served lunch, which was a light soup with bread and fresh vegetables from their garden. Everyone was anxious to hear what promised to be a miraculous story.

"Mr. Stevenson is your father?! This is incredible, Alaya!" Willemina exclaimed, flabbergasted.

"Do you know that he is a wanted man?" Nikolai added darkly. "The King has determined that he is highly valuable. He was asked to fill the post of Chief of Scientific Advancements shortly after the previous chief passed away under mysterious circumstances."

"Well, don't scare the girl quite so soon, my friend!" Frederick said. "That being said, he is right, Alaya. My machine was discovered on that final trip, and the King's men did their best to keep both myself and the machine in Batunia. They not only wanted to prevent me from escaping, but they also wanted me to dissect the technology and expand it to a whole fleet of machines. They may have found a way to keep me here, but I saw to it that the machine could never be duplicated. Even though it wasn't fit to hold passengers, I was still able to send it back home. That technology could be tremendously dangerous if it ever fell into the wrong hands."

"So what happened after the machine went back?" Alaya asked, eager to hear the rest of the story.

"Thankfully, Nikolai was able to get me away to safety. I owe him more than any other man I've ever met—I owe him my life." He turned to Nikolai and clapped him on the back.

"It was the only thing I could do. I was in the service of the King at the time, and I quickly learned what kind of man you were. I also knew what your fate would have been had you refused. You are a good man, Frederick. I sat back in silence and watched many suffer at the hands of our so-called King. No one should have to live like that." Nikolai paused, as though reflecting on a particularly troubling memory.

"Basically," Frederick tried to say between mouthfuls of bread, "Think of every horrible dictator you've learned about in history, Alaya. King Negash, and his predecessor, Ogapallos II, are right up there with the best of them. Negash has plans for total dominance, and is looking to expand his dominion by any means necessary. He's got this idea that I would be a great asset to his team, but you can imagine where I told him to go." Frederick chuckled to himself, and continued eating his vegetables and sipping the broth.

"You should still be cautious, Frederick," Nikolai said. The food in his bowl remained untouched, although he pushed it around with a spoon every few minutes. "We cannot be too careful. You know that he is still searching for you. The curfews are only growing more oppressive and between the King's Riders and the Neya Men..."

Frederick held his hand up.

"Nikolai, that's enough. I don't want Alaya to lose hope. She has only just arrived in Batunia; this is all new to her."

153

"Perhaps you are right, Frederick, but we have taken so much care to keep you safe and hidden. I would not want to see that it had all been for nothing." Nikolai shared.

Willemina spoke up. "At any rate, Alaya, I hope that this reunion has alleviated your memory illness?"

"That is a good question, Mrs. Iskinder," Alaya spoke up quickly, before her father had a chance to ask what Willemina meant. Still, a puzzled expression framed his face as Alaya explained herself.

"So much has happened, and we haven't had a chance to talk at any length. However, your family's hospitality over these last few days has been very wonderful. Now that I have found my father, I think I'll be staying with him. I'm sure that you understand," Alaya told them, hoping that would be the end of the matter.

"Yes, of course, Alaya. We understand completely," Nikolai's powerful voice boomed and Willemina agreed.

Alaya could see why her father and the Iskinders had become friends. They were kind, unassuming people.

"Frederick," Nikolai continued, "I know that you have only been supporting yourself these last few years. Ikbars run low for all of us, but if you need anything, just ask. We can spare a few things around here." Nikolai extended his palm to his friend.

Frederick shook his head.

"I appreciate your generosity, Nikolai, but Whalen has stayed with me on occasion, and I have managed just fine. I also doubt that Alaya will need nearly as much food as he does. At least, she never used to!"

"Dad!" Alaya said. Her father chuckled, and the joke spread to everyone around the table except Whalen, who only smirked at the comment. Alaya caught his glance and he quickly looked away.

"But, since you mention it, there is one thing. I am rather short on my supply of women's clothing and other…necessities," Frederick added.

"Of course, we certainly have that covered," Willemina assured him and rose from the table. "Hava can help as well, I am sure."

"Yes, Mother," Hava said, reluctantly rising from her chair.

"What can I do to help?" Whalen asked. Hava's eyes lingered on him before she left the room.

"Nothing too pressing comes to mind, but it may serve us well that you live so close."

Frederick turned to his daughter with a grin wider than the Nile River. "What do you say we head home?"

As everyone said their goodbyes, Alaya promised Max that she would return the next day to begin his tutoring sessions.

"I cannot wait! See you tomorrow!" Max replied with glee and waved goodbye.

Willemina sent them home with plenty of leftovers, so they would not need to cook for at least a few days. Alaya was grateful to have found such generous, sincere friends in this strange world.

As they walked through the forest, Alaya couldn't have been happier. Frederick led the way with his armor and supplies in tow, and Whalen carried a pack on his back that held the extra clothes and supplies for Alaya.

"I can carry that myself," she offered. "You don't have to be burdened with it."

"It's no burden," Whalen said.

His attention shifted to Frederick, who was slowing in pace. Occasionally, he glanced back over his shoulder toward Alaya and Whalen, and closely inspected their surroundings. *What exactly was he looking for?*

The forest was eerily silent, and Alaya suddenly realized how alone they were. There was no one else in sight. She felt the chill of the coming night begin to settle all around them. She drew her dress folds closer and hugged her arms together. Looking around, Alaya saw that the comforting glow of the lufaiyas were nowhere to be seen in the dense, dark forest.

"Do not worry, Frederick; we will be able to handle anything that comes," Whalen said. "She will be safe."

"I know, but we can never let our guard down, not even for a moment. Remember our lesson from earlier?" Frederick warned.

"Yes, of course. Shall I see you both in?" Whalen asked. Their pace slowed even further as they approached what Alaya only now noticed - a small wooden hut. It looked strange in the shadows, almost transparent as it blended into the forest beneath the dim moonlight.

"That is a very kind offer," Frederick said, "but I don't think that will be necessary. There is a very good reason Nikolai and I built this house of lichten wood." He walked up the steps to the front door.

"This is as close as we can come to having an invisible home. The full moon only shines once a month, so there is no need to worry. But why not stop by in the morning? It should be a nice, sunny day. You can show Alaya around the area; I'm sure she'd like that. I will have to go out hunting, since I now have an extra mouth to feed." He smiled at Alaya, gently patting her on the shoulder. She forgot how much of a jokester her father could be, especially in difficult situations. It was strangely comforting, to know he hadn't changed after all these years.

"Dad," she protested, "I thought that we could spend a bit more time together. I haven't seen you in seven years."

"I know, Alaya, but we will have plenty of time now. Besides, I did have a prior obligation to a friend." Frederick turned on his heel and waved. "Good night then, Whalen!" With the turn of a key in a lock she couldn't see, Frederick swung open a door and entered his home.

Whalen walked up the steps and reached down to touch her hand. "Goodnight, Alaya. Be safe." He retreated and was soon hidden in the thick brush just behind her father's home. She tried to follow his shape in the darkness, but he was already gone.

CHAPTER 22

Alaya followed her father into the house. Once inside, she was surprised to see that it looked just like any other, if not a bit smaller. The outside was the only part of the home that was nearly-invisible. It must have been because of the "lichten wood," whatever that was. Alaya made a mental note to remember to ask about this.

"Dad, where does he live? I see the path runs out just before your house."

"Actually, he lives right behind this one." He removed his overcoat and took a seat on a long, wooden piece of furniture. An oversized, red cushion served as the only comfort. Alaya sat down next to him.

"See?" He pulled aside a curtain, revealing another slightly larger house sitting behind them. "Many years ago, Whalen's parents were killed. They left behind a large plot of land and his uncle paid all their remaining debts and taxes to the king. Once Whalen came of age, that house became his property. His uncle rented out this house, but he soon fell into a deep depression. He doesn't come around anymore. I don't know much about the details and I haven't asked, but Whalen and I have both helped each other in a lot of ways. He has become almost like a son to me." Frederick stood and looked out a window, gazing out into the distance toward Whalen's house.

"He rarely talks about it, but I can only imagine what he has been through."

"That's terrible," Alaya said, trying her best to sound sympathetic. However, her true feelings defied her; she practically burned with envy. But it was not unwarranted. Alaya lamented the loss of her connection to her father during the crucial years of her childhood and resented the closeness Whalen now shared with him. *She* was his child, but Whalen had stolen that, in a way. He was able to enjoy her father's precious guidance and listening ear—something she had desperately craved for the last seven years.

Frederick thankfully interrupted Alaya's thoughts from drifting further down into the muck of her complex emotions of pain and loss.

"Never mind that right now," he said, turning his attention back to her. "We must celebrate these happy times! My daughter has somehow managed to find me after all this time!" They embraced again, and she was overcome by a surge of happiness.

The house had a warm, welcoming feel, although it was minimally decorated. Her father kindled a small flame in the stone fireplace. She had never lived in a house with a real wood-burning fireplace before. They had a gas fireplace at their home in Maryland, but it had always been more of a decorative piece. Somehow, this warmth felt more inviting and authentic. She drew close to the fire and soaked up the heat of the crackling, burning embers.

They both sat near the hearth, silently staring into the flames that danced wildly before them.

"Now, the real talking can begin," Frederick spoke. "Tell me, how did you do it? I want to know every detail." His expression turned serious.

"Mr. Miller," Alaya began, "he pretty much orchestrated the whole thing. I just did what I was told."

"I should have known the old dog was behind it right from the start. Of course, I'm not complaining. But why would be send my *only* child? Why did you do it? I wasn't even sure you knew who he was when you were younger; I can't believe you sought him out to find the answers. What a bright young woman you've become."

Alaya laughed. "Not exactly, Dad," she explained further. "Honestly, I only did it because Mom suggested that I get a job. I figured that his shop wouldn't be a bad choice."

At the mention of her mother, Frederick's face fell and he rubbed his brow with one of his large, calloused hands.

"Oh, Janice. She must be so upset with me...how has she fared over the years?" Frederick said, trying his best to keep a steady voice.

Alaya took a deep breath and sighed, unsure of how much to tell him.

"Janice *is* okay, isn't she? Or...is there someone else?" he asked. His voice almost quivered with trepidation.

"She's fine, Dad. And no, there's never been anyone else."

Alaya didn't know what to say. She didn't have the heart to tell him how she had become an alcoholic, assumed that her husband was dead, and now treated Alaya like a stranger on her best days and an enemy on her worst.

"She works at the hospital, lots of double shifts, but we've managed." Alaya kept things general, and as positive as she could manage. She wasn't sure how much her father could take all at once. They had only just been reacquainted and there was no use spoiling it with bad news.

"Besides, I'm old enough to take care of myself now, so she's had more time to focus on herself."

"Yes, my Janice has always known how to put her nose to the grindstone when she has to. But if I remember correctly, she was never able to handle stress very well. I'm glad that she has managed to stay strong...for both of you." Frederick sat back into his chair, obviously relieved.

"So she encouraged you to work for Miller?" he asked. "What about college? You should be what, nineteen now, right?"

"Well, I knew that it was time I started contributing to the household, and she told me that you two had been close, so I went for it. Maybe she thought I'd have a hard time getting hired anywhere else," Alaya shrugged her shoulders. "As for college...well, that's still in the works."

"Why would that be? You're such a bright star. Universities usually fight for students like you." Her father had always been very supportive of her, even as a child. But things had changed since his disappearance.

Alaya laughed again. "You're funny, Dad." She smiled, and then suddenly remembered what she held in her bag. "There is something else about Mr. Miller..." she reached into her bag to show him the troudare.

"Yes, I know he is really Matthias Negash. I was told that he stepped down from his service to the King for his own personal reasons. No one ever went into any detail, but that's part of what I've been unlocking—the truth. I know that Matthias kept his own secrets for his own reasons, but I respect that man above almost anyone. He overcame enormous adversity to get his wife Belina, and their child, out of Batunia." His tone had once again turned serious.

"What's that you have there?" he asked, staring at the glass orb.

"Matthias gave it to me so that we can communicate with him while I'm here. It's called a troudare." Alaya demonstrated how it worked.

"That's wonderful. May I give it a try?" He asked.

After several attempts, there was still no response from the other side.

"It may be late over there. Mr. Miller may be asleep. We can try again later," Alaya said.

They continued talking late into the night, laughing and enjoying one another's company. It was supremely odd; it felt as though no time had passed at all. Alaya wanted the night to last forever, but it was getting late. When she could no longer fight off the insistent deepening yawns, her father showed her to the spare room.

As she moved around the small room preparing her bed, he suddenly startled her.

"Alaya! The machine!" Frederick practically shouted, instantly remembering that not so small detail. "Where is it now? Is it well-hidden?" His eyes were once again wild with questions.

"Of course, I took care of that. It's hidden in the forest, buried in leaves. It is a good thing that it's autumn here," Alaya explained hurriedly, alleviating his concerns.

"I only ask because of what happened to me. It was all I could do to get away. Like Nikolai said, I've done my best to disguise myself over the years. When I'm not lugging around in protective gear, I usually wear an old cloak and walk with a cane."

His expression turned grave. "You must remember something, Alaya. In public, I am not your father; only address me as Frederick. If they discover our connection, it could mean trouble. I don't want to drag you into this mess. I couldn't live with myself if something happened to you. Do you understand?" There was a desperate note in his voice.

Alaya nodded. She understood the gravity of the situation, even though she didn't completely understand her father's place in the complicated mess of the kingdom.

"I understand that things may not be good here, but we have the machine now. You and I can leave here together, as soon as you like. I told Mr. Miller that I would find you and I'm not leaving empty-handed," Alaya stated.

Frederick paused. Alaya knew that face—something was bothering him—something serious. But she wasn't a child anymore, and she hoped her father recognized this too.

"You have only heard the very tip of things, my dear...just the smallest bit of the story. For now, why don't you get some rest? We'll have plenty of time to talk more in the morning. I have an errand to run in the village, but it shouldn't take too long."

He added one last thing, before retiring for the night.

"There is a great deal you still have to learn."

CHAPTER 23

The next morning, Alaya woke up to a gentle rapping on the front door. She jolted up; there were any number of horrible things that could have awaited her. Plus, the new surroundings did not help; she had to pause before remembering all that had happened the night before. Thankfully, she slowly remembered; last night had actually happened and her father was still alive.

"Dad?" Alaya called out, but there was no answer from his room. He must have left already.

She walked across the floor, feeling the biting cold even through her thick pair of socks. Slowly approaching the door, she asked, "Who is it?"

A familiar voice responded, "It is Whalen."

Alaya jumped, surprising herself. *How could I have forgotten?*

"Just a moment, please." She scampered back to her room to change. Just then, something caught the corner of her eye. On the small dining table, Alaya saw a scrap of paper placed in the center. It was a note in her father's handwriting.

"Be back as soon as I can. Love, Dad." Further down, there was a postscript: *"P.S. Stay out of trouble!"*

"Great," Alaya sighed, hoping things would not take too long. "Why can't we just go back home?" she asked out loud to no one in particular, crumbling the paper in both hands.

Her father had left a basin full of fresh water and she splashed cold water onto her face, fluffed out her hair, and combed it through with her fingers. Alaya twirled it up in a high bun - the perfect, no-fuss style. There was little else she could do in the way of personal grooming; after all, there was not a single mirror in the house, which made primping an impossible task. She pulled a new dress over her head, one that Hava had given her, and opened the door.

Alaya barely caught a glimpse of Whalen's outline before she was nearly blinded by the bold streak of sunlight, cutting its way through the open doorway. It was also a bit chillier than she expected and she shivered, feeling the air cut through the thin fabric of her dress.

"Wow! Good morning," she said, crossing her arms over her chest.

"Good morning, Alaya. I hope that it finds you well?" he asked, with what seemed to be a mix of curiosity and genuine concern. He didn't seem to notice the cold, not even flinching as a gust of wind whipped back the fronds of his nearly full-length coat.

"Yes, I'm very well, thank you. Do you mind waiting here for one more minute?" she asked, holding up one finger and darting back to her clothing stash. She slipped on some tight leggings, which were cleverly hidden under the length of her dress. She also grabbed a nearby cloak that her father had laid over the chair in her room.

Back outside, she stepped down from the small porch, immediately wishing that Mr. Miller had allowed her to take a pair of sunglasses. Although the sky was a stunning electric blue, the wind was a veritable tempest and she continued to shield her eyes from the powerful sunlight. She had never considered herself an "outdoors person," but that wasn't exactly acceptable in this world. In Batunia, video games, television, computers, and movies didn't exist. Aside from reading, there was not much to do if one opted to stay inside.

Whalen smiled, and Alaya interpreted this as him finding delight in her discomfort.

"The sun has a way of doing that—shining. The nerve it must have to do such a thing to *you*, though," he said, shooting her a sideways grin.

Alaya scowled, hardly amused.

He lightened up. "I have always admired how this house faces east. It is greeted by the sun every morning, a rare gift." He looked at Alaya, who continued shielding her eyes. "Well, perhaps not everyone might agree it's a gift."

"Most of the time, I love the sun, but I prefer it setting," she grumbled. "By then, I'm completely awake."

Whalen laughed. "Your father did mention that you might get a later start to the day than most. He told me that you have been that way since you were very young."

Alaya couldn't help but wonder what else her father had told him. What other snippets of her past had he shared?

"I hope I was not too early. I thought that you could use a bit of extra rest with all the excitement going on in the past few days." Whalen looked genuinely apologetic, and she smiled at his sweetness.

"I'm fine...really. It just takes me a few minutes to feel normal." She knew that once they got started, she'd perk up; the chill of the morning had already invigorated her. "Where are we headed?"

"I know that you were planning on meeting Max today, but I'd like to take you around Batunia. I thought you'd enjoy seeing a different side of the Kingdom, beyond

166

Neya Men and other evils." He looked on, past the bending trees. The wind was beginning to drop off, but Alaya could see small funnels of leaves swirling together, like flocks of birds that formed and collapsed in mere seconds.

They set out on a crude path that was a rough mix of gravel and fallen leaves. Although they were in the thick of autumn, the sun thankfully provided a warm reprieve. Alaya wished for a nice pair of hiking boots, instead of the thin ballet flats she now wore.

After strolling in silence for some time, Whalen began to ask questions. Although he was only making basic conversation, Alaya knew that she had to be mindful of her responses.

"So, what do you like to do?" he asked.

Alaya considered his question while the leaves crunched beneath her feet like potato chips.

"Well, just the normal stuff...I like watching mov...um, I mean, I like to read," Alaya insisted, catching herself. Whalen, like all of Batunia's villagers, would have no concept of movies, Hollywood, or the stars of the silver screen. Perhaps she would explain her world one day, but now was certainly not the time.

"I also like to go outside and exercise," Alaya lied, but stopped short when she saw Whalen raise an eyebrow. "Is there something wrong with that?"

"Oh, no, please don't think that I meant you should stay inside. I only find it intriguing. Women like Hava have work to do, but it is always to the benefit of the family. I suppose that without a family to support, you have time for other activities." He hesitated, probably hoping he had not offended her. "I think it is admirable that you came here to find your father."

Although Alaya was curious of the complexities of gender roles in Batunia, she decided it was best to ask her father instead.

"I saw you playing that sporting game with Max the other day. Soccer, he says you call it? It looks like fun."

"Yes, I learned that back in my hometown," she said, but quickly changed the subject, not wanting to have to expand on any details of where she was from. She wasn't sure how much her father had told him about his true background and she didn't want to ruin a seven-year cover story.

"What about you? What keeps you busy?" she asked casually. A few villagers had appeared on the narrow path, filling the space like small streams joining a larger river. Some were young and others were old; their destinations were unknown. Alaya noticed an elderly couple that blatantly stopped and glared at her as she walked past. But she kept looking forward; there was no point in concerning herself with rude people.

"Well, your father keeps me quite busy..." he paused before adding, "but as you observed the other day, I like combat. It helps me focus, and also to prepare." He grinned, knowing that Alaya had seen him the other day.

"Prepare for what?" she naturally asked. It didn't concern her, but she couldn't help but ask.

"You will know, soon," he said, but left it at that.

They continued further through the forest until the edge of a large river began to appear. Alaya grew uneasy; she recognized this area. The machine was buried less than a dozen yards from where they both stood. She tried not to attract too much attention, but slowed to search for the small mound of leaves. Once she discovered it undisturbed, she gave a small sigh of relief. The trees above must have shielded the machine from the worst of the rains.

They walked a bit further downstream, until they came upon a decaying footbridge that spanned the flowing water.

"Almost there," he said, striding toward the wooden crossing.

It now seemed that every person they passed gave Alaya strange or curious stares. She was beginning to grow uncomfortable; it couldn't simply be coincidence.

"Whalen, why does everyone keep looking at me like I have two heads?" she asked, quickening her pace to stay even with Whalen's long strides.

"You will see soon enough." He smiled down at her, smirking at her confusion.

Upon reaching the footbridge, Whalen went first. He seemed to effortlessly glide across the rickety, wooden planks, while Alaya was much more cautious. From the looks of it, the bridge had been around for decades without upkeep, perhaps even longer. Naturally, she was afraid. Even though she had been a strong swimmer as a child, the rushing water below was quite a bit different than the swimming pools to which she was accustomed.

Alaya slowly traversed the narrow path, looking down into the water with every step she took across the planks. She spied sharp needles of stone at the bottom of the shallow river. *How had Whalen done this?*

She was more than halfway across with no problems, until suddenly, one of the weak weathered planks cracked down the middle, nearly snapping in two. Alaya lost her balance and tried to regain control of her body, but she was unable to stop wobbling. Just as she had feared, she was about to fall into the frigid water below.

Although she hadn't seen him move, Whalen was suddenly by her side, wrapping his arm around her waist and pulling her onto more stable ground. She could feel her heart pounding against his chest.

"I have you. This bridge has been falling apart for years." He held her until they had safely reached the other side. "I should have warned you, I'm sorry."

Once Alaya reached the flat, unmoving surface, she sat down on a patch of grass and leaves. Only then did she allow herself to take a breath and calm her racing heart. She looked up into the sky, where only a few clouds lingered on the horizon.

"Where *are* you taking me?" Alaya asked. Her hands still clutched tufts of grass.

Whalen pointed toward something that she couldn't see, off in distance.

"There it is. We are here."

"Where?" Alaya asked, looking around as she stood up.

There were fewer people, but those who were nearby all stopped and stared at Alaya. They almost looked like they recognized her; as though at any moment, they might call out to her by name.

She began to feel uneasy and whispered to Whalen, "So now are you going to tell me why everyone keeps staring at me? This is starting to get creepy."

"In a moment, Alaya. Follow me." He held her hand, and led the way.

Rounding a bend in the trees, a stone fortress came into view. An intricately crafted metal gate stood before them, although it had been flung wide open. Apprehensive, Alaya allowed Whalen to lead.

As they stepped through the gate, another group exited. A child in the group boldly stopped forward to grab Alaya's hand as they crossed paths, and she placed Alaya's hand against her forehead. The girl couldn't have been more than three or four years old. Alaya smiled at her cuteness, but she was unsure of what this was all about. This small act of kindness must have meant the world to the little girl; she beamed like she had just received the gift of a lifetime, and then skipped off to catch up with her family.

"What was that about?" she asked.

Whalen watched the girl as she left.

"Alaya, this is the Circle of the Soranayum. Many people used to come here to worship, but now only a few practice in the old ways."

"That name is familiar to me. I remember Willemina mentioning this place at dinner." Alaya meant to ask Hava more about this, but she had forgotten until now. "Who are they?"

"I will show you," Whalen said, and they continued walking in silence, moving with quiet grace through each twist and turn of the labyrinthine corridors. They eventually came upon an open archway that stood in the center of the maze. Standing within the archway were three stone statues. They appeared quite sad and reached out for one another with extended arms, as if seeking an embrace that would never come.

Whalen explained. "These are the higher powers of this world, ancient goddesses who have stood since before time began. There are three goddesses: Sadenia, who has her hands and feet bound by the enemy, who continues to bring evil. The second is Flouridia, who is blind to the world of the living, but not the realm of the spirits. The third is Lysteria, who is mute. Although she is silent, she understands all. There were previously four, but one was stolen away many years ago. Alone, they are limited, but together, they are all powerful."

Alaya looked at the statues; there was a strange aura surrounding them, inspiring awe down to the core of her bones. She moved closer and noticed that small pieces of the statues were beginning to erode and chip away. Although their appearances had been marred by the slow degradation of time, they were strangely beautiful. The archway was imposing and the women filled it with their magnificent presence, a trio of constancy in an ever-changing world.

"People have come here to pray for years, in the hopes that Batunia could still be saved, yet nothing has changed. If anything, it only seems to get worse. Naturally, people have all but lost hope." Whalen intoned with sadness.

"Although the villagers' plead and make supplications, nothing has happened. We cannot blame them for losing faith. Now, there is something else you must see." Whalen walked toward the wall behind the archway, but Alaya wasn't ready to leave; something about this place drew her in like a magnet.

Finally, when Alaya walked toward him, she saw what he had been looking at - an old portrait of a woman in a golden frame. The woman looked vaguely familiar; she had long dreadlocks and beautiful dark skin. She seemed to glow with a regal fire. And then suddenly Alaya remembered where she had seen this woman before…she was the statue in Mr. Miller's basement.

"Her name was Velda. She passed away many years ago. I was only a baby when she died, so I do not remember her reign. This woman was a former Queen to King Ogapallos II, and she helped restore hope to the people of Batunia when all seemed lost. But there was something else. Velda was the last Ramajian the world has ever known, and the people loved her. Some had even begun to worship her, which is why this portrait was placed here, in the most sacred place of the old ways."

Looking up at the portrait, Whalen's next words took her completely by surprise.

172

"Perhaps now you understand why people have been staring at you, Alaya. The resemblance is uncanny."

She looked hard at the decaying portrait. Parts of it were so faded that she could barely make out the whole image.

"I don't know, Whalen. It's hard to tell. I can see how the imagination could find a match, but I don't see it. I know there aren't many people with dark skin in Batunia; perhaps people just think that we all look alike." Alaya laughed at the joke, but Whalen found no humor in it. After all, there was a fair amount of diversity in Batunia. Apparently, jokes based on skin color weren't part of the Kingdom's comedic landscape.

"You are free to hold your own beliefs," Whalen said as he turned back to the portrait of Velda, "but even though I haven't been here in a long time, it remains one of the only places I have ever truly felt at peace." He reached out and touched the frame.

An unsettling feeling began to swelter in the pit of Alaya's stomach. Under no circumstances did she ever want to be worshipped. But still she wanted to know more about the goddesses. *What was this evil that bound Sadenia?* And *was* there actually a link between her and the woman in the portrait, Velda?

Her questions would have to wait; a loud scream echoed from off in the distance, tossing them both from their moment of contemplation. Although it came from afar, it was still much too close for Alaya to feel safe. She scanned the area, looking for answers when Whalen took off in a hurried sprint. She struggled to keep up with the long strides of his legs.

"What was that, Whalen?" she asked between breaths once she caught up to him.

He slowed his pace as they reached the entrance to the Circle of the Soranayum. She could feel his body tense beside her, and he spoke with an uneasy tone.

"Keep silent and stay close to me." They listened for a few more moments as the screams intensified and drew nearer. He grabbed Alaya's hand and they skillfully maneuvered to a large patch of bushes nearby.

"Stay low. You mustn't be seen," he instructed, still holding her hand as they kneeled behind the shrubs.

A group of heavily armored men thundered past them on horseback and Alaya saw the source of the screams - a little boy on the back of one of the men's horses, near the front of the pack. He kicked and screamed, but there was no one around to help - no one except Alaya and Whalen.

"We have to do something," Alaya whispered desperately. "We can't just hide here and let this happen."

"And what exactly do you intend to do?" Whalen asked. "Of course I want to help, but it is not safe for either of us right now. We have no weapons, and I cannot put your life in jeopardy. Your father has entrusted me with your care, which means I protect you from harm, not draw it out."

His words were an unattractive blend of chivalry and condescension. She wasn't exactly a helpless child, but the little boy was clearly defenseless.

"How can you say that, Whalen? That child is being kidnapped. We can't sit by and let it happen; we have to try and help!" Alaya raised her voice to an angry whisper. "I thought you were brave, but it seems that I was wrong," she said with a harsh tone.

Once the words escaped her mouth, Alaya wished she could take them back. Whalen's expression tightened, like he had just been stricken across the face. But still, he said nothing. He intently watched the men, who were now gathered in a small circle about thirty yards from where they were crouched. Alaya noticed that his fists were tightly clenched, including the one that still held her hand.

The man who had grabbed hold of the child raised his fist, and the other men fell silent. He leaned over and said something to the boy, then slapped him hard across the face. Even though the blow was visibly hurt and shaken, he stopped screaming. The man's hand fell three more times, but the boy didn't let out another sound. Instead, his face began to contort as his eyes squeezed shut from pain. Small cuts turned to deep gashes, and the small blood droplets were now turning into a puddle collecting on the ground. He tried to fight back tears, but they streamed freely down his chin, mixing with the blood. *Why would anyone do such a cruel thing to a child? What was his crime?*

Alaya turned away; she couldn't watch the brutal scene play out.

"If we aren't going to do anything, then let's just go, Whalen." Alaya said, disgusted by the unwarranted violence.

"In a moment," Whalen said, still watching the men.

Once the man was finished with the beating, he kicked his heels into his horse and resumed riding; the group of armored riders dutifully followed. They headed west, towards the palace.

"They are gone," Whalen said and helped Alaya to her feet. "There is something that you must learn, Alaya. Batunia has had its fair share of trouble in the past, but things have gotten much worse. The Neya Men are not the only source of our problems. Those were the King's Riders." He quickened his pace again, walking in a new direction as Alaya hurried to keep up.

"They have grown bored of their usual pursuits, and have now found new ways to keep themselves occupied.

Sometimes, King Negash even takes part in the madness." Whalen was practically vibrating with anger.

So abducting children was commonplace. No wonder there was no outcry, or fight initiated on the child's behalf. In fact, it seemed as though everyone else had disappeared as soon as the screaming had begun. Alaya's mind was reeling around the implications of this backwards world. Alaya was flooded with emotions. She wanted to apologize to Whalen, she wanted to rescue that child, and she wanted to crawl into her bed and weep.

However, in that moment, she could do nothing but stop in her tracks. For better or worse, they had to make a choice, even if it meant doing nothing. Speaking out could have cost them their lives.

Alaya had a great deal to think about. The reunion with her father still seemed surreal, and she was already calculating how soon they would be able to leave. She didn't like the vicious reality of Batunia, and the longer they stayed, the more likely something terrible would happen. Now was the time to leave; that much she knew. Yet, why did she feel a strange tug in the pit of her stomach? It was as though there was an enormous anchor tethering her to the depths of this world.

Whalen looked back and saw Alaya frozen and lost in thought. She looked bewildered, as if she had been bound and stricken by muteness, unable to speak. He came to her side and put a hand on her shoulder.

"I am sorry, Alaya. There was nothing that we could have done." He gently brushed a tear from her cheek, and led her away from the scene of devastation.

CHAPTER 24

As they walked on in silence, Alaya felt the air grow thick with humidity. The sun was consumed by a dull fog, which cast an eerie feel to the path. She hoped that they would be able to get to the Iskinders home unscathed; she didn't think she could bear to witness any more tragedies. Truthfully, she wanted nothing more than to head back home—her real home—where they could put all of this behind them.

Whalen reached a long arm into one of the tree branches that curled high above them. His height allowed him to do so with minimal effort. He grabbed a branch and gave it a gentle shake.

"What are you doing?" Alaya asked, still upset, but curious.

"Looking for mongpayas. They are usually in season by now. You would be able to see them on the ground, but the leaves have probably covered them. The best tasting ones just fall off the tree naturally." He smiled, trying too hard to lift her veil of sorrow.

"What are mongpayas?" she asked.

"You do not have them in your village? That is odd. I thought that they were spread throughout the world." He gave another branch a quick shake, with no luck. "They happen to be the most delicious fruit that you will ever taste."

He jostled a third branch above her head, and a large fruit tumbled through the leaves. Whalen caught it just before it hit the ground and handed it to Alaya, who inspected it closely. The skin of the fruit was bright magenta and its shape resembled a pomegranate, yet it had the texture of an orange. She held it to her nose; the smell was divine. It was a light, sweet scent that reminded her of a blend of strawberries and blueberries.

"If you pick them, they are usually too sour to eat, but that one should be just right," Whalen explained. "Would you like to try?"

"Sure. Don't we need to peel it first?" she asked, handing it back to Whalen.

"Peel it? No, of course not! The outer layer is the best part." He bit directly into the thick skin. "Here, try it," he offered, handing the odd fruit back to her. Juice seeped out of the fruit where he had bit into it. Alaya held it to her nose, and was taken aback. The scent was intoxicating, even through the skin.

"Alright..." She hesitated. The small pores on the skin were almost exactly like an orange, but there was not as clear a distinction between the inner flesh and the skin, like there was with an orange. She looked at the fruit with a bit of curiosity, but thought *what the heck*, and gave it a shot. After all, how often would she get the chance to try a new species of fruit?

Wiping the juice from his mouth with his sleeve, Whalen encouraged her.

"Go ahead! The flavor is unlike anything you've ever tried. Trust me."

Alaya sunk her teeth into the mongpaya. The flesh felt incredibly mushy between her teeth, like an overly ripe

178

plum. As soon as she took the bite, her mouth seemed to swell in ecstasy. The skin of the fruit contrasted beautifully with the meat and her taste buds immediately watered for more. It tasted exactly like a strawberry and blueberry blend, but there was something else as well. She couldn't quite put her finger on it at first, so she took another bite and it clicked. *Marshmallows!* The combination was bizarre, but undeniably delicious; she couldn't get enough.

"Whalen, you weren't joking. This is really good!" Alaya said between bites of the quickly disappearing fruit. Once she had finished more than half of the mongpaya, she looked up at Whalen apologetically. "I'm sorry, it's almost gone."

He smiled. "No, you can have it. This is your first one; it would be a crime to take it away from you now."

Soon, there was a rapid sound of hooves striking the earth. It began as a slow rumble but quickly intensified into a heavy stampede. A dense fog had crept over the path and was now silently swirling around them. Alaya hadn't noticed until now; but she immediately stopped her feasting and dropped the fruit, forgetting about it before it even hit the ground. Whalen instinctively crouched like a lion preparing to pounce on its prey, and he pulled Alay down to safety with him. He had one arm protectively blocking her and the other held in front of him, tightened in a fist.

"Whalen, what is it now...?" Alaya asked, panic filling her voice. With the thick fog on every side, neither of them could see more than a few inches in front of them. The hooves drew closer still and her heartbeat quickened. *Not the King's Riders again, please...* However, this felt different. The terror felt like icicles freezing her veins, as if injected by a needle.

The wind picked up, sweeping the fog away and revealing a clearing just ahead of them. The shape of a woman appeared just as four dark horses descended upon her. They were mounted by four men, wearing armor and cloaks. Alaya looked over at Whalen for direction, but he was staring intently at the woman in the center of the group.

"Shah," he said softly to himself and slowly shook his head. "They have her."

Alaya remembered that name from her first night at the Iskinders' home. Shahara was a friend of Whalen's that had become connected to the Neya Men in some way. Alaya fell silent, not wanting to presume anything about the situation — they both tried to hear if anything was being said. Thankfully, they were beneath a mongpaya tree, so they had some cover behind the low-hanging branches. Alaya wondered what was going on and what Shah's involvement was, as well as what those men wanted with her.

"Don't move," Whalen whispered through clenched teeth.

Alaya nodded her head a fraction of an inch. She had nothing to say and her mouth had dried up like a rain puddle in July. The fog was continuing to clear, which would reveal them to the riders if they weren't careful.

What Alaya heard next was something she would never be able to scrub from her memory. The young woman emitted a piercing shriek from a few yards away, which seared into her head like a razor-sharp power drill. It was a primal scream of terror; bestial and desperate.

"Please... please! Do not take me away! My family will come to find me and stop you all!" she begged and threw out a slew of threats, but it was futile.

"We hope they do," a surly voice said. A man in dark clothing pushed Shahara to another of his comrades, who had just dismounted from his steed.

Alaya glanced at Whalen from the corner of her eye, and saw his jaw grind with rage. The men each wore a black cloak, along with black gloves, body armor, and heavy helmets to obscure their faces. Heavy metal weapons hung from their waists and dangled from the saddles of their overburdened horses. It was enough to put any modern military to shame.

"No, please don't do this! Whatever you want, it's yours. Money? Clothes? Food? Anything! Just please don't make me do it. My family…they can make an arrangement with you, but please spare me!" the young woman begged with every ounce of effort that remained in her petite frame.

"Oh, we will spare you. For a time, at least," the man's voice was muffled and sinister. "You made your choice long before today. You came to us when you needed a skill and you knew the price. Today we are collecting on your debt. You must come with us now. Unless, of course, you would prefer that your family join you? What do you say to that?" the man asked, joining the others in a cacophony of laughter, mocking the sobs that vibrated through her entire body.

All too early, it was beginning to grow dark. Alaya struggled to adjust her eyes to the menacing group, who now began to circle around Shahara like sharks in a tank.

Alaya kept an eye on Whalen, who was in the same position with fists at the ready and poised to fight. Alaya reached for his hand, to caution him against whatever he might have been thinking. He looked at her for a moment as though shifting out of a trance, and then quickly diverted his attention back to the group of men. Alaya was beginning to feel sick to her stomach. Being witness to a second kidnapping in a single day was too much to bear; she couldn't sit by and watch this happen all over again.

Without warning, one of the men lunged at Shahara with full force. She let out a cry of pain and struggled with what little strength she had left, but it was no use. He easily hoisted her into the air, impaled on the end of his spear. A faint, final scream, erupted from Shahara's body, followed by the gurgling rattle of death.

The man tossed her body to the ground and knelt over it, as though he was whispering something into her ear. Smoke began to rise from the body, slowly at first, and then her clothes ignited in a burst of powerful flames. Whalen looked away, but Alaya couldn't. Simultaneously mesmerized and horrified by the scene, Alaya had to consciously remind herself not to vomit on the roots of the tree behind which she was hiding.

The remaining men descended upon the body, and gathered more closely around the charred corpse. The spear-wielding man waved his hand and the fire died just as quickly. The men waited for the smoke to clear, and like beasts, they began to devour the poor woman's body. They ate with violent ferocity, like a pack of wolves that hadn't eaten in weeks. Alaya could hear bones snapping like twigs and she pushed down another wave of nausea. Still, she couldn't look away; her eyes were glued to the scene like she was watching a live-action movie.

Through her clothes, Alaya could feel her heart beating uncontrollably, faster than if she had just ran a mile at a full sprint. She felt they should've done something — anything — but what? Within minutes, the men were finished and they mounted their steeds, racing off as quickly as they had come. The leader of the group was the last to rise from the grisly feast looking triumphant, like a satisfied king who'd just consumed a lavish meal.

He reached down and slung something over his shoulder before mounting his horse. No, not something — but *someone*. Alaya had just seen those men set Shahara on fire and clean their teeth with her bones, but now the same woman looked perfectly alive. Her skin had basically returned to normal, although it was as pale as paper; the damage from the fire was nowhere to be seen on her body or dress. Her hair had faded to a stark white, to the point where it almost glowed with brilliance.

As the final man rode off, Shahara was no longer screaming. She took on the dull, stoic appearance of a zombie. Her movements were exaggerated, like she was a ragdoll who no longer had control of her body.

The man rode off while she was still slung over his shoulder, and she bobbed up and down, like an apple in water. Slowly, Shahara lifted her head. With milky-white eyes, she stared straight through Alaya, as though she sensed that she was being watched.

Alaya felt an intense chill ring through her bones, down her spine all the way to her toes, and she shivered. The pale eyes staring back at her were haunting, even from a distance.

Suddenly, a cold wash of guilt flowed over Alaya, and she thought she might collapse. She could do nothing but look away from that soulless stare and immediately broke eye contact.

"What have they done?" Alaya asked aloud, unsure if she'd get a specific answer. She was stuck in a state of disbelief.

Whalen slowly rose to his feet, coming out of his own fit of horror. Alaya was almost startled by his presence, but was glad to see he was okay. His eyes were riddled with a mix of despair, anger, and grief. Alaya could only imagine how distraught and broken he must have felt—powerless to help his friend in her time of dire need.

The forest was now a silent, abandoned haunt, forsaken by all who may have once watched claimed refuge within its spaces. Alaya couldn't escape from the high-pitched shrieks that still rang in her head. She walked through the brush without speaking a word; Whalen leading the way.

***

They returned to her father's home without any further incident, and stood just outside the door, awaiting Frederick's return. Alaya had plenty of time to think on their trek back. She refused to believe that there was nothing they could have done to save Shahara. She wanted to blame Whalen, but some part of her knew that was unfair.

"Are you okay?" Whalen asked, startling her. His voice was low and calm, but Alaya still jumped. Her nerves were frayed and wild from their ordeal.

"There was nothing we could have done...I know that," Alaya stated without turning to face him. She knew that the Neya Men had done something horrible to that girl, but what was it? Alaya had seen her fair share of horror movies, but this was far more terrifying than anything she had ever imagined. They had transformed Shahara into something outside of humanity. Her body and soul were surely lost, but yet her body had risen, taking a different form. *But what was it?* Alaya knew that there was something else, something far more dangerous, at work.

A big part of her wanted to drag her father back to the machine as quickly as he returned, so they could both just return home and put this behind them like the terrible nightmare it was. At the same time, she was paralyzed by uncertainty. She felt despicable. Earlier, she challenged Whalen's bravery, but now, she was the one who was the coward.

"Alaya," Whalen sighed, "believe me, there is so much that I wish I could do—so much that I wish *we* could do. Your father and I, along with the Council, train as much as we can, but there are limits. Our numbers are too few and people are growing more afraid to join. Things like what we saw in the forest happen more often than any of us care to admit. If you fight back, you will be killed on the spot or will disappear—never to be seen again. Once they choose a target, it is only a matter of hours before they find you." He said.

"But how can anyone stop them?" Alaya asked. Her back was turned away from him, and she was staring blankly out into the forest. The leaves rolled end over end, cartwheeling gently in the wind.

"I...I do not know." He came to stand beside her and looked off into the distance. His presence provided a sense of comfort that she desperately needed. She wanted to feel his touch...

"Shah!" He slammed his fists into the windowsill in anger, causing Alaya to jump. "Why would she turn to them for help? She knew better than that!" Whalen pounded his fist again; he hadn't shown any emotion since watching his friend be mangled by those monsters.

Alaya didn't interrupt him; it was clear that he needed time to process what had happened. Shahara was his friend. They had grown up together, shared memories and laughter, and were possibly even more than friends at some point. However, all of that had been taken away with abrupt, vicious finality. Now, she would forever be a stranger to him.

After another tense moment, he turned to face Alaya.

"I'm sure you've guessed what you saw today. Those were the Neya Men. Once they come for you, your fate is decided. No one ever gets a second chance. Once they come to collect the debts they are owed, your life belongs to them." His face hardened.

"But why do they do this? And what did they do to her?" Alaya asked.

"The Neya Men have powers; some say that they were given those powers by one of the Soranayum, the one called Sadenia. As that version of the story goes, she felt sorry

185

for them. They desperately wished for gifts, or talents, like the Ramajians. But the problem was, even though Sadenia meant well, she did not consult with her sisters. The Soranayum always work together as one unit, but not that time. And they paid the consequence as a result.

"What made it worse is that Sadenia had a tendency of being gullible and naïve. She gave them powers of simple magic that seemed benign at the time, but they twisted those powers into something else entirely. Soon, others wanted powers like them, so the Neya Men began giving out 'talents' in exchange for money."

"What kind of talents?" Alaya asked.

"Some people are given the power of sight, which allows them to tell the future, but the revelations are puzzles and riddles. Others are granted physical beauty, although it rapidly fades after only a few years. They have even opened shops just outside the marketplace, so customers can seek their services in private, but these talents are not what they seem, Alaya. They entice villagers with illusions. Some foolishly believe their families will reap the benefits, and they believe they can be careful. It is an easy choice for those people who are desperate or weak.

"But recent years have been difficult in Batunia. The people have grown desperate for relief, no matter where it comes from. With magic, nearly anything is possible. But this is only temporary. And what's more, nothing in this world comes without a price. The Neya Men have continued to grow more and more powerful through illicit practices like deals with demons from the underworlds. Those are the Neya Men that we are dealing with today. They collect on debts by stealing souls."

Alaya shuddered and wrapped her arms together. Thinking she was cold, Whalen draped an arm over her. There was something magnetic about his touch.

"What can be done?" Alaya asked. "That can't simply be the end of it, right?"

"Well, the Soranayum have tried to stop them, from what I understand. It did not take long for Sadenia to realize that she had made a terrible mistake. She told her sisters what she had done and together, they sought to remedy the situation. The three goddesses cursed the Neya Men, but they should have destroyed them."

"What did the curse actually do?" she asked again, almost fearing the answer.

"Many believe that it actually made things worse. Some of the Neya Men lost their souls, while others lost their human appearance. That is why they typically come out at night wearing masks, cloaks, and armor. However, as we saw today, they are growing bolder...and far more powerful." He dropped his head before continuing.

"I knew that things were bad, but I never thought Shahara would seek them out for talents. We were making progress with her brother's illness; some of the treatments seemed to be taking effect. We would have found a way to get more ikbars, if only she..." Whalen fell silent again. In the space of that silence, there was a shuffling sound heard off in the distance.

Alaya and Whalen both looked up, immediately on their guard. Once they saw the shadowy figure of a hunchback man with a cane emerge, they relaxed.

"Hello, you two! Back so soon?" Frederick asked.

CHAPTER 25

Frederick entered the house first, threw off his cloak, and set his cane aside.

"I expected you to be at the Iskinders, Alaya. I checked there first, but they said that you hadn't stopped by yet. Is everything alright?" Her father looked concerned.

"We saw the Neya Men today, Frederick." Whalen spoke first. "They have taken over Shahara's body, and Alaya saw the transformation." Whalen took her hand into his, and lightly kissed the back of her hand.

"I must go, but I will stop at the Iskinders' home later tonight. If you are there, we will speak more. But if not, I will understand." He turned to say goodbye to Frederick.

"Thanks for keeping her safe, Whalen." He said.

After Frederick closed the door, he immediately turned to Alaya.

"I won't blame you if you'd rather not relive the horrors of what happened here today," Frederick said, cutting to the heart of the matter. "But tell me, how much did Whalen explain about what you saw?"

Alaya appreciated his understanding, and explained everything that had happened: the kidnapping of the small boy, what Whalen had told her about the Soranayum, and the origin of the Neya Men. She didn't mention the portrait of Velda, as she still didn't know how she felt about that particular mystery.

"What exactly are the Neya Men, Dad? Vampires? Zombies?" Alaya asked.

"Not in the slightest. The Neya Men aren't limited to walking the forest at night, and they aren't mindless eating machines. They have a specific purpose—feeding on human flesh gives them strength to morph into a more powerful being. That is all. And since the King's Riders no longer meddle in their affairs, the Neya Men have grown both in number and bravery." Frederick said.

"Did he tell you how the Soranayum have come to look like they do today?" Her father asked.

"You mean they weren't always like that, made of stone?"

"Not at all. From my research, I concluded that the Soranayum were actually once corporeal beings. They were living goddesses that walked among men. Granted, this was probably hundreds, or perhaps even thousands of years ago. I'm starting to believe that Velda was in fact, one of them."

He took a seat, and Alaya sat down next to him. She wondered if she should have mentioned the statue in Mr. Miller's basement. But her father had more to tell.

"There is something else you must know. Do you remember the charm that I gave you? The one that was in the shape of a key?"

"Yes, of course," Alaya said, pulling the necklace out from under her clothing. It flickered, reflecting the pale orange of the candles in the room.

"I never took it off, just like you told me. It's always been my good luck charm." She said, but immediately wanted to take it back. "I mean, I used to pretend that it brought me good luck when I was younger. Of course, I don't believe in those kinds of things now." She unclasped the necklace, and handed it to her father, who delicately plucked it from her palm.

Frederick smiled. "Who knows, you might be right. After all, you found me, so maybe it is true."

Alaya wanted to smile, but she simply couldn't. There had been nothing lucky about what had happened today.

"Dad, it's silly, but I thought it would always protect me. But now, I'm not so sure."

Alaya watched as her father inspected the necklace, paying particularly close attention to the key's tiny handle. She began to wonder what the necklace had to do with Batunia.

"Is something wrong?" she asked.

Frederick held up his right hand, pulled out a thin knife from a fold of his cloak, and sliced a deep cut right down the center.

"Dad! What are you doing? What's the matter with you?" Alaya nearly screamed. She couldn't believe her eyes and her breathing came sharp and frightened. Droplets of dark blood began to stream down to the wooden floor, forming a dark, thick puddle of red.

Faster than lightning, Alaya was up on her feet carefully holding his hand up, above his heart. She frantically searched the room for something to dress the wound. Her eyes spotted a piece of cloth nearby, and although it wasn't ideal, she took it and wrapped it tight around her father's hand. She was thankful that Janice had taught her how to stop blood flow after one of her many drunken tumbles that left a gash or a scrape that Alaya was left to tend.

Alaya began calling out orders, almost instinctively.

"We need to get some bandages and some alcohol to sterilize the needle. Why didn't I remember to pack that first-aid kit before I left?" Alaya moaned, trying to quell the mild panic in her head by staying busy and running on automatic. She did the best she could with the cloth, but the thick red liquid was already starting to saturate.

All the while, in a stark contrast, Frederick remained strangely calm.

"Alaya, dear, you know I don't have anything like that. Can you imagine what someone would say if they saw a Band-Aid or Neosporin? It's dangerous enough you have brought the machine back." He paused, glancing down at his wound and the blood-soaked cloth. He removed it and tossed it expertly into a bin near the large washing basin.

"Dad! It hasn't stopped bleeding yet!" she scolded and went to wash the cloth so she could wash and reapply it. "Seriously, what is going on? Has this place driven you crazy after all these years? Geez!"

"You know, Alaya, now that I think about it, perhaps there is something you can do," Frederick said. "Think about it. Just use your head."

"Okay, okay...just give me a minute" she said aloud and began pacing. "Um, do you have any kind of ointment? Do any herbs grow around here?"

"No, no. That's not what I meant," he chided. "Come here, next to me." He motioned to her and she sat.

"Now, I need you to listen to me very carefully. Try and concentrate. Concentrate only on my cut. Visualize it healing. Imagine the blood disappearing and the wound becoming smaller and smaller, until it is nothing more than a fading line of light, and then only a distant memory. All that will remain may be a small scar, but it will fade in time. I know that you can do this."

His strange confidence behind those words was almost disturbing. *What was he talking about? Perhaps he actually is losing his mind...*

"Dad, that's ridiculous. Are you talking about healing through hypnosis or something? There's no way something like that could work. This isn't magic; this is real life. And in real life, your hand is bleeding all over the place." Alaya was reluctant to say anything else. Enough time had been wasted already, and he was still bleeding out.

Frederick's demeanor noticeably changed. His shoulders sunk and he looked as though he was a child whose kite had just been pulled apart in a storm.

"Please, Alaya. Why don't you humor me, huh? Just try it. After all, what's the worst that can happen? If it doesn't work, then I'll drop the whole thing and we can try to find something at the marketplace."

"Dad, this is--" She started, but couldn't finish her sentence.

"Trust me, Alaya. Besides, you cannot possibly make this cut any worse. At least, I don't think that it works that way."

"Dad! Quit joking around!" Alaya said, clearly irritated. She needed him to stay rooted in sanity. The world had flipped upside down in the past few days, but she needed something normal—something firmly planted on the banks of reality.

"Okay, just try. No *further* harm will be done, but the benefits might be great," he reassured her.

Alaya relented. She obviously could not convince her father of how foolish he sounded and he had his mind firmly made up that something was going to happen. She decided to give it a shot, but she would at least take the higher road and not gloat when whatever he expected, amounted to nothing.

Closing her eyes, Alaya concentrated on the things that her father had mentioned: the hand, the blood, the cut, and the fading scar. After what felt like nearly a minute,

Alaya opened her eyes. Blood was still flowing from the wound, just as fast as before.

"This is pointless." Exasperated, she continued frantically searching the house for something to wrap the cut. She began tearing off a sleeve of a shirt that she'd packed. It was old, and she wasn't likely to wear it anyway.

"Please, Alaya. Try once more, and really focus more on what you *want* to see happen, not what you expect to see. Hold my hand as you imagine it healing. Just once more, and then we'll forget the whole thing, okay? Humor your old man."

"Alright!" She practically shouted. "Only because I don't want you to pass out from blood loss; but after this, we're going to wrap that once and for all," Alaya said sternly.

Her father nodded in agreement, like an acquiescent child. Alaya could not understand why he was being so persistent, but she closed her eyes and gripped his hand a bit tighter. With all her energies focused, Alaya poured all her thoughts into the wound. She eliminated even those small, nagging voices that tried to preach to her about how silly this entire endeavor was. She was alone with the cut on his hand, and she gradually watched it close up into a red line, then fade to a light line of white.

Alaya's eyes remained closed, locked on that moment of closure, until her father spoke.

"Look what you've done!" he said with astonishment, sounding more stunned than he intended.

"What?" She asked, with eyes still closed. It was almost too terrifying to imagine what she might see. "It's not worse, is it?"

"Certainly not, Alaya, open your eyes!" he said, with excitement now cutting through where shock had been only moments ago.

Frederick held out his hand and touched her. Alaya hesitated, but finally cracked open one eye and then stared down at his hand in disbelief. The wound was not only gone, but there was not even a scar left behind. It was as though the wound had never existed at all.

"What did you do? How did you fake that, Dad? Let me see your other hand? There's no way that was real. How are you doing this?" She grasped wildly at both his hands, but there was no trace that he had ever cut himself.

"Alaya, it's okay. Your mind doesn't want to believe that this is real. But this is very real indeed. You saw it with your own eyes — the knife, the blood. But you were able to fix it. You healed that wound with the power of your mind."

Alaya shook her head viciously. She wasn't buying this nonsense. *This is right up there with those crazy mid-morning talk shows that feature people speaking to their dead pets.*

"No, Dad, you're wrong. Something like that would be impossible. You can't expect me to believe that I'm capable of…of…magic! And have never known until this moment."

Frederick walked back over to the table near the couch, and picked up the knife. Alaya became uneasy, wondering if he was going to force her into another demonstration…*What is he doing now?*

"When you were a little girl, your mother and I had plenty of questions about you. You probably don't remember now, but you were a very special baby. There were times when I'd see you hit your head so hard that it would leave a knot the size of a golf ball. Instead of crying for hours as most babies would, you would just rub it and the knot would disappear. I don't mean over the course of days…I mean within seconds. I thought that my eyes were just playing tricks on me until Janice said that she had seen things like that happen too. Do you remember any of this?"

Alaya shook her head.

"I have no idea what you're talking about." Her father took a step forward and she took a step backwards.

He gave another example from her bizarre childhood, and then another. He took one final step closer. For the first time in her life, Alaya was slightly afraid of her father.

"Your mom once banged her elbow into a cabinet, and she couldn't bend it without this excruciating pain shooting down to her wrist. It was going on for more than a half an hour and we were thinking of going to the hospital. You walked into the room and could tell that she was in pain. You offered to kiss it and make it all better. Do you remember that? Most kids say it, but you actually *did* make it better. The pain was gone instantly." He fiddled with the knife in his hands, running his hand from the tip of the smooth blade, back to the handle.

"I remember that day," Alaya said, "but how do you know that she wasn't just playing? I'm pretty sure she only pretended that I helped. Parents do that all the time. *Kiss the boo-boo to make it all better*," Alaya said dismissively.

"Your mother had been writhing with pain for nearly an hour. After you kissed her elbow, the pain was gone. Why would she have a reason to fake something like that?" He asked. Alaya had to admit, it was illogical.

"That can't be true though..." Alaya began, but her father interrupted, and grabbed hold of her right hand.

"Dad, what are you do--" Alaya started to pull her hand away, but it was too late. He sliced into her hand with the knife, but Alaya didn't scream, nor even wince. In fact, she felt no pain at all. When she looked down at the cut, red blood threatened to break outside of her skin, but the wound had closed in the blink of an eye, like nothing had ever happened. Not a drop of blood had escaped onto her skin.

"What?!" she gasped. "What is this? Am I some kind of demon, like those Neya Men? Dad, what's going on?!" Alaya shouted. She glared at her father, who sat smiling back at her, allowing her confusion to burn and then fizzle.

She couldn't believe what her father had been willing to do to prove a point. She wondered if he had legitimately lost a few marbles over the past seven years, but there was no time to dwell on that. He needed to get back home, to help her mom get back to normal. Their family needed to be together. They had stayed in this mad world long enough.

"Alaya, no. You are not a Neya Woman. In fact, you are quite the opposite. Thanks to you, my hand has been healed; they would never do something like that."

"But you just saw that, right? How did my hand heal so quickly? It didn't even hurt." Alaya turned away from her father, becoming more pensive. "People always talk about pain, but I don't honestly know if I've ever felt it," Alaya asked. "Can you please just tell me what's going on?" She wanted answers. No more riddles and no more magic tricks. Frederick was still beaming, his smile as wide as ever.

"Alaya, I know that you have no idea what's going on. But please know this. At the very least, you are a healer. You are a rare human. You likely have more powers than you have ever imagined." He said with pride.

"Got it. That makes *perfect* sense!" she said sarcastically, and swung back around to stare her father in the eye. "Dad, get real. None of this makes *any* sense. What would you call me? An alien? Witch? Some new species that doesn't exist?" she asked. Her sarcasm of a moment ago began to crack as she heard the words coming out of her mouth. *This might not be a joke...*

"I'm sure they have been called all of those things at some point, and more, no doubt," he said simply.

"Who?" she asked, shifting to straightforward questions so he could stop ducking and dodging.

Frederick calmly grabbed her shoulders, looking straight into her eyes, and spoke as plainly as possible.

"Alaya, when you were a little girl, your mother and I noticed that you never seemed to hurt yourself. Not so much as a scratch. You rarely cried. We took you to the doctor and they diagnosed you with something called congenital analgesia, which is a condition that doesn't allow you to feel pain. It is extremely rare in our world, but it is not so rare here in Batunia. There's more: you can heal wounds with the power of your mind, although we didn't get that diagnosis from a doctor. Instead, we realized it through observations, like the night with your mother's elbow. I had figured that much out early on in your life, but I had to find more answers. My research led me to some very strange places and introduced me to some even stranger people, one of whom was Mr. Miller. You are the reason why I came back here to Batunia so frequently, sometimes without telling Mr. Miller."

"Okay, and you're telling me all this because...?" she asked, although she could already feel the last tumbler about to fall into place to unlock the secret.

"What I am saying, my dear, is that you are not an alien...Alaya, you are a Ramajian."

CHAPTER 26

laya was confused and out of sorts. Could any of this really be happening? Although she had heard about Ramajians, none of this made any real sense. Was her father projecting her into a character in one of his made up stories? Was all of this, in fact, a magnificently constructed fantasy because she could not face the horrible truth that her father was actually dead? Alaya was drowning in these uncertain waters.

Or, what if this *was* real? Were there other Ramajians back home or was she the last of her kind? Alaya thought about it. *There had to be others.* Otherwise, why would Mr. Miller have created this whole charade? Or had Alaya only imagined him too...?

"Wake up...wake up!" Alaya began to say. She even pinched herself a few times. "Mr. Miller, I'm ready to get out of here!" she said and rushed to her bag to find the troudare.

"You aren't dreaming, Alaya, this is all quite real, I assure you. I can only imagine how overwhelming all of this must be for you. Why don't we talk to Mr. Miller...perhaps we should see what he says."

Frederick activated the troudare after pulling it from her bag. She was in a mild state of shock; she couldn't have resisted him if she wanted to. Mr. Miller's face appeared moments later in the small orb.

"Hello, old friend!" Frederick said. "It's wonderful to see you again!"

"Ah, Frederick! I knew it!" Mr. Miller said, cheerful as ever. He didn't seem nearly as shocked as she would have expected. "I knew that she would find you. I'm assuming that you are still in Batunia, yes? I should expect to be seeing you two quite soon then, I hope?"

"Listen, Mr. Miller…uh…Matthias. I have a favor to ask. I know that we have a great deal to catch up on, but something has come up. Alaya has just learned that she is a Ramajian, and—as I expected—she is having a hard time with it. I never expected any of this to happen, but if the truth ever came out, I knew that it would be difficult for her to accept. Would you mind telling her a bit more? Perhaps about Velda?"

"Wow…things have certainly developed quickly. Are you there, Alaya?" Mr. Miller looked like he was craning his neck to see her.

Frederick handed the troudare over to his daughter so she was staring directly into Mr. Miller's face. "Yes, I'm here. Nice to see you again, Mr. Miller."

"Glad to see that you are still alive and well. There is no reason to mince words, so here goes. When you came to interview for the job at the antique store, I hired you for more than the obvious reasons."

She shrugged her shoulders. "Such as?"

"Well, your father may have told you already, but that necklace belonged to Velda. She was one of the most powerful Ramajians in the history of Batunia. Frederick may not have had much research on her, and rightly so. She kept to herself for most of her life. I was among the fortunate few who could call her a friend."

Alaya leaned forward, finally getting the information she wanted.

"Velda came to my family when I was still small, just a boy of eight or nine. My parents were never terribly wealthy, but things were getting worse for everyone. It was becoming more difficult for my father to support the family and my mother. She had become bedridden early on in her pregnancy with my younger brother, and was far too weak to do anything most of the time. Without the extra help, my father struggled to keep us fed and cared for. One night, a stranger showed up on our doorstep. She was a beautiful woman with dark skin and long dreadlocks, though she appeared weary and abject. She said that her name was Velda, but she needed no introduction. We instantly recognized her as the former Queen.

"Apparently, she had become homeless and had been going door to door, looking for work. Ogapallos II had put an order out for her execution and she needed a place to stay. No one wanted to take her in, because that would have constituted high treason against the king. The particulars of her exile were unknown, but did it matter? Treason by one is treason by all. But there was a silver lining. She knew that those who lived outside the borders of Batunia were not very fond of the King and she had no other choice.

"Velda told us that she could clean, take care of children, teach, or do anything else we needed to earn a place to stay. My family was not usually one for pawning work off to a nanny, but the price she asked was practically nothing, and my mother and father took pity on Velda. She helped my father with the crops and harvesting, while also teaching me basic things like reading and writing. She cared for my mother, and assisted her throughout the pregnancy. She was willing to do all of that for no more than food and shelter, but my parents refused to have her work without some additional pay. Each of us in the family developed a unique bond with Velda; she became a part of our family.

"She typically kept to herself, but along with the money from my family, we helped her build a small home deep in the woods made of something called lichten wood. Velda said that she had discovered it in her father's hometown in Silandria, but I never believed it. Silandria wasn't too far away, yet I had never before seen wood that was practically invisible. The only time it appears fully solid is when the glow of a full moon hits. For that, and many other reasons, some began to think of Velda as someone to be stared at from a distance—a circus freak. Over time, they wanted nothing to do with her. So naturally, outside the walls of our home, she remained a very private person.

"Although my family didn't want her to leave our house, Velda said that it would be best if she didn't come around too often. Townspeople began to whisper about her and made up tales, considering her to be some sort of witch. Some even believed that she was a Neya Woman, while many others thought she was something far more dangerous. Many believed that this was why King Ogapallos II wanted her killed, but none of it was true. It actually couldn't have been any further from the truth.

"Velda was caring, loving, and best of all, she had the wonderful gift of healing—she was a Ramajian. Velda later told me that without the mercy of my parents, she probably wouldn't have survived. But the feeling was mutual. We all knew that without her, my mother wouldn't have survived. However, as you may have guessed, healing was not her only power. She was much more than a healer.

"Since I had the good fortune of being in my parents' home when they welcomed her in, I was able to witness many of her talents firsthand. After Velda finished helping my mother with chores around the house, she would teach me things, much the way a governess taught children in the Victorian era. However, she often went beyond our basic lessons of reading, writing, and arithmetic. She also taught me about people…she told me about life.

"Velda and the King had been married for the few years after I was born, but it lasted a very short time. It was an odd thing for a woman to marry so young; she couldn't have been a day over fifteen, but he had a weakness for beautiful women. We are certain he didn't know that she was a Ramajian. At least, not right away. I don't blame her for trying to hide the truth, but once he found out, he demanded that she bear him a child. The King wanted his bloodline to not only be royalty, but to also possess the mystical powers of the Ramajians as well. Unfortunately, she was never able to become pregnant; many believed her to be barren. Perhaps this was by some sort of unknown design of the Soranayum, who we believe created her. But, I never got a chance to ask Velda about her parents.

"Despite her inability to become pregnant, King Ogapallos was not deterred. He desperately wanted to take advantage of her powers in some way and refused to give up so easily. So he ordered her to find a way to transfer her powers to him. I have never heard of this sort of thing, and perhaps he hadn't either, but he believed that it could be done. He said that many of his leading thinkers, today's equivalent of scientists, had documented evidence that it was possible. I still don't believe that any of it was ever true.

"So what happened?" Alaya asked.

"She told him that it couldn't be done so he banished her from the palace and kept her locked away in the dungeon with other forgotten prisoners. Her sentence was to stay there until she found a way to share her power with him. If not, then he was prepared to let her rot. In the meantime, he remarried. This is when the rumors of his connection with the

Neya Men began swirling throughout the Kingdom. In his blind obsession with Velda's power, he went in search of others with obscure talents. Day and night for two years, although Velda tried to extract her powers, she was unable to do it. It felt as though they were attached to her very soul, and without them, she would also cease to exist. She endured beatings and constant threats of death, but it was impossible.

"There was a young, inexperienced guard who developed a soft spot for Velda. He saw how cruel she had been treated and wanted to help. They developed something of a friendship through the dungeon walls, although they never spoke. He only came in to offer her food and a basin of water to wash up in once a week. After a few months, he would enter her room and open a tiny window near the ceiling. He sometimes left it open all day and night so that she could smell the fresh air of the changing seasons, and feel the sun's rays on her skin. Soon, he started bringing her extra leftovers from meals served above, in the palace. Though he did all this, he never spoke a word to her.

"One night, after all the other guards were sleep, he was on skeleton duty and opened her door to hand her a meal. Unlike every other night, he turned to leave. But this time was different. He didn't lock the cell behind him. Velda carefully walked to the open door and looked up at him, but he only nodded.

"Just like that," Mr. Miller snapped his fingers, "this young man had facilitated her escape. He guided her out of the dungeons and beyond the walls of the city. The night air was chilly since it was winter, but Velda didn't care. She did not know his name, or why he did it, but she was eternally grateful. When they parted, she stopped to look back at the city and back at him, one last time. She wanted to thank him, so she took a step forward. That was when he finally spoke, but it was an admonition, not an acceptance of gratitude.

"'Go far from here. Deep into the woods. He will not stop searching for you until he has your head on a stick.' He said nothing more, and then turned his back and closed the small gate through which they had escaped.

"That's wild," Alaya said.

"She did exactly as he had told her, and a few nights later, we heard that fateful knock on our door. Soon afterward, we learned that Ogapallos II had that young guard executed. Such a tragedy."

Alaya flinched. She could almost see it happening in real time. She looked over at her father, but Frederick was looking out the window, lost in thought. Yet, she knew he was listening. The sun had set, but there was still a pink glow hanging on the horizon. In the distance, the moon was already gleaming on the dark world. It would be full soon.

"After her escape, Velda was hunted by King Ogapallos, right until the very end. It was a shame. From what my parents told me, Ramajians were once highly respected individuals in the community, but if history has taught us a single lesson, it is that time and time again, things inevitably change. By this point, most Ramajians had fled due to the massive hunt from both the King and others who had followed the king's example and chased them out of the kingdom. At the same time, the Neya Men began to grow in numbers.

"Velda was the last Ramajian who remained in Batunia. She often told me that her powers were both a blessing and a curse, but I saw nothing but blessings in abundanace. She never caused anyone or anything harm. I watched as she made flowers bloom in winter simply by singing. I have seen her make a plea to the clouds for rainfall, but then later implore the sun to shine all the next day for us to enjoy. She did these things so effortlessly, selflessly, and I still wouldn't believe it if I had not witnessed such things with my own eyes. It was like something out of a Disney movie.

"When I was 12 years old, Velda told me that I was no longer going to be taught by her. Obviously, I was devastated. She only said she had to go away for a while, until things got better in Batunia. Only, they never did. As a matter of fact, things became much worse.

"The years passed, and the cruelty of Ogapallos II only seemed to grow. My younger brother, Fendrel, began to take a more sympathetic view toward the King, which was strictly against my parents' wishes. He started attending meetings and demonstrations in favor of the King's actions, and then he made the decision to join the Royal Guard when he came of age. Eventually, he became a member of the King's Riders. My parents were in denial; after all, how could he want to do such a thing? We had all seen early on what the King was capable of and none of us wanted to support it, nor be part of his tyranny. My parents feared for Fendrel's safety, and cried every night for him to return. I, on the other hand, dedicated myself to bringing him back. I hoped that he would return to his senses.

"However; after a few years, I met Belina. Once she came into my life, I began to distance myself from Fendrel. She was Velda's younger sister and the same age as me. I knew her as a child growing up, but it wasn't until Velda's disappearance that we became close. Their kinship was unknown to most, since Velda's family didn't exactly embrace her—not after what had happened. Her family thought that making such knowledge public would cause too much trouble, so they refused to let her stay with them. They were a proud family from Silandria, with strong ties to Batunia's royalty. They didn't want their family name besmirched by the controversy their daughter had caused when she escaped the King's palace."

"So what happened to Velda after that?" Alaya asked. "If she fled the kingdom, then how do you even know that she died?"

Matthias paused, and a flash of pain skipped across his brow. "Because I was there when it happened."

CHAPTER 27

laya couldn't take her eyes off Mr. Miller, but he turned away from the troudare. It seemed as though it took every ounce of his mind to wrestle back the wave of emotions that had begun to surface. Even though this had happened many years ago, some wounds would always remain raw.

Finally, when Mr. Miller spoke again, he sounded rejuvenated. Perhaps talking helped him process through the painful feelings that he kept locked away for so long.

"Many years later, Belina and I were newlyweds when Velda returned. She looked very much the same, if only a bit wiser and hardened by the road. It was Belina who told me that her sister had finally come back to Batunia. She refused to meet her or seek her out, for fear of jeopardizing her family's secret, but I immediately went to see Velda at her old house in the woods. It was difficult to find at first in the direct sunlight, but I still remembered how to find it, even after all that time. When I arrived, Velda was huddled in a chair with a blanket wrapped around her, although I remember that the room had been well warmed by the fireplace. She said that she didn't have much time, but that she wanted to tell me a story."

"A story?" Alaya asked.

"Yes, her words were a surprise to me as well. It had been fifteen years since we last spoke, so that was hardly what I expected to hear. But, she held a book in her lap. It was shabby and frayed at the edges. She said that it was her journal. I had it here in the store all these years, but it seems to have recently gotten up and walked away," Mr. Miller said, looking around the basement as though he had just dropped it and would be able to spy it from his seat.

Alaya squirmed in her chair. She immediately felt herself becoming flushed as she thought of that green journal in her sack. *Did Mr. Miller know that she took it?*

Perhaps not. He continued on as if he hadn't noticed Alaya's discomfort.

"Velda wrote down the accounts of her travels, but she also told me things. She told me that she was the last surviving member of the Ramajians in Batunia...perhaps in the entire world. While she was away, Velda had searched for others like herself, but the quest was fruitless. In spite of that apparent failure, one part of her trip was successful. She had found a way to separate her power from her soul, and she wanted me to keep it."

"How did she manage to do that?" Alaya asked.

"I don't know...I couldn't believe it was possible. And to think, she only entrusted it to me. Not to her parents, or to a trusted friend, but to her young student from years past. Belina was as delicate as paper and Velda knew she would crumble under the lightest of storms. She was not a Ramajian; and was quite grateful for that fact.

"I asked Velda why she was telling me this, which was when she removed the blanket. That is when I saw it. They had found her after all. Some coward had decided to take her life in the name of the King. She never told me who was responsible, or how she got away.

"While attempting to rise from her chair, Velda stumbled to the ground. I pulled aside her dark robes, which were soaked through in blood. A large gash ripped across her stomach and there was a spreading puddle of blood beneath the chair. It was everywhere and there was nothing I could do to stop it. There, right before my eyes, Velda was dying. I told her, as though she had forgotten, 'You can heal yourself!' She said that it was too late, even if she wanted to. She told me that this was going to be the end for her.

"It was hard to believe, and I still didn't understand why she was giving up. As a Ramajian, she should have been able to do something to stop the flow of blood. She shouldn't have felt as much pain as I could see twisting her face. But it was no use. With her dying breaths, Velda explained that when she separated her power from her soul, she lost the ability to heal. Her Ramajian magic was gone, and she would soon die.

"In that horrific moment, I heard voices rapidly approaching from outside her hut. It was the King's guards and they were led by a familiar voice. Painfully familiar, in fact. That was when I saw my brother, Fendrel — the leader of the search party. They began calling for her to come out and show herself. They heard rumors that she was back in town and wanted to see for themselves. At this point, Velda quickly clasped my hand. 'They're coming closer, Matthias. You must return here as soon as they leave. I have hidden my power away and you must take it. Now go! Run!' and she pushed me toward the small door at the rear of her cottage.

"I ran as far and as fast as my terrified legs would take me. I didn't want to leave her, but I knew that there were a dozen men, and I was nowhere near a match for them. That moment was doubly painful; I knew that my brother was too far under the lies of the king to have mercy on me. I was forced to admit that he had gone mad with power and had been blinded by years of serving Ogapallos II.

"Thankfully, the darkness enveloped me, concealing me within the shadows beyond their sight. But the shadows were not enough for Velda. After I had reached a safe distance, I watched in horror as they descended upon her home to finish the job. I felt powerless as I watched the men moving in her house; my imagination conjured up nightmarish scenes of what could be happening. Eventually, I couldn't bear it any longer and I turned away. I never heard a single scream from her mouth. She had welcomed death with open arms. I am sure that those beasts had tortured her, or perhaps they had been eager to deliver the last, fatal blows on behalf of their King. The horror lasted but a few minutes. Then, exiting her home with a cruel laughter ringing through the forest, they left.

"I snuck back inside a few minutes later, once I was sure that they had gone, only to find that it was almost unrecognizable. The neat home that had been inside only moments prior, was now destroyed. I moved cracked wooden planks, stepped through broken glass shards, gently overturned pieces of furniture, and carefully navigated around the rubble to find her body. She had been bloodied, beaten, and broken, but her eyes were still open, haunting and defenseless. She was staring up at me in a pleading mask of death, begging for justice. I may as well have been guilty of the murder myself. I felt that I had let her die. I told her that I was sorry and I closed her eyes, leaving her in eternal sleep.

"Remembering what she had told me, I searched through her house. In all the rubble, it was difficult to know where to begin looking. Besides, I had no idea *what* I was looking for exactly, so I just went from room to room. When I entered Velda's bedroom, I saw something glistening on the windowsill. It seemed to call out to me and as I wrapped my hands around it, it was warm to the touch, far warmer than the metal should have been. When I opened my hand, I saw that it was a key—the very key on that necklace you are wearing around your neck, Alaya." He pointed to her.

Alaya looked down at her chest, seeing the glittering key on her necklace with new eyes. "This belonged to her? But then how did my father get it? And what does it open?"

"I gave your father that key. And as for the other, more complicated question, we have one idea of what it opens. I can only assume that's why your father went back, right Frederick?"

Frederick finally turned away from the window and slowly nodded.

Mr. Miller continued, "I'm not even sure it really exists. It could have just been a legend for all we know."

"Not sure what existed?" Alaya asked.

"There are those that believe the key around your neck unlocks a chest that holds the power of the last Ramajian. Since Velda was so powerful, some believe that it provides the means for one to achieve immortality. That's what the key was supposed to keep locked away. That being said, it has never been proven that the powers of a Ramajian include such a thing. After Velda died, a great deal of attention turned to Belina. Her family had left Batunia years earlier, and Velda's death ended all chance of their safe return. My dear Belina had become afraid as well. Rumors flew that she had powers of her own. Whether intentionally withheld or unknown, latent talents, some who supported the King believed Belina was waiting for the right time to reveal her true self."

"Over time, Belina became fearful for her life. She often spoke of fleeing the kingdom, as though once we had left Batunia's walls, we would be free, but Ogapallos never stopped expanding his realm. For a time, it seemed that his reach was practically endless. After overthrowing the King of Silandria, our only hope was a small neighboring Kingdom to the south, known as Zodaire. It would have taken us two weeks to arrive. But she was several months pregnant, and a long journey through the wilderness simply wasn't feasible. Besides, even if we had made it, who could say whether our lives would have been any better?

"I tried to search for answers among Velda's things, but I barely found anything of interest. However, I was able to find proof Velda had found a way to transfer her powers. There was an old, crumbled piece of parchment buried deep beneath the rubble; it had likely been hidden beneath the floorboards. The letter turned out to be instructions that spoke of a secret weapon contained within a chest. But I never found the chest. I can only presume that the King's men had taken it. That's the most reasonable explanation we've been able to come up with. However, if the instructions were to be believed, then the chest has never been opened, because they would have needed that key hanging around your neck."

"That's incredible," Alaya said. As had become normal in recent days, her head swam with details.

"Indeed it was. But there was something else. Before she passed, Velda had given Belina a priceless gift. Her sister had bestowed upon her a single token. It was unlike any other type of currency throughout the kingdom, so naturally, we were unable to spend it. Velda never explained what it was to be used for, nor what its value was. She only told Belina to keep it with her at all times, and that if she ever needed to escape, that token would lead the way. Belina did not understand it back then, but when the time came, we finally knew what to do. There was only one token, which presumably meant that only one could escape. I told Belina that it should have been her, and that I would find a way to follow on, but she refused.

"A few weeks later, Belina came running to me from her post in the palace kitchen. Things had gotten so bad; she wanted to run away and begged for me to come with her. I was more than happy to, but we couldn't come up with a suitable destination. Besides, in her condition, it would have been tough. She was already showing her pregnancy, but said that it didn't matter. As long as we left Batunia behind us, it would surely lead to a new, happier life. She won me over; I was never able to refuse her wishes. We packed as much as we could, but then we heard them.

"The guards had followed us and we were trapped in our own home. Belina was to be punished for leaving her post. No one was allowed to do such a thing without permission from the head guard, or directly from the King himself. There was no negotiation, nor a trial. In those days, punishment meant that we were to be made an example of, as a way of deterring others from the same behavior. Our fate was already determined—execution by hanging. There was nothing else to do, so we took off running.

In hindsight, I'll admit that it was foolish, but we hardly had time to think. We fled out the back door and ran as fast as we could. As we ran, Belina told me why she couldn't stay in Batunia even one more day. Earlier that day, the guards had "punished" her best friend Aricela for dropping food on the rug in the main hall. When Belina saw guards dragging Aricela's limp body from the kitchen, Belina ran without thinking, not knowing where she was headed.

"Our attempted escape was futile, as I had feared it would be. The guards soon caught up to us and we were commanded to halt. We were surrounded. I shivered at the thought of what they might do to my wife, as well as our unborn child. I swung around; attempting to shield Belina with my body, but it was useless. I had no weapons and I barely knew how to throw a punch, let alone how to take on a small army. All the same, Belina never let go of my hands. She clutched my fingers so hard that I could feel the fear coursing through her short, jagged nails as she pressed them into my skin. Then I heard her say something very softly. She whispered to me, if I can remember correctly, 'forgive me if this fails.' Then, Belina shouted, 'take us away from here, as far away as possible!'

"The next thing I knew, I woke up in a park that was surrounded by lights in a strange, new world. Belina was by my side, and I could feel her nails still digging into my skin. Her eyes were closed so I gently kissed her, and she opened them."

Alaya had to ask a couple of burning questions. "That's unbelievable, Mr. Miller. So why didn't you just return to Batunia with Dad? Once you had the machine, you two could have searched for the chest together."

"Two months after we arrived in your world, Belina died in childbirth and I lost my son. After that, I wanted nothing to do with Batunia. It had taken everything from me. I wanted nothing more than to start a new life, so I got a job at this store. The owner and I developed a close relationship. So when he passed, he left the store to me. When I met your father, I instantly knew he was a very clever man and had a hunger for the unknown. Once we became acquainted, after the sharing of many secrets I had buried in my heart, we invented the machine. I am sad to see that things have certainly not changed for the better in Batunia. So in short, I have no desire to return, Alaya. *This* is my home now." Once he was done speaking, Mr. Miller looked weary and tired, quite unlike his usual self.

Frederick walked behind his daughter and picked up the troudare.

"Thank you Matthias. Sorry to have taken up so much of your time. I know that it's getting late. We will speak again soon."

They said their goodbyes and the troudare went dark.

"Just a few more minutes, Alaya. That's all I need. After that, you are free to go back home, if that's what you want. We can make our way back to the machine and you can forget all about this — forever," Frederick said.

Alaya noticed that her father had said nothing about returning with her. She had no choice but to hear him out; she certainly owed him a few minutes.

"Okay, let's hear it," she said, preparing herself for the worst. After hearing Mr. Miller's story, she was open to just about anything.

"You know," Frederick began, "believe it or not, I didn't understand any of this either at first."

He began to pace around the room, grasping for the right words.

"It's just...Alaya, answer me this: Have you ever wondered if there was something more to it? To all of those 'special cases', as doctors like to call it? I don't mean your case of 'congenital analgesia', but other things. What about autism, dwarfism, and all those medical 'abnormalities' that science clings to in order to explain the world? What if everyone had a purpose? What if no one was 'wrong'? What if those conditions are just outside the comprehension of our limited perspective?" Frederick asked, sounding more philosophical than she could ever remember him being.

This was hardly a subject that she had given any thought to, so what did he expect her to say? She simply observed him pacing up and down the room like a madman, like someone who was desperately clinging by fingertips on the cliff of reality, slipping with each digit.

Frederick continued, attempting to explain himself further.

"Your mother always said you were special, that perhaps you had some sort of gene that allowed you to heal much faster than other people. I suppose that could have been true, so I agreed, but I never stopped wondering if there was more to it. It didn't explain why certain…other things happened and I needed answers. I wanted to know what was going on with my daughter."

"Wait…what other things?" Alaya asked.

Frederick stopped pacing. "Things that just didn't make sense. At least, not until I came here. That was when everything began to fall into place." He leaned down to her level and looked directly in her eyes.

"There are answers, Alaya, but only if you want them. At home, in the attic, is where I kept most of my early research on the Ramajians. Do you remember when I would read some of it to you? They were only bedtime stories to you, but in fact, they were very real. I didn't know nearly as much as I do now, but there is more to it than even Matthias is aware."

Alaya slowly nodded. She thought back to those hazy memories of her father reading to her from those papers. She had always thought of them as fairytales, like *Cinderella* and *Hansel and Gretel*, but she had been mistaken. They were the tales of Batunia's history…of other Ramajians like her.

"I remember, Dad. I even brought some of them with me. But what does he not know?" Alaya asked, worried about secrets being kept between Mr. Miller and her father.

"It's about the chest. Matthias, as well as many others in Batunia, believe that it holds the secret of immortality, but I have reason to believe that it contains something else entirely. I didn't mention this to Matthias just yet, because I'll need more time to work out some of the details, but I plan on telling him about it soon.

"Since I've been here in Batunia, I've discovered that there is a very powerful talisman that might be the answer to all of our problems. It is called the Orb of Shoraiva, and it is what Velda was trying to find before she was killed. If what Velda and I both think is true, then the orb is the only way to destroy the Neya Men. Like Matthias said, she had the key to open the chest, but someone must have found out and stopped her before she had a chance to find the chest and open it."

"But what is the Orb of Shoraiva?" Alaya asked.

"Right…sorry. I'm getting ahead of myself! Let me back up a bit. You have heard the story of the Soranayum?"

Alaya nodded. "Yes, Whalen told me about it when he took me to see the statues."

"Well, after Sadenia granted the Neya Men their talents, she almost immediately realized what a terrible mistake she had made. With her sisters' help, they came up with a way to destroy them. Unfortunately, they had to use dark, forbidden magic to forge the Shoraiva, which is why they were turned to stone. As higher beings, that was the price they had to pay."

"But what does this have to do with us? Why are we even involved?" Alaya asked.

"What you saw earlier today, with Shahara, was a soul-consumption ceremony. Very few in Batunia have ever seen this happen up close and lived to tell of it, but I have interviewed some who have witnessed it firsthand. What you described was almost exactly the same as the others: the fire, the smoke, the feast, and the return of the victim as some sort of zombie, for lack of a better word. The Neya Men drink human souls in their bid for immortality. Not all of them have fallen so far into evil, but the worst among them do, which stops them from aging. Since no one ever stands up against the Neya Men, it effectively means that the problem of the Neya Men will *never* be solved. If they continue unchecked, they could destroy every soul in this kingdom…and it wouldn't stop there. Their plague would spread without limit. We have to stop them, Alaya, but only a Ramajian can activate the orb."

Alaya had begun to involuntarily shake her head in disbelief as her father grabbed both of her hands.

"Listen, Alaya…remember when you told me that you believed this necklace was a good luck charm? It doesn't sound silly to me at all. The key likely has special properties that only you can sense, ones that have always hinted that it may contain some sort of power. Do you see those jewels around the key?"

Alaya looked down at the key on the chain. The jewels glimmered as she moved the key around in the candlelight which illuminated the room.

"I believe that parts of this key were actually forged from the Shoraiva. Through her years of travels, I believe Velda found the Orb, but she must have known that she was being hunted. So she created the key and placed the Orb in the chest until the time was right for the two to be rejoined. Alaya, you were meant to unlock that chest."

"There must be someone else who can do this. Don't you want to go home and get away from this place?" she begged, but she already knew that it was futile. Her father's mind had been made up a long time ago.

"It makes sense, doesn't it? Alaya, the Soranayum would only have trusted the Ramajians to destroy the Neya Men, because a Ramajian would never seek to harm anyone with their power. They were treated with respect and compassion long ago, but it came with a cost. And Velda, she paid the ultimate price. That is why most of them fled. As

Matthias said, Velda's own family didn't want anything to do with her. Furthermore, even if there are others out there, how could we possibly find them and convince them to do this? They will have successfully been in hiding for years, even decades. Do you see any other options?"

Alaya withdrew her hands from her father's grip and folded them across her chest. She was out of ideas, but she wasn't quite ready to concede defeat. "So what you're really saying is, I have a connection to Velda?" Alaya asked. "How is that possible?"

"The truth is, I haven't quite figured that part out yet." Frederick softened toward his daughter.

"Look, Alaya, you may not be happy about it, but this is where we stand. There's something else you must know. As a Ramajian, you cannot physically hurt anyone. I know that you want to learn how to fight, but you cannot. It's for your own safety."

"That's ridiculous," Alaya scoffed. "What do you mean I can't hurt anyone? I seriously doubt that. Besides, I can't feel pain, so what's the problem here? It sounds like an ideal combination, actually," Alaya said dismissively.

"Okay, try to hit me, Alaya. Go ahead," Frederick said. He stood up, motioning for her to do the same.

"Dad, I can--"

"Alaya! Just hit me! Or, at least try to," he practically mocked.

Alaya let out a deep sigh. She knew that it was futile to try and back out of this; he was as stubborn as she was. Obliging him, she balled her right hand into a fist, and aimed it square at her father's stomach. Once he nodded in approval, she drew back her arm and hit him as hard as she could.

Instead of Frederick reacting, however, Alaya collapsed on her back. The wind had been knocked clear out of her chest. She writhed on the ground, and for a moment, she couldn't even speak. Alaya was terrified; it felt like she couldn't breathe. It was the first time that she had ever felt such a sensation. *So this is pain...*

"Unnnggggghhhh!" she moaned, still keeled over on her side. A few more moments passed before she was finally able to speak.

"Why did that happen?" Alaya tottered to her feet and back into the chair, clutching her belly. She drew her legs up and pressed her knees to her chest, which seemed to help diminish the nauseating feeling swirling in her stomach.

"I am sorry that you had to find out like this, but I've noticed that you tend to trust your eyes more than your ears." Her father knelt down next to her.

"That is perhaps the one flaw of Ramajians. You may heal quickly when others hurt you, but you are unable to harm *anyone*, no matter how hard you try. Like I said, it is against the very essence of your nature. Some believe that the Soranayum created Ramajians to be protectors over the people of this world, rather than destroyers. I don't know if that is true, but you will never be able to hurt anyone physically without harming yourself first. I didn't feel a thing," Frederick said. "It's as though your fist stopped a hair's breadth away from my body."

Alaya thought hard about all of this. She had killed bugs more times than she could count, and she had stepped on her cat's tail a few times when she was a little girl. All of those things had happened without a reaction; a giant hand hadn't swatted her into the ground like a fly. Granted, she had never been in a fistfight before, and she had never felt a desire to physically hurt anyone. As an only child, even sibling squabbles and the occasional tussle hadn't been part of her development.

"Again, I am sorry, Alaya. I just want you to be fully prepared for what this means," Frederick explained.

"I get it," Alaya said, slowly straightening up now that she had begun to feel normal again. "Basically, whatever is in that chest is very bad news for the Neya Men."

Her father nodded solemnly.

"And you think that it actually contains the Orb of Shoraiva, which has the power to destroy them, but it's up to me to open it?"

"Precisely. I believe that the Neya Men are keeping the chest somewhere, because they know that it is the only thing that can actually *stop* them. The most likely place to keep it would be where it could be best protected — their lair."

Alaya sighed. *Of course they have a lair,* she thought. "So what happens now?"

"The only thing left to do. We go and stop them." Frederick answered confidently, but she could hear the slightest twinge of uncertainty in the depths of his voice.

CHAPTER 28

As a little girl, Alaya loved fantasy. The idea of faraway, magical lands occupied much of her imagination. She often dreamed of kingdoms where princesses were rescued from fire-breathing dragons to live happily ever after with their handsome heroes.

However, once her father went missing, everything came to a crushing halt. Instead, she became drawn to the truth of reality, along with the shadows that occasionally come along with it. Horror and psychological thrillers soon became her only source of comfort. Zombie survival movies were her favorite subgenre.

It wasn't until Alaya seriously considered all that she had heard from both Mr. Miller and her father that she made up her mind. She finally realized what purpose her strange fascination had really served. It had done far more to prepare her for what she was about to face than any happy ending fairytale could have ever done.

That night, Alaya tossed and turned in bed. It didn't help that the frame was creaky and the room felt cold beyond measure. Her nerves were stripped bare from worry. She lay there looking out the window, wondering what the next few days might bring. How could she face the Neya Men and expect to survive?

Alaya awoke the next morning to the smell of her father making breakfast. The sun had crept rather high in the sky, but she felt like she had barely slept. Her blankets were tangled and tossed halfway onto the floor and her hair tie had come out, leaving her hair a wild, knotty mess. It had been a rough night.

The smell grew stronger once Alaya swung her legs out of bed. As far as she remembered, her father had never been one for cooking. In fact, he despised it. But after surviving for seven years on his own, he had apparently found a hidden calling — it smelled delicious.

Turns out, he was making scrambled eggs. Alaya wondered for a moment what animal they may have come from; but then decided it didn't matter.

"That smells wonderful, Dad," she said, still feeling groggy.

"Cratine eggs," Frederick said, bending down to take a whiff of the scent. "They taste just like chicken." He said with a smile of contentment.

"Cratine huh?" Alaya raised an eyebrow. "You know what? I don't even care. I'm starving."

"How'd you sleep?" Frederick asked. He looked somewhat concerned, as though he could already tell how rough of a night it was by her tousled appearance. "I hope last night didn't scare you too much. I know it was a lot to take in so quickly. I can't imagine what you must be thinking."

"It's okay, really. It was obviously a bit of a shock at first, but I'm fine." She said, and she was right. She was surprised herself by how well she was taking these new revelations.

Frederick scooped the eggs onto a plate and they sat down to eat.

"You will have help, Alaya. We have the Warrior's Council, perhaps Nikolai and Whalen told you about it. After Nikolai left the Royal Guard, he began secretly gathering likeminded people to join him. It is meant to help the people of Batunia, much the same way that police protect citizens back in our world."

"Why was Nikolai part of the Royal Guard? They don't sound all that great." Alaya questioned.

"It seems that there is little choice in the matter. Once a young man turns twenty-one, he must serve the King in some capacity for ten years. It's a way for the King to maintain absolute control and inspire loyalty. If you wanted your family to eat relatively well, then you became a member of the Guard. Some choose to stay after their ten-year mandate to continue providing for their family, but it began to wear on Nikolai. After fifteen years of service, he left."

Alaya thought back to when Hava and Max had been talking about school. This must have been how Nikolai had been able to afford to send Hava.

"So Nikolai was able to leave that easily?" Alaya asked.

"No. I suspect that is how Nikolai lost his eye, but he doesn't talk about it," her father replied.

"That's terrible. I had no idea…" Alaya instantly felt guilty; she knew that she had consciously stopped herself from staring on more than one occasion.

"It's actually for the best. Nikolai is very discreet and always kept to himself – even back then. What's more, he has vast insider knowledge. He knows things about King Negash that few others do. For example, we believe that his Sage, the right hand man of the king, is actually King Ogapallos II."

"Really?" she asked. "But I thought he was dead."
She shook her head in wonder; Batunia was more
unpredictable than the soap operas Janice watched.

"True. Many believed that he was killed shortly after
Velda's murder, but a body was never found. We think he is
secretly still leading, influencing King Negash like a puppet."
Frederick stuffed the last of the eggs into his mouth.

"But no matter. We have work to do, and the Council
will join us. We have about twenty members now: Myself,
Whalen, Nikolai, Hava, and a number of others that you
haven't met. They are all good, but not all have been as well
trained as I would like. It seems Hava has done fairly well,
but I think she may have had other reasons for joining."

"I think you're right about that." Alaya said. She had
a pretty good idea it had something to do with Whalen.

Frederick continued. "A few of our best will
accompany you into the Neya Men's lair, but you must
know — this is not going to be easy."

"I understand," Alaya said, "but I feel better
knowing that you will be with me."

There was a knock on the door, and they both
jumped, as though the enemy heard every word. Alaya was
surprised to see Frederick's nerves were also on edge,
although he tried his best to hide that fact.

"That must be Whalen. Perfect timing."

"What are you going to tell him?" she asked, a note
of doubt creeping into her voice.

"Don't worry, Alaya. It will be much easier this time.
I won't have to slice my hand open again to prove a point."
He smirked and she returned the grin.

"Okay…just checking." She said.

***

Ten minutes later, Whalen knew that Alaya was a Ramajian, although it didn't seem to surprise him. Alaya thought this to be curious.

"I knew it," he said matter-of-factly, turning down breakfast that Frederick offered.

"How?" Alaya asked, not wanting to be the only person who hadn't known.

"Your resemblance to Velda. Think about all those stares you get, Alaya. People probably think that Velda has risen from the dead, and I don't blame them."

"That's ridiculous," she quipped. "Dad, what do you think?"

"I can certainly see it. I've been to the Circle of Soranayum many times. It makes sense, but the hair doesn't match up!" he joked, tousling Alaya's wild curls. "Willemina thought so too, but she didn't want to scare you — what with the amnesia and all." He smiled, and then turned to Whalen.

"I need to ask a favor. There are a few things that I must do to prepare us for the journey, but would you mind taking Alaya to the Iskinders? I think that it's time she had a talk with Nikolai. He's been waiting for a chance to tell her more about the Council. I will join all of you shortly."

"It would be my pleasure," Whalen said.

"I know that I don't need to tell you this, but be careful," he said in his fatherly tone. Even after all these years, it had come back to him quite naturally.

"You too, teacher. It will be a full moon tonight." Whalen cautioned.

"Don't worry about me, Whalen. I will join you long before nightfall."

CHAPTER 29

Back home, Alaya always had a terrible sense of direction, and relied on GPS navigation systems to the point where she could get lost in a paper bag. However, in Batunia, there was no choice but to learn the old-fashioned way, which required a basic awareness of one's surroundings and landmarks. She and Whalen soon passed the tree where she saw the lufaiyas on her first night. A little further up, she saw the large mound where the machine still remained buried.

"Alaya," Whalen spoke, disturbing her reverie. "Do you see that?"

She looked around, not really sure what she should have seen. The woods had grown thicker the further they walked. There were now thin slivers of light slicing through the thick clusters of leaves overhead. It must have been nearly noon.

Suddenly, they both heard ruffling from a nearby bush at the same time. Alaya spun on her heels and saw a rabbit dart out across their path.

"Is that what you were so afraid of?" Alaya asked, pretending she wasn't jumpy herself.

They both broke into gentle laughter and resumed walking in the warm afternoon.

Before they had taken another five steps, the ruffling in the leaves had started again, only louder. This time, Alaya knew it couldn't have just been another rabbit.

"Well, well...look at this. What a beautiful sight," a strange man said as he boldly emerged from behind a thick tree.

"Who are you?" Alaya asked. "What do you want?"

The man said nothing but took another confident step closer.

"Alaya, get behind me," Whalen said. His eyes were keenly studying the newcomer.

The man took a swig of amber-colored liquid from a glass bottle that hung from between his fingers.

"Oh! Could it really be?" he paused, momentarily looking as though he might be sick, and then let out a loud belch. "How have you been, boy?"

Whalen spoke through gritted teeth. "Alaya, this is my uncle, Grommet Travinian."

Once Grommet was a bit over a foot away, he stopped and closed his eyes, then leaned forward. He took in a deep whiff of Alaya's scent like he was sampling a perfume in a department store.

"Mmmm...you smell as delicious as you look."

Grommet leaned forward and stretched out his hands, in a slimy attempt to greet Alaya. Although, he had far less finesse than she'd hoped. Almost immediately, she recoiled in horror.

Though he was still inches away, the foul, sharp smell of alcohol was enough to knock Alaya sideways. Grommet licked his lips, as though he was about to partake in a seven-course meal after days without food. Apparently, he liked a challenge.

Reaching out, Grommet began touching Alaya's hair, wrapping a single curl around his finger. She slowly took a step back as he reached for her shoulder and she slapped his hand away.

"Uncle, that's enough--" Whalen began, and stepped forward to get between them.

Before the words had even left Whalen's mouth, Grommet spun on his heel and crashed the alcohol-filled bottle onto his nephew's head. Whalen crumbled into a pile of leaves, knocked out cold.

"How dare you interrupt me? You should know better than that, boy. Or maybe not," Grommet stumbled and nearly lost his footing, but he was persistent. "Your parents passed before you had the chance to learn some manners, I suppose." He hardly seemed aware that Whalen was unconscious.

Grommet lunged forward again, and Alaya jerked back, doing her best to dodge his advances. Despite being so intoxicated, Grommet had excellent reflexes. Although he missed her body, Grommet had caught Alaya by the back of her hair. He swung her around and clutched her from behind. Once more, he inhaled sharply; his nose hairs tickled the side of her neck. Alaya fought back the urge to vomit as the heavy mixture of body odor and alcohol drowned out everything else around her.

From somewhere deep inside, Alaya began to feel a new courage muster up.

"Let me go!" Alaya said and struggled to push the man away, but it was no use. She was terrified and her heart was rapping against her ribs so fast; she thought it might burst. All she wanted was for him to take his hands off her, but rather than let go, his grip tightened.

"Stop it, please!" Alaya writhed and screamed, twisting the man's arm as she fought for freedom. She bit down hard on the man's forearm, but rather than releasing her, she felt a searing pain scald her own forearm. Suddenly she remembered. *Right, it doesn't work this way.*

Grommet laughed and tossed her to the ground.

"Just what do you think you're doing, little girl?" He kissed her cheek, and his hands began roaming. "You know what I would love to do to you?"

Alaya certainly didn't want to wait and find out. She thrashed and spun her body until she was free, and then rushed over to Whalen's side. He still wasn't moving. She gently moved his hair to the side and immediately saw the wound. Blood stained her fingers as she stroked his temple. She didn't know how this was supposed to work, but she focused all of her energies into healing Whalen's wound. Much in the same way she had with her father's cut.

From behind her, Alaya heard the sound of jangling metal and the light thud of something hitting the ground. Grommet laughed as he tripped while trying to remove his pants and shoes all at once.

Unsure whether any of this was working, Alaya grew desperate. *Please...work!* She pleaded silently with whatever unseen force was supposedly inside of her. Minutes seemed to pass, although it was probably only seconds. Just when she thought that all hope was lost, Whalen's eyes flicked opened. The wound had begun to close and he moved to get up, but she held him down.

"Be careful," Alaya whispered and Whalen nodded, quickly understanding what had to be done.

Grommet was struggling to pull his shirt over his head when Whalen leapt to his feet. With a light foot, he snuck up on Grommet from behind.

The man cried out for assistance with his shirt halfway stuck over his head, caught on his chin. He stumbled back and forth, like a tree that was about to fall over. It was a mildly humorous sight, but the scene had little comedy.

Just then, Whalen pulled out a small knife and stalked his way forward until he was right behind his uncle. With a quick hand, he sliced a shallow line diagonally across Grommet's back.

"Ouch! What was that? Was that you, little girl?" Grommet said, making jerking movements with both arms raised, as though the shirt had become possessed. Whalen didn't speak, but kept his knife at the ready.

"Answer me! What was that?" he demanded, pain beginning to slip into his voice. He had successfully pulled his shirt back down over his head and he reached down for his pants.

"You'll pay for that, you little coward! Come here!" Grommet began to chase after Whalen.

"Alaya, let's go! We can outrun him!" Whalen shouted, and reached out for Alaya's hand.

"Oh yeah?" Grommet spun to see them already moving toward the underbrush. "Where do you think you are going?!" he shouted in rage. Blood had begun to soak through his shirt, but he didn't seem to notice.

Whalen and Alaya ran for several more minutes until Alaya's chest burned from heavy wheezing.

"Are you alright?" he asked, still grasping her hand tightly.

"Yes, of course," she said. "I think he's in far more pain than I am." She nodded in the direction of Whalen's uncle, who was stumbling through the underbrush some ways away, leaning on trees and rubbing blindly at his back. He looked all around, like he'd lost his traveling party.

Whalen only laughed, but stopped when he saw her arm. "Is your arm okay? Your father says that you heal quickly, but that looks terrible."

Alaya pulled her hair back into an elastic band and stretched out her arm. The teeth marks were still there, but they were already starting to fade.

"It doesn't work as well if I cause the pain, but I'll be okay," she said, still trying to catch her breath. "Do you think he'll catch up to us?" she asked, looking back toward the crashing of leaves and branches.

Whalen was silent. His facial expression was a mixture of anger and sorrow. He bent down, seemingly fascinated with a random tree branch. Alaya didn't know what to say. She couldn't imagine how he must have been feeling; he had never mentioned his uncle before.

"Has it been a long time?" she crouched down next to him. "Since you've seen him?"

"Not long enough." Whalen broke the tree branch in half and stood up straight.

"Well, I'm glad that you were there. I don't know what I would've done if I had been alone. I know he couldn't hurt me, but--"

"You are wrong, Alaya. There are other ways to hurt a woman." Whalen tossed the broken pieces of the branch far off into the distance. They heard Grommet lunge forward, towards the direction of the fallen branch pieces.

"I shouldn't have stayed for even a moment. I should have known that he would try something like that. And to think, he used to be a member of the Warrior's Council. Frederick tried to help him, but he chose his bottle over his friends. Now you've finally met him—the town drunkard. I swear, if he had—"

"Stop, Whalen. It's over. It does no good to beat yourself up like this," Alaya said, trying to sound comforting. "You can't control other people...only yourself."

"Look at this place, Alaya. I used to love it here," Whalen said, sounding almost disgusted. "You know, as a

232

kid, I used to climb these very trees. I could stay in them for hours without a care in the world." He looked up, and Alaya followed his eyes.

"But that's the problem now…nothing is safe or sacred anymore. My home is no longer safe, especially for someone like you." He locked eyes with her and she didn't look away.

"You mean…for a Ramajian?" Alaya asked.

Whalen hesitated for a moment.

"I suppose, yes. It's not that you couldn't handle things yourself. But, what I mean is that you are an inexperienced fighter. Not to mention…a beautiful one." He turned his gaze toward the path ahead, and Alaya felt suddenly flush.

"I know you cannot fight without hurting yourself. Trust me; I will never let something like that happen again. I will never leave you, Alaya. Do you understand?" Whalen looked deeply into her eyes, and she could feel the intensity of his words. It touched her at the very core. He was willing to go to the end for her, and there was nothing she could do about it. She nodded with understanding.

"Good. We are almost there. I can see the Iskinders' home up ahead." He trudged forward, not looking back. Perhaps that was for the best.

CHAPTER 30

Before Alaya and Whalen could reach the house, Max came running out to meet them.

"Alaya! And Whalen, too! Look, Hava, they are back!" he shouted, skipping out to greet them.

Hava emerged from the east corner of the house. She quickly put her hair in order and wiped her hands hurriedly on the small apron attached to her dress.

"Why, hello there!" Hava said, first greeting Alaya and then Whalen.

"How are you two?" Whalen asked, smiling. He swung Max above his shoulders, looking far more carefree than he had mere moments ago. Alaya was impressed with how quickly Whalen had overcome what had just happened, which made her consider something quite disturbing. *How many times has he had to overlook the shortcomings of his disgraced uncle?* It was a wonder that Whalen didn't take that sort of frustration out on anyone else.

"Our parents went out to town, but they will return shortly." Hava said.

"There they are now!" Max pointed and ran through Whalen and Alaya's legs, sprinting toward his parents, who had just arrived at the edge of the path.

Once inside, Willemina began to prepare a light lunch for everyone.

Alaya ate, but she couldn't taste the food. She had no appetite after the morning's events.

Willemina placed the empty dishes into the washbasin as the rest of the family gathered in the living room.

"How is your father, Alaya?" Nikolai asked.

"Oh," Alaya gave a start; she wasn't expecting Nikolai to speak. Small talk hardly seemed like his forte. "He had to finish something back home, but he will be joining us soon."

"We look forward to seeing him," Nikolai replied, and leaned back into silence on the old sofa.

"What a day we have had!" Willemina blurted out. It was clear that she had been meaning to bring this topic up for a while, waiting for an opening.

"What do you mean, Mother?" Hava asked.

"It is the King. He appears to be on a mission to continue the work of his mentor and predecessor, King Ogapallos II. He is simply...wretched."

"Willie..." Nikolai cautioned.

"I know. We must not speak ill of him so freely, but he is such a foul man. He has done nothing to help Batunia. He always leaves us just enough to survive for one more year," she said, shaking her head in disgust.

"I cannot believe that he reclaimed a quarter of our money in taxes this past season." She nearly screamed in frustration. Alaya had never seen Willemina this angry.

"That man is evil," Hava added. "How can he sleep at night while his people starve?"

"Very soundly, I am sure," Whalen snarled and then stood like he was about to leave.

"Are you okay, Whalen?" Max asked.

"I am sorry to interrupt, but Nikolai, may I speak to you outside?" he asked.

Nikolai didn't flinch. "Of course." He led the way to the exit at the rear of the house.

"Alaya, would you join us?" Whalen asked softly.

Willemina and Hava looked at one another, but didn't speak. However, Max hadn't quite developed such tact.

"What is going on? Can I come too?" He wore a look of longing, like a puppy that had been left outside in the cold for too long.

Nikolai turned and gave him a cold stare that clearly said, *don't ask questions.*

Willemina took the hint. "They will be back soon, Max. Why not stay here and keep Hava and I company?"

Max had no qualms about pouting as he watched them walk out the door.

***

Outside, it was chilly, but the sun felt good on Alaya's face. Whalen wasted no time in getting right down to the business at hand.

"Nikolai, it is time. I have spoken with Frederick, and he believes that we are almost ready." He looked all around, ensuring they were in fact alone. "We must move soon."

"Our men will be ready," Nikolai answered confidently.

It sounded like they were making some sort of shady transaction that Alaya wasn't sure she wanted to witness. She began to wonder why they had even asked her to join them when Whalen turned to Alaya.

"Would you like to tell him?" He asked. "It is okay, Alaya."

Alaya looked at Nikolai. Aside from his typically hard expression, his stone-cold face was unreadable. She did

236

her best to focus on his remaining good eye, remembering what her father had told her.

"Well, Nikolai. I might as well just come out and say it. I am—"

Nikolai cut her short. "You do not have to worry, Alaya. I know that you are a Ramajian," he said nonchalantly.

"I...yes. But how did you know?" she asked, genuinely stunned. Apparently, everyone had known except for her.

"The way you look is not something one forgets. I had only seen Velda in portraits when I worked in the palace, but it makes perfect sense. Willemina often visits the Circle of the Soranayum. After you came to our door, she said the same thing."

Whalen continued. "Frederick believes that the time is near. Alaya must journey to the Neya Men's lair. She is the only one who can do it." He said with a note of sadness.

"So you have it then? It exists?" Nikolai asked, speaking faster and with more enthusiasm than she had ever seen from the usually brusque, patient man.

"You mean this?" Alaya pulled the necklace out from under her shirt, revealing the dangling key. The jewels from the Orb of Shoraiva twinkled in the now-dying sunlight.

"No one but the Council must know about this," Nikolai warned, hardly able to tear his eyes from the key. He turned to Whalen and began giving orders like a military commander. "We must gather our best men for this journey. There is no telling how dangerous this will be; no one has ever done this and returned to speak about it. However, we still need a few from the Council to stay behind and keep watch over things here. The King's Riders will not let up, but neither will we."

"I understand," Whalen agreed, nodding. "I have already decided; I will accompany her."

"It should be a smaller group to prevent detection, but we should have more. Perhaps no more than five, including Alaya. I believe that at least, Frederick and I should go," he advised.

"Are you sure, Mr. Iskinder? What about your family?" Alaya asked. She wouldn't be able to live with herself if Nikolai was hurt while trying to defend her. She could think of nothing but Max and Hava; she had known the feeling of having her father ripped away at a young age. No one deserved such a thing. And there was Willemina. Nikolai had a family, and they needed him.

"Willie has known that this day could come in our lifetime—the time to fight. I have been the leader of the Warrior's Council for many years and I keep no secrets from her," Nikolai answered firmly.

"Alaya makes a good point, Nikolai. Perhaps someone else can go in your stead?" Whalen asked, wearing a look of concern.

"Whalen, you are a fine warrior, but you are still learning. We need more experience with whatever we will be facing down there." Nikolai said. He was clearly not interested in debating the issue. "You may have seen the worst that the Riders can do, but the Neya Men are like nothing you've ever experienced. No one knows what we will be up against."

"Nikolai, I have no family. I have chosen not to marry for this reason. My life has been dedicated to changing this world. In a few more months, I will be twenty-one years, and the King will recruit me to serve in his palace. I cannot live with myself if I am forced to fight for his cause. I would rather die for something *I* believe in." Whalen was resolute; it was the most confident Alaya had ever seen him.

Nikolai let out a deep sigh. "Alaya, what do you think? Your opinion matters the most, I suppose. After all, you are being asked to place your trust, as well as life, in our hands." He asked.

Alaya thought long and hard. How could she be expected to make such a decision? She had seen Whalen fight, and although it was true that he was still learning, Whalen had eventually been able to overcome Grommet. On the other hand, she had never seen Nikolai fight. Plus, he had lost an eye, which may impact his abilities. However, he had served for fifteen years on the Royal Guard. He would not have had such a position if he didn't earn it.

Still, Alaya thought back to the family sitting inside the living room, unaware of what was being discussed mere feet away. She thought about Max, so curious and eager about the world. He was even younger than she was when her father had gone missing. There would be no amends and no amount of apologies Alaya could give Hava or Max if they lost their father to a cause that they had no control over. *That settles it.*

"I would like Whalen to accompany me," she said. "Please, Nikolai. I think it's best for you to stay behind."

"Very well, then," Nikolai said, without debate. This worried Alaya. "Let us go inside. I have the maps you will need." Nikolai turned around and headed back inside the house.

CHAPTER 31

oments after they stepped inside the house, a brutal pounding on the front door followed them inside.

"My goodness! Who could that be?" Willemina said, jumping to her feet. She looked worried.

Nikolai rushed to the front window. Cautious, he peeked through the curtain before opening the door.

"It is Tabari," a man said. His breathing was heavy, like he had just run a long distance.

Nikolai swung open the front door. Tabari was out of breath and bent over with his hands on his knees.

"What is wrong, friend?" Nikolai asked. "Are you alright?"

"Nikolai...I was out in the woods just now. Yes, I know that it was foolish of me to be alone, but I saw the King's Guard. I thought they were making their typical rounds, not disturbing anyone. But then I saw the King himself! Can you believe it? King Negash was out in the forest!" Tabari's voice rose with excitement.

Nikolai invited Tabari inside. Alaya recognized the tall, dark man. She had seen him before at the marketplace, the same night the protester was killed.

They both had a seat and Willemina brought Tabari some herbal tea. He held the cup with both hands and took in deep gulps. Alaya saw that they were quivering.

"That should help with your nerves," Willemina said; her lips were turned into a line of worry.

"Thank you, Willemina. There is something else, Nikolai…something much worse." Tabari's hands were still trembling, but it began to slowly subside. "They have taken him…Frederick."

"What?" Alaya asked, stepping forward without thinking. She hoped she hadn't heard him correctly.

"Of course," Nikolai said to himself, and pounded a fist into his hand. "It is not quite twilight, yet it is nearly a full moon. They must have seen his house, but how did they know where Frederick lived?"

Tabari didn't answer Nikolai, but he addressed Alaya; now noticing her standing before him.

"You —" he began.

"What can you remember, Tabari? How many men were with the King?" Nikolai asked, refocusing his friend.

"You are his daughter, then?" Tabari stood to greet Alaya, ignoring Nikolai's questions.

Whalen placed the maps on the nearby table. "Tabari, how did he look? Was he harmed at all?"

"Right, I'm sorry everyone. Whalen, I do not know exactly, but Frederick did not resist. There were at least half a dozen men…he was powerless…" Tabari hesitated, but it was clear there was more.

"I am sorry to say this Whalen, but you must know. Grommet was with them. I saw them hand him a bag of money and he lurched off like the snake he is. Although I tried to stop the Guards, I was overpowered. They said he was a wanted man and that we would both be tried for the same crimes if I continued to stand in the way of justice. The

King never even spoke. He just kept his eyes on Frederick like he was some sort of wild animal." Tabari reached out to Whalen to offer consolation, and then turned his attention back to Alaya.

"He wanted me to tell you something, Alaya. He kept shouting, 'Tell her not to worry about me. Focus on the mission.' I do not know what that means. I am so sorry to be the bearer of this news."

"No, thank you," Alaya said softly. She began to feel numb. Part of her wanted to run away; to take off that instant and not stop until she was right in front of the palace. However, another part of her wanted to crumble to pieces right where she stood. She had only *just* found her father again. *How could this be happening again?*

Alaya felt her knees begin to buckle, and she practically collapsed into a nearby seat. The room began to grow wider, and the Iskinders, Whalen, and Tabari suddenly felt distant. It was as though she was stranded on an island, and everyone had begun fading far away...

Everyone in the room fell silent. Willemina began speaking some words of comfort, but Alaya wasn't able to make sense of them. She felt the soft touches on the back from her friends, but she could barely feel or see anything.

Suddenly, Alaya felt as though a giant hand had swooped down and pulled her up from an abyss. In a shock to everyone including herself, Alaya erupted like a volcano, and rose to her feet. She couldn't sit back and wallow in self-pity. She had to move...she had to do *something*.

"I have to go, Nikolai. Whalen, we have to go save him!" She shouted, looking around the room and seeing individual faces once again, but no one moved. "Fine then! If none of you will come with me, then I will have to offer myself to the King. Maybe once he learns who I am, as well as what I am, then I would be able to convince him to release my father, right? Perhaps I can offer myself in exchange."

Alaya knew that none of this made sense. She knew she was being rash and illogical, but what choice was there? Her father was in danger. He was probably being tortured or held against his will in a dungeon, forced to create new inventions to aid the King's twisted interpretation of Manifest Destiny.

"Alaya, that is not possible," Nikolai admonished. "We cannot risk you going anywhere near the palace. Do you know what King Negash would do if he found out anything about you?"

"Yes, he is right Alaya. I know how you must feel, but as Tabari said, we still have our mission. Only you can help us now. Your father understood that." Whalen added.

Nikolai explained their plan to Tabari, and mentioned that he would need to assemble the most skilled of the Warrior's Council. The remainder of the Council would find a way to rescue Frederick in the meantime.

While they talked, Willemina, Hava, and Max never left the room. They learned the truth about everything, including the work of the Council, its members, and Alaya's true identity. After all, the family had a right to know everything that was behind Nikolai's willingness to sacrifice his life.

"Alaya, a Ramajian? Hava and I thought the whole thing was made up!" Max squealed. "That's amazing!"

"Max, leave her alone. I am sure that Alaya has enough to worry about right now," Hava chided him. She walked over to Whalen. "I cannot believe that you are going to do this. Have you really thought this through?"

"Yes, *have* you all thought about this?" Willemina supported her concern, looking back from Nikolai to Whalen. "This is unbelievably dangerous. The Neya Men? What chance do you have of surviving? Has *anyone* ever gone into their territory? How do you even know if those maps are correct, Nikolai?"

Alaya had wondered all this herself. What if they were walking straight into a deathtrap?

"Willie, do you remember when I served in the King's Guard all those years ago? Well, one night in particular, will live forever in my memory. I remember the exact night, because it was peculiar how low the temperature had dropped. I couldn't stop thinking about how much I would have rather been indoors, but my shift was almost over. At one point, I noticed strange voices off in the distance. There was a man in a dark cloak and he was talking to someone that I recognized as very high up in the ranks within the palace. I believe that he was one of the King's advisors."

"At the time, I did not know much about the Neya Men, except that they were generally repugnant characters who were rumored to practice black magic. Some thought they were mythical, but I knew better. They may have only come out at night, but I could almost feel their presence.

"But that night, something happened to the King's advisor. From a safe distance, I saw him pull something out of a bag. He handed it over to the cloaked man, who looked very pleased. I could not get a good look at first, but the cloaked man leaned down, and began to eat. I assumed that the advisor had been smuggling food from the palace, which was hardly a serious crime, so I looked the other way.

"I tried to mind my own business, but soon, I could hear the advisor struggling. He was saying 'I do not want to; I cannot do this.' Naturally, I rushed over to the advisor. He looked hurt, and I wanted to provide any assistance. Just before I could reach them, my entire body froze. To this very moment, I have no idea what happened to me, but I was powerless for what came next.

"The cloaked man looked directly into my eyes and although I do not remember seeing a weapon, he actually burned a hole clean through my left eye. I have never been able to forget that face or the look of hatred he had scarred on it. His skin was practically invisible and blue veins scaled the outside of his face like trails of ice. His eyes were crimson pools of blood, which matched the blood from the flesh that was still dripping from his lips. I nearly tripped over my own feet trying to get away. As I ran, I heard the King's advisor calling back to me, telling me to return, but how *could* I? After what I had seen? I didn't stop until I was safe inside the palace, where I crudely dressed my wound. Hours had passed before I returned to my post, but they were both gone."

Nikolai's voice broke. Nearly everyone in the room leaned in; he seemed deeply shaken by the powerful memory.

"Go on, dear," Willemina encouraged him. "They have to know what they're up against."

"Days later, I was in bed in the palace infirmary, waiting for my eye to heal when the advisor came to visit. He wore a large bandage around his neck and chest, and covered it with a high collar shirt. I am not sure what lie he told to cover it up, but I knew the truth. He told me that it had been a huge misunderstanding, and that he was grateful for my discretion. Then, he handed me this map." Nikolai pointed to the map Whalen placed on the table moments earlier.

"He said that he never meant for things to get to that point. He had drawn the map from memory in order to make atonement for what he did. I didn't ask what he meant. I do not know what he expected me to do with that map, but I knew that whatever it was, I could not do it alone. While I didn't agree with his path, I respected what he was trying to do. He couldn't live with himself for killing that innocent child—the sacrifice for his talent. The leader of the Neya Men had told him that it was needed for the soul transformation ceremony, which was to take place the night I saw them together.

"Later, I learned the King's advisor flung himself out of the tower window that night. He had already begun the initial stages of the transformation, but he could not go through with it. Eating that child's flesh would have been the final step." Nikolai fell silent and placed his head between his hands, rubbing his temples as if to shake the haunting thoughts from his mind forever.

"Nikolai, please let me know how I can help," Tabari said. He spoke for everyone.

Nikolai's frame, which had once seemed like a towering figure of strength, now looked burdened and tired. Unfortunately, the fight had only just begun.

"I know that I need not even ask, Tabari, but please...look after my family."

CHAPTER 32

Nikolai silently packed his bags while Willemina looked on, occasionally pleading with him, but it was no use. She looked as though she might burst into tears at any moment. Hava asked to go with him, but of course, Nikolai answered with a fervent no. When it came to fighting Hava was like a toddler asking to learn to swim in the deep end. Nikolai knew it just wouldn't make sense for her to be tested so early.

Max, in contrast to everyone else, was clearly proud of his father's heroism. He was eager to help Nikolai any way he could, so he packed clothes and other small essentials into a bag.

Nikolai moved the family couch to one side and shook a loose floorboard until it popped up, revealing a rather large collection of weapons. There was everything from swords, shields, axes, spears, pocketknives, throwing daggers, and miniature crossbows.

"Father, has all of this always been in the house?" Hava asked, stunned by the excessive amount of weaponry that had been lying beneath their feet for years.

Among the options, Nikolai chose a sheathed sword and throwing daggers, which he slid into the bag. He swung it over his back with ease, like this was just another day at the office.

"Hava, I have had these since before you were born, so in answer to your question – yes. I took them with me when I left the palace. Willie?" He turned to his wife. "Would you mind packing some food? We will need enough to last the journey; monocrant jerky and some dried fruit will do nicely."

She wavered and looked around at the rest of her family. No one was saying much of anything.

"This is it then? Just like that, we are to pack you some food and see you off to your death? How can you do this Nikolai? What will I do if something happens to you?" she asked. Her eyes were now almost full of moisture.

Nikolai ceased packing and sighed heavily before turning around to face his wife.

"Whalen, Alaya...you should both gather some things as well. I will meet you at Whalen's house shortly, and we will head out from there. It will actually be best to travel after dark. We do not have too far to travel, so pack lightly. One more thing: stick together at all times. This is no time to be separated in the forest," he warned.

"Of course, Nikolai," Whalen agreed, nodding. "We will see you soon."

***

They both took great care while traveling back through the forest. The sun was beginning to set on the horizon, but that didn't matter anymore; they were going into the belly of the beast. Alaya couldn't begin to imagine what they were about to encounter, but strangely, she wasn't afraid. She tried desperately to keep her mind off her father's plight, but it continued to rise in her like a bubble of pain that she had to constantly push beneath the surface.

Nikolai was right; they had to stay focused now. The sooner they stopped the Neya Men, the easier it would be to topple the King and rescue her father. All of it felt surreal, like this was happening to someone else and Alaya was simply reading pages from a book. However, if things grew too painful or frightening, she couldn't just close the book and walk away.

While treading through the forest, Whalen kept a few inches ahead of Alaya. This was when she noticed the daggers poking out of his back pocket.

"Are you any good with those?" Alaya asked, trying to lighten the mood. The gravity of what they were about to face was almost starting to be too heavy to bear.

"With what?" Whalen asked but he didn't turn around, nor even break stride.

"Those knives. I thought hand-to-hand combat was your thing," Alaya said.

"That is why I practice hand-to-hand so much; it's a weakness of mine. Besides, you have never seen me do anything else, so your knowledge of my skillset is limited."

Whalen gave a brief chuckle, although he still didn't turn around or take his eyes off the surrounding night. Regardless, it was good to hear laughter again.

"Why the laughter? That was a serious question. I don't want to have to keep healing you every five minutes. It's tiring, you know?" she teased.

That last joking jab got Whalen's attention; he turned around and smiled.

"Pardon me! It was only once, thank you." His smile slipped slightly. "Are you sure that you're okay, Alaya?"

"You know…it's hard to say for sure, but I feel fine. I knew that this wouldn't be easy, particularly from the way Dad worked to prepare this morning." She smiled, reflecting on his perfectionism. "He was always such a hard worker. It almost makes me wonder if he knew that something like this might happen."

"It is possible. However, even Frederick could not have kept his guard up all the time," Whalen tried to comfort her. "No one can sleep with one eye open every night."

Once they safely reached Frederick's house, the straw roof was nearly fully visible. High above, the moon was nearing its peak and the sun was on the horizon. Whalen scouted the house for intruders for good measure. From outside, Alaya watched near the front door while he stalked from room to room, searching for any signs of a straggler. After several minutes, he returned.

"All clear," he said, gesturing for her to enter the house.

"Did you check under the beds?" she asked, and stepped inside with caution. If horror movies taught her anything, it was that terrible things could be lurking anywhere, including beneath beds. Or inside closets.

Whalen laughed; Alaya hadn't realized how much she had come to enjoy that sound until now.

"I'll put it this way; it doesn't *appear* that anyone was in here besides yourself and Frederick. Look," Whalen pointed to the table, "his work is still here, untouched."

Alaya went over to examine the notes. They were disjointed, but Alaya could tell that they concerned the Orb of Shoraiva. Her father had mentioned getting his ideas down on paper for Matthias. She also saw some of his older notes from interviews he had conducted with people who had seen the Neya Men and survived.

"Good," Alaya answered. "I don't think the King or his men were ever inside. They must have gotten my father while he walked through the forest. These papers would have been far too valuable to leave behind." She collected them into a pile to bring along, just in case.

"I suppose we deserve something in the way of luck. Alaya, I will return very soon. I must go and gather my things, but I will not be long. Shout if anything happens; I'm not far," Whalen warned. He looked tenderly at her, making sure that she understood.

Something overcame Alaya in that moment. It was a new feeling, best described as a strange combination of longing and restlessness. She didn't know how to explain it, but it felt like a small, fluttering sensation emerging from somewhere deep inside her stomach. Alaya felt it more and more frequently whenever Whalen looked at her like that...with those eyes.

"Whalen?" Alaya called out. He turned around, stopping in his tracks just before reaching the door.

"What is it?" he asked, instantly concerned.

"I..." Alaya struggled. She couldn't find the right words. *What do I need to tell him?* Alaya wanted him to stay with her, but she knew that there was work to be done. It was foolish for her to waste time, especially with such an important mission looming before them. This wasn't like her at all. Maybe Hava, or some other silly girl from school, but not her. *She* didn't do this sort of thing.

"Never mind...it...it's nothing," she said, shaking her head and releasing a nervous laugh. She knew that was untrue. It *was* something, but Alaya had a hard time forming a sensible thought, let alone a coherent sentence. Whalen must have sensed her strange shift in mood as well. He returned to join her at the table.

"He will be okay. You must know that. Your father is one of the toughest men I have ever met," Whalen said the encouraging words, and placed a hand on her cheek. His touch sent another electric pulse throughout Alaya's body.

"...Maybe...but what about us?" Alaya asked. She found herself drifting toward him, as natural as a moth circling a flame in ever-smaller circles.

"Alaya, I will not leave your side until the end, whatever it brings. I swear it." He held her gaze, looking deeply into her eyes.

Their bodies drew together like magnets with opposing charges. By that point, Alaya was incapable of breaking away, but more importantly, she didn't want to. This was the first time that she had actually noticed something unique about his eyes. They were deep brown, but they also had small flecks of blue, like tiny bursts of sapphire. Had his eyes always been that way?

"Your eyes...they're incredible," she laughed softly, and looked away.

Whalen smiled. "They only reflect what I see."

Alaya felt Whalen's hand gently bring her cheek closer to him. Soon afterward, their lips met and in an instant, they were lost in one another's spell. Whalen's lips were gentle and his stubbly chin was rough against her face. Alaya felt that small fluttering in her stomach erupt into a raging wildfire. This was her first kiss. She had never even imagined what it would have been like before. In fact, she had always thought it was silly to romanticize such silly things, but she had never expected this.

This was actually the first time Alaya had ever *wanted* to kiss someone. She felt Whalen's other hand find her own and their fingers linked. She inhaled Whalen's scent and their bodies drew closer. Alaya felt the strength in his toned, broad chest and arms as he embraced her frame. She could have stayed like that forever. It seemed he wanted to as well; he held her tight like she might disappear at any moment. Kissing him felt almost like she was dancing on a cloud.

All too soon, however, Alaya felt herself returning to reality. Their time was running short. She knew that Nikolai could be arriving at any moment and they still had to pack. Reluctantly, she put a hand on his chest and began to pull away from his embrace. It wasn't easy.

Whalen immediately became apologetic. "I am sorry, please forgive me."

Alaya also felt the odd urge to apologize too. He wouldn't have stayed if she hadn't stopped him from leaving earlier.

"Whalen, you didn't do anything wrong. There's no need to apologize." Alaya paused, debating whether to finish her thought. "I...I wanted you to do that," she admitted out loud. There was no use in pretending otherwise. The temporary haze and the memory of his lips began to lift from her head, clearing her mind.

Did that really just happen? She had thought of Whalen as a good friend, nothing more, but at some point, that had clearly changed. Alaya just couldn't pinpoint when it happened, but it did.

Whalen interrupted her thoughts. "I should have never done something like that without first asking permission. Alaya, please forgive me. That was rash of me." Whalen continued, clearly distressed by his behavior. He kept his gaze focused on the ground and both hands were clutched behind his back, as though holding the other one away from her. She could only imagine that there must have been some moral code he had broken. Perhaps all Batunians followed a societal norm when it came to kissing, and she just wasn't privy to it. *Go figure.*

"Listen to me," Alaya said, stepping close enough to feel the heat from his body radiating, calling out to her. But she stayed focused — she had to.

"It wasn't dishonorable. It was sweet. I promise that I am *not* angry. Now, I believe that we have a kingdom to save." Alaya said.

Whalen looked relieved and he nodded firmly in agreement.

"I should go get my things. After all, we do not want Nikolai to leave without us." He curled his lips into a half-smile and left. She went to the window to look after him; her heart was still beating with excitement. His thin shadow quickly mixed with the coming darkness and she began to pack her bag.

CHAPTER 33

Whalen returned to Frederick's house much faster than Alaya had expected. He carried a heavy-looking pack with a long strap and tossed it onto the nearby table.

"What do you have in there? Bricks?" Alaya asked. She moved to lift the bag, but found that it wasn't nearly as heavy as it looked. She pulled the drawstrings back and peered in at the contents. The leather rucksack held an intricately designed quiver, bow, and a sheaf of arrows.

"This was left to me by my father," Whalen explained, perhaps a hint of pride in his voice.

"You certainly pack light," Alaya replied, not seeing much in his bag or on his person besides weapons and light armor.

"Only the essentials. Do you have everything that you require?"

"I have everything except a weapon, but since I can't fight, it wouldn't serve much of a purpose." She said.

A light rapping was heard from the front door and Whalen got up to answer it, one hand instinctively poised on the dagger at his hip.

"I apologize for the delay," Nikolai said to both of them.

He had a single sack slung across his back. She wondered how he was able to fit all the weapons, clothing, and food into such a manageable bundle. Willemina must have helped, Alaya concluded.

"It is never easy, of course, saying goodbye. Even though I have done this hundreds of times before, it is still difficult each time, particularly now that the children are older. And Willie…" Nikolai didn't finish his sentence. "She wanted to pray for us at the Circle tonight, but I convinced her to stay behind. It is just too dangerous. Let us hope that the goddesses will hear her call."

"This will not be a goodbye, Nikolai," Whalen assured him.

"Exactly right, Whalen," Alaya agreed, wanting to move away from a subject that instantly conjured up images of her father. "Shall we go?"

***

Walking into the darkness of the forest was slightly less daunting with the bright light of the moon shimmering overhead. Before they turned at the bend in the path, Alaya glanced back at Frederick's house. It now appeared just as solid and clear as any other house. For the first time since being in Batunia, she saw that his house was the same color as their home back in Maryland—light peach. Although she didn't want to parse through that complicated emotion, the realization made her happy.

Nikolai led the way down the pebble-strewn path. Although cautious, he walked with a determined gait, the folded map in hand. However, he rarely referred to it, which made Alaya wonder if this was actually his first trip. She slowed her pace a bit to sidle up next to Whalen.

"I am not certain, but I do know that he has had a few encounters with the Neya Men. Only once or twice, and it was when he was in the Guard. They generally try to stay out of each other's way," he answered her question about Nikolai's experience with the soul-stealers.

Suddenly, Nikolai whispered in a furious growl, "Get down!" He quickly disappeared under a thicket of bushes as though he had never been there at all.

Alaya dropped to her knees right where she stood and Whalen followed suit. She looked around on her line of sight, but she could see nothing. Suddenly, she heard strange, awful noises coming from overheard. She looked up, but there was nothing to be seen. Yet, the noises continued. They sounded like the squawks of buzzards, mixed with calls of a beast in the wild.

Alaya remembered when the Iskinders referred to the gramongles on that first night together, but she had forgotten to ask anything further about them.

"Whalen, I know this isn't the time, but what is a gramongle?" she asked, barely audible.

"They are horrible beasts—pulled straight from a child's nightmare. The Neya Men use them for surveillance, but the gramongles have been known to pursue their own…amusement," he didn't elaborate.

Alaya wondered what he meant, but she didn't have to wait for long. From high up in the night sky, she saw a winged creature that looked like a flying lion, except its skin was a dull and scaly gray hue, pitted like stone.

The gramongle circled dangerously close, as though it was watching them, but it never came down to surface level. Alaya felt an eerie chill come over her, even though she was wearing a heavy coat. The temperature had dropped significantly once night fell, but she knew that the cold had little to do with her trembling body. Finally, after several minutes of making its ominous rounds, the gramongle left.

Alaya rose from the ground. She had kneeled in a puddle, so part of her dress was covered in mud. She attempted to wipe the stain away with her hand, but this only served to further smear it across the dress. At least it was dark.

"What was that about?" she asked. "Where are they going?"

"Surveillance," Nikolai answered, emerging silently from the shrubbery. "One of the functions of the gramongles is to keep watch over the Neya Men. If a threat appears, the gramongles have been known to hurt and even kill humans. However, it is the eyes you must avoid. Some say that they can paralyze a man with a single glance; turn him to stone." He trudged along, undeterred. "We are getting close."

Alaya noticed that the forest was beginning to gradually change. What was once a lush green forest now looked barren and dreary. Skeletal tree branches surrounded them as they walked along the gravelly path, which had become far less defined. Alaya looked all around her; the lufaiyas were nowhere to be seen. She thought back to what Hava had said about the Soranayum no longer watching over Batunia. Perhaps she was right.

"Stay close, Alaya," Whalen said. She looked around and realized that she had fallen behind her companions.

"This place...it feels so... abandoned," Alaya said, hurrying to catch up and rubbing her arms together. It was not something she did for warmth; it was for comfort. Whalen hung back and held her hand.

Nikolai provided a response to her rhetorical comment. "This land has been destroyed. Many years ago, when the Neya Men were cursed by the Soranayum, they were chased underground. The Soranayum, with all their might and prowess, scorched the land with magical retribution. Nothing could recover from such an act, especially since it had been delivered by the three goddesses. It was only fitting that this became their land," he explained.

Suddenly, the sound of rotting hooves emerged, and they were rapidly approaching. But there was nowhere to run; they were cornered.

The first man to speak jumped off the side of his horse and landed with thick, black boots. Once Alaya saw the official seal on their torso; she grew frightened. These men were part of the King's Riders.

"Well, well," a strange voice said. "I cannot believe my eyes...Nikolai?"

"Brumley, and Richard is with you too. Still touring together, I see. To what do we owe this pleasure?" Nikolai asked, addressing the two men. Brumley, the first man to speak, was perhaps fifty years old. He had streaks of grey peppering the sides of his head, but the top was as black as slick tar. Still, despite his age, he looked to be a picture of health. He was large, but it appeared to be muscle.

"That is right, old friend. It is much more difficult to find loyal friends these days. I have never had to question Richard's dedication." Brumley said, and spat off to the side. Alaya saw he was chewing something—it reminded her of tobacco, but she couldn't be sure.

A second man steered forward on a horse, it must have been Richard. He was slightly younger than his partner, but just as brawny.

"Brumley, it appears that he has not forgotten about us after all," Richard said. Then he nodded toward Alaya and Whalen. "Are you going to introduce us to your friends?"

It was more than apparent that Nikolai was struggling with something internally. Maybe he was thinking about running, or maybe attacking. But he didn't move. With each minute that passed, Alaya felt a growing ominous feeling circulating in the pit of her stomach, but she didn't know what to do.

"Whalen, I think you already know." Nikolai gestured towards Whalen, who was now slightly standing in front of Alaya, blocking her from the men.

"Yes, of course. Good to see you again, Whalen. We have been looking forward to a chance to work with you. It will happen soon enough, I suppose. I have heard great things about you; I am sure you will be a great asset for the Guard. You will see that for yourself in a few months." Brumley said.

"Where *did* the time go?" Robert taunted. "Guard Age just creeps up, does it not?"

"And your other friend? Who is that little gem?" Brumley asked, nearing Alaya.

Whalen spoke this time. "She has lost her tongue and cannot speak. But Nikolai recognized her from Hava's schooling days."

"Is that right? Would you like to come with us girl? We can get you to wherever you want, much faster than these two can." Brumley said, stepping forward still.

Nikolai jumped between them.

"That will not be necessary. We are almost there." He said, stiff as a board.

"Nikolai, cut the act. Where were you three really headed tonight?" Brumley asked. "Certainly not where it appears you are going. You know that place is off-limits to Batunians, right? It is for your own safety." He began circling around Nikolai, Whalen, and Alaya.

Nikolai did not answer Brumley. He seemed to be fighting the overwhelming urge to lash out with a weapon. *That was probably for the best,* Alaya thought.

Richard now hopped off his horse like a young teenager. He was surprisingly fit, despite his age. He stalked slowly up to Nikolai until they were only inches apart. Alaya had always thought Nikolai to be exceedingly tall, but Richard stood slightly taller and seemed to enjoy looking down at the man standing before him.

Brumley suddenly gave Nikolai a push from behind. Nikolai steadied himself, tensed his body, and clenched his fists, but nothing more. Richard began to laugh with a sadistic twist.

"What is it Nikolai? Have the Neya Men got your tongue too?" Brumley mocked. Richard began cackling even louder, and then grabbed one of Nikolai's arms.

"You need to come with us. I am sure we can help you find whatever it is you're looking for." Richard said in a patronizing drawl.

"Or, if not you, then perhaps this young lady will suit our needs...just fine." Brumley slid his eyes over to Alaya and began to saunter toward her as though he was propositioning a prostitute.

"I would not do that if I were you." Whalen stepped forward, shielding Alaya behind his lean but muscular frame.

"Ho now! And what are *you* going to do, farmer? Wrestled any rabbits lately?" Brumley spat a large wad of murky black goop into Whalen's face. Then he reached for the crux of Whalen's neck, but at that moment, many things began to happen all at once.

Whalen took a step back and pivoted with his shoulder, hitting Brumley in the back of the head with his elbow, and then flinging Brumley down to the ground. In the space of a breath, Whalen was holding Brumley's face inches from the puddles of mud in the marshy land.

Richard, who still had one of Nikolai's arms, instantly clutched harder and swung Nikolai around. Once

Alaya got a better look, she saw Richard held a knife to his throat.

"Let him go, Whalen. Or Nikolai dies," Richard shouted.

"Please, stop!" Alaya pleaded with the men, her eyes flicking back and forth between the two groups.

"Well! It's a miracle! The little birdie can speak, after all! I wonder what other lies you all have been telling. Whalen, if you know what's best, you will let go of Brumley, nice and slow-like," Richard demanded.

"With pleasure," Whalen answered and dropped Brumley's face into the largest of the puddles. Brumley struggled to lift himself upright. Once he emerged, he shook his face, which had been covered in thick, brown muck. Alaya wrinkled her nose. His face had dislodged whatever foul odor had been trapped beneath the filth.

In a move of rash stupidity, Richard pushed Nikolai to the side, unsheathed his sword, and lunged straight toward Whalen. With lightning speed, Nikolai pulled a small dagger from his own belt and threw it with a sharp flick of his wrist. It slammed into the back of Richard's head with a sickening thud. Richard froze and his own sword fell to the ground. He collapsed face first like a heavy tree, landing dead in the mud beside Brumley, who had only managed to make it to his knees.

"I suggest you leave now, Brumley," Nikolai warned him calmly before walking to Richard's body and unceremoniously wrenching his dagger from his skull.

Nikolai cleared off the mess from the dagger, and returned it to his belt, concealing the knife and other small weapons with his long leather jacket.

"I am sorry you had to see that, but we have no time to lose," he said. "We must keep going."

Whalen and Alaya exchanged a look. *Nikolai just murdered someone in front of them,* she wanted to say. This had taken her by complete surprise; her expression must have been riddled with terror and worry. Was this a glimpse of what was to come? Whalen said nothing, but looked nearly apologetic. His expressions said something else; this wasn't the first time he had seen death. *How much more death would they see?* Alaya shivered at the thought.

CHAPTER 34

As they continued even deeper in the barren wasteland, Alaya looked around. The area was eerily silent, as though every sound had been sucked up with a large, powerful vacuum.

"We are nearing the entrance...stay close now," Nikolai hushed them from the lead.

Alaya looked around. The path had now blurred to the point of nonexistence. It was nothing more than dead leaves lightly pressed into the ground. Upon closer inspection, she saw that the leaves were a dull, faded gray. Their outlines were white, as though they had been frosted over, but it wasn't that cold in Batunia. In fact, all of the foliage in the area had a ghostly, lifeless appearance. The world had been shot by a low-vibrancy setting on a camera.

Just then, there was a crack in the brush from somewhere behind them. Alaya swung around, squinting her eyes to see what could've caused it.

"What was that?" Nikolai whispered. "Everyone, get down."

A few minutes passed, and the sound of crushing leaves grew closer. It didn't sound like an animal—in fact, there were no animals to be seen.

"Oh no…" Whalen said, "Nikolai, look."

Nikolai nearly launched up from his hiding space once he saw the figure emerging from the shadows.

"Hava! What are you doing here?! I expressly forbade you to come along."

Hava jaunted over to them, panting. "I had to… You need more people than this."

"I have told you, Tabari is sending more men to join us, but we have no time to waste. Once Alaya's father is rescued from the palace, it will only be a matter of time before the Council is no more. We have to act now, and you should *not* be here." Nikolai said forcefully.

"Father, I'm staying. Would you really want me to go back home now? I saw what happened to those men back there." She pointed behind her, and at that point, she knew she was going to stay. How could Nikolai argue after that? Dangerous though this mission would be, it would be far more dangerous for Hava to return home alone. And they couldn't risk losing Whalen or Nikolai. Their small group was already parsed down enough to the point where the odds of survival were against them.

Alaya and Whalen exchanged a look. Although Alaya wanted Hava to be safe back at home, she had a point. They did need more people, and from what she heard, Hava did have some skill fighting.

Whalen asked Nikolai for the map and took a quick look. They were indeed quite close; a few more minutes and they would be in front of what should have been the entrance to the Neya Men's lair.

"Alright, I cannot stop you now, but we must keep moving." Nikolai said, clearly perturbed.

***

Sure enough, they were soon upon the boulder, just like the map indicated. Except, this was no ordinary boulder.

This was apparently the door that led to the underground area belonging to the Neya Men. Alaya and her small group of bodyguards would soon be in hostile territory.

"Nikolai, how are we to get inside?" Whalen asked. They found a few smaller boulders nearby, and took shelter behind them to formulate a plan.

"We will have to wait. Someone is bound to either arrive or exit sooner or later. When the door opens, unless it's an army coming out, we run straight for the entrance. Got it?"

Everyone nodded; this was simple enough to understand.

"Won't we get caught?" Alaya asked, worried. "There are four of us."

"I'll take care of that," Nikolai replied. "The rest of you just run."

Suddenly, a grating, screeching sound ripped through the sky overhead, piercing their ears. It sounded like a large bird, but it was much deeper in pitch. Alaya had heard this sound before. She looked up into the sky, but Nikolai and Whalen instinctively fell to the ground, shielding their heads with their coats.

Hava shouted out, "Alaya, hurry!" She tugged on Alaya's dress, but it was no use.

Alaya wanted to fall into the shadows, or even run away, but she simply couldn't. She froze in her steps, unmoving. The gramongle appeared in an instant and was swooping down toward her. Its eyes were as red as blood and its mouth looked to be something straight from a horror movie. Blood trickled from its sharp fangs and Alaya shivered. But one question remained. *Why couldn't she move her body?*

"Alaya, get down!" Nikolai called, but it was far too late. The gramongle had spotted her. It was flying down toward her at a great speed; much faster than a beast that large should have been able to fly.

"I'm sorry, everyone. I'm so sorry, but I can't move!" Alaya cried out. "I didn't mean for it to catch all of us!"

"Never mind that now, Alaya," Whalen said. "Just look away and run." He grabbed her by the shoulders and literally turned her body around. Once her eye contact was broken with the creature, she was free to move.

"Whalen, you have the map. Lead the way, quickly. Hava, whatever you do, stay with them!" Nikolai shouted, and they all sprinted away.

Alaya heard the gramongle disappear into the canopy of trees high above, but thankfully, she had lost sight of the monster's eyes. Her body was once again limber and swift; no longer under the gramongle's spell. The creature was shuffling through the trees, darting back and forth like an eagle ensnaring its prey.

Whalen and Hava began to run, but there was one problem. Nikolai remained firmly planted into the ground. Once Alaya saw this, she stopped in her tracks.

"What are you doing? Come with us, Nikolai!" she urged.

"No more of this running. You two just keep going; I will take care of this wretched beast. I have grown immune to the power of the gramongle's stare." Nikolai reached into the pack slung across his back and reached for his long sword, but it was too late.

Giant claws sprung from the gramongle's thick, almost reptilian skin and the creature tore into Nikolai's back.

"Agghhhh!" he cried out in pain as the claws disappeared into his shoulders.

"Nikolai! NO!" Whalen shouted, turning back and running toward one of his mentors.

In the next moment, the gramongle swooped up into the sky and Nikolai was gone. A heavy gust was left in his wake; creating a burst of wilted leaves encircling the place where Nikolai stood. Seconds later, something fell from the sky. It was his pack. *He's now without a weapon*, Alaya thought, but didn't know if that would make any difference at this point.

"Dad...Dad!?" Hava cried out, searching the dark, bleak sky. Then, she suddenly turned to Alaya, "Look what you've done! Since you've come to Batunia, everything has just fallen apart!"

"This is all my fault. Hava I'm so sorry!" Alaya said, mournful as Hava crumpled to the ground like a deck of cards. "I knew not to look into their eyes, but I couldn't stop myself. I didn't mean for any of this to happen."

"Of course you didn't. That's why I had to come. I knew something bad would happen." Hava snarled.

"Hava, that's enough. Like Nikolai said, we have to keep moving. Besides, we don't know that he's dead." Whalen said, trying to be the voice of reason. He reached out for Hava's hand, and she graciously accepted.

Alaya reached out for Nikolai's pack lying a few feet from her on the ground. How could she have been so stupid? What kind of Ramajian gets their friends killed, or even kidnapped? Alaya couldn't shake the nagging feeling that she could've done something to stop it.

"Alaya," Whalen whispered. "We cannot stay here. We were spotted. The Neya Men will not be far behind their beasts. I am sure that gramongle will warn others."

Whalen took a closer look at the map. If they backtracked, they would come upon a small pond. At least they could find a fresh water supply, as well as a place to lay low for a while and regroup.

***

Once they found the pond, they all sat right beside it. In the dark, the water looked clean enough, and only smelled a bit odd. Still, stagnant water was better than none at all.

They unloaded their sacks and took out some dried meat. Alaya only gnawed on the food, but it was tasteless. Her thoughts were wrapped up in the chaos of recent events, and at the same time, trying to figure out what to do next. Hava didn't speak to Alaya at all, but it was understandable. With Nikolai gone, the mission parameters had certainly changed.

"Eat, Alaya. It will help," Whalen said, noticing she hadn't eaten much of anything. He offered her a bit of dried fruit.

Alaya looked at the dry mongpaya, but the thought of eating anything made her feel sick to her stomach. What were they going to do now? They hadn't even made it into the lair before something terrible had happened. Had they already failed before they had begun?

"He is stronger than you think, Hava. Do not fear for Nikolai just yet. I know that it is hard, but we have to think of a plan." Whalen began speaking as he looked around, getting a closer look into the pond.

It was not at all what Alaya had expected. The "water" was actually a light brown sludge, which slowly slithered along like hot lava flowing down a mountainside.

"This must have been the same stuff that Brumley fell into. It stinks," Alaya said, plugging her nose and waving with her other hand. Whalen cracked a smile at her comment.

Hava looked into the sky. "It will not be dark for much longer," she said, and she was right. Once the sun rose, moving unseen in the forest would become far more difficult. If something was going to happen, it had to be now, whether they liked it or not.

"Right," Alaya answered, sounding weak. When she tried to get to her feet, she nearly toppled over. She hadn't realized how tired she had become until now. "Let's go."

"On second thought, your eyes are beginning to droop." Whalen said, and pulled out a soft mat to sleep on. "I know this may not seem like the best time, but perhaps we should all get a bit of rest. Once we enter the underground, there will be no time for sleep, and we'll need all the strength we can get."

This made Alaya worry about Nikolai all over again. What about his safety? What about his strength? Hava settled in next to Whalen, who looked at Alaya with a frown of worry. But she was grateful he didn't ask about her welfare. Hava was in need of comfort, so it made perfect sense for them to be together.

Alaya tucked into her sack the best she could, considering the circumstances. Yet, try as she might, Alaya couldn't turn off her racing mind, and struggled to get even one minute of precious sleep. *What will I tell Willemina? Or, or Max, or...*

"Alaya! Alaya, wake up!" Whalen whispered frantically and gently shook her limp body. Alaya struggled to regain consciousness. A loud sound rumbled in the ground. She realized that it was the sound of hooves stamping on the earth, and they were very close.

"I think it is them. They must be returning now that the sun is almost upon us. This is our only chance!" Whalen was gathering what little belongings they had, and slung on Nikolai's pack as well as his own.

"Let's go you two! Here they come!" Hava said, growing impatient. Alaya saw she was fully prepared.

Carefully, they trailed the Neya Men from a safe distance. It helped that their horses were panting and making quite a ruckus with their trotting. Otherwise, it was

270

completely silent in the woods. There were only two of them, which was a relief. One wore armor from head to toe, while the other wore a long, black cloak. One was a warrior of physical strength, and the other one preferred to fight battles using dark magic.

"Do you think it's really him?" a slimy voice emerged from the man in the armor.

"Yes, the Sage told me," the cloaked man responded. "After all these years, they finally found him. I knew he must have been hiding in a house made of lichten wood. No matter now. He will soon be ours."

The cloaked man approached the boulder and slid off his horse. He stopped directly in front of the large rock and made a huge circling motion in opposite directions with both hands. Slowly, the boulder began to crunch over the dead leaves and rolled to the left.

"Yes. The Guard plans to investigate his house once morning comes. We will soon have all his secrets." They both entered the lair.

Seconds after they disappeared inside, the boulder began to slowly move back into place.

"Now!" Whalen said, and tumbled forward. Hava followed closely behind him. The opening was nearly closed, barely a sliver, when Alaya sucked in her gut and squeezed through.

"Not without me!" A voice came from behind Alaya. She swung around on her heels, only to see Nikolai's broad bulk slip in at the very last moment before the boulder closed with a loud crash. This was it; they were now sealed off from the outside world, for better or worse.

"Nikolai! Where did you, how did you...?" Alaya whispered, not needing the answers as long as he was safe. "Oh, I don't even care. Thank goodness you're okay!"

Upon hearing her father's voice, Hava swung on her feet.

"Father! You've made it!" She said, trying her best to keep her voice down amidst her excitement. She threw her arms around him and Nikolai recoiled.

"Are you okay?" Hava asked.

"Never mind me. That gramongle was tough, but I was tougher." Nikolai said. Alaya noticed that he walked with a slight limp, and his shirt was torn. He had a large gash on the side of his waist.

Alaya quickly offered to heal him. After all, it was the least she could do.

Nikolai continued. "What they do not tell you about gramongles, is that while they may look frightening, they are actually quite stupid. I was able to fend it off and kill it before I became its dinner."

They didn't ask for any more details; just imagining the idea of struggling with a monster in mid-air was enough to make Alaya feel nauseous.

"I am glad that you all picked the same opportunity to enter. I have been waiting near the entrance for quite some time, hoping to spot you." Nikolai asked. He held up an arm while Alaya healed the deep gash in his torso. She was amazed that he hadn't expressed more pain.

"I am glad to see you back, safe and sound." Whalen said. "Here are your things." He handed Nikolai his pack, still cinched shut.

"I am grateful for this, Whalen. Now, where do we need to go from here?" He asked, ready to get back into the thick of the mission.

After reviewing the map, they determined that the Orb of Shoraiva would most likely be hidden somewhere deep within the center of the underground labyrinth. It would be the most heavily guarded area, which meant that it would also be the most dangerous.

"Once we are close enough, I think we should split up. Alaya, you may need to go into that final room alone, while the rest of us hold the others off. At least until backup arrives." Nikolai suggested, although he didn't sound particularly keen on the idea.

Alaya couldn't believe what she was hearing. "There's no way that I can fight for myself, Nikolai. What if there's someone in there guarding the chest?"

"I do not believe there will be. The room is no larger than a bedroom, for which there is a good reason. If someone makes it that far, then the Neya Men have already lost. The guards will most likely be outside this room." He pointed to the middle of the lair map — dead center.

Alaya took a deep breath and sighed.

"I suppose you're probably right. Let's finish this."

CHAPTER 35

The Neya Men's lair was like a massive, underground cavern. Everywhere that Alaya looked, soaring, dark colored walls surrounded them. It seemed like it should have been warm, or even hot, but it was chilly and damp, growing colder the deeper they plunged. Alaya's skin quickly grew bumpy from the cold, and she began rubbing her hands together for warmth.

They walked along the narrow corridors between the walls for some time, but eventually, her suspicion was confirmed - they had entered an intricate maze. However, this maze was unlike any other. She had been trying to keep track of their progress based on the color of the walls they had passed. The map was no help; it seemed to disregard the maze, and only pointed to direct routes.

However, after connecting other visual clues in certain areas, Alaya realized that the walls were actually changing. She explained this to the group, who were becoming frustrated with their apparent lack of progress.

A new clue came from an unlikely source –Alaya's nose. She smelled water, possibly large amounts of it. The smell grew stronger with each step, but where could that much water be? From the looks of the map, the lair was not large enough to hold a lake. Perhaps there was a smaller pool somewhere?

They had been walking for almost two hours, and most of that time had been retracing their steps in circles. However, things started changing; their surroundings seemed different.

After some time, Whalen suddenly stopped walking and held up a hand. He turned and crouched down, then urged them to peer around the corner and look into the distance.

"What is that there?" Hava asked, and pointed toward what looked like a jagged scar on the cavern floor, perhaps a hundred meters away. Alaya craned her neck and finally recognized what the scar actually was—steps which led further underground.

Looking more carefully, Alaya could see a long staircase that led directly into a small pool of water. There was, however, one problem; a pair of heavily armored Neya Men guarded the foot of the steps.

"Leave this to me," Whalen said. "Hava, would you join me?"

"Of course," Hava said with a smile.

Out of nowhere, Nikolai started mumbling indiscernible words. Alaya struggled to make sense of the strings of random words, until he suddenly shouted, "Scoundrels! The lot of you!"

Alaya couldn't ignore this; she spun around and instantly clapped a hand over his mouth.

"Nikolai, what are you doing? Someone will hear us!" she scolded.

"I am sorry. I do not know what came over me." Nikolai began to apologize profusely, and Hava rushed by his side.

"You healed him, didn't you?" Hava asked, addressing Alaya directly for the first time since her father's disappearance.

Whalen and Alaya both looked at one another, and then back at Nikolai. His forehead was beading with sweat and his cheeks were flushed, even though it was still quite cold and damp in the lair.

"I am sorry," Nikolai repeated, shaking his head. He almost looked like he was coming out of a trance. Several lines of sweat were now dripping down from his brow. "I do not know what came over me."

"Nikolai, just have a seat. You are probably exhausted after everything you've been through." Whalen suggested and Nikolai obeyed. He then pulled Alaya to the side, although it probably wasn't necessary. As soon as Nikolai sat down, he resumed his blank stare, looking intently at one blank space.

"Alaya, do you know anything about your healing powers for illness? Who knows what infection Nikolai may have picked up from the gramongle, but he is certainly not himself." Whalen asked, under his breath, so as to not alarm either Hava or Nikolai.

"I'm not sure, Whalen, but I will try my best. In the meantime, be careful—both of you." Alaya said, and watched as they headed towards the spiral staircase.

Alaya kneeled down to Nikolai and placed both of her hands on his head. She did her best to concentrate on healing whatever illness had struck him, visualizing a clean, healthy glow around his body. Imagining a wound healing was far more normal and tangible than eliminating an infection. She didn't know how far her powers extended, or what role the visualization had, but it was worth a shot.

From the corner of her eye, Alaya saw Whalen pull out his full quiver and longbow, and Hava retrieved a long

276

sword. Whalen shot first; he drew back his arrow and released it into one of the guards. She could hear the whistle of the feathers soaring through the air, just before it hit its target.

Off in the distance, a cry of pain rattled to the ceiling. Whalen and Hava took cover, but before long, he quickly drew another arrow from his quiver and let it fly towards the other guard.

"What is going on here?" Alaya could hear a voice, perhaps of another guard that had shown up. Alaya watched from her place with Nikolai. The guard was searching frantically; trying to identify the assailant responsible for dropping his comrades from the shadows. "Who is--" But the guard fell silent before he could even utter the sentence; Whalen's third shot hit the bullseye.

Alaya closed her eyes. She didn't want to see Whalen killing anyone; hearing it was bad enough.

He slung his bow back across his shoulder and turned, but it was just in time. Hava sliced through the armor, reaching the neck of a nearby assailant. Once the job was done, Hava pushed him over the ledge, to join his companions below. Soon, they rushed back to help Nikolai to his feet.

Hava spoke first this time. "It is over, Alaya. Shall we go?"

"Yes, I'm ready," she answered. "I did as much as I could for your father; his fever appears to be gone."

The way ahead grew increasingly dark and musty. Whalen held Nikolai by the shoulder, and Hava led the way with the map. Alaya was overcome by a mild coughing fit and covered her mouth to muffle the sound. There were swirling eddies of disturbed dust dancing all around them.

As they ventured deeper into the dark corridor, the air became increasingly thick; it felt like something sticky was being pulled into Alaya's lungs. The dust mixed with the moist air to leave a filthy sheen on their skin.

At length, they reached the staircase, which actually ascended for a small stretch before plummeting deeper into the earth. At the foot of the staircase, they could see a fork in the road. One path led off to the right, while the other veered left. It wasn't difficult to make a choice, since both options looked exactly the same — dark and unwelcoming.

Nikolai finally seemed as though he had returned to his normal self and offered to take the lead. He no longer needed assistance walking.

"I will go down ahead, and let you know if it is safe." Nikolai carefully stepped over the trio of corpses at the top of the staircase, and placed his foot onto the first step.

Before he could take his second step, a cry shattered the silence.

"Intruders! There they are!" Someone from up above shouted. "Raise the alarm!"

Looking up, Alaya saw the source of the voice. He was approaching from behind via a winding path they hadn't noticed before. The speaker was wearing a red cloak and was followed by two other men in armor. "Seize them!"

Alaya, Hava, Whalen, and Nikolai charged down the steps, eager to put as much distance between them and the riders as possible. Thankfully, they had some distance between them and the enemies, which evened the odds considerably.

"Which way?" Alaya asked as they neared the bottom of the steps.

"Does it matter?" Nikolai asked, following closely behind. "If one does not work, we can try the other. At the moment, it doesn't make a difference."

For no particular reason, Alaya chose to take the path bearing left. But she soon came to regret her decision. She

278

wouldn't have thought it possible, but the air seemed even more viscous and suffocating than it had been in the cavern above. They drew in air through thin breaths, gaining the tiniest bits of precious oxygen. Somehow, the walls seemed to grow shorter and narrower. Or was it simply her imagination? At that point, it was hard to tell. They could hear the clanging steps of the armored guards rapidly approaching, but they were still a ways away.

Soon, they came upon a small, brown door at the end of the corridor. It was so small, in fact, that Alaya was convinced that the only way through it would be if she inched her way like a worm. It would have been almost impossible for the others to get through, except maybe Hava. Alaya looked back, wondering if they should turn around and try the other path. If this door locked from the other side, then she would have no way of turning back.

"Alaya this is it!" Whalen shouted, looking down at the map. "I don't know whether it was dumb luck or if the goddesses are simply on our side, but this is the room. You have to go in alone. We will hold them off until you return."

"I will hurry!" she shouted. Against her better judgment, Alaya gently pushed on the door and it cracked open like it had been waiting especially for her arrival. Alaya thought this was incredibly odd; she had expected at least a lock.

Alaya slithered her way through the narrow passage, when she heard the loud, earsplitting sound of metal against metal. Quickly, she looked back and caught a glimpse of the first armored man as he raised his sword and charged at Nikolai. So it had begun. Trusting that they could take care of themselves, Alaya could do little else but press on. Once making it inside the small room, Alaya shut the door behind her three guardians and looked around the dark room.

It was very nearly pitch black, but once her eyes adjusted Alaya saw a smaller door staring back at her. Not wasting any time, she pushed this door open and was met with yet another door. It looked very much like the previous two. *Am I going in circles?* She thought. This must have been some sort of a trick, but these silly games weren't going to stop her. Alaya didn't know how many doors she would need to open, but she knew that they couldn't go on forever.

However, once Alaya pushed this third door open, she found it was much more difficult than the first two. She used the force of her entire weight and leaned into it, and she was able to crash through, tumbling to the ground. When Alaya stood, she found herself facing a solid brick wall.

"Now what?" Alaya asked aloud, exasperated.

She ran her hands all over the brick wall, feeling for any sort of loose opening or hidden lever. After what felt like hours, she finally managed to pull out a loose brick. A foul, pungent odor drifted through that small passage, and brought on a powerful wave of nausea. Alaya wondered what it could be, but she knew time was of the essence. Her friends' survival depended on her quick retrieval of the Orb of Shoraiva.

Quickly, Alaya broke several more of the bricks away until she had created a wide enough opening to tumble through. It was quite dark and Alaya could barely see ahead of her own hand, but she pushed through the opening. She almost immediately tripped on something sharp and hard, but stepped over it, only to stumble on something else and fall to her knees.

At that moment, Alaya was grateful that she could not feel pain or injure herself, since she could feel several sharp objects poking into her skin. She got closer to the ground to get a better look at what was on the ground.

When Alaya finally realized what she had been walking on, she stumbled over and nearly screamed.

Alaya's eyes continued to adjust to the darkness but to her horror, she saw what had to be hundreds of fresh corpses and rotting skeletons. They were tossed haphazardly, toppling one another. She could only guess how many layers deep this enormous grave went. Alaya wasn't prepared for the sight, and her stomach flipped as the stench of rotting flesh invaded her nostrils. Some of the bodies had actually been nailed to the ceiling or impaled from spikes on the walls, where condensation and toxic dew dripped from their bare bones. Alaya realized that this must have been where the Neya Men kept the discarded bodies once they had finished feeding and extracting souls.

Unable to hold it down any longer, Alaya bent over and was sick between her shoes. As unpleasant as that feeling was, she had to allow herself that one, small piece of humanity. Her knees began to buckle, but she steadied herself, rationalizing the wave of fear that had threatened to consume her. After all, no human being would have been able to get through such a room without a similar reaction.

Did the King know about this? On second thought, she realized that it probably didn't matter. Even if he did know, what would he actually do to stop the Neya Men? What could *anyone* do?

Off in the distance, Alaya was certain that she could see another door. Keeping both hands and part of the cloak over her nose and mouth to ward off the stench of death, Alaya slowly pressed on, determined to see what lay ahead. She was careful not to disturb the corpses; they deserved at least that much.

After Alaya traversed the sea of bodies and reached the far door, which revealed a small stairwell. She had already come this far, so, throwing caution to the wind, she stepped onto the first stair. The staircase was made out of wood, which meant that it was frail and showed signs of probably rotting in places. A thick layer of dust settled over each stair; it didn't look as though it had been used for years — possibly longer.

Alaya's legs began to shake as soon as she set her first foot down, followed by the other. She instantly became terrified. She remembered back to the bridge that she had crossed with Whalen. Except this time, there was no water around to catch her fall.

Before Alaya plowed on, she silently prayed that this one wouldn't similarly buckle or crack under her feet. Carefully, she passed one step at a time. Once Alaya reached the bottom of this staircase without any further incidents, she was plunged more confidently into total darkness. She was grateful that there were no more doors; perhaps she was reaching the end of this bizarre maze.

Alaya's eyes adjusted after a few moments. She took a look around and immediately felt something strange. This had to be it — the final destination. It was the room that held the chest.

CHAPTER 36

large problem became immediately apparent...the chest was nowhere to be found. Instead, Alaya stood before a large body of water, quite a sizable lake. There was no telling how deep it was, but it was certainly not shallow. What was worse: the water looked murky and emanated a foul, stagnant stench. Alaya could only imagine what was down in that muck. The other things that stood out to her were the tall, cement pillars sitting high above the water. There was no other option. In order to find the chest, Alaya had to cross the lake using the pillars. The only direction to go was forward.

Alaya crept up to the lip of the lake; the first pillar was mere inches away. *Come on Alaya, how hard can this be?* However, as her eyes traced the pillar path across the lake, she saw that each successive pillar was a little bit farther apart than the one before. Indeed, the last pillar was nearly four or five feet away from the other side of solid ground.

This is insane! Alaya grew worried, anxiety beginning to rise in her throat. Why couldn't she have been a gymnast in school instead of a brain? However, there was no use regretting her past choices; it wouldn't do any good. She thought about her friends, who had been left behind fighting for their lives. She also thought of Hava, who cared so much for the mission, that she would disobey her parents and sacrifice her life on Alaya's behalf. Yet here she was, afraid of a little water. An image of Nikolai rose in her mind. Although he'd fallen ill, he was still willing to fight for her. She pushed her doubts aside. She *had* to do this...for their sake.

Alaya noticed something hanging from the ceiling fairly low, and a small bit of hope returned. There were dozens of long bars hanging down that reminded her of the monkey bars from grade school. They hung slightly above the pillars, meaning that she would have to jump rather high to reach them — but it was doable.

Now that Alaya had a plan, she stepped forward onto the first pillar. *So far, so good.* Alaya then made it to the second and third pillar without difficulty. However, the fourth pillar and the remaining five or six were not going to be so easy. Looking above her, Alaya knew that she had to reach the bars above. Being careful not to fall off the pillar, she jumped straight up, but her fingers slipped off the bar. The slight tug on the bar also caused a small chunk of the cavernous ceiling to break off.

The jagged section of the falling rock bounced on the pillar and tumbled off the edge toward the water below. Alaya's eyes followed the rock, despite the wave of vertigo that caused her vision to swim. She expected a splash, but when the stone hit the water, the entire body of water began to rumble, as though it was coming to a boil. The water began to rise, or perhaps the pillars began to sink. The water didn't seem to sizzling from heat; it appeared to be bubbling and hissing like powerful acid.

The piece of rock that had fallen was instantly devoured, disappearing in a puff of acrid smoke where it had landed. This was no ordinary lake. Whatever Alaya did, she knew that falling from these pillars was not an option; no amount of swimming would save her from that plunge.

Alaya's heart began to rattle hard in her chest, and her palms grew sweaty with anxiety. Against better judgment, she began to think of everything that could go wrong. What if she missed the bar above, slipped off the pillar, and fell into the acid-filled lake below? She had to stop for a minute to regain composure and began talking to herself.

"Get it together, Alaya. Sweaty palms won't help."

After a few minutes of attempting to focus, Alaya felt she was ready. She put as much power into the jump as she could muster, and leapt for the bar again, elevating as high as her legs would allow. She felt one of her calves overstretch, but as usual, there was no pain. She caught hold of the bar with one hand, and clutched onto it as hard as she could until she could bring her other hand into place. Carefully, Alaya began to swing her body back and forth like a gymnast in the Olympics.

Once she had the rhythm down, Alaya swung out and released herself from the bar, delicately landing on the next pillar. She did the same and followed suit for the last two. Alaya saw large blisters forming on her hands, but that didn't matter. She had made it safely across.

Alaya looked back. There was a faint, but distinct sound of clanging metal. Had the Neya Men been able to follow her through the narrow passageways? She had to hurry.

A large wooden door stood before Alaya, although this one was quite a bit larger than the others had been. Metallic borders rounded the edges and a large knob hung in the center of the wood. She placed her hand on the knob, but noticed that it wouldn't turn left or right. Looking beneath the knob, Alaya noticed a small keyhole and immediately knew what to do.

Removing the necklace, Alaya inserted the key into the hole, and pushed the doorknob. Like butter, the door easily swung open.

As soon as Alaya stepped inside the room, she saw a strange pod suspended in mid-air in the center of the room. Although she couldn't be sure, the pod seemed to contain the silhouette of a person. On the ground just below the pod, Alaya finally saw it—the chest. There was an opaque string that connected the two and the chest almost glowed, oddly hovering between a solid state and liquid transparency. When Alaya stepped closer to the pod, she couldn't believe what she saw.

The silhouette of a person that she had seen in the pod was a woman, encased in what looked to be water. The woman's eyes were closed, but her look was unmistakable. A shiver ran across her skin; the woman seemed to resemble Velda.

Wondering what the woman's purpose was, Alaya stepped forward and attempted to touch the chest, but her hand passed directly through it. *What's going on? Why can't I touch it?* Alaya wondered. She was clearly missing something, but what? Alaya wished she had the map, but realized that it probably wouldn't help.

Carefully approaching the woman, Alaya hoped for some sort of revelation. She felt a strange energy around the pod and actually became dizzy as she drew closer.

"Do not fear, my child," a soft voice suddenly resonated in her head.

"Who said that?" Alaya asked aloud. She immediately became on guard and looked in all directions. When Alaya looked back at the woman in the pod, she nearly jumped out of her skin.

The woman's eyes had opened and were gazing down at Alaya, with her long locks slowly moving in the water. How was she speaking? She obviously could breathe in the water, and more importantly, she was dead. *Wasn't she?*

"Was that you talking just now?" Alaya mustered up the courage to ask the woman in the pod, not expecting an answer.

The woman's head nodded up and down. "Please do not be frightened. Difficult times have befallen all of us, young one; perhaps you most of all. I am afraid that you are being hunted. Even now, they pursue you, but you must not be afraid."

"What can I do?" Alaya asked. "I know that I'm supposed to destroy the Orb of Shoraiva, but I don't know how."

"I do not have much time left," the woman said. "But I must tell you, the Orb of Shoraiva is the source of life for the Neya Men, but their leader is an important piece as well. As long as they both exist, the Neya Men cannot be stopped. Their leader discovered long ago that he could use my power as a Ramajian to keep the Orb sealed away. Protecting the orb, combined with his power, means that their race will never perish. Also, while I am here, you cannot open the chest."

"Wait...Velda? How are you talking to me right now? Weren't you...um, you know..." Alaya couldn't bring herself to say the words. It felt insensitive somehow.

"Killed? Yes. In a way. Although my physical body was destroyed, my spirit was taken captive. I have kept this chest locked away so that no one could open it, but I have been here for nearly twenty years. My spirit is breaking down and I will soon fade away. The Neya Men have grown afraid that someone new may come in and steal away their existence. You must break the Orb and end this conflict before they capture you and force you into the same fate as mine." Velda said, speaking with concern in her voice.

"How can any of this be possible? This orb, is keeping them alive? How can I destroy it?" Alaya asked. "I can't even touch it," She cried out in desperation, as she reached out again and demonstrated how her arm could run straight through the middle.

"Once my spirit fades, you will be able to open the chest with the key. This is going happen very soon now...I am growing so tired. Once you unlock the chest, you must destroy the orb immediately. Do you understand, Athaliah?" Velda said, now sounding exhausted.

Alaya stopped cold. "How do you know my real name?"

"My journal contains everything that you need to know. Matthias should have kept it for you. Inside, you will find the truth in the final pages." Velda paused. When she continued, her voice sounded sad, as though she was in pain.

"I wish we could have had more time together. Farewell, dear Athaliah...I am very glad that I got to meet you before my end. Just as it was foretold...on your twentieth birthday." Velda's face shifted again, as though being relieved of a great weight. Her spirit began to fade away, escaping in another way since she had been unable to slip the bonds that held her.

"Velda, wait! Don't go just yet!" Alaya called out, but it was futile. She wasn't ready to say goodbye. There were still dozens of unanswered questions waiting to be asked, but Alaya would have to find the answers without the help of Batunia's greatest Ramajian. Velda's spirit was beginning to literally fade away before her eyes.

In the distance, Alaya heard voices and heavy boots — they may have just descended the fragile wooden staircase. People were heading her way, but she could not tell whom, or what their intentions might be. The woman in the pod was Alaya's only concern at that moment.

"It makes me joyful to see the woman you have become...my beautiful...daughter." With those final words, Velda's spirit disappeared, and with it, so did the pod. The chest below suddenly became solid.

Alaya remained completely still. She was stunned, confused, and unable to comprehend Velda's last words. *Why had she called me "daughter?"*

"Alaya, do it now!" a voice shouted from just outside the room. Whalen's voice followed moments later. "The chest, Alaya! Open the chest!"

CHAPTER 37

"Get in! All of you!" A third, unfamiliar voice rang out. Another strange voice squealed triumphantly, sounding far too happy with himself.

Alaya quickly opened the chest, and grabbed the orb. Thankfully, it was no larger than the troudare, so it fit comfortably into the folds of her clothes. She then quickly ran to the edge of the room and looked out across the water. Her heart began to race when she saw her father, Hava, and Whalen being held by armored Neya Men, with swords pushed against their backs. Nikolai was nowhere to be seen. Perhaps he was able to get away and find help?

Any happiness she would have felt from seeing her father alive, was quickly subdued by the fact that he was still facing imminent danger. She could tell that they were all hurt very badly. Her father could barely stand and was bleeding from a number of wounds. But there was someone else beside them. Alaya couldn't be sure, but it looked like Grommet was also there.

"Imagine finding you *here*, at this very moment." The strange man said, stepping out of the shadows. "I could not have asked for the timing to be any more perfect. I suppose

Matthias was right all along; this could not have worked out better."

What did he just say? Alaya wondered what he meant. *Perhaps there was another Matthias?*

"He knew that it was only a matter of time; eventually you would find your way into this room. At first, I had my doubts, I must admit. We have never had a Ramajian get this close. I had often wondered if I would live to see the day. How fortunate for me. We have all been waiting for you, Athaliah." he cackled.

"Who are you?" Alaya shouted across the water.

"I apologize, Athaliah; we have never formally met. My name is Ogapallos II, the former King. And of course, you remember my companion." Ogapallos extended a thin, withered hand toward the back of the group.

A second voice emerged from behind the armored men.

"Hello, my young explorer." Matthias stepped forward. "It's good to see you again. And Frederick, of course."

"What?! Mr. Miller? What's going on?" Alaya's heart nearly dropped. She was beginning to feel dizzy and nauseous at the same time. *How could this be happening?* If this was a dream, then Alaya hoped she would wake up soon. She closed her eyes. Any second now...

"It was easy. Almost *too* easy. Think about it. The troudare? It was more than just a communication device. I was able to track every move you made. The GPS technology of your cell phones was a great idea. Not to mention—your end had a microphone that was never muted. Obviously, it made for hours of boring material, but it was worth it. I overheard every conversation you had with Hava, every plan you made with Frederick and Nikolai, and all of your awkward moments with your sweetheart over here." He jerked his head in Whalen's direction. "All of that, and you were none the wiser. In fact, you thought I was *helping* you!" Matthias emitted a savage laugh and Alaya shivered. It was a *cruel, mocking* laughter.

"Mr. Miller...how could you?" Alaya asked in a weak voice. She sounded like a small child. Each word he said to her was like an individual stab wound, creating emotional pain, rather than physical.

"Such a silly girl! Do you remember that night when your father tried to reach me, but there was no answer? I didn't respond because I was here. I have always had a second machine. I didn't come to Batunia much, as I couldn't risk someone seeing me. However, my brother and Ogapallos had much to discuss. More specifically, we had to figure out how to get you to Batunia and to the chest—fast. After all, Velda's time was running out and your twentieth birthday was getting closer all the time. We needed another Ramajian to take her place and seal away the Orb of Shoraiva forever," Matthias said. "I know that you took the journal, so you should have seen what was there all along. The prophecy, the Orb...everything. Although, I have to say, it helped with your friend tipping us off to Frederick's whereabouts." He said, nodding to Hava.

Alaya didn't understand, and her mind was replaying all the old clips of conversations and events, desperate to piece the puzzle together. How could Mr. Miller have tricked her, without her father noticing that something was amiss? And Hava? How could she have betrayed them? Worse than that, how could she have gone through her whole life without knowing that she was actually adopted?

Alaya thought back to all the times that her mother had seemed cold and distant. She had always assumed that it was because she missed Frederick, but to add taking care of a daughter that wasn't hers on top of losing her husband...had

Janice even *wanted* a child? Or had Frederick convince her? As mad as this all seemed, some other things started to make some sense…or so she thought.

Ogapallos inched forward and raised both arms, revealing two white skeletal twigs covered in thin, papery skin. There was no denying that he was a member of the Neya Men. Gradually, the distance across the water began to shorten. The pool significantly reduced in size and the columns had basically become stepping-stones. Against her will, Alaya was being brought to within feet of her enemies. She got a closer look at her friends. Hava was cowering in a corner; unable to meet Alaya's eyes.

"I'm so sorry, Alaya," Hava blubbered between sobs. "They offered me the ability to fight. I couldn't turn that down…I just, couldn't. I was nothing special before that. You have to understand."

"I have nothing to say to you, Hava." Alaya snarled.

Ogapallos reached out a thin arm, and began to take steps forward. Matthias looked on in delight, like he couldn't have been more pleased with this outcome.

"Stay away from me," Alaya snarled. "All of you."

Ogapallos only smiled. "Ah, afraid are we? That's no way to talk to your friends. And what if I do not want to stay away from you? What will you do then?" His voice reminded Alaya of a hissing snake.

Alaya struggled to think quickly. If she destroyed the Orb of Shoraiva now, the lives of her father and Whalen would be in jeopardy. That still wouldn't help her with identifying and destroying the leader, since she was unable to fight without hurting herself. However, if she didn't, they would force her into the pod in order to keep the Orb sealed away forever. *What am I supposed to do?* Suddenly, a calming voice echoed off the high walls nearby.

Patience, dear.

Alaya looked all around, searching for the source of the advice. But then she realized what it was; Velda was somehow speaking to her. No one else seemed to react. Perhaps they had not even heard the voice? Alaya wondered momentarily if she was going crazy, but dismissed that notion. Life was a bit insane, but she certainly wasn't. There was no rhyme or reason to it, but somehow, she and Velda were linked. Whether through blood or magic, it was the only reasonable explanation for how they were able to communicate, even after death.

"We can all walk away from this unharmed," Alaya said, not really knowing why she had made the oddly bold statement. Following the suggestion of Velda's voice, Alaya decided to stall. She used the most authoritative voice she could manage, but it still felt like a farce.

Unwittingly, Ogapallos was beginning to break down her confidence. The former King had an intimidating, frightful presence, and darkness seemed to be closing in around her just as the opposite side of the room was closing in on her position. She felt her skin grow cold and prickly with fear. The room began to spin all around her, and grew in speed. She had to shut her eyes to make it stop. *Perhaps this was the former King Ogapallos II's talent...the one he had procured from the Neya Men in exchange for his soul.*

Matthias spoke casually, as though everything was completely under control, which it certainly seemed to be for him at least.

"Of course, how could I have forgotten such an important detail? The very thing you have been desperately searching for this whole time?" He took a step forward onto the first pillar, bringing the edges of the gap between them even closer. Alaya hoped that he wouldn't notice how loud and quickly her heart had begun to race. She struggled to open her eyes.

"Now," Matthias said, snapping his fingers. Suddenly, a cloud of smoke began to fill the room as though it was creeping in from the outside. The haze began to move toward the center of the room. Alaya started to unconsciously back away slowly. So slowly, in fact, that one might not have noticed. The fog quickly consumed the room and overwhelmed Alaya. She was finding it difficult to draw anything deeper than shallow, haggard breaths.

"What is this?" Alaya said through jagged coughs.

"You will see soon enough," Matthias answered with another sinister laugh.

Alaya shut her eyes and dropped to the floor, barely able to breathe below the rising smoke cloud. She drew her knees in to her chest to form a shell of protection around her body. There was no use trying to hide it. They knew that she had the Orb of Shoraiva, and they were going to get it from her, one way or another.

"Hello, Alaya. I believe you have something I need," a new voice spoke.

Thankfully, the choking smoke begin to thin. Once it finally cleared, Alaya saw a new man standing in front of the crowd. He was dressed in the finest jewels and had a lavish crown perched confidently atop his brow. All of the men around him dropped to one knee and covered their faces.

This was King Negash.

"My, my...what an exotic beauty. You were right, dear brother." He looked over at Matthias. "She does resemble Velda. It was a good thing that Belina defied you and took her away all those years ago. If she had remained in Batunia, I would have surely made her my new Queen by now. We were lucky though. No one had the chance to poison her mind, or else she would have run away like the rest of those cowardly witches. You actually found a way to make her *want* to return! I am quite impressed," King Negash said before turning back to Alaya.

"So you are the special little girl everyone has been talking about all these years. The one true manifestation of Velda's harnessed powers; the one she called her daughter. And to think she was once believed to be barren." The assembled guards and kings all enjoyed a good laugh at this.

"The only one who can open the chest, isn't that what I've been told?" King Negash continued. "Well, let us see about that." He looked up at her expectantly, clearly not a man used to his requests being refused, but Alaya remained affixed to her spot and didn't move a muscle.

"The Orb, Alaya. We know that you have it!" Ogapallos sneered.

"Just tell me this one thing, Matthias. Why? How could you do this to me? And Dad," Alaya turned her anger toward her father. "All this time, I didn't know that I was adopted. Why didn't anyone tell me?" She knew that this probably was neither the place nor time, but since everyone seemed to be coming clean, she wanted answers.

"Alaya, honey, I am so sorry." Frederick pleaded. "Janice and I, we weren't sure if it was a good idea to tell you. As far as we see it, we *are* your parents. After all, the adoption agency had no records. They say that they found you in the back of their lot one morning. You were left with only a letter that stated your name and the fact that this necklace was a family heirloom. It was to stay with you no matter where you were placed. Once we saw you in that horrible place, all alone, we knew that you were *ours*. Sweetheart, please believe me. I can't imagine what it feels like to find out like this. But, I suppose that now, at the end of things, you should at least know the truth," he pleaded with her, looking as though he might weep at the thought of being rejected as a father.

"Oh yes, that was a nice touch, wasn't it, Frederick?" Matthias taunted. "All that time, you thought I was only interested in you for your research and brilliance. What you didn't realize is that I had been following you to keep track of Alaya for all those years. It was just icing on the proverbial cake that you were a celebrated archaeologist and naturally thirsted to learn more about Batunia. We knew that Velda wouldn't be able to seal away the Orb of Shoraiva forever. However, we knew what the prophecy promised. We had twenty years before Velda's spirit disappeared. After that, we would need another Ramajian. Quite fitting that it would end up being her daughter—Athaliah."

Matthias turned back to Alaya.

"I never told you the rest of this story, but perhaps I owe you that much. When Velda was murdered, I told you that I found the necklace. Well, I also found the chest that night, as well as one more thing—you. She had kept you well-hidden, and you never cried, not even once. The only way I knew that you were there was because of the letter she wrote. Velda had written that she wanted Belina and I to raise you as our own. It is true that I lost a son when Belina died, but I didn't want to raise a child on my own. Especially one wearing that necklace every day. Neya Men cannot touch the cursed thing." Matthias held up his hand, revealing a small bit of smooth, red skin in the shape of the necklace.

"Remember when I touched your necklace, back in the shop? You dropped it into my hand before I had a chance to stop you. Thankfully, being a germaphobe isn't too unrealistic these days in your world..."

It all came flooding back to her now, and Alaya suddenly felt so stupid. *How could I have been so blind?* Everything was starting to make perfect, tragic sense.

"What do you want from her?" Whalen spoke up and struggled against the brute strength of the armored men, but they only clutched his arms more forcefully. One man kicked him in the back of the knees and he crumpled to the ground.

"Alaya ought to know something about this. Back when I first revealed the machine to you, I mentioned Pompeii. It was a sad story, indeed, but it was real. That is what Batunia has become, only, no one has discovered it. Our beautiful kingdom was buried centuries ago by someone named Athaliah. Many believe that name to be a mythical Goddess, but think about it, Alaya. It was *you*. You are the woman fated to destroy everything that we know and love in this world. If you do destroy the Orb, no one will ever know of us, or of you, but it doesn't have to be that way! That is why you must preserve it. Our land must thrive…that is the only way our people can survive."

"He's lying! Do not…listen to him…Alaya!" A weak, broken voice trailed forward from the back of the crowd. Everyone turned around to see the new visitor.

"Nikolai!" Frederick shouted. "Are you alright?"

Nikolai struggled to make his way down the stairs. He looked terrible, on the verge of death, or at least collapse. His skin was pale and blotchy, and his face had begun to take on a gaunt appearance, as though he hadn't eaten in weeks. Alaya couldn't believe it. He seemed fine earlier.

"I see that the transformation has begun. Soon, Nikolai, you will be one of us." Ogapallos jeered. "I knew that we would get you back on our side…one way or another."

"Never," Nikolai said. Then he addressed Frederick, Hava, Whalen, and Alaya. "I have done my part. Now, please, do me this one favor…tell Willie and Max that I love them. I never got around to saying that as often as I should have." He began to cough with such violent convulsions that his entire body shook. Spittle shot from his mouth and his hand clutched at his chest.

298

"Father, hang in there!" Hava called out, racing to him. "There must be something we can do!" Several guards almost tackled Hava, and clutched Nikolai's arms.

It was then that Alaya came to the sad realization: although she had done her best to heal him, she failed. Her powers must be unable to completely undo the dark magic that transforms a person into one of the Neya Men.

Alaya shouted to Ogapallos and Matthias, with fury on her face.

"*You* can stop this!"

"You are in no position to negotiate, young lady. Unless you want to take up Velda's old post," Ogapallos mocked.

Without thinking about all the ways this standoff could play out, Alaya removed the Orb of Shoraiva from the inner folds of her cloak.

Holding the treasured item high above her head, Alaya felt a rush of adrenaline and looked straight at Ogapallos.

"Are you sure about that?"

CHAPTER 38

The moment Alaya held up the Orb of Shoraiva, Matthias ordered his men to stand down. The men holding Whalen, Nikolai, and her father eased their grip, but kept their swords drawn.

In that quiet moment, as every eye was locked on the necklace's shining jewels in Alaya's hand, a low rumble could be heard through the cavern.

"What is that?" King Negash asked. For the first time since appearing, he seemed slightly unsure of himself.

Several men suddenly burst through the wooden door and charged down the steps to join the fight, taking the dozen or so men by surprise. She recognized one of them, Tabari from the Warrior's Council. He had brought the remaining members of the Warrior's Council with him and they began hacking into the Guards with reckless abandon. Chaos ensued and the small space was almost too small for anything to happen with swords swinging in wide, dangerous arcs.

The Neya Men were confused and the two kings appeared to be waiting to see how things played out, ringed by a pair of their burliest private guards.

In his weakened state, Nikolai limped forward to Whalen's side. "My job is done." He almost collapsed onto the floor, but managed to hold himself up, using whatever last bit of strength he still had.

"Hold on, Nikolai," Whalen urged, "I will get you out of here. I promise you that. Just stay with us."

Whalen tried to swing Nikolai over his shoulder, but Nikolai refused. He dug his heels into the gravel, and moved his weight against Whalen like a stubborn bull.

"Remember what I said about my family. Tell them what happened here. Tell them what this meant. As for Hava, I will leave that revelation up to her; she can tell Willie if she chooses." Nikolai burst into a violent coughing fit. Even at a distance, Alaya could tell that there was blood in his hands.

"My time has expired, Whalen. The transformation...cannot be stopped. The gramongle did his best, and I thought I beat him, but..." Nikolai lifted up his jacket, and then his shirt. To Whalen and Frederick's surprise, a large bite mark could be seen, but there was no blood. There were only white, sickly bite marks that slashed across Nikolai's torso.

"I was wrong. They Neya Men are not the only ones who can change someone. But that doesn't matter now...I *refuse* to accept this outcome." He grabbed Whalen's shirt to draw him closer. "I will *never* become one of them. Do you hear me?!" He leered at the Neya Men nearby as they fought against members of the Council – Nikolai's council. "I will die on my *own* terms while I am still a man. Make sure to thank Grommet for me. He was able to do what I could not."

Reluctant to move, Whalen eventually dropped his hands to his sides and took a step back. "Goodbye, my dear friend. May the Soranayum watch over you and may peace follow your spirit, forevermore."

"Nikolai, don't!" Frederick shouted, but it was too late. Nikolai took off in a hobbling run. Frederick lunged forward to catch him, but missed his friend by mere inches. It almost seemed like slow motion; Alaya watched Nikolai hurl himself over the edge and plunge into the pool of acid. His body was consumed almost immediately, leaving behind a belch of smoke. Her eyes stung painfully, but it had nothing to do with the rising cloud of vapor.

"Nooo!" Hava screamed and collapsed to her knees. "Father, please forgive me!"

In that instant, Batunia had lost a great warrior and an even better man. Alaya remained silent, paralyzed, watching the bubbling pool. Even though his body had begun to mutate, which certainly caused his thoughts to begin working against everything he had fought for over the last fifteen years, Nikolai had never been one to give up. She couldn't imagine what a struggle his final hours must have been, yet he still found a way to help. She could never repay him for that, but she would try for the rest of her life.

Whalen and Frederick were both badly injured, but not enough to stop them from avenging their fallen friend. Hava crumbled into a corner; she had lost her will to fight. Frederick picked up a nearby sword, and began slashing and hacking his way through bodies cloaked in black. In that sort of blood rage, she wondered if he would know when to stop. King Negash and Ogapallos II had begun backing toward safety, unsure of how things would now play out, but Matthias confidently stayed behind.

As the groups brutally fought on, Alaya came to a sobering realization: only one of the two factions was going to leave the room alive. No other outcome was possible.

Alaya scanned the dwindling crowd, only to see her father and King Negash engaged in a heated battle. She saw that everyone else was preoccupied with their own frenzied matchups.

Carefully, Alaya made her way across the pillars, gently stepping amidst the battling men and monsters. Although she couldn't fight, she could still heal her father and the others whose blood was sprinkling the battlefield. However, the moment she moved to lay her hands on someone, she was engulfed in flames.

"And what do you think you are doing, my young explorer?" Matthias asked.

"Let me go!" she demanded. "Shouldn't you worry about protecting your baby brother, the King?"

Alaya's attention remained focused on her father. In his weakened state, he was unable to defend himself against the onslaught of blows unleashed by Negash. Her father was no match for the brutality of the enraged king; it was only a matter of time before things took a turn for the worse. On top of this, Alaya spotted two men who were slowly sneaking up behind him. She saw Whalen nearby, who had just finished up another of his endless stream of opponents.

"Whalen, my father…behind you!" she shouted through the ring of flames.

With lightning speed, he flung three daggers through the air, which plunged straight into the two men's backs. They stumbled to the side and collapsed through a small opening in the ground, falling into the acidic water below.

"Take the girl!" one of the Neya Men shouted.

Suddenly, it seemed to be raining weapons as many of the armored men rushed toward her. The flames died suddenly and Alaya scrambled to find shelter. Knives, rocks, arrows…none of the Neya Men held anything back, despite the protection that the remaining members of the Warrior's Council were trying to provide her. She was powerless against the barrage. Although Alaya could heal quickly, she didn't know if she would be able to survive this type of assault.

Alaya retreated behind a nearby boulder. She crouched down, shielded her neck, and froze. She was more terrified than at any other point in her life.

Matthias crept up from behind and her skin crawled when he spoke into her ear.

"You know, Velda trusted me, right until the end. It is a shame, really. I knew of the assassination plot from the very beginning, of course, but I didn't stop it. Neither did Belina. She knew that there was no future in remaining associated with Velda. She, along with her parents, completely renounced her. Once alone, it was far easier to kill Velda without a fight." Matthias whispered.

"You're despicable. I can't believe that I ever trusted you," Alaya said, struggling to speak. The level of betrayal was almost too much to bear.

"That seems to always be a weakness of Ramajians, isn't it?" he asked, not expecting an answer. "I suppose that you are no exception. You know, not a single person came to her defense before I broke her neck. How she struggled...it really was such a pity." He moved closer still. Alaya now felt his hot breath on the back of her neck.

"Now, as I was saying. Since I couldn't touch the key, I tried to have my brother do it. I asked Belina, and even King Ogapallos, but nothing worked. We wanted to find a way to remove its power our *own* way, so it could no longer have a hold over us. Suddenly, there you were. The silent baby we discovered in the other room. That is when we realized what Velda had done. *You* were the only one who could open that chest. But you were also the only one who had the power to guard over it, to keep it sealed. It's funny, actually, thinking back. I wonder if Velda realized that things would end this way." Matthias began laughing, but what he found so twistedly comedic, Alaya could only guess.

"I pretended that I didn't want Frederick to use the machine, but really, I was elated when he returned to Batunia. It finally meant that he would learn the truth about you, and we could be done with this silly Orb of Shoraiva, once and for all. As long as the Ramajians existed, they threatened our survival. You needed to come back to Batunia, so we could finish you off, one way or another," Matthias finished with contempt.

Alaya didn't want to hear any more. Every time he spoke, it felt as though her heart was being stabbed over and over, until a pulp remained. She could see how much Matthias reveled in her mental anguish by twisting the blade.

"Oh, and the sibling rivalry thing...that was genius, wasn't it? The truth is that Fendrel and I have always been close. It was very difficult for me to leave, but we were among the few who saw the benefits of an alliance with the Neya Men. This is the superior race; there is no denying that any longer. It's only a matter of time before everyone sees it, even back in your world, Alaya. Our plan worked out beautifully for everyone; well, everyone except my dear Belina. Toward the end, she began to feel remorseful. She began to bond with you, and I daresay, she had grown to *love* you. After all, you were her niece. It was bad enough that she tried to kidnap you in order to keep you away from me and the others. She said that I was becoming a 'monster', and tried to escape Batunia without me. Can you believe that? It was good fortune that I caught her arm just as she disappeared with the token. As soon as we arrived in that new land, I did what needed to be done. I couldn't let anyone ruin our plan...not even her."

Alaya cringed. She didn't how much more of this she could take. Everything she had ever heard out of Matthias' mouth had been a lie. *Everything.* But there was still more.

"After that unfortunate hiccup, I needed to regroup and form a plan. Frederick and Janice were all too eager to have a child of their own. They were overjoyed to accept you into their home, and I made sure to find a way into your life. It was perfect. Frederick was an avid collector and archaeologist and I owned an antique store. Later on, when I told Frederick about the machine, I pretended that I didn't want him to use it. I made up the tales of woe and constructed the false stories in the scrolls in order to convince him that it was all true. It didn't actually take much work," Matthias spat out those final words with sickening pride.

"So, Alaya, make your choice. You have opened the chest. We have won. But continuing this fighting is quite silly. You have lost. Go on, you can try to destroy the orb, but remember one thing. I am standing right behind you with a dagger pointed at your heart. I know that you can't feel pain, but all it will take is one fatal blow. Not even your mother could have healed quickly enough for that." He leaned in closer to whisper in her ear. "I would know. She was dead in seconds."

Alaya's eyes flooded red. She wanted to spin around and strangle him until every spark of life escaped from his body. Unfortunately, she knew that it would never work; she would only end up strangling herself instead. *If only I had more time!* The things she would have liked to ask...she still had so many questions...but Velda was now gone forever. She would never have the chance to connect with her birth mother.

The hatred Alaya felt for Matthias at that moment was like nothing she had ever felt before. There was such a flood of rage, a tsunami of anger...it felt like her blood was on fire. She hated him for what he had done to Belina and to her father, along with the painful reminder that she would never know Velda because of her murder at his hands.

"We only need your soul," Matthias said. "We have the men here who can retrieve it."

That was when Alaya saw them. The cloaked Neya Men were the only ones who could perform the darkest depths of magic—the soul extraction of a Ramajian. They slowly approached, as though they were attending a funeral procession.

"If you will not go willingly, then you will be terminated." Matthias pushed the dagger further into her back, and directed her towards the cloaked horde. "I will have you to thank for the Neya Men's continued existence—either way."

"I don't think so," Alaya said. "I'm done with your games. This ends now."

CHAPTER 39

"I do not care to hear any more of your words," King Negash said. He must have overheard their conversation. "You have two choices: come with us and you live for eternity in the life source pod, or be killed. Either way, we win."

"You're forgetting choice number three," Alaya shouted back defiantly.

Just then, an arrow shot past Matthias, taking his left ear with it as it passed. He screamed with rage, and Alaya managed to wriggle herself from his grip. She ran toward her protective duo of fighters; Whalen and Frederick.

"Please, King Negash, leave my daughter out of this!" Frederick said, growing steadily weaker.

"Silence!" he roared. "There is no other option, Frederick. She has made her choice. This is the last I will tolerate from you. As an escaped prisoner, you are already in line to be executed for high treason if you do not die here tonight!" King Negash screamed and ordered his men to attack.

So many things began to happen that Alaya could barely keep up. Men scrambled to surround her; some from the Council to protect her, others were Neya Men who lunged with gleaming spears, and some may have even been from the Royal Guard. A group of men threw themselves at Frederick, while others began beating Whalen with their fists.

Soon, King Negash came upon Frederick, and his opponents disbursed. Frederick wobbled on his knees, struggling to stand straight. King Negash struck him over the head with the hilt of his sword. Alaya watched in horror as her father fell to the ground face first, and didn't move after that. She feared the worst, thinking he was either unconscious or something else; she couldn't tell from her vantage point. From the corner of her eye, she saw a flash of movement; however, she couldn't quite make out what it was.

King Negash raised his sword, preparing to deliver a fatal blow to Frederick, but before he could strike, Whalen leapt forward and pushed the King with his feet. Alaya rushed over to move Frederick's limp body to safety, but his eyes began to open.

"Thank goodness you're alive, Dad!" She cried.

"Never been better." He tried to smile through the pain. "Tell me where they went." He said, trying to sit up

"Dad, I don't know--"

But it was too late. Whalen tossed a weapon at Frederick's side—a double-ended spear. Whalen chose to wield two small swords, and together, they both rejoined the increasingly bloody battle. The ground was slick with the blood of both sides.

"We can take it from here, Alaya," Whalen said with urgency. "Go somewhere safe and destroy the Orb!"

"Right!" Alaya said, and ran, trying to find a place to hide. She had to jump over bodies; some dead, others badly injured. It was too hard to tell the difference. Some moaned and reached out to her as she passed. As much as Alaya wanted to heal the injured, there was no time. She heard bodies falling into the acid pool and sizzling to their ultimate end.

"You are *not* getting away with this, traitors!" King Negash barked.

Alaya ran as fast as she could, when a strange man reached out a hand and grabbed a hold of her foot. She caught her balance just in time.

"Over here, girl!" the injured man said. He was kneeling over a fallen comrade. She was torn, but after looking into the man's pleading eyes, she knew that she couldn't turn them away. Forced back to the battlefield, Alaya immediately worked to heal them both. Fortunately, the man who waved her down was only slightly hurt and healed quickly. However, his friend was not so lucky. Alaya held his head between her hands, and watched him take his last, dying breath.

Alaya heard a loud cry from a voice that she recognized. She turned to see Whalen being cut from his mid-torso to his shoulder by King Negash's blade. A deep, dark red stain immediately appeared through his shirt. He stumbled forward, struggling to stay on his feet.

"Whalen!" Alaya screamed and immediately jumped up, racing toward him.

"No...Alaya...stay back. Finish..." Whalen struggled to get out the words as Frederick helped him safely to the ground. She saw her father turn and lash out savagely at King Negash with intense vigor and strength. She could hardly believe her eyes.

Alaya reached Whalen and knelt by his side.

"It's not too late. It can't be. You're going to be alright, Whalen," she repeated and stroked his head. Alaya didn't have much time to think. She only knew that it was time to act. Frederick still fought King Negash only feet from where she was, but she could only concentrate on healing Whalen's broken body.

Alaya felt someone hovering over her shoulder, and whipped around.

"Is he going to be okay?" Hava asked.

Although Hava was the last person Alaya wanted to see, she felt a little sorry for her. after all, she had just lost her father moments earlier.

"I think so, but we could use some backup," Alaya said, never taking her eyes off Whalen.

"Alaya, I--" Hava began, struggling to speak her peace. "I never meant for things to get this bad. I'll admit that I was jealous of you. The way he looks at you; it's what I always dreamed would happen to me. But I know that can never happen now. I can't make up for what has happened, but I hope my father can forgive me...wherever he is. I hope *all* of you can, someday." Hava said, and touched Whalen's forehead. He barely moved. Slowly, she took a step back, then another, and took off full pace towards the heated battle.

Alaya placed her hands directly onto Whalen's chest. Thick blood splattered everywhere; on her cloak, on her arms, and even on her face. Yet, none of that mattered. Whalen began to lose color in his face and she could see his eyes beginning to roll to the back of his head. Her hands trembled as she worked.

"Stay with me...you're going to make it," Alaya cried through the tears that blurred her sight. She spread her arms across his body like a physical blanket hovering just above his skin, moving back and forth. The blood stopped flowing and then very slowly, his wounds began to mend right before her eyes.

Alaya let out a deep sigh of relief. She had gotten to him just in time. The color began to return to Whalen's face, and he opened his eyes. He was smiling, and although Alaya wished that he wouldn't speak to conserve his energy, he did anyway.

"Alaya," he whispered as he stared up at her, his smile as bright as one could expect in such circumstances.

"Yes, it's me. Now take it easy. You're going to be fine," Alaya replied.

"Noooo!" Alaya heard Tabari shouting from a distance, and Alaya heard Ogapallos II's disgusting cackle break through the chaotic sounds in the room. *What now?* She thought and spun in the direction of the shouting.

Alaya immediately saw King Negash holding a long sword in front of him; it was stuck through a man's midsection. Except, this was not just any man. Negash slid the sword out with a cruel jerk and Alaya watched in horror as her father was dumped to the ground, falling first to his knees, and then onto his face. He did not move.

"Dad, no!" Alaya cried out. She ran as quick as a jaguar to his side, but she already knew that it was too late. There was nothing she could do. There was just so much blood, *too* much blood, in fact. Frederick was dead.

Alaya held her father's head in her lap, cradling it tenderly. Blood spilled from nearly every orifice and trickled from the corners of his mouth, leaving dark streaks across his skin. His eyes were open, but distant, far away from everything and everyone. Alaya stared deeply into them, glancing back and forth from eye to eye, hoping that at any moment he would blink or show a spark of life. They remained glassy and still. His eyes were devoid of life, like two glass balls trapped in a fleshy shell.

"Dad! Daaad!" Alaya screamed at the lifeless body, but of course, there was no answer. She grew hysterical and shook him, screaming even louder, begging for him to wake up. Still, there was no movement and no breath. Alaya could hear the unmistakable sound of a few men quietly sobbing in the background, while others ramped up their outrage through violence. As is always the case, every man dealt with his grief in different ways. She heard Whalen's roar of rage as he picked up his weapon and rejoined the fight, thanks to the power she held in her hands. If only it had been enough for her father as well.

At that moment, Alaya wanted to give up. It had all been for nothing. Returning to Batunia, fighting for its people; it was all pointless if she couldn't save him. She tugged her father's body up, close to her chest, and rocked him back and forth. She had temporarily forgotten what surrounded her, and her mission was being blown into the back of her mind by a tragic wind. Everything and everyone was disappearing in a fog that rolled and billowed out of her mind.

Frederick's body felt stiff and heavy, but she was surprised by how warm he was to the touch. *Maybe he isn't really gone?* She thought about how her father used to pull tricks on her. *Maybe he was only faking it?* She knew how ridiculous that sounded. She also remembered how dangerous hope could be; she had already experienced a lifetime of hoping that her father would come back to her, only to be disappointed time and time again.

Alaya kept her eyes closed for a long time, squeezed shut to block out the world, but she opened them when she heard Whalen shouting for King Negash.

"You will pay for what you've done! I do not care *who* you are!" Whalen raved, his eyes swirling with madness. He struck Fendrel in the back of the head with a large rock, and he fell to the ground like a toppling tree. The King's sword clattered beside him, slipping from his fingers as his skull crashed into the solid floor surrounding them. Leaning down, Whalen grabbed the King's sword, and with fury fuelling his eyes, he drew back and thrust the sword straight down through King Negash's skull. The sword stuck into the ground and remained standing upright, quivering.

"Traitor!" A nearby member of the Guard shouted. "What have you done to our King?!"

"What should have been done a long time ago," Whalen retorted, looking extinguished. He made his way to Alaya, slicing and ducking past the remaining warriors that still had blood in their veins. He knelt by Frederick's side and searched for a pulse.

Everything grew quiet around Alaya; the rushing sound of wind in her ears stopped and the fighting in the background seemed to fade into darkness. She felt dizzy and could no longer hold her head up...

"Keep steady there...I have you." Whalen's voice caressed her ear, and he wrapped an arm around her.

Slow, clanking footsteps could be heard nearby, but Alaya didn't even look to see who was coming. Her energy was practically spent and even the effort to raise her head or open her eyes felt far too taxing.

"So what happens now?" the voice asked. That specific voice sent a surge of anger and energy back through Alaya. Staring back at her was Atreus Ogapallos II, his hateful eyes burning straight into hers. Those red pits of fire were unnatural and disturbing, just as they would have been for Nikolai all those years ago on the night he lost his eye.

Whalen pulled away from Frederick's body and shielded Alaya from Ogapallos' eyes.

"The Orb," Alaya whispered very softly. "This won't stop until I destroy it."

Whalen nodded. "Do what you must. Just be careful—please."

"We'll have your back, Alaya," Hava said, finding her purpose.

Alaya slowly backed away from the scene; Whalen covered her exit as he turned to face Ogapallos. She had to find a way to destroy the jewel without being distracted or attacked in the process.

Alaya snuck to the rear of the large room, trying to avoid notice by any of the groups of men still holding swords and looking for flesh to cut into. She crouched down and pulled the Orb of Shoraiva from the folds of her dress. It still vibrated with a dim, insistent glow; the Neya Men's life source was still surging through it.

Alaya laid the jewel on the ground in front of her and reached for a spiked hammer that had fallen nearby. She ignored the blood that spotted the weapon as she lifted it above her head. She was ready to finish this, once and for all.

As she moved to strike, the hammer refused to move. Her arms strained against the invisible force that had suddenly taken over the hammer's path. She tugged desperately, crying out in frustration, but it wouldn't budge. Alaya whipped her head around and her heart plummeted.

Matthias was standing a few feet away, watching her every move.

"And just *what* do you think you're doing?" He asked, addressing her like a father would chastise a child. "Did you think I wouldn't notice you sneaking off?"

Alaya didn't answer; the last thing she wanted was another delay or any more horrific stories from the man she had once known as Mr. Miller.

"Stay back!" Alaya warned, and bent down to scoop up the Orb. She held it close to her chest as she stood. "You can't stop me, Matthias!"

However, when she raised her eyes to meet his, Matthias was nowhere to be found. Instead, he seemed to have transformed into what stood before her—a massive creature, wrapped from head to toe in solid steel. It stood several feet taller than her and had white glowing eyes that seemed to pierce Alaya's skin from within the steel helm. The small areas of his skin that weren't covered appeared black and scaly. Bones jutted out in strange positions throughout his body. His teeth had transformed into long, gleaming fangs. Saliva dripped from the tips of the fangs and fell to the ground. He snarled and gnashed his teeth at Alaya, who nearly dropped the Orb of Shoraiva at the sight of this new, hellish version of Matthias.

"So, you really were the leader all along?" Alaya stepped back and braced herself, knowing that this might very well be the end for her. She had no idea what she was up against and her heart was bound in fear.

The giant beast spoke in a deep, ominous tone. Its tongue lashed through its teeth as it formed the words. Alaya almost refused to believe this was the harmless, quirky antique shop owner she had once known.

"Alaya, once I've killed you, I will emerge from the depths to finish off the rest of the fools that stand against us. Batunia, and the entire world, will soon belong to the Neya Men!"

Alaya looked all around her; scattered fighters continued battling, along with Whalen, Tabari, and Hava, who were still fighting off the others. Occasionally, Whalen turned a worried eye on her. She could tell that he was trying to make it to her, but he had been blocked in. The acid pool was not as far as she thought, and while Nikolai's death was tragic, perhaps there had been some wisdom in that sacrifice. If only she could make a run for it...

She never had time to make a move; Matthias snapped his head toward her, leading with his teeth, and she barely dodged his attack. Some part of his armor had torn into her arm and blood poured from the wound. She instinctively covered the wound, which healed over almost instantly.

A few Council members approached from the mouth of the entrance, warily measuring the situation.

"Alaya, we have come to help," an unknown man shouted. "We received word from above ground and came as quickly as we--"

The beastly Matthias struck the man square in the chest with the flat end of his sword, sending him soaring straight into the cavern wall. Alaya heard the wet, cracking sound of blood mixed with snapping bones. The man didn't move from the ground; his neck was turned at an impossible angle.

"Attack!" another man shouted and they charged as one toward Matthias, their weapons flashing in defiance.

Matthias waved his arms and swatted the men away like flies, barely noticing their attacks. A few rose to continue fighting, but their weapons proved useless against Matthias' impenetrable armor. He moved between them, slicing and hacking like a medieval surgeon, unforgiving and merciless.

"You cannot defeat me. My only match here is far too afraid to face me," Matthias growled; the sneering comment about Alaya was lined with disgust.

"That's not it," Alaya said as she watched him crush the life from the remaining men. He stomped others with his heavy feet, crushing their bodies like shards of broken glass. "I have only been waiting for the right time."

"I am right behind you." Whalen had moved next to her, preparing to attack.

Alaya tried to warn him. "Whalen, the weapons seem useless against him; he's far too strong."

"Do not give up hope, Alaya," Whalen spoke quickly, while dodging the first swinging blow from Matthias. Alaya felt like they were caught in a dangerous game of chicken. A new group of fighters swarmed Matthias, allowing Whalen and Alaya to slip a few meters away. Shortly afterward, Hava joined them.

"Before father left home to meet up with you and Whalen, he told Tabari the secret of defeating the leader of the Neya Men," Hava said. "You must use a weapon forged from their own demonic sorcery. Only the dark magic of the Neya Men is powerful enough to undo their souls."

"So we need a weapon that they have used?" Alaya asked.

"Yes. These are weapons forged from dark elements that are unique to their user. However, there is a catch; the one who wields the weapon runs the risk of becoming poisoned by it. The power is said to be wildly exhilarating; some warriors have even turned against their own men," she explained, and unfolded a cloth wrap, revealing a sharp, double-edged sword.

"You can't run forever, Alaya!" Matthias bellowed as he tossed another warrior into the sizzling pool of acid; the number of her allies was dwindling.

Alaya gave the sword a quick look; it was unlike anything she had ever seen before. It was perhaps 4 feet long, but seemed easy enough to wield. The hilt was sleek and narrow, although the sword itself was black steel with small barbs sticking out haphazardly along the length.

"Whatever you have to do, Hava," Alaya said. "I want to end him."

"Okay," Whalen said. "I will distract him. Try and find an opening to attack."

Whalen began to distract Matthias while Hava got a better look. She wrapped the cloth around the hilt of the sword and brandished it with care, as though waiting for some surge of power to take over her body.

"Hava, wait!" Alaya said. "Whalen cannot stand to be attacked again, but I can. If he sees you with his sword, he may immediately try to kill you. He will know that we have discovered his weakness. I will draw his attention so you can get close enough to finish him."

Hava nodded and Alaya took off, sprinting in Matthias' line of vision so he was sure to follow. She tried to run in a zig-zag pattern, leaping over bodies. With all of that heavy armor on, Alaya knew that Matthias could not move as quickly.

"Fool! You are only delaying the inevitable!" Matthias said as he turned awkwardly to pursue her. He moved surprisingly fast and had cornered her in seconds, but that is what she had been counting on.

As Matthias moved in to take her, Whalen crept up from behind and leapt onto his back. As Matthias realized what was happening, Whalen gripped a groove in the back of Matthias' armor to hold on. Just below his helm, Alaya saw a dark band of flesh at the back of his neck.

"Hava, his neck!" she shouted.

"Oh no, you don't!" Matthias roared and reached behind him with an armored fist to grab Whalen. He tossed him aside like a rag doll.

Just then, Grommet stepped in, catching Whalen.

"What? Grommet? But, why are you —"

"No time for questions, my boy. Let's just say I came to my senses, eh? I gotcha now! Come on, that ain't all you've got left, is it?" Grommet said, looking rejuvenated from the battle. Sweat mixed with blood painted his brow, but he had more spunk than Alaya would have expected. She was grateful he turned down the bottle and rejoined his brothers and sisters of the Council.

"Now!" Alaya yelled. Hava had to make this count; it was almost certainly their last chance. She quickly climbed onto Matthias' back, while Whalen and Grommet attacked from below.

"There will be no mercy," Matthias said, and struck a glancing blow towards Hava, who was now near his shoulder. The angle of attack meant that Matthias couldn't put his full power behind the swing. Hava managed to endure the blow, but Alaya could see that it had still done a great deal of damage. A shower of blood fell to the floor, but Hava didn't stop.

Somehow, she managed to maintain her grip, and leaned in to speak directly into Matthias' ear.

"You're right. There *will* be no mercy. But I have to thank you and your men for this talent; the one that killed you." Hava said, and plunged the sword deeply into Matthias' neck, forcing the blade out the front until her wrist was pressing against the back of Matthias' head. The tiny barbs of the evil sword left a jagged trail of muscle and bone as they tore through the front of his throat. Alaya had to turn and look away; it was too grisly of a scene.

Hava jumped herself off of Matthias' back and took the sword with him, severing Matthias' head. It fell to the ground with a heavy crunch. At the same moment, Alaya opened her hand, which she had been clenching for what seemed like a lifetime. She cocked her arm and tossed the Orb of Shoraiva into the burning pool of acid a few feet away, following its path until she saw that tell-tale puff of smoke. It was gone.

It was soon clear, however, that this was not over. The pool began writhing and surging, sparking from beneath the acid surface. A blinding web of electricity shot through the room, winding its way past the members of the Warrior's Council, but entangling the remaining Neya Men in blue and white bolts of power. In moments, the Neya Men began to shake uncontrollably and explode. Pieces of armor blasted in all directions and just like that, it was finished.

"Nooo! This is impossible!" Atreus Ogapallos said from the side of the room, backing toward the exit, his allies defeated.

Tabari emerged from a pillar next to Ogapallos. He was wounded, but still standing. He said nothing, but spun his sword once and slid it through the former king's abdomen.

It was finally over.

***

"Hava, Whalen are you two okay?" Alaya shouted, and ran over to the charred ruin of the body that had once been the leader of the Neya Men. Hava still held the sword in her hand, but was lying next to the corpse of the monster, struggling to breathe. Her eyes were fading in and out of consciousness.

Alaya breathed a sigh of relief to see she was still alive. Hava's eyes opened slightly at the sound of her voice.

"Is it done? She asked, and began to moan with pain.

"Yes, almost. There is one more thing that I need to do," Alaya said and began to heal her wounds.

CHAPTER 40

"ow is that?" Alaya asked. Hava sat up, still clutching the barbed sword.

She hopped to her feet, much faster than anyone expected. A moment later, her face held a smirk.

"Feeling better?" Whalen asked.

"Much better. Thank you. For a minute there, I..." She didn't finish her sentence.

"Hava, are you okay?" Alaya asked.

"Thanks...you did the right thing, healing me...you tireless wench! I should've killed you a long time ago!" Hava shouted, and grabbed Alaya by the throat with frightening strength. She pushed Alaya hard against a wall, and held up the barbed sword, prepared to strike.

Suddenly a dagger plummeted into the back of her head. Hava's grip immediately slacked, releasing Alaya to the floor.

"I'm sorry, but it had to be done." Grommet said, and went over to scoop up Hava's body. "The transformation had begun. I saw her lose her grip on the covering once she was struggling with that monster. She stood no chance."

Alaya grew petrified, and was shaking. Hava was one of them; she was remorseful. Why did this have to happen *now?*

"Alaya, there was nothing we could have done. She must have been able to withstand the transformation long enough to bypass the Orb of Shoraiva's destructive powers." Whalen said, and leaned over his fallen friend. "I am sorry it had to end this way, Hava. Your family will know of the bravery you showed tonight. I promise you that."

Alaya could barely hold back anymore; tears began to fall freely down her face and she wept. Like a child who had just lost its way, Alaya was inconsolable. Whalen held her while she sobbed. He must have understood exactly how she was feeling.

***

Tabari joined up with them and they surveyed the battlefield around them. Tidal pools of blood were everywhere, enough to make even the most battle-hardened men sick with grief. There were far too many casualties to consider this a victory. The Council members had been able to defeat most of the Royal Guard, and the rest had fled once they saw King Negash struck down. As for the Neya Men, once Matthias was killed, they were leaderless. Destroying the Orb did the rest.

Alaya suddenly remembered something from her conversation with Velda. She retrieved her sack from the room with the opened chest. Whalen followed closely behind, not wanting to leave her side.

She pulled out Velda's journal and feverishly scanned each page near the back. She eventually found what Velda must have been referring to before her spirit vanished. As her eyes continued down the page, she found that she could hardly speak. She looked up at Whalen and handed him the open journal.

"What is it?" he asked, holding it open, but she said nothing. She knew what had to be done.   Looking down at the page, Whalen read. His face was expressionless, and he silently handed the journal back to Alaya.

"I am ready," she said. "Take me to him."

***

"Are you absolutely sure that you want to do this?" Whalen asked, standing behind Alaya. "There may not be a second chance. This seems to be a one-shot kind of deal."

"Yes, I am sure," Alaya answered confidently.

"Alaya, I am only saying that perhaps you should think about this. If what this book says is true, then you will give up your powers — permanently," he pressed, trying to be the voice of reason.

Alaya and Whalen walked back over the pillars to search for Frederick's body. Grommet and Tabari helped them search. The piles of bodies strewn like broken dolls were horrific and she felt a wave of guilt crash over her all over again, the guilt for losing Nikolai, Hava, as well as all the other men that she had been unable to save.

"Are you sure that this is something Frederick would want for you?" Whalen asked. "Think of all the good that you could do for Batunia, not to mention the rest of the world, if you remain as you are."

"Don't try to convince me otherwise, Whalen. This is not your choice to make. He's my father...I can't just leave him here like this."

Whalen seemed to struggle with the next words he chose.

"Alright. If you are certain, then I am in no position to stop you. I respect your decision." He stepped back into the shadows as they reached Frederick's body, which lay bloodied and battered where he had fallen.

Alaya knelt beside her father's body and closed her eyes. She reached out and touched him softly. He was cold and stiff, but she did not focus on that. Instead, she concentrated on the task at hand. She placed one hand on his heart and the other on his forehead. These were the two most essential organs for life. If any healing could happen, it had to start there. It took a great deal of effort, but after several minutes, Frederick's wounds began to heal.

Each wound began to mend itself back to fresh, unmarked skin, as though he had never even fought in a battle. After his wounds were closed, Alaya focused intently on the far more difficult task of reawakening his heart and brain.

"I think it is working," Whalen whispered.

Alaya didn't speak. She continued to pour her focus into his body, directing all of her energies through the contact her hands had on his skin. She imagined hearing his voice, seeing his smile, and feeling his warmth when they embraced. Alaya pushed forward until she began to break out into a sweat. She could feel resistance to what she was attempting to do; it felt as though she was being drained of her life force. At one point, she must have blacked out from exhaustion. Alaya felt Whalen catch her, breaking the fall and laying her head on the cold stone.

"I have you," he comforted her. "Are you okay?"

As she struggled to sit upright, they both heard a deep gasp and a gurgle of breath rattling through lungs.

"Well, aren't you two a sight for sore eyes," a familiar voice said from her side.

Alaya's exhaustion was no longer a concern. She quickly found enough strength to speak.

"Dad! Thank goodness, you're back!" she said, and crawled forward to hug him. "I can't believe it worked!" She didn't have much energy, but Frederick squeezed her tightly enough for both of them. She didn't want him to let go, out of fear that he may disappear at any moment.

"Back? You mean I went somewhere?" he asked, although whether he was joking or not, Alaya didn't care. It wasn't important. All that mattered was that her father was now alive and well.

"Here, try healing this," Tabari offered, stepping forward to reveal a small cut on his forearm.

Alaya looked into his eyes, afraid of what would happen. She laid her hands on his arm, but try as she might, she could not heal the wound. She concentrated harder still, touching his wound with both hands. Still nothing; the wound remained unchanged.

"I guess that's it then," she choked out with a little sadness. Everything that had made her special was now gone. The power of the Ramajian was no longer hers to claim.

"What is it? What happened, Alaya?" Frederick asked, immediately concerned for his daughter.

"You were dead, but now you are not," she answered simply as she wiped away a few tears.

"Oh, my dear girl. I am so sorry that you had to go through that." Frederick reached over and wrapped Alaya in another embrace. Soon, he pulled away, as though he had remembered something very important. "We should get out of here. There's nothing left for us in this place." Alaya couldn't have agreed more.

CHAPTER 41

In what seemed like no time at all, the small group made it safely made it back to Frederick's home, although it had basically been destroyed. Tabari and Grommet said their goodbyes, and parted ways. Together, they headed back to the Iskinder's home, to inform Willemina and Max of the outcome of the battle, and to offer their condolences.

"So, what next?" Frederick asked in a solemn tone.

Alaya hesitated; she didn't know how to answer that. The three of them took a walk down to the edge of the forest, where Alaya had hidden the machine. Somehow, through everything that had happened, it still remained hidden beneath the piles of leaves. In fact, the pile seemed to have grown over time.

"Alaya?" Frederick looked at her, now clearly concerned. "You've been very quiet. Is everything okay?"

"Dad, I...I want to stay here." She was admitting it to herself just as much as to him and everyone else. Her father was silent for a few moments and then he grinned.

"Sweetheart, I know," he replied, to Alaya's surprise. "This is where you were always meant to be. There is something that I've wanted to tell you ever since you were a little girl. It's my last bit of research, and the reason why I was so drawn to Batunia. Just promise me that you won't read it until I am gone," Frederick warned.

Alaya nodded. "I have found a few good reasons to stay. Batunia could use some help rebuilding, especially since we've destroyed the entire government and all," she said with a smile. "One other thing, Dad. I've met someone; you probably remember him." She tossed a glance over to Whalen, who looked just as surprised as her father.

Whalen looked at Alaya and she nodded. He stepped forward to stand before Frederick. "Nice to meet you, sir," he said reverently. They shook hands as though they were meeting for the first time.

"You're sure about this, Whalen?" Frederick asked.

"It is one of the only things I am sure about, right now. I know the world is chaos, and we have a lot of rebuilding to do, but...I am in love with your daughter. Having her in Batunia is the greatest blessing I can have," Whalen answered humbly.

"Well," Frederick sighed, "I cannot stand in the way of love. Plus, can't say that I'm surprised. Not even a little." Frederick said. Alaya changed the subject before any further awkwardness had to be undergone.

"I'm sure that Mom will be so happy to see you. She has missed you so much. After all these years, she never lost hope. She has had me around my whole life; perhaps it's time for you to catch up on lost time," Alaya said, suddenly wishing that she could see Janice one last time. At least now, she truly understood that her mother *did* love her. In fact, both of her mothers loved her.

"Yes, you may be right. I would love to see my Janice again, but how will I explain your absence? Or mine?" Frederick asked.

Alaya shrugged. "You'll have plenty of time to think of something. Besides, I guess you will both have to get back here sooner rather than later. I'm sure that Mom would love it here," Alaya suggested and Frederick began laughing.

"Yes, and this time, it won't take me seven years to do it." He laughed and hugged his daughter. "I promise, Alaya, I will tell your story. History books will know of the Ramajians. They will know how my daughter, the last Ramajian, saved her father's life. I will tell your story — Batunia's story — to the world."

Alaya smiled. "Thanks, Dad. That would be something, wouldn't it?"

With that, they said their final, private goodbyes. After a very lengthy embrace and a handful of fallen tears, Frederick stepped into the machine. With a final wave and a twist of all the appropriate dials, the image of her father grew hazy, the light bloomed to illuminate the forest clearing, and he disappeared.

Epilogue

After several years, Batunia was rebuilt into a bustling, profitable hub that helped spur growth and prosperity to its neighboring kingdoms. It flourished, and actually became quite popular with tourists from distant lands. People came from far and wide for a glimpse of the Queen who, if the stories were true, had defeated the most perilous threat to the world in recent memory.

True to his word, Frederick had written many books about Batunia. However, it was confirmed that Batunia was never part of the history she knew; but it was in fact, a new world altogether. So, rather than being known from history books, Athaliah became a type of goddess; not unlike Aphrodite or Venus. She was okay with this; it meant she and her parents were both still in existence at the same time. Also, the machine was still able to travel between worlds, so they were able to visit Batunia often.

***

It was a sunny spring day, and the sky was unmarred by even a single cloud. The lake surrounding the palace was placid and soothing, betraying not even a ripple from the gentle wind. Alaya stood on the precipice of the palace balcony, looking out over the Kingdom of Batunia. Although no longer a Ramajian, she felt happier than she had ever been.

Standing there, Alaya thought about her life before her journey to Batunia, when she had no clear direction or purpose. No matter how hard she tried, no hobby or career goal had ever sparked her interest.

However, all of that changed once she arrived in Batunia. Even if someone had sworn it to be true, Alaya would have never believed that she would eventually be the Queen of a thriving, successful kingdom.

It had been exactly six years since the Neya Men were defeated, and Batunia had never been more beautiful. Even the area of the forest that the Neya Men had once inhabited had been restored to its natural beauty. Many believed that the Soranayum were once again protecting and guiding the lives of Batunians.

Alaya closed her eyes and let her skin drink in the warm rays of the sun. The King, Whalen Travinian, stepped out onto the balcony to join his wife. In his arms, he held their daughter, Florencia, who had recently turned three years old.

"How are you today, my Queen?" Whalen asked. He greeted Alaya with a kiss on the forehead. Florencia squirmed to be put down, and she stood next to Alaya, clutching the fringes of her simple dress and smiling up at her mother.

Alaya smiled at the touch of Whalen's lips. "Your Queen is *very* happy. And how are you, my King?"

"Perfect. Everything is absolutely perfect," he answered, holding his wife contentedly in his arms.

"Look mommy, look!" Florencia cried. She giggled with excitement in the cute way that young children do, and pointed up to the sky.

Alaya looked up in shock; a strange half-scream, half-laugh erupted from the royal couple.

"Oh wow, Florencia! How did you do that?" She bent down to her daughter's level, and placed her hand on Florencia's wild, curly hair. "It's a rainbow, but there aren't any clouds in the sky!" Alaya smiled, shocked to witness her daughter's unusual talent for the first time.

"Like mother, like daughter?" Whalen said, questioning.

Alaya only smiled. She was overjoyed to know that the power, beauty, and grace of her heritage had not been completely lost when she exchanged her powers for her father's life all those years ago.

"Dad says we can go to the Circle of the Soranayum today. I want to see Grandma Velda. But before we go, will you read me the story again, Mom? Please?" Florencia begged. Her brown eyes tugged at Alaya's heartstrings; refusing her was nearly impossible.

"You must've heard that story a dozen times by now," Alaya replied, but she didn't mind. She liked the story almost as much as her daughter. "Alright, sweetheart...have a seat."

Whalen reached into a hidden pocket sewn into his royal coat and handed Alaya an aged piece of parchment wrapped around a scroll.

"This was given to me by your grandfather many years ago, before you were born. He found it near the Circle, back when he was traveling extensively. This is what it says:

'A little girl will soon arrive, who will be our answer. A girl who will be formed, but never born. In her soul, I will impart the will and bravery of a warrior, the patience of a Goddess, the kindness of a mother, and the power of a healer. She can do no harm to others, unless they seek to harm her. She will know nothing of evil, nor commit crimes for selfish gain. For those things are not in her nature.

She will grow into a great and powerful force for Batunia. She will receive the key, which will help her rise up and defeat the evil forces in the final hour. She will be the answer to Batunia's greatest questions. In the darkest hour, she will be empowered to give a final sacrifice, the last gift any Ramajian can give. Just as I have done. Athaliah will be my legacy, and Batunia's destiny.'" Alaya lowered the parchment and smiled down at her daughter.

"I really like that story, Mom," Florencia said, grinning up at her parents.

"I do too, Florencia. I do too." Alaya said, and drew her daughter and husband close; allowing the gentle sun to wash over them.

Acknowledgements

I'd like to thank my family, on both coasts of the U.S., who have supported me in the publishing of this book. Also, I must extend thanks to my mother, who taught me the true meaning of dedication, and to my father, for his unconditional support.

I would also like to thank the "the twins" for their astute editing. Also, I would be remiss if I did not thank my husband for igniting the spark which eventually led me on this path.

Finally, this book is dedicated to the blessings who have yet to grace us with their presence.